THE SCROLLS
The Missing Eighteen Years

THE SCROLLS
The Missing Eighteen Years

James W. Mercer

Hardcover ISBN 978-0-557-97329-3

Paperback ISBN 978-0-557-97328-6

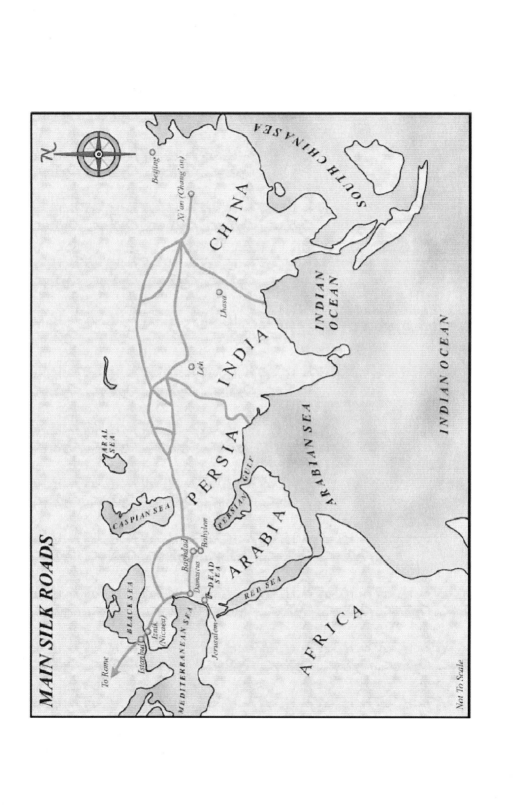

MAIN SILK ROADS

Not To Scale

About the Author

James W. Mercer works in the area of hydrogeology and has published numerous technical articles. In 1985, he was awarded the Wesley W. Horner Award of the American Society of Civil Engineers for work performed at Love Canal. In 1994, he received the American Institute of Hydrology's Theis Award for contributions to groundwater hydrology. *The Scrolls* is his first novel. He currently lives in the Washington DC area.

Acknowledgments

I am indebted to my ever-supportive wife, Misia Mercer. The idea for this book formed as I was reading *The Tao of Zen* by Ray Grigg. Misia encouraged me to fulfill a longtime desire to write a novel by telling me to "just do it." She helped edit *The Scrolls* and provided numerous ideas. Thanks also go to Ania Wieckowski, my sister-in-law, a book editor by profession. Her skills enhanced the storyline and readability of the book. I also would like to thank Christina Paugh for preparing the map of the main Silk Roads, which shows the locations of many of the places discussed in *The Scrolls*. Special thanks go to Joanna Wieckowski, Doreen Larson, and Robbi Jones for their helpful comments. Like a metamorphic process, they helped transform my writings into a more substantial book.

I acknowledge those who unearthed the wealth of ancient history, a source for me to draw upon. During the writing process, I was surprised at how well disparate pieces of this history fit together. In ancient times, storytellers often embellished the truth by spinning entertaining and memorable yarns. Following this tradition, I have taken liberties with certain historical facts and cherry-picked Biblical verses, a common practice in the religion business, in hopes of creating a more interesting tale.

How to Order

The Scrolls is available at Lulu.com, Amazon.com, Barnesandnoble.com and Amazon.co.uk.

Prologue

If an all-powerful, benevolent God allows untold suffering, then that God is either not all-powerful or not benevolent.
                                                    —Mark Malloy, 2003, Geologist

Spring, Second Century CE, Dead Sea Region, Israel

Aharon sat on a rock in the cool shade of the cave's entrance, intently focused on the task at hand. Hunched over, he carefully tapped a small hammer with his right hand. All that could be heard was the soft ping ping ping of the hammer as it hit the delicate chisel firmly gripped in his left hand. After every three taps, he painstakingly repositioned the chisel on the metal sheet that lay on a soft wooden board, which was stretched across two larger rocks in front of him, forming a low table.

The thin sheet, almost pure copper, was an open-hand-width wide and several hand-widths long. The copper had been mined in the Timna Valley, north of the Gulf of Eilat, from the oldest copper mines in the world. The movements of Aharon's chisel and the subsequent tapping produced a text in Aramaic. His father, Yared, also had hammered out text, but in Greek, a language he had learned from his father, Eran the Vigilant. Eran, now deceased, was the reason for the current project.

Eran had been one of the best caravan guides to navigate the trade routes, doing so without the aid of maps or a compass, relying on his knowledge of the desert, landmarks, and the stars. Having traveled extensive portions of the trade routes, he was adept at packing and managing camels, the ships of the desert.

On one of Eran's long journeys, he met a person who forever changed his life, like a strong fever infecting his entire body. It was a fever that Eran passed on to his son, Yared, who in turn passed it on to his son, Aharon. The fever was Christianity and the source, the man who Eran met, was Jesus Christ. Eran had been fortunate to spend several months with Jesus, listening to and memorizing his intensely inspirational stories.

Once home, Eran told and retold these stories to Yared, who in turn told them repeatedly to Aharon. Now they were recording these stories and others they had heard on copper sheets that would be rolled in to scrolls and placed into clay jars. They performed this task out of love and fear—love for Jesus and fear of their fellow Christians.

The Romans still occupied Judea despite several Jewish uprisings. The Jews had been soundly defeated, their temple destroyed, and many dispersed throughout the Roman Empire. Now relative calm existed between Jews and Romans, so Yared feared neither of them. Christians, however, were growing in numbers and forming many competing groups with diverse beliefs. When Yared shared his father's stories about Jesus with some of these groups, certain members became angry, almost violent, to the point that Yared feared for his life and that of his son. He felt an urgent need to preserve the stories, so Yared had purchased the copper sheets, determined to record what he had learned from his father.

After months of tedious work, with the task finally complete, Yared placed the jar containing the last scroll deep into the cave. He rose. Standing over the jars and admiring his work, he thought, *Now the world will know the truth about Jesus.*

Chapter One

If something is in me which can be called religious then it is the unbounded admiration for the structure of the world so far as our science can reveal it.

—Albert Einstein, *The Human Side*

Spring 2002, Dead Sea Region, Israel

Looking down, Mark checked his watch. It was just after 1 PM. They were running late.

"Watch out!" cried Gilda as Mark drove quickly around a hairpin curve on the gravel road.

"What are those?" he asked, looking up in amazement and simultaneously hitting the brakes. In the middle of the narrow road were several deer-like animals he had never seen before. The wheels locked, causing the Range Rover to slow and fishtail slightly, just missing several of the animals.

Bracing herself in response to the sudden stop, Gilda shook her head, smiled, and replied, "They are ibexes, common in this area." Pointing, she continued, "Those huge, round horns are typical. Ibexes are similar to your North American mountain goat."

Her slight accent, which Mark found appealing, gave away her Israeli origins. She added, "As you can see, they are large animals and would cause considerable damage if we hit one."

Mark counted eight. Cautiously, he made his way through the herd, surprised the vehicle didn't frighten them.

Once past the ibexes, he hit the accelerator and inadvertently kicked up gravel.

Feigning distress, Gilda's response was immediate, her tone playful, "What's the hurry? Where did you learn to drive anyway?"

Mark again looked her way. She was smiling, a look that strongly affected him. He responded a little sheepishly, "Sorry." He added, "I learned to drive in the Florida panhandle, but not in a Range Rover."

"Huh," responded Gilda. "Driving a Range Rover is a piece of pie."

"You mean 'a piece of cake'," Mark grinned.

"Whatever," she said testily. "Pie, cake … what difference does it make? Range Rovers are easy to drive."

***

Dr. Mark Malloy, an American geologist with Florida State University (FSU) in Tallahassee, was on sabbatical working with the Geological Survey of Israel (GSI) studying the formation of sinkholes. His interest in these often treacherous depressions stemmed from their occurrence in his home state, where they were known to swallow up entire homes.

His research included studying the impacts of geological processes on early civilizations. These processes, such as the formation of springs or earthquakes, often influenced ancient man's decisions and his myths or religions. For Mark, working in Israel was exciting and would lead to publications. His university definitely adhered to the adage "publish or perish"—perish like the dinosaurs, a colleague had once told him. He had been working in Israel for several months now and planned to remain until midsummer, when his sabbatical would end and he would return to FSU in time for the fall semester.

As others who traveled to this part of the globe, Mark took an avid interest in religious history, especially Biblical history, and now he was in the area where much of that history had unfolded. Rock formations were visible in all directions, and he felt he was in his element. Geologic processes shaped these formations, profoundly influencing stories in the Bible. He looked forward to exploring the relationships between Biblical stories and the geology surrounding him.

Good-natured, his sense of humor often took the form of teasing. At age thirty-four and still single, Mark was considered handsome by many of his female students. Almost six feet tall, he had a thick crop of brown hair peppered with streaks of gray, a premature condition inherited from his mother's side of the family. What caught the attention of most people were his dark, expressive brown eyes, where the colors of his pupil and iris merged as one.

***

Driving north along the southwestern edge of the Dead Sea, Mark periodically scanned the recent aerial photograph lying in Gilda's lap showing the locations of a cluster of sinkholes on the west side of the ancient salt lake. Many of these sinkholes had formed since 1980. Mark and Gilda's destination today was a line of sinkholes that had collapsed within the last two weeks.

Ruts resembling the wavy surface of an old-fashioned washboard caused the Range Rover to bounce violently. Gilda's body shook, her sunglasses nearly falling and ending up at the tip of her nose.

She steadied herself, placing a hand on the dashboard. Peering at Mark over tortoiseshell frames, a twinkle in her eye, she said mischievously, "I don't know about driving in the Florida panhandle, but here in Israel, it helps to slow down when there are bumps in the road, especially when carrying expensive and sensitive equipment."

That's twice she's poked fun at my driving, he thought, gazing at her full lips as she spoke. His comeback was delayed as his thoughts lingering on her lips. After a moment, he said apologetically, "I didn't see those ruts back there. I'll slow down, I promise." In jest, he added, "I didn't realize you considered yourself expensive and sensitive equipment."

Gilda cracked a smile and said, "You know I was referring to the geophysical equipment in the back, but I, too, am valuable cargo who does not like to be shaken by a terrible American driver. If you want, I will be happy to trade places."

"Hmm, now that I know I'm carrying such precious cargo, I'll be more careful." He couldn't help himself—he was grinning from ear to ear.

***

His passenger and teammate was Dr. Gilda Baer with the GSI. Although having spoken previously on the phone, they had met earlier that day. His friends at the GSI had warned him about this single and attractive colleague who socially avoided all male geologists. Gilda was not only an expert on the geology of the area, she also had experience in archeology.

Their conversations flowed easily, and Mark felt an instant camaraderie with her. However, he was unprepared for Gilda's effect on him. She was a striking, black-haired woman, also in her early thirties, who could hold her own in a field dominated by men. At five feet, six inches, she kept a trim, athletic figure. Intelligent and articulate, there was something in her manner that intrigued him. When he kidded her, she teased him back, providing a stimulating repartee.

GSI had a health-and-safety policy of always studying sinkholes in teams of two or more. As he interacted with Gilda, Mark grew more appreciative of this rule and her company.

***

Their study focused on sinkholes located west of Mount Sodom, a salt formation off to their right as they drove north. It wasn't a large peak, but it appeared imposing with the bright sun glistening off exposed salt crystals.

For Mark, the formation triggered a question, "Weren't the towns of Sodom and Gomorrah near here?"

Following Mark's gaze toward Mount Sodom, Gilda answered, "Yes. Some believe this salt formation was the inspiration for the Biblical story about Lot's wife, who was turned into a pillar of salt for looking back on Sodom and Gomorrah while they were being destroyed by God."

Before today's trip, Mark had read about the local geology. Many thousands of years ago, a large prehistoric lake, Lake Gomorrah, filled the basin that was now occupied by the much smaller Dead Sea. Over geological time, many tons of sediment had been deposited in Lake Gomorrah. The weight of these sediments squeezed buried salt deposits upward, forming Mount Sodom. Subsequent erosion left behind columns of salt.

As Mark looked to his right, out of the passenger window beyond Gilda, if he squinted, he could actually see salt columns resembling standing people. Maybe, he thought, ancients saw people in the salt as well, giving rise to the story of Lot's wife.

"How do you think Sodom and Gomorrah were really destroyed?" he asked keeping his eyes fixed on the road.

Summoning from her memory, Gilda responded, "The Bible described the destruction of Sodom and Gomorrah by fire and brimstone. Geologists who studied this area, however, determined that the two towns were actually destroyed and partially submerged by a major earthquake around 2150 BCE or Before the Common, Christian, or Current Era."

"Ah, I know what BCE means." Mark said shaking his head. He also knew that in Biblical times, ancient people didn't understand earthquakes, so describing the disaster resulting from an earthquake as God's wrath in the form of fire and brimstone seemed reasonable.

He explained his thinking. "I can see how some people linked fire with earthquakes. In ancient times, the shaking knocked over candles and lanterns, starting fires that quickly got out of control. The damage would be blamed on fire not the earthquake. And where there was fire, to ancient man, brimstone, a rock associated with lava, must be nearby."

Momentarily distracted by potholes in the road, he slowed, then resumed the conversation. "Even in modern times, earthquakes damage natural gas lines, which lead to fires. The 1906 San Francisco earthquake was referred to as the San Francisco fire for years because a large portion of the city burned when waterlines were broken and fires could not be extinguished."

Gilda nodded in agreement, thinking of her childhood. As a girl, her greatest thrills were taking field trips with her father to visit archeological sites. These trips often included enthusiastic discussions of natural sciences, especially geology, and they had a profound influence on her career choice. Now, as Mark spoke, she experienced a feeling of contentment and déjà vu.

"You know," Mark said, "when I think about the activities in Sodom and Gomorrah, I'm reminded of some of the televangelists we have in America."

Gilda looked at him quizzically. Even though they had only been together since the morning, she was growing accustomed to Mark's religious discussions. She asked, "Why is that?

Mark responded. "Because their behavior is as bad as that in Sodom and Gomorrah. Take the husband and wife team of Jim and Tammy Faye Bakker of the PTL Club for example."

Gilda remained silent. He turned to see a blank expression on her face.

"Haven't you heard of them? Tammy Faye wore loads of makeup. Remember?" Mark asked.

"No. I don't know who they are, but America seems to have more than its share of religious leaders who are not what they seem." She went back to studying the photo.

Undeterred, he continued, "Some rightfully thought PTL stood for Praise the Lord while others joked it stood for Pass the Loot because of all the money the PTL Club collected. Much of the money was used for personal gain instead of helping the needy. Their vast ministry collapsed after Jim's affair with a PTL staffer was exposed."

Gilda sat quietly and looked at Mark, shaking her head in disbelief. She returned to studying the air photo.

Mark thought of another televangelist. "What about the self-aggrandizing Jimmy Swaggart? Surely you've heard of him."

Gilda shook her head.

"Swaggart exposed a fellow minister who was having an affair with another pastor's wife. Competition for the church dollar is cutthroat and if you can eliminate another minister, there's more take for you."

Recalling the rest of the story, Mark said. "In retaliation, the ousted minister had Swaggart followed. A private detective caught Swaggart in a motel room with a prostitute."

Gilda was not particularly interested in American televangelists. "Sorry, I haven't heard of him either. If it helps, I have heard of your Jim Jones and the mass suicide using cyanide-laced Kool-Aid."

"Yes, he was product of American fringe Christianity." Considering Swaggart's behavior, Mark thought, this reality bests any fiction. He muttered under his breath, "Sex, religion, and money are a bad combination. You have to wonder what's going on with other televangelists."

Gilda listened, amused at Mark's fascination with sex and religion. Most men she knew were the silent type, but not this American. When she first met him in the morning, she thought he was brash and overconfident—traits she disliked. As the day progressed, however, she found herself vaguely attracted to him despite her best efforts to the contrary. There was something about his grin, his eyes.

"I guess we should get back to business," Mark said. "How much further to those new sinkholes?"

"*We* should get back to business?" asked Gilda sarcastically. "I think you mean *you*." After a short pause, she answered, "Not far. See that marker in the distance? We'll turn left there and follow the small trail. At the end, we should be close."

The marker to which Gilda referred was a conical stack of rocks, a cairn, along the side of the gravel road. Turning left at the cairn, the small trail rose and headed west toward the distant Judean hills. The air was dry, and the vehicle kicked up dust in its wake, some of it entering their vehicle.

Gilda rolled her window up part way. She turned to Mark, "We are driving away from the Dead Sea, which is almost fourteen hundred feet below sea level. Topographically, this part of the Jordan Rift Valley is the lowest place on earth." The Rift Valley is a long linear feature caused by the earth's crust being pulled apart in the vicinity of the Dead Sea.

Mark reached for a bottle of water and took a sip. "Man, is it dry," he commented, "not like Florida where I grew up. I'm used to heavy humidity and abundant greenery. But I have to admit, the desert possesses a wondrous beauty."

"It is beautiful," agreed Gilda, "and arid. Precipitation around the Dead Sea is less than a handful of inches each year. The Jordan River, where Jesus was baptized, flows from the north and terminates in the Dead Sea. During the last half of the twentieth century, large amounts of water were removed from the river and used for irrigation and water supply. As a result of these diversions, the volume of water reaching the Dead Sea has significantly declined."

Mark was generally aware of what Gilda was telling him, but enjoyed listening to her accent. He was certainly interested in the subject matter. So he encouraged her to continue, "And the consequences of this decline are?"

She explained, "This reduction of river water entering the sea, combined with a high evaporation rate, caused the sea level to drop dramatically. The lower sea level pulled in adjacent groundwater. This produced a lowering of the underground water table surrounding the sea, which, in turn, is contributing to sinkhole formation. The inflowing groundwater and low flow from the Jordan River cannot sustain the Dead Sea, which is shrinking. It someday will disappear altogether if current conditions continue."

"You know what's ironic," said Mark, not really expecting an answer. "West of here in Egypt, there's too much water. Irrigation produced a rise in the water table beneath just about every temple in Egypt, including the one at Luxor. Even under the Great Pyramid of Giza and the Great Sphinx. The high water is damaging the bases of these structures, requiring dewatering projects to lower the water table. Too bad that excess water can't be moved here where it's needed."

"True. Have you heard?" asked Gilda. "There is a proposed project to import water from the Red Sea. If proven feasible, water from the Red Sea may someday be used to augment the Dead Sea."

"That's an interesting idea," thought Mark aloud.

***

As the Range Rover crested a low ridge, the small, gaping openings of several newly formed sinkholes came into view. "There they are," Mark said, pointing to the holes, which were probably associated with a buried fault where the earth's rocks and sediments had been disrupted by geological activity. He knew that west of the Dead Sea lay a buried layer of salt. Fault openings allowed groundwater flow, resulting in localized dissolution of salt over thousands of years, leaving behind empty pockets that formed cavities and caves.

Parking, he turned to Gilda, "Bet Archimedes wasn't thinking of sinkholes when he came up with his principle on buoyancy."

They both got out and looked around.

Gilda understood Archimedes' Principle but chose not to comment. She simply nodded. She knew water provided an upward buoyancy force, as enumerated by the Greek mathematician. A cave ceiling submerged in groundwater is effectively supported, in part, by the groundwater. When the water table drops below the ceiling, the upward buoyancy force is lost, but gravity continues pushing down on the ceiling, which can collapse if it loses structural integrity. That is exactly how the sinkholes they were viewing had formed.

"What a spectacular view," observed Gilda, looking over the horizon. "I count approximately a dozen sinkholes." The sinkholes stretched over a distance of about a half-mile, with the undulating Judean hills looming in the background.

The contrast of the reddish brown desert floor with black holes against the cloudless dark blue sky reminded Mark of modern art he had seen in the National Art Gallery in Washington DC. He recalled a Biblical passage in Numbers: "And the earth opened her mouth, and swallowed them up, and their houses, and all the men ..." He couldn't help but wonder if the origin of this story was a sinkhole.

***

It was early afternoon, and they hadn't eaten since morning. Gilda asked, "Are you ready to eat before we start work?"

"Sounds like a plan." During lunch, Mark wanted to talk on a personal level with Gilda, but he wasn't sure how to approach the conversation. Instead, he chose a more comfortable topic, saying, "How do you like working for the GSI?"

Gilda finished chewing a bite of her sandwich. "I enjoy it very much. It's the perfect job—a good balance between working in the office and spending time in the field, like today. I didn't major in geology to spend all my time behind a desk. I especially appreciate the opportunity to be outdoors doing fieldwork. This area is hard to beat for interesting geology and beauty."

"I agree," replied Mark. "This is the perfect place to perform fieldwork. In the desert, the geological formations are clearly exposed. Back home in Florida, large amounts of rainfall produce heavy vegetation, covering the geology and making it more difficult to interpret. Unlike here, the geology in Florida is less stimulating visually."

Mark wanted to ask Gilda if she was seeing anyone, but he didn't have the nerve. They finished their lunch in silence, enjoying the view. Overhead, the dark blue sky was marred by several growing white contrails, the telltale indicators of passing jets, adding to the palette of colors and geometric designs on nature's canvas.

***

Following lunch, they gathered their equipment and began methodically investigating the sinkholes. Mark grabbed his backpack, which he took everywhere. The first sinkhole they came to was typical of the others.

As Mark took off his backpack and laid out the equipment, Gilda carefully approached the hole to inspect it. Leaning forward, she peered into the fifteen-foot opening. The cavernous hole was dark inside, preventing her from seeing the bottom. She leaned in a little closer. Still not seeing the bottom, she took another step.

Abruptly, the ground beneath her shifted. Dirt cascaded into the opening. Losing her balance, she began falling forward into the black hole. She flung her arms out to regain her balance. Suddenly, Mark grabbed her right arm. He pulled her back toward him just as the sinkhole expanded its diameter to where she had stood.

Moving quickly away, a shaken Gilda said, "I can't believe that happened to me." A moment later, she added, "Thank you. I didn't know you were so close. I thought you were working on the equipment over here."

"I was, but when I saw you approaching the sinkhole, I moved closer, just in case."

"Good thing you did," said Gilda, her body shaking. "We need to be very careful near those openings. The ground is obviously unstable." She was numb, and her words were rote.

After a few moments and sensing she was okay, Mark released his hold on her. She stood awkwardly in silence.

Slowly recovering her composure, Gilda said, "I'm fine. Let's get started."

"Are you sure?" Mark asked.

"Yes," she assured him, and she began preparing to work.

They used a global positioning system to map the locations of the sinkholes. Exploring the surface, they took samples, then mapped and photographed geological observations and sample locations. Cautiously, they moved from one sinkhole to the next, moving steadily away from the Range Rover. One of them always stayed back as the other approached an opening to take measurements.

Working as a team, each seemed to anticipate the other's needs. The tedious work was physically demanding. Both Gilda and Mark stripped down to tee shirts and shorts in the warm midafternoon sun. Gilda kept reminding him, "Be sure to drink plenty of water."

"Yes, mother," he responded and did as told.

He could not help but notice Gilda's dark, well-toned body. He tried not to let the vision of her female form interfere with the work at hand, but it was difficult. *Thank goodness for sunglasses*, he thought. It seemed his eyes had a will of their own and would find her and linger even though he commanded them not to. He feared she sensed his eye problem, but she graciously said nothing.

Observing her, willingly or unwillingly, made the time pass quickly. Performing fieldwork with her was sheer pleasure. On occasion, their work brought them close together, even touching. During such occasions, Mark's senses became heightened, and he was keenly aware of her close presence, even her smallest movement.

Toward the end of their study, they conducted surface geophysical surveys, allowing them to see into the earth and map anomalous features like caves and cavities below land surface. The surface geophysical tool was analogous to a doctor using an x-ray machine to see into a body. And just like with the x-ray, some interpretation was required.

Based on preliminary results, Gilda observed, "These sinkholes are definitely connected by a linear cave system. With the geophysical results, we should be able to create a comprehensive map of the caves."

"Agreed," responded Mark, pleased with their findings. "The main cave is aligned north to south, but there are several offshoots, including a significant linear feature that heads off toward the west over there." Pointing, he added, "These secondary caverns don't seem to play a role in the sinkholes formed thus far. It will be interesting to determine why some of these linear features produce sinkholes while others don't. Maybe we can develop a method for estimating where the next sinkholes are likely to form."

It was late afternoon, and Gilda was ready to call it a day. "We should pack up and head back. We can analyze the rest of the data in the office."

"I'm ready," Mark concurred as he pulled on his shirt. "We should leave while we're ahead—no one fell into a sinkhole."

Suspecting this was a reference to her near mishap, Gilda smiled demurely as she began gathering the equipment.

Packing, Mark looked up and noticed a new hole further off to the west.

Chapter Two

Scientific research is based on the idea that everything that takes place is determined by laws of nature, and therefore this holds for the action of people. For this reason, a research scientist will hardly be inclined to believe that events could be influenced by a prayer, i.e., by a wish addressed to a Supernatural Being.

—Albert Einstein, *The Human Side*

Spring 2002, Dead Sea Region, Israel

Squinting to see better, Mark pointed and said, "Look, Gilda, up the hill about five hundred yards. Isn't that another opening?"

Looking westward, into the sun, Gilda shielded her eyes with her hand. "You're right. It appears to be aligned with that western linear feature we just mapped." Energized by the sighting, she dropped her gear and said, "Let's go check it out."

Heading up the hill, Gilda called back over her shoulder, "Are you coming?"

Catching up to her, Mark needed to walk briskly just to stay beside her. When they reached the hole, they saw signs of weathering or aging in the opening.

"This isn't recent," said Gilda. "It's been exposed to the elements for some time."

"I agree." Bending over to examine the rock, Mark said, "Look, this is limestone, not salt. We've moved up the hill enough so that we're above the salt formation." He added the obvious, "This isn't a sinkhole; it's a cave."

Excitedly, Gilda said, "Let's explore inside."

"Huh, okay," agreed Mark unenthusiastically. "Do you think it's safe?"

"With the proper equipment, we should be fine."

Mark wasn't as confident. Some of his friends in Florida were spelunkers. They explored caverns, even diving into submerged caves with scuba gear. He repeatedly declined invitations to join them.

Squeezing through narrow passageways below ground, unsure what lay ahead, did not appeal to him. Plus, people periodically died diving in caves. So it was with reluctance that he finally agreed. "Okay. Let me carry our mapping equipment back to the truck and retrieve what we might need."

It took Mark fifteen minutes to make it back to the truck almost a mile away. He drove the Range Rover off the small trail and parked as close to the cave as he could, careful to avoid the sinkholes and linear features they had just mapped. He returned to Gilda carrying hardhats, mining headlamps, flashlights, and rope, most contained in his backpack. They had been unsure how long their fieldwork would take, so they had brought equipment for almost any situation, including camping equipment in the event they were out longer than planned and had to spend the night.

While Mark was parking, Gilda explored the area around the cave entrance, looking for signs of recent activities by animals or man. She found none.

She put on her hardhat and headlamp, preparing to enter the cave.

Mark, lost in her smile, finally remembered to put on his own hardhat and headlamp.

"If you're ready," she said, "let's go."

"I'm ready," replied Mark. "After you." With a dip at the waist and a swing of his arm he motioned in the direction of the cave entrance.

They walked single file through the narrow cave passage with Gilda in the lead. As Mark crouched slightly to avoid bumping his head, the light from his headlamp fell directly on Gilda's derriere. The view momentarily belayed his fears of narrow caves and the unknown ahead. Trying to focus on their task, he asked, "What are we looking for?"

"These caves have been used over the centuries by locals for a variety of purposes. You never know what artifacts, if any, this cave could hold." Gilda continued with excitement in her voice, "The ancient settlement of Qumran was located north of here. Caves near there yielded the Dead Sea Scrolls."

Hearing this, Mark's enthusiasm for cave exploration increased somewhat. Deeper in the cave, the ceiling was higher and he was able to stand up straight. Adjusting his headlamp, he said, "I've heard of the Dead Sea Scrolls, but don't know much about them." Half kidding, he asked, "Are they the missing books from the Bible?"

Gilda stopped, turned, and looked at him questioningly. "Which Bible? Yours or mine?"

Mark, playing along, said, "Okay, enlighten me."

"Mine is the Hebrew Bible, corresponding roughly to your Old Testament."

"I knew that. Isn't your Bible called the Torah?"

"No, the Torah, or Teaching, is only part of the Hebrew Bible called the Tanakh. The other two parts are the Nevi'im, or Prophets, and Ketuvim, or Writings."

"So," said Mark, "my Bible, the Protestant Bible, encompasses your Bible, presenting Jewish history and teachings before Jesus Christ and the New Testament, which includes history and teachings after the birth of Christ." He paused, before adding, "I guess bigger must be better."

"Only if you believe what a bunch of church bureaucrats in Turkey decided should be included in the New Testament," retorted Gilda, somewhat irritated.

Mark noticed her irritation, which, in a perverse way, he enjoyed. There was something about the sparkle in her eyes and her mannerisms when she was slightly perturbed that appealed to him.

"Now it's my turn to enlighten you," he said with a slightly superior tone. "What I think you're referring to is the Council of Nicaea, which took place in Nicaea, present-day Iznik, Turkey, during the fourth century CE or Common, Christian, or Current Era. The bishops who attended that gathering decided things like 'Is the Son of God equal to God?' Oh, they also wanted to separate Easter from Passover."

"Didn't want to share a holiday with the Jews, huh?" jabbed Gilda. "And I know what CE stands for." She realized he was getting back at her for earlier defining BCE.

Smiling but ignoring her question, Mark continued, "It's believed that they didn't decide the contents of the New Testament as you suggest. That the bishops decided what should or should not be included in the New Testament is considered a myth by many in the church. It is interesting, however, that a complete and universally recognized New Testament was not compiled until the fourth century CE, sometime after the Council of Nicaea."

Mark interrupted himself. "Is that a coincidence or what? I don't usually believe in coincidences. Anyway, up until that time, there were multiple Christian documents that were not necessarily consistent in their stories and beliefs. Some of the documents were included in the New Testament and some were not. Someone had to make those decisions. If it wasn't bishops making them, then I wonder who did."

He paused from his ramblings and thought a moment, ultimately displaying mock surrender. Reluctantly, he said, "You know, you may have a point after all."

Gilda grinned at him in a told-you-so fashion, then turned and walked farther into the cave, saying over her shoulder, "Now that we are clear on that, do you want to know about the Dead Sea Scrolls or not?"

Deeper into the cave, there was little natural light, and the air was cool. Catching up with her, Mark declared, "Sure, of course."

She stopped and faced him, the light from her headlamp falling on his chest. "The Dead Sea Scrolls are the only known surviving copies of Biblical documents, with some as old as 150 BCE. They were found in multiple caves and contained portions of almost every book of the Old Testament. Written in Hebrew, Aramaic, and Greek, like in your New Testament, there were inconsistencies within these documents."

She paused for a moment and added, "The study of the Dead Sea Scrolls shows that the Hebrew Bible was not finalized until about 100 CE, only about three centuries before your New Testament. Relatively speaking, your bishops tended to move much more quickly to finalize the New Testament than we Jews did with the Old Testament."

Teasing him, she said, "Moving so quickly, one can make mistakes."

"You confuse quickness with efficiency," Mark rejoined. "I can't help it if your rabbis were not efficient." He had a big smile on his face, thinking he had just one-upped her. Yet he knew there were mistakes and inconsistencies in the New Testament, although he doubted haste was the reason.

They continued walking and reached a wider portion of the cave, beyond which the passageway narrowed. Here, they encountered a blockage where roof debris had slumped down and effectively prevented further entry. Gilda hesitated, then turned around and began to examine the floor of the cave.

"What are you doing?" Mark asked.

"Just looking for any clues that people may have been here."

"I'm going to check this mound to see if there's a way through it," Mark said.

"Okay, but be careful."

Taking off his backpack with trepidation and unease, Mark climbed onto the rock debris and looked for a pathway deeper into the cave. Slowly picking his way up the mound, he slipped and almost fell, catching himself by pressing his body against the pile of debris.

The sound of rocks cascading caused Gilda to look with alarm toward Mark. "Do you need help?"

"No. I just slipped on some loose rock. I'm fine."

Gilda returned to her exploring while Mark continued his climb. Finally, near the top of the debris and the cave ceiling, the clearance became very narrow.

He tentatively ventured to his left, trying to squeeze through a small opening. *This is exactly what I didn't want to be doing*, thought Mark. Suddenly, the debris beneath him gave way. Down he went. Attempting to grab something stationary, his arms reached out. Nothing was there. Falling farther, his lower body became wedged into an extremely narrow space. His upper body was pummeled by dirt and sharp rocks, which jabbed him, producing severe pain. Panicked, the realization hit him—he was being buried alive. Then everything went black.

Gilda turned to see Mark disappear through a small hole in the cave floor. All she could see was dust exploding up from the newly formed jagged opening. The rumbling stopped almost as soon as it began. Instinctively, she ran to the edge of the missing floor and yelled down, "Mark, are you okay?" Fearful, she waited a moment, and then asked, "Can you hear me?"

No response. The dust prevented seeing anything other than the blunted stream of light from his headlamp. The dulled light beam was about ten feet below her and stationary, indicating Mark was either not moving or he had lost his hat. A ten-foot fall could easily be fatal. Even if Mark were just injured, how would she rescue him? Concerned, she kept calling out, panic creeping into her voice. Her heart pounded.

***

Mark lay in the dusty darkness, disoriented and covered with debris. He heard moaning, then realized the sound was coming from him. Dazed, he may have lost consciousness momentarily. He wasn't sure. Pain engulfed his body. Dozens of pressure points worked in concert to crush him. Trying to remain calm, thoughts of dying intruded his reasoning. Pushing those thoughts aside and reconstructing what happened, he discovered that he could only move his right arm. The rest of his body, except for his head, was buried. Feeling around with his free hand, he retrieved his partially buried flashlight. Barely penetrating the dust, the light shown on the surrounding wall, only inches away from him. Claustrophobia engulfed him. Fighting off nausea, he closed his eyes to calm himself. Soon his fear dissipated, rapidly replaced by anger.

He heard Gilda in the background and wondered why people always ask if you are okay after something like this happened. He continued to hear her calls more clearly now, and coming out of his fog, he finally responded. Angry with himself, he lashed out at her, yelling back, "No, I'm not okay. I was just swallowed by a sinkhole!"

"Are you hurt?" she asked.

But there was no answer, the terrible silence continued. She now could see two dulled light beams but little else. Gilda had to wait for either Mark's response or for the dust to clear to see. She felt helpless.

Mark was stuck, unsure if he could free himself. Another wave of panic came over him. Controlling his fears, his response was Darwinian—a determination to survive. Slowly with his right hand, he began removing debris from his other arm. After a few minutes, he was able to pull it free. He yelled up, "Gilda, I'm stuck but my arms are free. I'll try to work on the rest of my body."

Gilda hated the waiting, the uncertainty. She wanted to know what was happening. She yelled down, "Can I do anything to help?"

"No," Mark called back curtly. Then all she could hear was rock and dirt being tossed.

Gradually Mark dug away more material from around his body until his arms could reach no deeper. Pushing down on both hands, with great effort, he tried to pry his legs out of the narrow hole where he was wedged. He struggled, failing to budge on the first few attempts. Finally, on the fifth try, his body moved slightly. It took him several more attempts, each time moving himself upward in small increments, the earth closing under him. Eventually, he pushed himself free and crawled on top of the debris.

To Gilda, an eternity passed. All she could hear were Mark's grunts, then silence. The lights below were no longer moving. Had he lost consciousness? Again, she yelled down, "Are you okay?" There was no response.

Exhausted, Mark sat against the wall catching his breath. Thankfully, after checking various parts of his body, he found himself unhurt except for some bruising and a catch in his lower back. The right side of his face felt as if he had been in a losing fist fight.

He looked up and saw the light from Gilda's lamp. Luckily, the fall was only about ten feet. It was fortunate the collapse wasn't any deeper. Only some of the debris had caved in and covered him. More luck, he thought. Breathing a sigh of relief, he was grateful for his hardhat.

He heard Gilda cry out again and finally had enough air in his lungs to respond. "No, I'm not hurt badly, just startled and maybe a little winded." This time he was more polite. "Thanks for asking."

After a pause, he said, "I brought the rope. Can you please pass it down? It's in my backpack that should be nearby."

Gilda found the backpack and took out the rope. Fortunately, it was long enough. She dropped one end of the rope down and tied the other end around her waist. "Wait until I brace myself."

Finding an indentation in the cave wall, she wedged herself in. "Okay, try to pull yourself out now."

The strain on Gilda was great as Mark started up the rope. He was only up a couple of feet when her boots slipped on the dusty floor and Mark fell back to the bottom. "Let me try again," she called. This time she placed one foot against the wall, pushing hard to stabilize herself. She yelled out, "Okay, try pulling yourself up again."

With considerable effort and constant encouragement from Gilda, Mark climbed slowly out of the hole. When he finally reached the top, he lay on the cave floor trying to catch his breath. He lifted up to a sitting position unsure what to do next. Looking down, he was covered in dust, and his shirt and pants were torn in many places. His legs were covered with scratches and small cuts.

Breathing heavily, Gilda rushed over and sat beside him, staring wide-eyed. She slowly ran her hand down his dirty cheek, causing him to shiver.

Shining her light on him, she could see purple bruising on his left arm. His right cheek was beginning to swell. "Are you sure you're okay?" she asked with concern in her voice, looking straight into his eyes.

"Yes," he said awkwardly, ignoring the pain and touched by her kind gesture.

Embarrassed, he looked away toward the back of the cave. At that point, he noticed the cave was no longer blocked. The debris had fallen through the hole, yet the cave roof held.

"Look," Mark said, pointing with renewed interest, "the collapse opened the cave." His pained face brightened.

Gilda glanced toward where Mark pointed and turned back to him. She studied him. "Are you okay to continue?"

Steeling himself against the pain, Mark replied excitedly, "Yes." He stood up, almost falling over. Slowly, he regained his balance. Dusting off his clothes and bending his legs to test them, he said, "Come on." Mark grabbed his backpack, shoved the rope in, and moved further into the cave. They edged their way around the almost five-foot-wide hole in the floor, reaching the other side unscathed.

Mark said with unease, "We should limit our movement. I don't want to trigger another collapse. I may have used all my luck back there." He looked back and shined his headlamp on the hole in the cave floor through which he had fallen moments earlier. It looked like a gaping mouth wanting to be fed, and he didn't want to be swallowed again.

Once past the hole, they stood still and slowly took in their surroundings with the aid of their powerful flashlights. It was still dusty, making it difficult to see and breathe, but it appeared the cave opened up into a large room. As the dust settled, their flashlights penetrated further. Against the cave wall toward the back, their headlamps suddenly fell on a number of regular shapes, each about a foot tall.

"Over there!" Gilda cried excitedly as the light from her flashlight revealed dusty, ancient-looking jars.

As they approached the clay jars, Gilda recalled, "The Dead Sea Scrolls were found in containers like these. As the story goes, a Bedouin shepherd threw a stone into a cave to scare out stragglers from his sheep herd that may have wandered into the cave. Instead of hearing animal noises, he heard pottery breaking so he went in to explore. He found jars similar to these."

Mark stopped, looking intently at the jars; he was overwhelmed. Staggered by the many possibilities these jars might represent, he finally said, "These were probably never found before because the passage was blocked. Who would have thought that a sinkhole could lead to this discovery?"

Gilda bent down examining the jars more closely. After clearing away the dust, she removed the lid and peered into the nearest one. Inside, she saw deteriorated linens that appeared to be wrapping material.

Trying to remain calm and keep her hands from shaking, she told Mark, "We need to be very careful to preserve this finding. However, we need to determine what exactly is inside. Do not shine your flashlight directly on the contents of the jar."

Carefully, she removed the object and the linen surrounding it from the jar. Setting it on the ground, she next removed the fragile linen to reveal a scroll made of what appeared to be copper.

Gilda gasped in astonishment. "Most of the Dead Sea Scrolls were written on parchment with some on papyrus. One scroll, however, called the Copper Scroll, was found."

"I wonder how old this scroll is," Mark thought aloud.

"It's hard to tell, but given the location and similar condition to the Dead Sea Scrolls, it is possible they date back to the same time period," she reasoned.

Mark's mind raced, and his excitement built. He knew this could be the discovery of a lifetime.

Gilda carefully rewrapped the copper scroll and placed it back in the jar. "We need to leave the cave and notify my boss of these findings so that proper archeologists can study this site and remove the jars for examination in a laboratory."

"That doesn't seem fair," said Mark, half kidding. "We found them."

"I think we can stay involved, but this requires skills beyond our capabilities."

"Why don't you make your call while I stay and take some photographs?" Mark suggested.

"Okay, but be careful."

Gilda turned and cautiously made her way out of the cave. When she reached the truck, she called on a satellite phone.

Meanwhile, Mark took pictures of the twelve clay jars.

Carrying his backpack in one hand and the rope in the other, Mark exited the cave as Gilda hung up the phone. "Well, what did your boss say?" he asked.

"First, we can stay involved, but we have to comply with a secrecy rule, meaning we cannot discuss the existence or contents of these scrolls with anyone. This isn't unusual. There was a similar rule for those involved with the Dead Sea Scrolls. I guess I should say the Qumran Dead Sea Scrolls because now we have—"

"The Mount Sodom Dead Sea Scrolls," Mark finished her sentence, adding, "I'm not sure I'm willing to go along with a secrecy rule."

"Then you may not be able to stay involved," Gilda informed him. "I'm not enthusiastic about this condition either, but I don't think we have a choice."

After briefly thinking about it, he reluctantly said, "Okay. I guess I can't object for now because I definitely want to remain involved in learning the scrolls' content."

"Second," continued Gilda, "archeologists from my government will be here first thing tomorrow morning."

"So what are we supposed to do until morning?" asked Mark.

"That's the third thing. To insure the scrolls' protection, we need to spend the night here."

"Unlike the secrecy rule," replied Mark cheerfully, "that's a condition I can live with."

It was getting late, and Gilda said, "We should set up camp. This is as good a place as any."

They pulled out sleeping bags and a cooler with food and drink for dinner, and then set up camp next to the Range Rover. As he settled, Mark became aware of an ache in the small of his back related to his fall. His entire body throbbed. He stretched by bending over and moving from side to side, but he couldn't eliminate the pain. Finally, he said, "You know, during that fall in the sinkhole, I think I may have injured my back. How are you at therapeutic back massages?"

Thinking he was teasing again, Gilda said, "Don't push your luck, wise guy. You don't know this about me, but I trained with the Israeli Army and know the art of self defense." All Israelis serve in the army, including women, so Gilda's threat was real but not serious.

"Okay, okay, I give up." Pushing the pain out of his mind but holding his back, Mark continued to think about the scrolls, wondering what stories they told. He watched his Israeli partner, trying to assess why she affected him so.

Chapter Three

I cannot imagine a God who rewards and punishes the objects of his creation, whose purposes are modeled after our own—a God, in short, who is but a reflection of human frailty.
—Albert Einstein, Obituary in *New York Times*, April 19, 1955

Spring 2002, Dead Sea Region, Israel

During the day, white light from the sun is scattered by atmospheric particles into violet and blue colors to produce blue sky. At sunset, the sun's white light travels a greater distance through the atmosphere, a trek during which even more light scatter occurs. The result: only the color red, thanks to its longer wavelength, reaches our eyes, yielding the exploding ball of crimson that precedes dusk. This was Mark and Gilda's view.

The temperature dropped rapidly in the desert as the sun began to set. Gilda slipped into a light jacket while Mark lit the gas stove. They had come prepared to spend the night if need be, packing cans of stew and mixed vegetables, which Mark began to heat. Gilda sliced up fruit and cheese, gathering plates and utensils for eating. Focusing on their food preparation, neither one spoke. Eventually breaking the silence, Gilda said, "What a beautiful sunset."

Looking up from the stove, Mark soaked in the setting sun, which had turned the red landscape a deeper, more vibrant red. The shadows cast by rock outcrops became longer and longer. It was as if the shadows came alive and moved across the desert floor. It was an enchanting setting for dinner. The sun was almost down when dinner was ready. Mark and Gilda sat on a couple of large rocks next to each other with food-laden plates on their laps. They ate by muted light cast from a flickering camp lantern.

Searching for conversation, Mark complimented Gilda, "Your fruit and cheese taste really good." He thought everything tasted better when eating outside in the fresh air.

"I'm glad you like it." Then she added, "It's nice to have a man help cook, even if it is just warming up the contents of a can. Do men in the United States typically help with the cooking?"

Mark wasn't sure how to respond. He began hesitantly, "Growing up, my mother was the main cook, but being a bachelor, I have no objections to cooking or other household chores. Maybe it's a generational thing. I certainly enjoy cooking outdoors."

While eating, they drank beer, a last-minute addition to their supplies purchased along the way. Mark would have preferred wine, but the beer tasted fine. From time to time, he held the cool beer can next to his swollen face, providing some relief from the slight but constant throbbing. Looking out over the horizon, he asked, "So, what's it like growing up in Israel?"

"It's wonderful, in general. As you know, the study of geology here is very interesting, as is history and archeology. The climate is as close to perfect as it gets. And we have beautiful beaches."

Becoming more serious, she added, "Unfortunately, terrorist attacks are the downside. Last year, we had thirty-four attacks resulting in eighty-five deaths. So far, this year the rate of attacks and deaths is even higher. Suicide bombings have increased, and some recently involved child bombers, a new tactic we have not seen before. Because we live under the constant threat of these attacks, you have to always be vigilant, reporting unattended packages or suspicious-looking people. After a while, the continuous stress takes a toll on your nerves and well-being."

Mark thought about Gilda's description of Israeli life, knowing that religion was a major factor in the violence. The wounds of history are difficult to heal. Trying to make a point, he carefully selected his words.

Somberly, he said, "The Israeli-Palestinian conflict is an extremely difficult situation. While many Muslims don't support violence, there are some fundamentalists who promote it. These groups base their violence on the teachings of the Qur'an and on the sayings and examples of the prophet Muhammad himself. Initially, Muhammad, as the legend goes, was approached by the archangel Gabriel to preach the message of one God, the God of Abraham, Moses, and Jesus. While Muhammad taught this message and gained many converts in Mecca, his new viewpoint was not always popular, and there was an attempt on his life. He escaped."

Gilda stopped eating. Staring at Mark, she wondered where this conversation was going. She was about to respond but didn't. The look on her face was response enough.

Mark swallowed, noticed Gilda's intense look, and continued, "Muhammad, who had been a merchant in Medina, became a warrior, attacked Mecca, and converted the population to his new religion, Islam."

Shaking her head, Gilda said, "I'm not sure I see your point."

Mark explained, "Because he was forced to become a warrior, some of his teachings have messages of violence, not that dissimilar from some of the teachings in the Old Testament, where the Israelites were forced to fight and take back land after being exiled in Egypt."

"I'm having a hard time making that connection," responded Gilda, bemused by the comparison of the two religions.

He tried again, "My point is that it's too bad that Islam, and for that matter, Judaism, don't have the equivalent of Jesus' teachings found in the New Testament like the Christians have, focusing on loving one's neighbor, peace, and harmony as a path one should follow. Israel and some Muslim countries have many things in common; one of those is a nonrelinquishing desire to occupy the same land. This unfortunately leads to violence."

Gilda looked at him for a moment and then argued, "You make some good points, but even though Christians have Jesus' teachings in the New Testament as a guide for living in peace and harmony, they often choose not to follow that guidance. Look at the Spanish Inquisition; that was not a peace-and-harmony event. Or take the Crusades; those were hardly peace-and-harmony events. Or take your country … in how many wars has your Christian-dominated country participated?"

Mark did not immediately respond, realizing Gilda made effective arguments against his thesis, but he still believed Jesus' message was a significant turning point. He adjusted his sitting position on the rock and countered, "You're correct. Many Christians take their guidance from the Old Testament rather than the turn-the-other-cheek life of Jesus in the New Testament. But the New Testament is still available as an option for one to follow."

Gilda, slightly annoyed, again refuted Mark, saying, "The Old Testament also has many good passages that one could elect to follow. Most notably The Old Testament introduces the Ten Commandments, one of which is 'Thou shalt not kill.'"

Again, Mark had to agree with Gilda, saying, "You're right, but I still think the New Testament marked a change in philosophy from that of the Old Testament. After all, Luke indicates that Jesus' mission on earth was to spread peace and good will toward men. That is my point."

Placing his plate on the ground and standing, Mark continued to promote the New Testament but with a new tact, focusing more on Jesus. "Battles and tumultuous events were common in the times of the Old Testament, and they were just as intrusive into daily life in Muhammad's time. It is no surprise the guidance in both the Old Testament and the Qur'an is somewhat militaristic. Jesus was not a warrior. He went from past teachings about 'An eye for an eye and a tooth for a tooth' to teaching a more peaceful approach for humankind. It is as if Jesus became enlightened in a Buddha-like or Hindu sense."

Gilda, drawn into Mark's point, remained seated on her rock, picking at her food and thinking. She had studied the New Testament and was aware that not all of it was consistent with the enlightened message to which Mark referred. Gilda completed her thoughts, saying, "You may be correct about Jesus, but the New Testament contains more than Jesus' teachings. The four gospels—Matthew, Mark, Luke, and John—provide the main part of the New Testament describing Jesus' life. Not included in the Bible are several other gospels that were never canonical. Much of the rest of the New Testament are letters or epistles, twenty-one in all. These letters, along with the Book of Acts, serve as a bridge between Jesus' life and the emerging Christian churches of the late second century CE. The authenticity of several of these letters is questioned by some scholars."

She paused, giving Mark an opportunity to respond. When he did not, she continued, saying, "At the time of the letters, the early Christian churches were in competition with Judaism. As a result of this competition for converts and, for that matter, for Jewish history itself, the content of some of these letters does not always conform to the enlightened philosophy of Jesus. There are some who believe these letters may have even influenced the writings of the gospels."

Again she paused, waiting for a rejoinder.

Mark simply said, "I agree with everything you're saying." Adding, "Are you finished?" He began to pace, considering further what Gilda had said.

She cleared her throat, "Not yet. For example, Paul the Apostle, or missionary, is credited with writing thirteen of these letters or epistles, but scholars question whether he wrote all of them. The book of Acts discusses Paul's travels and deeds, but it contradicts Paul's own epistles. We don't know much about his life, but he never knew Jesus. He was born Saul, a Jew, who, by his own admission, 'violently persecuted' Christians until his conversion to Christianity on the road to Damascus. Do you remember?"

"Yes, the metaphor 'On the road to Damascus' is often used to describe an event that causes someone to change his or her opinion." Mark continued pacing, clearly savoring the moment. "Some thought Paul manipulated Jesus' message for his own gain and glory. Had there been television back then, Paul might have been the first televangelist." Mark smiled at his comparison.

Gilda finished her beer and continued. "Paul's writings are inconsistent and actually can be interpreted in opposite ways. Based on these writings, some consider Paul to have been a woman-hater, homophobic, and anti-Semitic. None of these descriptors can be applied to Jesus. My point is that not all of the New Testament is as enlightened as Jesus' teachings."

Mark now recalled that Thomas Jefferson, third president of the United States and America's first wine connoisseur, was a critic of Paul and once wrote that Paul was the "first corrupter of the doctrines of Jesus." Mark knew many other corrupters of Jesus' message followed Paul, including some preachers today in the States.

Mark agreed enthusiastically. He was enjoying the stimulating discussion. "You make some interesting points. When I think about the New Testament, I tend to focus on Jesus to the exclusion of everything else. I will try to correct that from now on."

Then he added, "I agree with you. Jesus' words have been misinterpreted and corrupted by many, perhaps starting with Paul. I focus on what Jesus said, but we don't know what he said exactly. So I tend to follow the intent of Jesus' message, which I believe is more peaceful and enlightened than earlier messages in the Bible." As he finished his statement, Mark thought again about those who corrupted Jesus' message today. Jim and Tammy Faye Bakker came to mind.

Silence ensued; Mark stopped pacing and scanned the horizon, deep in thought. Gilda stood up, stretched, and began gathering dishes and cooking utensils.

He changed the topic as he helped with the dishes. "What do your parents do?"

"My parents were killed in a car accident many years ago when I was in college. Before that, my father taught high school science in Jerusalem."

Mark stopped and stood looking at her. "I'm very sorry. I know from personal experience how hard it is to lose a parent at a young age. I can't imagine losing both parents."

"Thank you. I went through a very hard time, but I survived. My brother, who is two years older, lives nearby and is very supportive. I know he is always there for me. He has a kind, gracious wife and two adorable children." Gilda paused, "And what about your parents? What do they do?"

"My father is a lawyer. My mother passed away when I was in high school. She died of colon cancer. It had a profound effect on me. As she was dying, her body withered around a very sound mind. I hated seeing her suffer, and I prayed to God to either take her or let her get well. But the all-powerful, benevolent God did neither. She continued to suffer. I began to think that either God is not all-powerful or God is not benevolent. Both prospects called into question what I had been taught, and I began to question my faith. Since my mother's death, my religious beliefs have never been the same and certainly not as strong as they were prior to her death."

Gilda put a hand on his shoulder. "I know what you mean. My parents' deaths had a similar affect on me."

They remained quiet. It was an awkward but, at the same time, an oddly pleasing moment, sharing similar personal experiences. Finally, Mark asked, "Where did you go to college?"

Gilda removed her hand from his shoulder and answered, "I did my undergraduate work at the Hebrew University of Jerusalem in the Institute of Earth Sciences. My graduate work was at the Technion-Israel Institute of Technology in Haifa. How about you?"

Mark regretted her moving her hand from his shoulder. He said, "Those are both very good universities with excellent geology programs. My undergraduate work was at Florida State University, which at the time had quite a renowned geology program. For my graduate work, I attended the University of Illinois."

Not wanting the conversation to lapse, he asked, "Have you lived in Jerusalem all your life?"

"Yes, except for the time I spent in Haifa. Where did you grow up?"

"I was born and grew up in Panama City, Florida. It's in the northwest part of the state, an area called the panhandle. Panama City has beautiful white-sand beaches and is a hundred miles west of Tallahassee, where FSU is located. It was a fantastic place to grow up, especially if you like the water. They say once you get the saltwater in your veins and the sand in your shoes, you won't want to leave. After my mother died and I went to college, my father relocated to Tallahassee."

Mark hesitated and then asked a little awkwardly, "So, are you involved with anyone at the moment?" *There*, he thought, *I finally got it out.*

Gilda put away the last of their dinner utensils. "Actually, I'm not and haven't been for almost a year now. And you?"

A glimmer of hope leapt into his heart. Excited by her answer, he blurted out, "I'm not involved at the moment either." Then he added with uncertainty in his voice, "Perhaps when we return to Jerusalem we could have dinner together." Instantly, he realized his response was too rapid, caught up in the fervor of the moment.

"Are you asking me out on a date, Dr. Malloy?" Gilda asked, sensing his discomfort and seeing an opening to needle him. Mr. Confident was not so confident right now!

A moment passed as Mark tried to seize on a witty retort. But before he could speak, Gilda asked, "What's the matter, dog got your tongue?"

Trying to regain some control of the situation, Mark fired back, smiling and saying, "Well, we don't have to go out. We could stay in and one of us could cook." As the words left his mouth, he realized in a flash how weak the response was. Before she could answer, he smiled and added, "And it's 'Cat got your tongue.'"

"I'm just glad you finally found your voice. What if I told you I don't cook?" Gilda said jokingly, still sensing she had control of the conversation. In actuality, she was an excellent cook.

This wasn't going the way he envisioned. Enough banter, he wanted to close the deal. "In that case, Dr. Baer, it's a date and I'll take you to a great restaurant I discovered for an excellent dinner with a fine bottle of wine because I don't wish to cook either. I guarantee it'll be better than the stew and beer we just had."

Gilda smiled, "In that case, Dr. Malloy, I accept, but I'll bet your restaurant won't have a better view than this." As the words exited her mouth, doubts immediately followed. Was a date with this brash American a good idea?

"How true, the view and ambiance here can't be beat." Mark replied and then he added, "After a meal like this, I like to go for a walk. Are you interested?"

"Yes, a walk sounds great," nodded Gilda, still contemplating her prior commitment.

They finished cleaning up, packed away the stove and started walking down to the small dusty, rock-strewn trail on which they drove earlier in the day. It was a clear night, with a half moon allowing them to see the Dead Sea reflecting in the light.

"It really is beautiful here," observed Mark.

In addition to being remarkably clear, the air was quite cool; the only sound was gravel crunching under their feet. Gilda pressed close to Mark for warmth, saying, "Do you mind if I get close?"

"Not at all," replied Mark, happy for the low air temperature. He used it as an excuse to put his arm around her. "Is that better?"

"Yes."

Even though Mark was in his thirties, Gilda caused him to act like an awkward teenager. He couldn't believe the effect she was having on him, and he was sure he was not making a very good first impression.

They turned and walked back up the hill. Mark noticed his legs ached slightly from his encounter with the sinkhole. They stayed close together, with his arm still tightly around her. When they reached the truck, Gilda said, "Even though I'm not that tired, I think I will crawl into my sleeping bag to stay warm. Why don't you put your sleeping bag next to mine and we can talk for a while?"

After searching a while, they found a flat spot, put down air mattresses and laid their sleeping bags on top. Lying next to each other and talking, they looked up at the stars twinkling with such a fierce brilliance that they seemed close enough to touch. At one point, Mark pointed out a shooting star passing overhead and Gilda said, "You get to make a wish."

Mark did so.

"Well, what did you wish?"

"It's a secret. But it does involve you."

Gilda smiled and did not pursue the topic further.

They talked well into the night and eventually drifted off to sleep. Before Mark fell asleep, his mind vacillated from thoughts of Gilda to thoughts of the scrolls.

***

They awoke to a clear, crisp morning and the sound of roaring car engines. Two Range Rovers pulled up. It was seven o'clock, and it felt to Mark like he had just fallen asleep.

He and Gilda, slow to wake up, struggled out of their sleeping bags. The man who seemed in charge introduced himself.

"Hello, I'm Dr. Amos Meyer. I'm heading up the team of archeologists who have come to examine your discovery." Dr. Meyer stared at Mark's swollen cheek and black eye and then looked at Gilda.

Sensing the attention and wanting to ensure there was no misunderstanding, Mark touched the side of his face, saying, "I had a fall yesterday while we were exploring the cave containing the artifacts." He told them about his sinkhole experience.

Several of the men found the story amusing, but the venerated Dr. Meyer was concerned. He said, "I take health and safety while performing fieldwork very seriously. I am glad your injuries were not worse."

Dr. Meyer appeared to be in his late fifties, tall and distinguished with meticulous manners that generated admiration among the other members of his archeological team. His calm demeanor and wire-rimmed glasses bespoke an intelligent man. He was trim for his age. His team stood quietly by his side, respectfully awaiting his instructions.

They all shook hands and introduced themselves. Dr. Meyer offered them hot coffee and still warm freshly baked rolls.

"We stopped and picked up breakfast for you. I hope these rolls are adequate."

The coffee and rolls were a welcomed treat. It was just what they needed to get going. While Mark and Gilda ate, the members of Dr. Meyer's team unloaded materials from their trucks. Dr. Meyer directed the operation. Listening to the conversation, Mark noted that his team all referred to him as "Doctor." Mark assumed that Dr. Meyer preferred to be addressed by his title and decided to follow suit.

When they finished eating, Dr. Meyer asked, "So where is the site of your find?"

Gilda pointed in the direction of the cave, "It's over there, a little up the hill. We can take you there if you're ready to go."

***

While the archeologists gathered their equipment, including lights and ropes, Mark and Gilda prepared for the day. When ready, they all headed in the direction of the cave. At the cave's entrance, Gilda briefed them on what they would find inside. With hardhats, headlamps, and flashlights on, they entered the cool cave and retraced the steps Mark and Gilda had taken the previous day. Carefully negotiating the small sinkhole in the floor of the cave, they finally reached the back. There, they saw eleven clay jars in total, some standing upright while others lay on their sides. While Gilda and Mark watched, Dr. Meyer's team photographed the jars, then carefully removed them and carried them back to their trucks. His men cordoned-off the cave entrance with official-looking plastic caution tape, similar to that used at crime scenes, and posted a government sign indicating "No Trespassing" and "Danger" in Hebrew, English, and Arabic.

Back at their vehicles, Dr. Meyer explained, "We'll come back later to study the cave in much more detail, but for now, we have the main items of interest."

Dr. Meyer performed a cursory study of each jar and its contents. "All these scrolls are made of copper and appear to be written in either Greek or Aramaic. They seem to be in much better shape than the Dead Sea Scrolls found near Qumran. There is only minor oxidation of the copper."

Mark said with a slight grin, "By the way, we have named these scrolls the Mount Sodom Dead Sea Scrolls. What do you think? And how long do you think it will take to translate them?" Mark knew that the name he selected to describe the scrolls was a little ironic, but he hoped Dr. Meyer would accept it.

"That's as good a name as any, and it is consistent with a nearby landmark. As for your second question, it's hard to say how long the translation will take, but it could take as little as six months to a year, maybe longer," Dr. Meyer responded. "These scrolls are in very good shape, and that should certainly speed the process along."

"Because Gilda and I found these, we're interested in the findings. We would like to stay involved," requested Mark eagerly, turning to Gilda to see whether she concurred. She acknowledged with a nod of her head, saying, "Even though we are geologists, this is a project in which we are very interested."

Dr. Meyer smiled and replied, "When the work is complete, we will brief you both on our results. But right now, we need to head back to Jerusalem. I would like to get these into the laboratory as soon as possible."

As the archeologists loaded the scrolls into wooden crates, Mark and Gilda packed up their camp site. Then the caravan of Range Rovers headed down the trail and back to Jerusalem. This time, Gilda drove.

***

Mark felt crusty. "I don't know about you, but I'm ready to get back to Jerusalem to clean up."

Gilda looked over at Mark and said, "A shower and toothbrush sound good to me. We will be back soon. One thing about Israel; everywhere is relatively nearby."

Mark sat on the passenger side, glanced over his shoulder at his backpack and thought about the scrolls. He was impatient and didn't want to have to wait an entire year to learn the contents of the Mount Sodom Dead Sea Scrolls, but he understood that much work had to be performed. More immediately, he watched Gilda out of the corner of his eye as she drove. He would definitely keep his promise to take her to his favorite restaurant.

Chapter Four

Science is merely an extremely powerful method of winnowing what's true from what feels good.

—Carl Sagan

Fall 2002, Jerusalem, Israel

In Jerusalem, Mark and Gilda returned to their normal work routine. Dr. Meyer made it perfectly clear that nothing would be announced about the Mount Sodom Dead Sea Scrolls for some time, and he would contact them when appropriate. Don't call us, we'll call you.

Mark talked with Gilda periodically, keeping it short and business related, not wanting to be a nuisance. He hated early relationships where his every move was awkward. Keeping his promise, Mark asked Gilda out one Friday.

As the evening approached, Mark was filled with the thrill of anticipation. When he picked Gilda up, she was wearing a simple summer dress covered in sunflowers. It was the first time he noticed her with makeup, including dark red lipstick. It was unnecessary, he thought. Makeup did little to further enhance her natural beauty, although the lipstick attracted his attention more than once. She wore a short silver necklace with a pendant that caught his eye. "I like your trilobite," he said admiringly.

She brought her hand to the extinct marine arthropod that lived some 540 million years ago. "What, this old thing?" she said with a touch of mild sarcasm in her voice.

Looking up and catching her eyes, Mark smiled broadly at the geology reference.

At that moment, she checked out his wounds. Placing her hand affectionately on his face, she said softly, "Your eye and cheek look much better. You heal nicely."

"Thanks," was all he could manage, embarrassed and excited by her touch, his face reddening. *So much for trying to be suave*, he thought.

On the way to the restaurant, the conversation consisted mainly of small talk.

Over a bottle of Italian Amarone, Mark made a toast, "To our first date."

After touching glasses and taking a sip of wine, Gilda asked jokingly, "So is this where you bring all your Israeli women on the first date?" She smiled, waiting for his reaction.

He set down his wine glass and slowly leaned into the table. "Actually, you're the first," he responded. "But depending on how this evening turns out, I may consider bringing others here," he added, maintaining the repartee. Leaning back in his seat, he wondered what was coming next.

He didn't have to wait long.

"In that case, I'm not sure how well I want this dinner to 'turn out,'" she responded.

Her rule was not to date other geologists, especially ones in the GSI. Bemused, she didn't know why she made the exception with Mark. Maybe it was because he wasn't really part of the GSI and would be heading back to America in another few months.

Fortunately for Mark, their meals came at that moment, and he didn't feel compelled to respond to Gilda's comment. The restaurant lived up to his expectations—both food and wine were sumptuous. The conversation flowed easily. So far, Mark thought, the evening was a success.

Finishing their meal, he told Gilda, "Well, my wish on that shooting star has come true."

"You mean this date? You didn't ask for much," Gilda said, somewhat surprised.

"I guess it depends on your point of view. From where I sit, it seems like a pretty special wish." He sat looking at her with a big smile on his face.

Gilda couldn't believe it—she blushed. She wondered what it was about this American she found appealing. He was brazen, and focused at times on the topic of religion to the extreme, bordering on being politically incorrect. Yet to her amazement, she enjoyed being around him and actually found his religious discussions intellectually stimulating. She also enjoyed talking about geology with him.

After dinner, while drinking coffee, Gilda asked, "What have you seen of Jerusalem while you've been here?"

Mark stopped sipping his coffee, "Not much. I've spent most of my time working and settling into my apartment."

She paused for a moment, deep in thought, and then he asked, "What are you doing tomorrow?"

Mark had planned on catching up at work but that could wait. "I have no plans. Why?"

"How would you like a personal tour of the Old City?"

Mark quickly leaned forward in his chair and said, "I would love a personal tour as long as you're the tour guide."

"That's what I had in mind." Thinking a moment, Gilda asked, "Do you know where the Jaffa Gate is?" The Jaffa Gate, one of several gates into Jerusalem's Old City, was a stone portal through the historic walls surrounding the city.

"I think so," responded Mark. He wasn't sure, but he would definitely find it.

Still working out the details, Gilda said, "I have some errands I need to run tomorrow morning. Could you meet me there later, say, at ten o'clock?"

"Yes, sure," Mark responded, excitement building over the thought of spending more time with Gilda.

"Wear comfortable walking shoes and be prepared to spend the entire day," Gilda instructed. "Oh, I just thought of something else— bring a flashlight and a change of clothes because you will get wet." She emphasized the "will." Gilda's enthusiasm was apparent. She looked forward to spending the day with Mark and showing him Jerusalem's Old City, her city.

Why do I need a flashlight, wondered Mark, *and what in the world will we be doing that I'll get wet?* Instead of asking, he decided to wait until tomorrow.

Finishing their coffee, Mark paid the bill and they walked out into the cool, crisp night air. "Another beautiful evening in Jerusalem," Mark said. Turning to Gilda, he asked, "Would you like to go for a walk? It's not the desert but—"

"A walk sounds lovely. I know this area and can show you around."

They walked side by side through a popular neighborhood crowded with young and old alike. The night air was seductive. As they strolled, Mark heard conversations in Hebrew, Russian, and English. Walking by a variety of shops and crowded cafes with many people sitting outside, Gilda pointed out various places and people, explaining the ways of her country. Rarely speaking, Mark enjoyed watching and listening to her continuing dialogue while they strolled. He never tired of her accent. Her passion was contagious, and he could tell how much she loved Jerusalem from her manner and conversation.

He was especially entertained by the use of her hands as she spoke. He watched her hands and noticed that her fingers were thin and long. Her hands were feminine and very graceful. When she became excited about a topic, both her speech and hand movement became more rapid. He wondered if he held her hands, would she still be able to speak.

There was a break in the conversation, and Gilda noticed the time. Although it seemed they had just begun their walk, it had somehow become very late.

Surprised by the hour, Gilda said, "We have a long day tomorrow, and I need to get up early to run my errands. I should probably go home now."

"Okay, I understand," Mark responded, disappointed. Continuing to talk, they returned to Mark's car, which was parked on a nearby street. While driving back to her place, Gilda pointed out local highlights. Double-parked in front of her apartment complex, they sat in his car. It was an awkward moment, and both remained silent.

Finally, Gilda said, "Thanks for a lovely evening. I liked your restaurant choice." She paused. "There's a part of me that wants to invite you in, but it's late and I need to get an early start tomorrow. It is probably best if we say goodnight now."

With that said, she leaned into Mark and kissed him on the lips. His pulse quickened. It was a long kiss and there was definitely passion, thought Mark. A good kisser, her lips were moist and soft, yet firm against his. He was enjoying every aspect of their physical contact.

Slowly, Gilda pulled away smiling and quickly exited the car, saying, "See you tomorrow."

"I'll be there, the Jaffa Gate." Mark sat in his car and watched as she walked into her apartment building. He continued watching the closed door for several moments after she was out of sight. Thinking of her lips, he could almost taste her lipstick. Her scent lingered in the air as if she were still there. As it dissipated, he slowly drove away, images of Gilda replaying in his mind on a continuous loop.

***

The next morning, he was at Jaffa Gate by 9:30, anxious for their rendezvous. Gilda arrived early as well. She was dressed in tan pants and a blue top that clung to her body, accentuating her figure.

She greeted him with a "Good morning" and a kiss on the cheek. "You are early," she said with a smile.

"Good morning," he responded after the kiss. "Punctuality is one of my few virtues. Did you take care of your errands?"

"Yes, I was able to complete everything. We have a great day for your tour." It was sunny and warm with low humidity and a slight breeze.

She added, "So Mark, are you ready?"

"Absolutely," responded Mark, eager to begin.

Gilda led him through the Jaffa Gate into a small square. She pointed out, "This square is between the Christian and Armenian quarters. As you can guess, the Old City is divided into quarters and is important to many different religious groups." Next Gilda led him to the Ramparts Walk at the Jaffa Gate. This took them up the wall surrounding Jerusalem, providing a spectacular panorama.

"This wall was built in 1537 by the Ottoman Turkish Sultan Suleiman the Magnificent, but Jerusalem has had many walls over the years that have been built, destroyed, and rebuilt. According to the Bible, before King David's conquest of Jerusalem in the eleventh century BCE, the city already had a wall. I brought you up here for the view and to get oriented. Looking inside the wall, you can see the Old City, while looking behind you is the rest of Jerusalem," Gilda pointed out enthusiastically.

Mark scanned the horizon and took in all of Jerusalem. It seemed surreal to have a bird's eye view of a city he had heard so much about.

Gilda turned toward the Old City and continued, "The four quarters in the Old City are Armenian, Jewish, Muslim, and Christian. The Armenian quarter is the smallest, but their Christian Patriarchate remains very independent." Pointing, Gilda continued, "Over there is the Christian quarter. It covers the northwestern corner of the Old City. The Jewish quarter is over there, in the southeastern sector." Gilda swung around to point in another direction. "Finally, over there in the northeastern corner is the Muslim quarter, the largest section of the Old City."

Mark asked, "Why is there a separate Armenian quarter if they're Christian?"

"It's partly due to their long history with Jerusalem and their somewhat unique ethnicity. Ancient Armenia was much larger than present-day Armenia, was strategically located east of Turkey, and was the first state to adopt Christianity as its official religion in about 300 CE. Unfortunately, during World War I, Armenia was devastated, shrank in size, and ultimately became part of the old Soviet Union."

"Wow. I'm impressed with my tour guide's knowledge."

"So where would you like to start?" Gilda asked.

"I leave that decision to my capable guide," responded Mark with a grin.

"In that case, I suggest we start in the Muslim quarter. If you are ready, let's go."

Mark followed Gilda down the steps of the Ramparts Walk, through the small square, and slightly to the left down a narrow cobbled lane. They were in what Gilda called the Christian quarter. She walked quickly. Mark hustled to keep up with her. On occasion, the narrow streets opened into small squares filled with shops offering a variety of goods, including the religious souvenirs that were displayed everywhere. Mark noticed prayer beads, crosses with Jesus, crosses without Jesus, and pictures of Jesus in different positions always looking upward usually with a light shining down on him. He found it interesting that Jesus often was shown near a large rock.

After a brisk uphill walk, including numerous steps, they came to an open area—a large plaza with impressive architecture. Gilda slowed her pace, finally stopped, and turned back to Mark.

He was almost out of breath, but Gilda was able to speak easily, "This is the area we Jews call the Temple Mount. Muslims call it Al-Haram El-Sharif or Noble Sanctuary. See that octagonal structure over there with the golden dome?"

Mark looked in the direction she pointed. "Yes."

"That's the Dome of the Rock. And the mosque right next to it is the Al-Aqsa Mosque. This area is considered the holiest site in Judaism and the third holiest site to Islam, behind Mecca and Medina."

Mark was humbled by what he saw and by the religious importance of this small area to so many people. "Can we go and look inside either of those?"

"Yes, except on Fridays and Muslim holidays, but given our time constraints, I prefer not entering today." Pausing, she asked, "Do you know the history of this area?"

Mark thought for a moment and said, "I know some."

"Well, millions of years ago, this area was a shallow sea where limestone formed," Gilda said with a slight smile, waiting for a response from Mark.

He took the bait, "What is this, a little geology humor? I thought you were going to tell me about religious history. But it is interesting that the bedrock here is limestone."

"And rocks are part of the religious history. After all, it is called the Dome of the Rock," said Gilda.

"True, geology in action again," Mark interjected.

"The Dome of the Rock was built over the rock where Abraham prepared to sacrifice his son Isaac," continued Gilda.

"It's hard to believe that a merciful God would demand a father to sacrifice his son. But I guess back in those days many people believed in various kinds of sacrifices. I'm glad we got beyond that practice," Mark commented.

Gilda continued, "As you know, Muslims consider Abraham a prophet, and this location symbolizes the center of the world in Muslim geography. Muslims also consider Jesus a prophet, and there is a long epigraphic strip dedicated to Jesus in the Dome of the Rock. Here's the part you'll like; there is a cave under the Rock. It's called the Well of Souls, where tradition maintains that souls of the dead linger before disappearing."

"A lot of things disappear in caves, as I almost did recently. I see that the blocks of rock used for construction of the Dome are also limestone."

"Yes," said Gilda "There's a quarry nearby."

"What about the Jewish history of this area?" Mark asked.

"Well, there's the story we just discussed about Abraham and his son. Then there's the story of King David's son Solomon, who built a temple here in 960 BCE known as the First Temple. It was destroyed by Nebuchadnezzar II of Babylon. The Second Temple was built here in 19 BCE by Herod the Great, the Roman puppet. That's the temple that was here during Jesus' lifetime. That temple was destroyed by the Romans. All that remains of the Second Temple is the Western Wall, which is known as the Wailing Wall. We can go there next if you'd like."

As Gilda spoke, Mark looked around at all the beautiful structures. The Old City was an astonishing place; he couldn't help but wonder "Why here? Why did so much religious history occur in this location?" Finally, he replied, "Sure. I can see why this area is so hotly contested. It's remarkable how many religions developed from events that took place here."

They stood in silence observing the view for some time before Gilda said, "Come on, let's go to the Wailing Wall."

To get to the Western Wall Plaza, they had to pass through security. Once in the plaza, they watched in silence some distance from the wall as many Jewish men, some dressed in black and with black hats, went to the Wailing Wall and prayed, often swaying forward and backward. There were others who wrote on paper and placed it in the cracks in the limestone blocks. It was a very somber place. Not like being at church, Mark thought, more like being at a cemetery.

A gust of wind caused the ends of many mostly white scarves with fringes worn by some men to fly up as if saluting them in unison. "What is the scarf they wear?" Mark asked in a low voice.

Gilda replied softly, "That is a prayer shawl called a tallit. It's a religious symbol Jewish men use to cover themselves both physically and spiritually in prayer and celebration. A tallit combined with the Shield of David is the flag of Israel."

Mark continued to watch the men and said, "I didn't know that. Where did wearing of the tallit come from?"

"The wearing of the tallit was commanded by God in the Bible."

Mark thought about this out loud, saying, "I wonder why Christians who take the Bible literally don't wear a tallit?"

Mark and Gilda continued to people watch at the Wailing Wall, and after awhile Gilda whispered, "What you see is only a portion of the Western Wall. There is a tunnel that exposes an additional fifteen hundred feet of the wall. Would you like to see it?"

"I'm a geologist; of course I'd like to go into a tunnel," Mark whispered back, glad it was a tunnel and not a cave.

They found their way to the tunnel entrance and went in. It was well lit. About 150 feet into the tunnel was a sealed-off entrance called Warren's Gate. Gilda pointed out that this location was thought to be very close to the Rock under the Dome of the Rock and consequently was a very holy place. But what was most interesting to Mark was the Western Stone, the largest rock in the Western Wall, thought to weigh 570 tons.

By the time they exited the tunnel, it was well into the afternoon and Mark was hungry. "Are you about ready to eat lunch?" Mark asked.

"Yes, and I know a good place, but it is outside the Old City." They walked a short distance and exited the Old City through the Dung Gate and found a small cafe that Gilda liked.

"Let's eat quickly," Gilda said. "There is still so much I want to show you."

"Fine with me" responded Mark. "I'm curious, though, when will we get wet?"

"It's a surprise. Patience. You'll have to wait." Her eyes sparkled, clearly looking forward to what would come next.

Their lunch came right away, and they only spent a short time at the cafe. Mark then followed Gilda, first going to the right, then to the left, and eventually coming to the entrance of Hezekiah's Tunnel. They were still outside the wall surrounding the Old City.

Gilda instructed Mark, "Get out your flashlight. This is where you get wet."

They both pulled out their small, slim flashlights. When they saw that the other held the same light but with different colors, they laughed.

Gilda said, "Normally you need to go on a public tour of Hezekiah's Tunnel, but because of my GSI credentials, we will take a self-guided tour by ourselves."

"This must be the only perk GSI employees receive," Mark joked, knowing the benefits of working for the GSI were limited to working outdoors.

"True," said Gilda, then before entering the tunnel, she explained, "This is a water supply tunnel over five hundred meters long, constructed through the limestone under Jerusalem in about 700 BCE by King Hezekiah; hence, the tunnel's name. It was built in anticipation of a long siege, the possible result of the Assyrian danger from the east. The tunnel is under an area referred to as the City of David, named after King David, and connects the Gihon Spring discussed in the Old Testament to the Pool of Siloam discussed in the New Testament."

Gilda added, "When King David captured Jerusalem, he used the spring and passageway as a means to enter the city thereby avoiding the wall surrounding the city. You might say he used the geology of the spring to help capture Jerusalem." She paused, smiling at Mark to see his reaction.

Half-joking, Mark said, "Of course, geology contributes to everything. David even used a rock to kill Goliath. Was it a coincidence that a rock was used? I don't think so."

Gilda smiled and continued, "The Pool of Siloam is significant because it is a location where Jesus is thought to have baptized followers during his last days in Jerusalem."

Mark was thoroughly enjoying himself and knew Gilda said the part about "used the geology" for his benefit; she was kidding him about his intense interest in the subject. But he really did believe geology played an important role in many historical and religious events.

Because the lighting in Hezekiah's Tunnel was poor to nonexistent, Mark and Gilda entered the tunnel with flashlights on. Immediately, they were up to their knees in water. The tunnel was narrow and in places; Mark had to duck to keep from hitting his head. The trek through the tunnel normally took only about forty-five minutes, but Mark and Gilda were exploring all aspects of the tunnel so their tour was going to more than double the norm. They studied the rocks, looking for fossils, and joked with each other. Mark was having a fantastic time.

Toward the end of their excursion, the water reached waist high. Mark and Gilda began to laugh about their situation, and soon water was being splashed. It was unclear who started the water fight. Toward the end of the battle, they were both soaked. Falling into each other, Mark held Gilda close so she could no longer splash him. The cold from their wet clothes had penetrated them, and the warmth of each other's bodies felt good. In the semidarkness, Mark looked into Gilda's glistening eyes, and the next thing he realized they were kissing passionately. Losing sense of time, they finally parted lips upon hearing distance voices of a guided tour somewhere behind them.

Still holding each other, their eyes locked but neither spoke. To break the awkward silence, Mark asked, "Do you think King David would mind our kissing under his city?"

"King David had his own passions. He committed adultery with Bathsheba, so I think he would understand," responded Gilda as they slowly pulled away from each other. After a moment, she said, "We should probably keep moving. I'm getting a little cold down here."

When they finally made it out of the tunnel, Mark turned to Gilda and said smiling, "Well, that surely was the highlight of my day."

Gilda wasn't sure if he was referring to Hezekiah's Tunnel or their kissing or both.

She said, "I had wanted to take you to the Israel Museum to see the Qumran Dead Sea Scrolls, but given how wet we are, I think we should save that for another day. Why don't you follow me back to my place and we can change into our dry clothes and I'll make dinner for us?" Their dry clothes were in their respective cars.

"That would be a real treat. I gladly accept your offer." As he said this, Mark shivered, unsure if it was from the cold or because of Gilda's invitation.

***

They drove separately; Mark following Gilda. He sat on a towel, but his clothes were drying quickly. Making it to her home and parking, Mark met Gilda at the front of her apartment with a change of clothing in his backpack. She also had a backpack. This observation made them chuckle. With a devious smile, she said, "Come."

"Yes, ma'am." He followed Gilda into her apartment building and into her first-floor apartment. She closed and locked the door behind them, dropped her backpack, and grabbed Mark, causing him to drop his. As they kissed, they began removing each other's damp clothes. With each clothing item removed, Gilda pulled Mark one step closer to her bedroom.

Mark's first thought before entering her bedroom was that he may have fallen in love in a water tunnel through limestone beneath the City of David. Only a geologist would fall in love while standing in groundwater. His second thought was he hoped to get to know Gilda in a Biblical sense, meaning intimately, and that struck him as ironic given the day they just spent in Jerusalem's Old City. His last thought as they entered her bedroom was that his sabbatical was going to be over way too soon.

Chapter Five

A man's ethical behavior should be based effectually on sympathy, education, and social ties and needs; no religious basis is necessary.

—Albert Einstein
"Religion and Science," *New York Times Magazine*
November 9, 1930

Fall 2002, Oklahoma City, Oklahoma

Chester Weeks grew up poor during the fifties and sixties in Oklahoma. A humorless, often mean-spirited man, he was no fool. He had few opportunities to escape his working-class background. As a child, he and his mother attended church regularly, and each Sunday, the collection plate passed as he sat in his pew. At the time, to Chester, the plate seemed to contain enormous sums of money. He loved to attend church, not for the ineloquent sermons blasting from the pulpit, but to see all the money pass before his eyes. Afterward, he would fantasize about grabbing handfuls of bills and coins and stuffing them into his pockets.

He remembered asking his mother once, "Why does God need so much money?"

She explained, "Oh, it's not for God, dear, the money is for helping people in need."

That's when Chester determined he was "people" and clearly "in need."

"God must want me to have some of that money," he convinced himself.

Following the money, he volunteered to count the offering. His mother thought it wonderful that her son took such an active interest in the church. She beamed as she told neighbors, "Chester is such a good son. He's involved in the church, and his good deeds include helping count the money in the collection plates."

His counting, however, was imperfect as some money disappeared into his pockets each week; his fantasies came true. With his ill-gained money, Chester bought material items to impress his fellow classmates; he finally felt respected. On many occasions, he would say to himself, "God really does help those who help themselves." It was the beginning of his twisting of Bible mottos to serve his needs.

With time, he outgrew his position in the small church and moved to bigger and more lucrative churches, eventually winding up in his current paid position. He no longer needed to volunteer to acquire his money. Not a deeply religious person, Chester saw religion as a means to an end—a way to make money, and lots of it. At times, however, he played his role well, supporting evangelical causes, or as he considered them, "long-term investments."

***

Chester was the chair of the financial committee of the First Church of God's Chosen (FCGC), a charismatic megachurch located in Oklahoma City. "Committee" was a misnomer; its members were volunteers who simply rubber stamped Chester's decisions. In addition to their five thousand–seat sanctuary, the FCGC had a television studio where they broadcast daily on God's Chosen Network (GCN). The GCN reached every state in the union and parts of Canada, and the cable network was expanding. Chester was in a growth industry, and the more Christianity grew, the better it was for business, meaning more money could be collected.

Chester sat in his office behind his large, dark cherry desk thinking about his success and how far he had come from his childhood days. He considered himself a self-made man, learning from others in the business. He had a high regard for those who lead the way before him—men like Jim Bakker and Jimmy Swaggart who made large sums of money in the televangelist business. He felt badly they were caught having inappropriate sexual relationships, but their elimination from the televangelist business opened up opportunities for the FCGC.

Chester also learned from other televangelist organizations an insidious way to take money, that is, receive donations, from the elderly. He knew as people aged and approached death, they became susceptible to people like him requesting donations in the name of God. Old folks wanted to make sure they were right with God in preparation for their imminent death. Often, they would overcompensate for the sins of their youth by giving freely to the church. Using this susceptibility, Chester refined a tried-and-true scheme to obtain the homes of old people and sell them for a nice profit after their death. He would convince the elderly to sign over their home titles to the church, and in exchange, the church would pay their mortgage payments until they passed.

Chester only pitched this "opportunity to give your home to the Lord" to near-death folks who had their mortgages mostly paid off. Cancer patients, especially women whose husbands had preceded them in death, were his specialty, but to Chester's chagrin, new treatments had prolonged the lives of some of these patients, costing him money in additional mortgage payments. He hated Medicare. Nonetheless, the subsequent selling of the deceased homes netted him—that is, the church—tens to hundreds of thousands of dollars from which he took a substantial commission.

If the departed's relatives complained, Chester simply offered to pay the funeral costs. He had worked out a kick-back scheme with several local funeral parlors so he made money from every funeral the church financed. Paying for the funeral usually appeased the relatives, but if not, tough—he had a legal contract, and who was going to aggressively pursue money given to the church? Yes, thought Chester, *religion was definitely a good business.*

The financial papers and reports Chester just finished reviewing were carefully stacked on his desk; everything was in its proper place. He was in a good mood. The monthly tally for the FCGC was excellent, a 20 percent increase over last month. The current Republican White House administration was doing wonders for FCGC revenues, just as Chester had hoped when he helped with their election campaign. Chester was well connected politically, and that alone helped him generate revenue. Many politicians on Capitol Hill were acquainted with Chester and valued his political contributions. He always told his friends that it was a "you-scratch-my-back-and-I'll-scratch-your-back" world, and he was a master back scratcher.

His only concerns at the moment were several Republican senators who campaigned on family values, implying that their Democratic challengers were immoral. This moral-high-ground approach—or as Chester liked to think of it, holier-than-thou approach—garnered true Christian votes. Unfortunately, these particular sanctimonious senators were having extramarital affairs, one of which was not with the opposite sex. Chester didn't see the hypocrisy, but feared a negative reaction if word of the affairs became public. If Chester knew about these affairs, it was only a matter of time before the public found out. He would have to cut back his donations for he feared these individuals would soon be out of power and of little use to him. He didn't care about their transgressions; it was simply business.

One of Chester's creations was the Family Values Foundation (FVF) that ostensibly promoted "family values," which was code for no homosexuals and no abortions. Being antigay and antiabortion was good for business because railing against gays and abortion always increased contributions. As far as Chester was concerned, gays and feminists were great for the FCGC.

Each time the Hollywood crowd voiced their support for gay rights, it was an opportunity for the FCGC to rail against Hollywood, thereby generating even more money. It always helped to throw in the "liberal" media as part of the problem, even though Chester believed the media was not that liberal. He thought it ironic that being against something like abortion always generated more money than being for something like feeding the hungry. He knew what worked, and he gladly followed the path that generated the most dollars.

In reality, FVF was little more than a political action committee that supported politicians in tune with the FCGC agenda. Through his political contributions, Chester had gained substantial influence and power. He was an expert at moving money around so political goals were met and favors obtained while maintaining a semblance of separation of church and state. After all, the FCGC didn't want to lose its tax-exempt status, thought Chester.

In addition to having political connections in the current administration, Chester was personal friends with the Israeli Minister of Tourism. The FCGC alone was responsible for promoting over fifty thousand Christian tourists each year to visit Israel and see the place where Jesus lived and died. Their relationship was more than a religious alliance. It was a political and financial union, one promoting a strong and lasting Israel. This alliance provided a tremendous amount of money for the Israeli tourism industry. Although some may have viewed this symbiotic alliance between Jews and Christians as unusual, it was very necessary and good for business—Chester's and Israel's. Chester knew that he alone contributed greatly to Israel's gross domestic product, which offered him certain privileges within the Jewish state.

Chester was pleased with his organization, which had taken many years to build. It was strong and powerful. The weakest link in his business was Bob Bailey, or Pastor Bob, as he was commonly called. Pastor Bob was a very kind, good-hearted, middle-aged man, but was a few clowns short of a circus. Oddly enough, his low wattage brain appealed to many parishioners. Chester knew that dumbing down the messenger worked in politics, as the current administration proved, so there was no reason it shouldn't work for a preacher. Only Pastor Bob was not doing it intentionally.

From outside the church, Pastor Bob was viewed as the leader of the FCGC. Certainly, he was the spiritual leader and the face that drew the huge crowds. He was an excellent charismatic speaker who had the ability to captivate the crowds with his well-delivered bombastic sermons, conveyed with a slight Southern drawl. Pastor Bob was in his early forties with good looks and an appealing way about him. He performed his job well, but he knew nothing about what it took to maintain and grow an organization like the FCGC.

Fortunately for Chester, he was able to turn Pastor Bob's weakness into a strength. Chester was able to control and manipulate Pastor Bob. With Chester's guidance, Pastor Bob had become one of the most successful televangelists on TV. It was important for the front man to do well so the FCGC could flourish. All in all, it was a beneficial relationship—Pastor Bob generated the money, while Chester controlled it.

Chester walked down the hall to Pastor Bob's office. He found him diligently working on next Sunday's sermon.

"How are things going, Bob?"

"Things are going okay, Chester, but I'm having a bit of difficulty coming up with this week's sermon topic."

"Maybe I can help with that," Chester offered cynically, undetected by Pastor Bob. "Everyone loves your sermons on the Book of Revelation."

Especially me, thought Chester.

That topic usually generated more revenue than most other sermons. Chester had run an unofficial correlation finding that "fire and brimstone" sermons usually generated far more money than "be good to your neighbor" ones. You might say that sermons based on the Old Testament greatly outperformed those based on the New Testament, as far as money was concerned. Revelation was an exception. *Revelation is better suited for the Old Testament*, thought Chester.

Another moneymaking theme from the New Testament, one of Chester's favorites, concerned the difficulties of a rich man entering into the kingdom of heaven. *This theme was ironic*, thought Chester, *making rich people feel guilty so they give their money to me ... that is, the church.* But it always worked.

Every once in a while, the national headlines told of someone seeing the image of Jesus in a potato chip or a tomato, always resulting in increased contributions the following Sunday. Chester thought these occurrences hilarious, but that was one way Jesus stories did increase his revenues. "So keep those Jesus sightings coming," Chester would tell people close to him.

Pastor Bob interrupted Chester's thoughts, saying, "I'm not sure, Chester. Don't you think my flock is tiring of sermons on Revelation?"

Chester chuckled to himself and suppressed a smile. He always found the term "flock" a bit humorous when Pastor Bob referred to his congregation.

"Bob, your flock loves to hear you preach about the Book of Revelation. When you get to the part about Jesus seated on the throne floating above Jerusalem, your flock is in awe. Then when you preach about the believers being raptured up toward him in the sky, many in your congregation, uh flock, break down and cry."

And reach for their billfolds, thought Chester, *because no one wants to be left behind during the Rapture.*

The Rapture, a prophesied event by Paul, not Jesus, would occur during the Second Coming of Jesus Christ, at which time true believers would suddenly be taken from earth. Chester wanted to make sure everyone understood you couldn't be a true believer and be "raptured" unless you gave money to the church, which of course meant giving money to Chester. Fear was a strong motivator for generating revenue, and Chester liked to use it.

"Following the broadcast of your sermon on GCN, we can sell, uh offer, the framed pictures of the Temple Mount in Jerusalem showing the location where the temple will be rebuilt to herald the Second Coming of Christ. All God's chosen want at least one copy of that picture." That should generate several million dollars alone, thought Chester.

"This is also a good time of year to promote our quarterly FCGC-sponsored trip to Israel. My contact at the Ministry of Tourism assures me the best accommodations are at our disposal, and he recently expanded the Christian tour of Jerusalem's Old City just for the FCGC. We need to continue collecting donations for Israel. Remember, you can't spell Jerusalem without USA in the middle. It's important for us to support Israel to ensure that Jerusalem is not in the hands of Muslims when Christ returns to earth. You understand that as well as I do, Bob."

"I certainly do," said Bob assuredly. "The Book of Revelation it is. Sunday's sermon should be one of my best ever."

Chester would miss Sunday's sermon. It was the monthly celebration of Holy Communion. Chester had a thing about Holy Communion—he thought that drinking grape juice and pretending it was the blood of Christ and eating a wafer and pretending it was the flesh of Christ was symbolic cannibalism. Holy Communion always gave him the creeps, so he chose not to attend services on Sundays when it was given.

As Chester walked back to his office, he felt there was proper order in the FCGC and in the world. The war in Afghanistan, which began in October 2001, was going reasonably well. There were many reasons to support that war, Chester thought, but his primary one was that the Taliban and al-Qaeda did not fit his proper order. It was good to have more Christians in that part of the world, even if they were soldiers.

Now there was talk about invading Iraq, which meant another opportunity to bolster a Christian presence in the Middle East. *This is a good time to be in the business of Christianity*, he thought, *we just need to keep it growing.* As the number of Christians grew, so did Chester's bank account. He did not like it when conditions were out of proper order, and he would do whatever it took to maintain it.

Returning to his office, he admired his plush surroundings. Chester definitely liked his creature comforts. He looked down at his Alexander Amosu gray suit and pink accented silk tie, now askew. Grimacing, he straightened the tie with his right hand, a large diamond ring on his pinky finger.

On his wall, a portrait showed Jesus in a sitting position next to a large, impressive rock on which his arms were raised in prayer. In the painting, a light shown from above, highlighting Caucasian features and making Jesus look like a fair-skinned Western European. A Bible lay on his desk, mainly for display and rarely read anymore. Although familiar with its contents, Chester didn't take it literally, or figuratively for that matter.

The thing about Christian Evangelicals, he thought, is that they take the Bible literally. And if you know the Bible, you know their playbook and can use it to manipulate them. The Bible never changed and was part of Chester's proper order.

The phone on Chester's desk suddenly rang, startling him from his reverie. He picked up the receiver, and his receptionist notified him that the Israeli minister of tourism was calling. "Please connect him," he told her.

"Hello, Jacob, how are things in Israel?" Chester greeted the minister.

"Hello, Chester," Jacob Cohen responded with a heavy accent. "Overall, things are going quite well. Tourism is up for the year, and for that I thank you."

"I appreciate that."

Chester listened to Jacob's polite conversation, thinking that Jacob didn't sound quite right. His call was unexpected, causing Chester some apprehension. Hearing enough, Chester finally asked, "So what's on your mind, Jacob?"

"I am calling because there is a situation you should be aware of."

"Oh, really. What's that, Jacob?" Chester's senses were at full alert.

"Six months ago, several copper scrolls were found near Mount Sodom, along the southwest side of the Dead Sea," answered Jacob.

"I never heard about this find," said Chester, wondering what these scrolls had to do with him.

Jacob continued, "The find was subject to a secrecy rule, and nothing has been disclosed about their discovery and analysis."

Closing his eyes in thought, Chester hesitated, trying to comprehend the significance of Jacob's message. "And why, Jacob, should I need to know about these scrolls?"

"They date back to a period shortly after the Qumran Dead Sea Scrolls. They are called the Mount Sodom Dead Sea Scrolls to differentiate them."

Chester thought that "Mount Sodom" was an odd name that conjured up sexual thoughts. He didn't share this with Jacob. "Okay, and …?" Chester said quizzically.

"The Qumran Dead Sea Scrolls were early versions of the Old Testament. From what I've learned, the Mount Sodom Dead Sea Scrolls are the earliest know version of the New Testament."

"But Jacob, from what I understand, the Qumran Dead Sea Scrolls were found sixty years ago, and we're still waiting for the final analysis to be completed. By the time these new scrolls are translated, I'll be in heaven."

"That is not true," responded Jacob. "These new scrolls are all made of copper and were in a cave sealed from the atmosphere. The scrolls are in incredibly good shape and quite legible. The analysis and translation has progressed rapidly. The analysts are nearing completion of their evaluation of the scrolls."

The gravity of this situation slowly dawned on Chester and he asked with sudden apprehension, "Who knows about this, Jacob?"

"Several scientists in the Israeli government, and each is sworn to secrecy. One of those scientists is reporting developments directly to me. The only non-Israeli who knows about the scrolls is an American geologist, a professor at Florida State University who discovered the scrolls while on sabbatical. His name is Dr. Mark Malloy. A Dr. Gilda Baer from the Geological Survey of Israel was his partner when together they stumbled on this find. Dr. Malloy returned to Florida when his sabbatical was over. He likely will soon return to Israel to discuss the findings from the scrolls."

"You mentioned findings from the scrolls. What are they?" Chester asked intently.

"For that, you need to come to Israel. I don't want to discuss the translations on the phone. I assure you, this is information you need and will want to know."

Chester paused and thought about what Jacob told him. It was very clear he needed to go to Israel. "Thank you, Jacob. Please wait a moment."

Checking his calendar, he noted he had several meetings scheduled with prominent church donors. He hated to miss these, but they would have to be postponed. The trip to Israel was far more important. He informed Jacob, "I have no major commitments coming up so I'll arrange my trip as soon as I can. I'll call you in a day or so with my travel plans."

With that, the two men bade their farewells and hung up. Chester leaned back in his chair. At that point, he had a premonition that perhaps his proper order of things was being threatened after all.

Chapter Six

If people are good only because they fear punishment, and hope for
reward, then we are a sorry lot indeed.

—Albert Einstein

Fall 2002, Tallahassee, Florida

Professor Mark Malloy's large office featured a built-in bookcase
covering the entire back wall from floor to ceiling. The well-worn
room's creaky wooden floors were littered with books and strewn with
papers that overflowed like a glacier from the solidly stuffed bookcase.
Mark sat in his office on the third floor of the Carraway Building, a
1950s vintage structure housing the Department of Geology at FSU.
His sabbatical over, he arrived back in Tallahassee only two months
ago, having successfully finished his stint with the Geological Survey
of Israel.

Fall in Tallahassee was an exciting time. The temperature
dropped and, more importantly, so did the humidity. Football was a
huge part of fall, and so far the Seminoles, FSU's football team, were
undefeated, generating tremendous enthusiasm on and around campus.
The school year started with its typical influx of fresh, young faces. A
rebirth at the university occurred every September. Mark's teaching
load this semester was light, consisting of only one course. Plenty of
time was available to focus on research, including writing papers about
projects he pursued while in Israel. Being home, he should be happy,
but he felt an aching loneliness, making even simple tasks difficult.

He missed Israel—or more accurately, he missed Gilda. Being
separated two months was a short period of time, but it felt like eons.
Einstein's theory illustrated that the flow of time can change, but
Mark's theory concerning time involved the mind—it acted like a
filter, and with time, negative memories were allowed to pass through,
lost to the hidden recesses of the brain, while positive recollections
were retained, used by the brain to change your mood whenever it felt
like doing so.

Thoughts of Gilda drifted into his mind at the most inopportune moments, producing flashes of joy, only to be followed by a throbbing in the pit of his stomach when the realization of their separation flooded his mind like a dreaded tsunami. He didn't understand why she touched him so deeply. His thoughts of Gilda included their stimulating discussions, the memories of the warmth from her soft skin pressed against his, and their nights together. Then there were her shoes. Seeing them in his mind's eye, it was remarkable how many pairs she had.

To add to his gloomy mood, a tropical storm came to rest over Tallahassee, and it had been raining for the past two days. It was pouring now, sheets of rain drumming steadily against his office window and creating a water curtain that obstructed his view to the outside. Thunder rumbled in the distance. The rain made him long for the sun, bringing to mind the desert in Israel, where he had spent the better part of last year.

After discovering the Mount Sodom Dead Sea Scrolls, he and Gilda spent much of his remaining time in Israel studying sinkholes. They had collected and analyzed considerable data, even written a manuscript together and submitted it to a leading journal. Proud of his work, he felt they had advanced the understanding of these features. Mark believed this new knowledge had great transfer value to Florida, where sinkholes occurred frequently. FSU had gladly supported his sabbatical in Israel and would be rewarded with his research findings.

While back in his office with familiar reference material, Mark refreshed his knowledge of the Bible's history. This review was motivated by discussions with Gilda and his lingering curiosity. He read that the official Latin Bible of the Roman Catholic Church (RCC) was not compiled until the early fifth century CE. Minimal copies existed at the time because they were generated by hand. Consequently, the Bible was not available to the public, most of whom could not read Latin anyway. Only an exclusive club, the RCC, had access to and control of the Bible.

The RCC strongly discouraged nonofficial versions of the Bible, fearing others may translate or interpret the Bible differently. The first handwritten English Bible was produced in the 1380s by John Wycliffe. This attempt to make the Bible more accessible so infuriated the Pope that once he learned of the deed forty-four years after John Wycliffe's death, he ordered Wycliffe's bones dug-up, crushed, and scattered.

The printing press was invented by Gutenberg in the 1450s, and the first book published was the official Latin Bible. In 1516, however, Erasmus published a Greek Bible based on earlier manuscripts, revealing that the RCC Latin Bible contained numerous translation mistakes. Later, in about 1525, William Tyndale published the first English Bible, but the RCC burned every copy it could find, declared it replete with errors, and threatened those in possession of the English Bible with death by burning. The proverbial cat was out of the bag, however, and copies of the Tyndale Bible survived, available to commoners. For his efforts, Tyndale was convicted of heresy, strangled, and burned by the RCC in 1536.

The history of the Bible was complex and sordid. As a result of his recent review, Mark concluded there were at least four "divinely inspired" Bibles in use today. This did not include the "Jefferson" Bible produced by Thomas Jefferson, who focused on Jesus' message, removing supernatural portions and perceived misinterpretations from the New Testament.

Each group believed their Bible was the true version and claimed that the other Bibles contained mistakes. One used by Jews had twenty-four books or chapters. Others included the Protestant Bible, comprised of sixty-six books, not counting the Book of Mormon; the Roman Catholic Bible, which had seventy-three books; and the Greek Orthodox Bible, which contained the most with seventy-eight books. There were more books rejected and not included in any of the Bibles. After all, there were the Gnostic gospels discovered in 1945 in Nag Hammadi, Egypt. The fifty-two texts or treatises in this discovery included, among others, the gospel of Judas and the gospel of Mary Magdalene. These books never made it into the official Bibles. Mark wondered about the missing books, their content, and whether the Mount Sodom Dead Sea Scrolls contained them.

A soft knock at his office door caused Mark to look up to see a graduate student, his teaching assistant this year. Mark couldn't help but smile, given his recent experience in Israel. His assistant, a young man with a Hispanic background, was named Jesus (pronounced hay-soos) Lopez. A second-generation American, Jesus spoke fluent English and Spanish.

"Hello, Jesus. Come in. What can I do for you?" asked Mark, leaning back in his chair.

Jesus, a bright and capable student with whom Mark enjoyed working, had studied to become a priest before turning to geology.

Mark considered Jesus more than a student; he was a friend. "Professor Malloy, I just wanted to let you know that the laboratory curriculum for your class is ready, and I look forward to working for you again this year."

"Thank you very much, Jesus. I'm looking forward to a productive year. How's your thesis writing coming along?" Jesus was working on improved geophysical methods to more accurately map underground cave systems from the surface.

"I made significant progress while you were away and should have something for you to review in about a month."

"That's great. I can't wait to read it."

"Thanks, Dr. Malloy."

As Jesus was about to leave, he noticed something on Professor Malloy's bookcase behind his desk. It was on the uppermost shelf away from the window. It looked like a clay jar encased in glass. Pointing, he asked, "What's that, professor?"

"Oh, that's a replica of a jar similar to the ones in which the Dead Sea Scrolls were found. I bought it in a shop in Israel for fifty dollars. What do you think?"

Jesus studied it from where he stood in front of Mark's desk. "It looks very realistic."

"I thought so as well," said Mark.

Recalling the writings in the Dead Sea Scrolls, Jesus mentioned, "You know, Dr. Malloy, before I decided to major in geology, my divinity work included ancient languages. I became familiar with archeology, and I even learned Latin and Greek."

"I didn't know that." Mark straightened up in his chair and asked, "How well do you read Greek?"

"With a dictionary nearby, I can read most anything. I learned English and Spanish as a child. It seems to me that if you learn two languages simultaneously at an early age, new languages later in life are easier to conquer."

"I'm impressed. I do poorly at languages." Mark thought for a moment, and asked, "Is ancient Greek different from modern Greek?"

"From an oral perspective, they are different, but the written text is the same. Through time, ancient Greek writing has changed little, with Biblical Greek being the simplest. I can definitely translate Biblical Greek," Jesus responded with enthusiasm, proud of his language skills.

"I'll keep your Greek language skills in mind. I may have a project for you. I would pay for your help with a translation. Any interest?" Mark said.

"Sure, I'm interested, but you don't have to pay me," Jesus said, happy to help his professor.

"Let me get back to you. And for what I have in mind, I insist on paying you." Mark was pleased with the language resource, especially someone he could trust.

"Okay. I'll be around all semester. Just let me know what you would like me to do." Jesus looked down at his watch. With a start, he said, "I have to run now. See you, professor." With that, Jesus turned and left.

"Good-bye, Jesus. I'll be in touch."

Mark was aware of several very good baseball players named Jesus. He thought it was interesting that the Hispanic culture felt comfortable naming their sons Jesus. It was a respectful name in the Hispanic Catholic Church. Yet, it would likely never be used in the uptight Anglo culture.

Outside, the heavy rain continued. Mark leaned back in his padded chair causing it to incline backward. He locked his hands behind his neck, continuing to gaze at the torrents of water on his window rushing downward in sheets. Hypnotized by the rain, his mind drifted back in time.

***

Upon his return to the States, Mark visited with his father. He told his father all about his time in Israel and about his various projects, leaving out the part about finding the scrolls. One topic discussed was Gilda. From the way Mark described her, his father understood how special Gilda was to his son, more so than other women he had dated seriously.

While continuing to watch the rain, Mark reminisced about his time in Israel. He and Gilda found other caves in the area of their discovery and explored them with high hopes of locating additional scrolls. After all, the Qumran Dead Sea Scrolls had been found in multiple caves, so there was the possibility additional scrolls might be found. Unfortunately, they hadn't found any, and neither had anyone else.

Throughout that time, they worked closely together and saw each other socially. Their first dinner date was a memorable experience for both of them. Mark took her to the special restaurant he had promised. The meal and wine helped make the evening. The chemistry between them led to their relationship maturing quickly. Mark frequently thought about the tour Gilda gave him of Jerusalem's Old City, their exploring Hezekiah's Tunnel, and that first evening at her apartment.

By the end of his stay, they spent not only time working side by side but many nights together as well. On one of their weekends together, they made it to the Israel Museum to see the Qumran Dead Sea Scrolls, an impressive display. Upon his return to Tallahassee, they kept in touch almost daily, by e-mail or phone.

Gilda and Mark continued their interest in the scrolls, but the Israeli government kept quiet on the matter. Mark begrudgingly signed the secrecy rule, an absurd requirement, he thought. Now he wondered if the rule meant he was to keep the secrets of the scrolls, or if the secrets of the scrolls were to be kept from him, as he never heard from the researchers who were working on them. Even so, every time his phone rang, he thought it might be Dr. Meyer or Gilda with news about the scrolls. All he could do was wait; unfortunately, patience was not one of his stronger virtues.

What Mark did know was that a project team of Israeli government scientists headed by archeologist Dr. Amos Meyer was studying the scrolls. Dr. Meyer seemed very competent and was respected in his field, but most of his work was performed in secret, largely unpublished, and remained in government files not available to the public. Mark learned this from various contacts he made while in Israel and from information on the internet.

The scrolls were in surprisingly excellent condition, partly because they were copper and partly because of the way they had been stored in a somewhat air-tight cavity. The slumped debris blocking the cave helped in the preservation process. Geological processes contributing to the Biblical understanding once again, thought Mark. As a result of the good condition of the scrolls, translating them proceeded much more rapidly than for the Qumran Dead Sea Scrolls.

While still in Israel, Mark was told that the Mount Sodom Dead Sea Scrolls were the earliest known version of the New Testament, which meant the scrolls were about Jesus' life. The gospels in the New Testament, like St. Mark, the source of Mark's Christian name, told much about how Jesus lived and about his teachings. The scrolls should further expand upon the life of Jesus.

Mark knew from his study of Biblical history that some theologians made the case that the gospels were not a reliable account of history and Jesus' life. Even his namesake is grouped with Luke and Matthew and labeled the Synoptic gospels because their writings contain the same stories, the same order, and even the same wording, suggesting plagiarism. All the gospels were written long after the death of Jesus, so by that time, facts were fuzzy and based on oral accounts, told and retold, providing opportunity for error.

After all, Jesus was one of many Jews the Romans crucified as an insurgent during their occupation of Judaea beginning in 63 BCE and lasting for about 375 years. Historians at the time paid little, if any, attention to Jesus—just one more troublemaker executed for his seditious teachings and inciting large numbers of people. Jesus was a champion of the poor, and historians tended to focus on the powerful and wealthy. Under Roman occupation, there was a wide gap between the wealthy few, who often collaborated with the Romans, and the poor masses, which no one cared about.

Scholars don't even have the original writings of the New Testament, thought Mark, *only copies produced by fallible scribes with their own agendas*. Consequently, according to these theologians, there was considerable uncertainty in the history of Jesus for those who looked to the Bible as a history text. Given his scientific training, that was the way Mark saw it, too. The birthplace of Jesus was an example of this uncertainty.

Mark recalled the story of Jesus' birth, described today with great conviction. But in actuality, little is known. At the time the gospels were written, no one knew where Jesus had been born. There were even early copies of the gospels found at St. Catherine's Monastery near Mount Sinai, Egypt, implying that Joseph was Jesus' biological father. It's not even certain in what year he was born. At the time, no one cared about the birth of a peasant. An Old Testament prophecy foretold that the Jewish messiah would be born in Bethlehem. Mary and Joseph, mother and father of Jesus, however, lived in Nazareth in the Galilee, ninety miles north of Bethlehem. Although Jesus usually did not refer to himself as the messiah, the gospels, especially Mark whose text was written first, wished to make the linkage. Therefore, to be consistent with the Old Testament messiah story, the challenge was to get Mary and Joseph to Bethlehem for Jesus' birth.

The solution, some believed, was to create a story about a census for taxation purposes that required everyone to travel to the city of their ancestors, assuming everyone knew who their ancestors were and where those ancestors came from. Joseph was believed to be descended from the house of David, and as luck would have it, David's city was Bethlehem. *What a convenient coincidence*, thought Mark. The birth-location problem was solved with a dubious "tax decree."

Putting aside the disruption a mass migration of people this tax decree would have caused, the logical question was: Why would the Romans require Joseph to travel to Bethlehem where a distant ancestor had lived a thousand years earlier? It had the feel of a made-up story in order to conform to the Old Testament prophecy. Perhaps Jesus had been born elsewhere and the tales of his birth in Bethlehem were just that, stories, told and written to fit the account in the Old Testament. Mark hoped the Mount Sodom Dead Sea Scrolls would help resolve some of the uncertainty he felt still surrounded Jesus' life.

As he watched the rain, Mark continued thinking about the Bible and his beliefs. After his mother's death, he wasn't sure what he believed, but he thought the Bible was a beneficial document, providing background on important historical events, albeit only those that occurred in a small portion of the world. It also offered guidance on how to conduct one's life decently; however, he did not take the Bible literally. Biblical scholars had long questioned scripture accuracy, while those in the pews accept it without any challenge.

Mark came to the logical conclusion that the Bible had internal inconsistencies, making a literal interpretation impossible. An example was in Mark 2 where Jesus referred to the time of King David and the high priest Abiathar. That same story, retold by Jesus, was described in the Old Testament. In I Samuel, the high priest was not Abiathar but his father, Ahimelech. Either Jesus' memory was flawed and the New Testament was wrong or the Old Testament had the story wrong. To believe one passage meant you could not accept the other passage because one contradicted the other.

Mark found that many Christians did not accept the entire Bible as exact; instead, they carefully ignored portions not suiting their needs or applied its teachings selectively. He found their interpretations subjective, molded to fit their beliefs, like some in the South who used Biblical discussions on slavery to justify its use prior to the Civil War. Now there were Christians against abortion on the grounds that all life is sacred, yet they supported war or the death penalty. As far as Mark knew, the "Thou shalt not kill" commandment did not have a footnote allowing war or the death penalty as exceptions.

If the Bible was clear, a literal reading should produce consistent beliefs. Yet interpretations varied dramatically, as demonstrated by the plethora of Christian denominations. According to the United Nations statistics, in 1982 there were more than twenty-three thousand competing and often contradictory denominations worldwide, all based on the Bible. This fact caused Mark to recall the warning in the gospel Matthew to beware of false prophets and wolves in sheep's clothing. The image of some televangelists came to mind, and he recalled his early discussion with Gilda.

Mark wondered how and if the Mount Sodom Dead Sea Scrolls would alter his and the world's religious understandings and beliefs. Dr. Meyer had been reluctant to release additional information about the scrolls until the project was further along. When the Israeli government was ready, he would be informed. At that time, he would return to Israel to be briefed on the findings.

He didn't care about the Israeli government timetable; he was anxious to learn the findings. He wanted to know what was on the scrolls because of his scientific curiosity, but more importantly, he wanted an excuse to return to Israel to be with Gilda.

As if by wishing it to occur, his phone rang.

"Hello," Mark answered.

"Dr. Malloy, this is Dr. Meyer. How are you?"

Mark responded enthusiastically. "I'm fine, Dr. Meyer. How are you?" He quickly added, "And how is the project going?"

"I'm doing quite well. The project is the reason I'm calling. We still have work to do, but are far enough along that we are confident in some of our interpretations. Some of which are very interesting."

"Can you share this information with me?" Mark asked, excitement building.

"Yes, but I prefer to brief you in person. Are you able to come to Israel?"

Thrilled about the prospect of returning to Israel, Mark tried to remain calm. "Yes, I should be able to return, but I need to check with my department head. I'll also need to arrange for someone to handle my teaching load. I think I can be there in about a week or so. Does that work for you?"

"Yes, we will brief you and Dr. Baer when you arrive. Once you have approval for the trip and have made flight arrangements, please provide us with your itinerary, and we will set up a meeting. I look forward to seeing you," Dr. Meyer said.

"Okay, I will do that. I look forward to seeing you too, and I'm anxious to hear the update on the scrolls." There was silence at the other end of the phone, so Mark asked, "Is there anything else, Dr. Meyer?"

"No, I think that is everything. Hopefully, I will see you soon, Mark."

"You can count on it. Good-bye for now, Dr. Meyer."

"Good-bye," responded Dr. Meyer.

Mark hung up the phone. His glum mood changed to one of euphoria; he couldn't keep the smile off his face. Soon he would be back in Israel and with Gilda. Outside, the rain slowed, and the sun broke through the clouds. The weather matched his mood. The sky transitioned to robin egg blue. There was an expression in Florida, "If you don't like the weather, wait an hour; the weather will change and perhaps be more to your liking." Today's weather seemed to typify that expression.

As Mark considered what he would learn from Dr. Meyer, his thoughts turned to Gilda, his imagination running wild. Just thinking about her sent his mind off on flights of passionate possibilities.

Chapter Seven

What I see in Nature is a magnificent structure that we can comprehend only very imperfectly, and that must fill a thinking person with a feeling of "humility." This is a genuinely religious feeling that has nothing to do with mysticism.

—Albert Einstein

Fall 2002, Jerusalem, Israel

In the first-class section of the Boeing 747 headed to Jerusalem, Chester Weeks relished the meals fit for royalty with unlimited alcohol, mainly beer and whisky, which he consumed without fear of being spotted by fellow church members. "Only practice what you preach in the company of the masses you wish to control" was Chester's motto. He was able to sleep soundly, totally reclined, using the provided eye covers and earplugs. Being waited on by stewardesses was an additional perk; he refused to use the politically correct term, flight attendant. Best of all, he didn't have to share the bathroom with people from steerage, an expression used to refer to the lowest decks on a ship that Chester applied to the coach-class section of the jet. He arrived in Jerusalem two days prior to Mark, who would not be flying first class.

Chester's exquisite hotel, near Jacob's office, offered five-star meals and an elegant spa, where he could receive a full-body massage using new-age massage therapy. The therapy left Chester stress-free and relaxed. Following his latest massage, he lay on the padded floor mat, nude except for a towel covering his abundant midsection. Inhaling sweet-smelling incense and listening to soft sitar music in the background, he thought, "Now this is a religious experience."

When not enjoying the amenities of his hotel, Chester met with Jacob Cohen. Despite the secrecy rule, he was given a full debriefing by Jacob about the scrolls found by Mark and Gilda. Because of his government position, Jacob had learned about the latest findings concerning the scrolls from Dr. Meyer. Now it was Chester's turn to learn their contents because of the significant tourism money he generated for Israel and the possible threat the scrolls presented. *Money talks*, thought Chester.

The writings on the scrolls had yielded terribly disturbing information. Anything questioning the steadfast words in the Bible was unacceptable. Chester feared it might set the modern Christian world on its collective ear. As he was debriefed, he felt a tinge of panic. How would this news affect his business? His order of things was definitely being disrupted. The story of Jesus in the Bible was being challenged, his financial empire threatened.

His first thought was to destroy the scrolls and any other evidence of their existence. He knew the Israeli government wouldn't agree. Another option was to keep the information concealed, away from the public. He believed Jacob could control people within his government, including the Israeli geologist. The American geologist was the wildcard, thought Chester. Neither he nor Jacob wanted them to learn the words and ideas contained in the scrolls. He harkened back to the Middle Ages; in those days, the geologists could easily be killed for heresy.

Over the past two days, Chester and Jacob had discussed at length how to handle the situation. The minister of tourism was as concerned as Chester about how this new information might upset what Chester thought of so fondly as "the order of things," meaning a possible decrease in tourism and the dollars it brought to Chester and Israel. Beyond tourism, there were further reaching potential financial impacts at stake causing Chester great consternation. Even the hotel massages could not totally eliminate his anxiety.

"What if Dr. Malloy was to have an accident and disappear? I understand that he's a fan of sinkholes. Perhaps he could fall into one and never be found again," mused Chester at one of their meetings, unaware that Mark had already survived one such fall.

Troubled, Jacob thought Chester must be kidding, but he wasn't sure. "We are in control of the situation," Jacob quickly said, trying to assure him. "There is no need for such an extreme solution."

"Well, maybe not now," added Chester as he nervously rubbed his bald head. "But what happens if you lose control?"

"Our plan is to only provide Dr. Malloy and Dr. Baer partial information, hoping they will be satisfied and become disinterested," Jacob said without conviction.

"Why would they lose interest?" Chester asked.

"After all, they are geologists, not archaeologists," Jacob said. "Dr. Meyer has reluctantly agreed to cooperate with us, and I have directed him to deflect Dr. Malloy's curiosity about the scrolls. Dr. Meyer will tell them the scrolls only confirm the New Testament, which should pacify Drs. Malloy and Baer and maintain the scrolls' secrecy." Downplaying the geologists further, Jacob continued, "They are simply unimportant lose threads."

Chester thought Jacob was not taking the geologists as a serious enough threat. "Let me remind you, Jacob," said Chester, "it's important for both our sakes that what you've told me about the scrolls not become public. The impact this information could have on Christianity is difficult to predict. Anything that threatens contributions to the First Church of God's Chosen, not to mention all other Christian churches, also is a threat to Christian tourism to Israel. We both have too much to lose here. We must control the situation. Do you agree?"

"Yes, of course," replied Jacob with growing concern.

"What if your plan doesn't work?" asked Chester sharply.

"I have a backup plan," Jacob responded. "As I will explain, this plan involves you, or more specifically, for it to succeed it requires your financial support." Jacob knew from previous conversations that for Chester money was not a problem. Chester had numerous accounts from which to draw cash.

Chester had confidence in Jacob. Jacob Cohen was not only minister of tourism, he also was the brother-in-law of the prime minister of Israel. Israel relied heavily on money from tourism to drive its economy and contribute to the county's defense. Tourism generated about two billion dollars annually for Israel. That amount didn't include donations made to Israel simply because the Holy Land was located there.

The position of minister of tourism alone was powerful because of these sums of money, but that combined with being the brother-in-law of the prime minister meant Jacob Cohen was indeed one powerful man. That power is what initially drew Chester to him.

Jacob wondered how far his government would go to suppress the findings about the scrolls. He didn't want Israel to be seen as the country that caused chaos in the Christian world by releasing the findings. The relationship between Jews and Christians was delicate, and he did not want a backlash that could impact Israeli tourism or complicate international relations. There were those in America who still disliked Jews for the treatment of Jesus, and Jacob did not want to give them any additional reasons to dislike Jews. He knew Chester was influential and helped Israel financially. Chester had his quirks, but he was a good barometer of a potential Christian reaction. And what Chester was telling him was not comforting.

On the other hand, the Israeli government might not want to suppress anything as important as the material in the scrolls. A cover up of that nature could backfire, also causing damage to tourism and the Jewish-Christian relationship. Jacob felt he was in a difficult position with no easy solution. If only the scrolls had never been found! He blamed the two geologists for his dilemma.

"Tell me about your backup plan, Jacob," Chester inquired.

"The backup plan is to send Drs. Malloy and Baer on a fool's errand, wasting their time looking for antiquities that likely do not exist. Their goal would be to find corroborating information supporting that found in the scrolls. Hopefully, they get discouraged, give up and forget about the scrolls. An ingenious part of this plan is that Dr. Meyer will accompany them, reporting back to us. That way, we can track them, learning if they actually stumble upon anything important. At a minimum, this will buy us time. However, there is one critical part missing and that is where your role is crucial."

Jacob carefully described more details of his backup plan. He wrapped up by asking, "Chester, would you be willing to provide the financial support for this plan? This will ensure the plan can be executed quickly." Jacob paused, trying to gauge Chester's reaction, then continued with his coup de grace, saying, "Without your support, I will need to turn to other sources for money, and will not be able to guarantee your continued involvement."

Chester recognized Jacob's threat to terminate his access if he did not provide financial support. He appreciated Jacob's manipulative style but didn't take kindly to being blackmailed. Taking a few moments to assess his options, he concluded it would be worthwhile to stay involved. Chester responded frostily, "Jacob, you leave me little choice. I must agree with your plan, but I am willing to fund only reasonable travel expenses." Chester concluded that his financial investment would be small relative to staying involved and learning about any corroborating evidence that might be found. In addition, his investment would help keep the scrolls contained and away from the public.

Vigorously shaking Chester's hand, Jacob said, "You've made the correct decision, my friend."

Chester's mood thawed, his mind starting to work out money transfer logistics.

Following Chester's acceptance, Jacob told Chester, without being explicit, about the possible need for nonfinancial support, saying, "I trust you can take care of any circumstances that might threaten our plan."

"I'll do my best," Chester said with an assuring nod, confident he would think of other means to contain the scrolls, if needed. "Just be sure to keep me informed."

"You can count on it." Jacob said, happy with the deal he had just orchestrated.

Chester said good-bye and left Jacob's office. He liked the plan and at present had no better ideas. He would noodle it over to see if he could come up with any improvements. A massage would help him think, so he decided to walk back to the hotel. Before leaving the building, he spread sun tan lotion on his face and on the ever-expanding bald spot on the top of his head.

It was a sunny afternoon, typical of days in Jerusalem. At this time of the day, the streets were not crowded. As he walked, he tried to stay as much as possible in the shade. His thoughts turned to the American geologist. He didn't know Dr. Malloy, but Chester doubted he would give up easily. Chester began to appreciate Jacob's backup plan, thinking it just might have to be put into practice.

Perhaps he would need an additional backup plan, one more robust. He knew just the person who could implement this contingency. There was no need to share this plan with Jacob. He could take care of this second backup plan on his own, and it would guarantee the scrolls would never be released, that his order of things would not be disrupted.

Chapter Eight

There is nothing divine about morality; it is a purely human affair.

—Albert Einstein

Fall 2002, Jerusalem, Israel

The Jerusalem airport closed in 2001 due to security concerns, so Mark landed in Tel Aviv. When his flight arrived at Ben-Gurion Airport, the sun had fully set. Rising from his cramped coach seat, he stretched, retrieved his backpack, and exited the plane.

Leaving passport control and customs, his first view was Gilda, who looked radiant, like moonbeams glistening off the Dead Sea. He recalled their first night in the desert. She smiled with both her mouth and eyes. Mark reacted in kind. They hugged tightly and kissed passionately, not wanting to separate. The airport was crowded. No one took notice of the lovers. She felt so familiar. A mixture of excitement and a feeling of warmth and comfort swept over him. The two-month separation had done nothing to quell his feelings. That seemed to be the case for her as well. The spark was still glowing brightly.

"I missed you," she said softly when they finally separated.

"I missed you too," Mark replied as he took her by the hand and began walking toward the exit. "Let's get out of here." He had already claimed his luggage in customs and was ready to go.

"How were your flights?" Gilda asked. "And the food?'

"My flights were long but uneventful, the best kind. I did have a window seat and was able to get some sleep. The food, well, you know how airline food is these days. Not the best—edible—but to tell you the truth, I'm not all that hungry for food right now," he said with a silly grin on his face.

She pulled his hand, steering him to the airport's exit. "Come on, my car is just outside."

On the thirty-mile ride to Jerusalem, they caught up on a variety of topics. Finally, Mark asked in a more serious tone, "What have you learned about the scrolls?"

"Not much, probably the same as you. Dr. Meyer is very tight-lipped. We're scheduled to meet with him tomorrow morning at ten o'clock. Hopefully, we'll learn more then."

They arrived at Gilda's one-bedroom apartment, which seemed very familiar to Mark. He carried in his luggage. Before he could even open his suitcase, Gilda began kissing him. She continued holding him. She pulled her head back, breaking off the kiss. With a sly look, she asked, "After such a long flight, you must be in need of a shower."

"Actually, a shower sounds great," he said, looking between the bed and the bathroom, not sure which attracted him more.

"I can help with that," she said, pulling him lightly to the bathroom. She slowly removed his shirt, revealing his chest and trim abdomen. Next, she removed her blouse, revealing no bra. She had perfect breasts, and Mark immediately became aroused. He kicked off his shoes as Gilda began to undo his belt. She slowly removed both his pants and underwear together, leaving him naked and at attention. Finally, she removed her shorts and panties. Mark admired her from head to toe. She was striking, her nude body reminding him of a perfectly sculpted statue of the Greek goddess of love and beauty, Aphrodite.

"Are you ready for your shower?" Gilda asked.

They lingered in the shower, washing each other's bodies slowly and sensuously. Mark was ready to explode.

After drying each other, they practically ran to her bed, tumbling in. Despite Mark's exhaustion from his strenuous trip, he found a reserve of energy. In the aftermath, they lay askew in disheveled bed linens, pillows on the floor, trying to catch their breath. It was a rare moment when Mark was not talkative. Gilda took advantage and shared her life during the last two months without him. Mark listened as long as he could, but finally succumbed; he fell into a deep sleep in the middle of one of Gilda's stories.

Given his excitement of being with Gilda and of the prospect of learning the scrolls' contents, he awoke at seven the next morning and carefully moved out of bed, trying not to disturb Gilda, who looked angelic lying there curled up, continuing to sleep. Although short, his slumber was restful.

He closed the bedroom door behind him and went to the kitchen, where he made coffee and looked around to see what Gilda had in the way of breakfast food. He found eggs, bread, and some other odds and ends.

After making breakfast, he returned to the bedroom and began softly kissing Gilda on her neck and shoulders. She moved slightly and slowly opened her eyes.

Finally, after a long good morning kiss, Mark was able to catch his breath. "Hi, gorgeous. Are you ready for breakfast?"

She smiled at his thoughtfulness. "I'm famished. I feel like I put in a hard day's night. I wonder why?" Looking sheepish, Gilda rose and put on her robe.

They made their way to the kitchen, sat at her table, and began to eat. She looked up at him with a big grin and said warmly, "This is pretty darn good. You know, I think I might just be able to get used to having you around."

Mark blushed. "Thanks," he said. Slowly, he responded to her second comment, "I know what you mean." He was happiest when spending time with Gilda. They sat quietly, enjoying each other's company. They caught up on more topics: friends they had in common, places they shared, the paper they had written together.

Eventually, the conversation steered to the topic at hand. Mark asked, "Have you had any contact with Dr. Meyer since I left?"

"None. Like I said, he hasn't been very communicative."

"Is that normal? Is your government usually this secretive on archeological finds?" Mark asked, clearly frustrated.

"Not on most archeological finds. They weren't even this secretive on the Qumran Dead Sea Scrolls. The findings made the news, and the usual scientific papers were published. This total secrecy does seem a bit unusual."

Gilda finished eating her breakfast, clearly savoring her time with Mark.

"Have you any idea how today's meeting will go?" Mark asked.

"No. My sense is that we might finally find out what is on those scrolls."

"Can you think of any reason why your government would be so secretive and withhold this information from the public?" Mark persisted, finding the behavior hard to understand.

"No. I am disappointed with how my government is handing this," responded Gilda.

"I have to tell you I don't have a good feeling about this. I know I'm a scientist and should stick to the facts, but this just doesn't feel right and has not felt right from the beginning when we had to sign that silly secrecy agreement. I hope I'm wrong about this." Mark began clearing the table, stacking the dishes in the sink.

He turned and asked, "Where's our meeting this morning?"

"In Dr. Meyer's office, and with traffic as bad as it is, we should start getting ready," responded Gilda.

"Do we have time for … you know?" Mark asked with a broad smile and a mischievous gleam in his eyes.

"Given your silly look, I should say no, but then I would have to share in your punishment. So the answer is yes, if we hurry."

"I can be quick when I need to be," Mark said, grinning from ear to ear.

They made love again. This time, the bed linens remained intact. Lying there and wishing for more time, they reluctantly jumped out of bed and hurriedly got ready to leave. This included another joint shower.

Gilda drove across town to Dr. Meyer's office, which was in a government building. They had to pass through various levels of security that included soldiers carrying automatic weapons. Understandably, the Israelis took security very seriously, but it still intimidated Mark. With her government identification, Gilda was able to pass through quickly. On the other hand, Mark was scrutinized and probed at every checkpoint.

Finally through security, they headed for the elevator and up to their meeting with Dr. Meyer. Approaching Dr. Meyer's office, Mark felt his apprehension and excitement rising.

Chapter Nine

If God created us in his own image, we have more than reciprocated.

—Voltaire

Fall 2002, Jerusalem, Israel

"The meeting is being held in the conference room at the end of the hall," Dr. Meyer's matronly assistant explained. She led them down the corridor and knocked softly on the door.

When Gilda and Mark entered, three middle-aged men stood to greet them. A large conference table almost filled the room. Dr. Amos Meyer, whom they both knew from his visit to the cave where the scrolls were found, extended his arm to shake hands, saying, "Good morning, Gilda. Good morning, Mark." They responded in kind.

Dr. Meyer turned to the other two men and introduced them. "This is Jacob Cohen, the Israeli minister of tourism. And this is Chester Weeks, from the First Church of God's Chosen in the United States." Jacob was a small-framed man in his fifties with piercing eyes. Chester, also in his fifties, was heavyset and balding. Offering her hand, Gilda's handshake was firm as she looked intently at Chester. Following Gilda's lead, Mark also shook hands.

Expecting to meet other scientists, Mark felt like he had just stepped into the Twilight Zone, and the catchy theme song played in this head. He had heard of Chester Weeks, and he definitely knew about the First Church of God's Chosen. When he watched TV and flipped channels, he could not help but see parts of their programs. Always asking for donations, the GCN broadcast twenty-four hours a day and seven days a week over the cable airways. His immediate question was: *Why in the world were these men here? What did tourism and American evangelicalism have to do with the copper scrolls?*

Misters Cohen and Weeks seated themselves at the far end of the large rectangular table while Dr. Meyer moved to the front to begin his presentation. Mark, bewildered by the presence of these nonscientists, followed Dr. Meyer and addressed him directly in a quiet voice, "I appreciate your meeting with us, Dr. Meyer, but I'm at a loss as to why Mr. Cohen and Mr. Weeks are here, especially given the secrecy rule."

"Mr. Cohen is the senior governmental official overseeing this project. He reports directly to the prime minister on the scrolls project and has an interest in how the information in the scrolls may impact Israel's relations with other nations. Mr. Weeks is an interested party. His role here will become more obvious by the end of this meeting," responded Dr. Meyer.

Mark was dumbfounded by Dr. Meyer's response and demeanor, and he was still confused by the presence of the other men.

"Please be seated, and I will begin," Dr. Meyer told Mark and Gilda.

While settling in her chair, Gilda leaned over and whispered to Mark, "Jacob Cohen is not only minister of tourism, but also the brother-in-law of the prime minister." Mark was still unsure why either Jacob or Chester was involved.

Dr. Meyer looked around the room, gathered his thoughts, and began his presentation. "As you well know, eleven copper scrolls were found about six months ago by Drs. Malloy and Baer, whom we are pleased to have with us today. Until now, we have translated nine of them. Most of the scrolls are in Greek, but a few are in Aramaic. Most interestingly, unlike the Qumran Dead Sea Scrolls that contain material associated with the Old Testament, these nine scrolls contain material from the New Testament."

Dr. Meyer paused to let his words sink in. Continuing, he added, "The oldest known books of the New Testament or manuscripts containing the gospels are from the fourth century CE. The scrolls found by Drs. Malloy and Baer are from the second century CE and therefore are the earliest versions of the books of the New Testament ever discovered. They represent the fountainhead of early Christianity."

"How do they compare to currently accepted books of the New Testament?" asked Mark, glancing at Chester and Jacob and trying to size them up.

"The comparison is remarkably good with a few exceptions."

"And those are?" Gilda asked in a clipped tone.

"That's not important for now. We can discuss those later."

"What about the last two scrolls?" Mark quickly added. The withholding of information fueled his curiosity.

"We are still in the process of translating them."

"Why are those two scrolls taking longer? Are they more difficult to translate for some reason?" Mark asked.

"The difficulty is due in part to their content. We want to make sure our translations are correct, so it is taking longer," continued Dr. Meyer patiently.

"What is it about their content that's making you so cautious?" Mark asked, continuing the ping-pong dialogue and becoming increasingly skeptical.

Based on Dr. Malloy's questioning, Chester could feel their first plan to dissuade Dr. Malloy slipping away and knew that their backup plan would soon need to be put in play. Chester had trouble reading Dr. Malloy's eyes, but his words were clear. Dr. Malloy was being incredibly persistent, his interest too keen. Chester could tell from her body language that Dr. Baer was as intensely engaged as Dr. Malloy. Chester leaned toward Jacob, muttering under his breath, "I'm glad we devised that backup plan."

Dr. Meyer knew what he could and could not tell Mark and Gilda. He felt uncomfortable withholding information from his colleagues, but Jacob had been adamant about what information he could divulge. Now what he was about to say would likely upset Jacob. He began slowly answering Mark's question, careful not to reveal too much, saying, "Dr. Malloy, I believe you are familiar with the Bible, in particular, the New Testament?"

"Yes, of course."

"Then you know the New Testament provides a brief and intermittent account of Jesus' life from the time of his birth until he was about twelve years old. It is around that time, age thirteen to be exact, that Jesus would have undergone his bar mitzvah. You might think of the bar mitzvah as a rite of passage to manhood. It would have been a time when Jesus became responsible for his actions. An odd thing about the New Testament is that it does not resume the story of Jesus' life until he is thirty years old. In other words, there are eighteen years where a discussion of Jesus' life is totally missing from the Bible." Pausing, Dr. Meyer added slowly, "The last two scrolls address that missing eighteen year period in Jesus' life."

The conference room was utterly silent. Mark was stunned by what he heard. It was an unbelievable discovery. *To think we could finally find out what Jesus did during those eighteen years*, he thought. What insights this could shed on this person of such great stature!

What experiences had Jesus had during this period that helped shape his life and his message? Mark could feel his excitement rising.

He blurted out, "This is great news! A significant discovery like this should be made public. Does this mean the secrecy rule will be lifted?"

Gilda, as elated as Mark, added, "This momentous discovery is as important as the Qumran Dead Sea Scrolls. The Mount Sodom Dead Sea Scrolls should be made available to other scientists to maximize scientific studies, creating the potential for further discoveries within the scrolls' text."

That was exactly what Chester did not want to hear. He had already evaluated this "momentous discovery" and had concluded the impact on his wallet would not be a positive one. In his mind, this information needed to be hidden from the public. *The less thinking about Jesus' life, the better*, thought Chester. What was known in the Christian world for almost two thousand years had worked up until now. The Bible was a constant. Why change it? The scrolls could only spell disaster for the current state of Christianity. He was displeased that Dr. Meyer had revealed so much.

"What was found in these two scrolls is not in the current version of the New Testament. Some believe the release of this information at this time could be extremely disruptive to the Christian community," Dr. Meyer stated evenly, trying to calm Mark and Gilda.

Hardly able to believe what she was hearing, Gilda looked at the others in the room and asked impatiently, "Why? What is so disruptive about this information? What did Jesus do?"

Dr. Meyer pursed his lips, deciding to divulge a little more, "These scrolls indicate that Jesus traveled toward the east and spent eighteen years outside of present-day Israel."

"How is that information a threat to Christianity? Where did he go?" Gilda inquired with frustration in her voice. The information provided was selectively ambiguous. This was not the scientific debriefing she anticipated.

"We are not yet sure of all the details," responded Dr. Meyer quickly, looking down, uncomfortable with his answer. "We still need more time to work on the final two scrolls." This was technically true, but he knew he was giving an impression that was not accurate. He disliked the conditions Jacob had placed on him.

Dr. Meyer knew much more than he was revealing. The translation of the final two scrolls had been completed several days ago. The scrolls had contained considerable details about Jesus' extensive travels, but these details would not be given to Mark and Gilda. Dr. Meyer was a scientist, and part of him wanted the information contained on the scrolls to be released, but he also was loyal to his government and believed he must follow Jacob's plan. He felt very conflicted.

"So what's it going to take for you to release this information? When will it be circulated?" demanded Mark.

Okay, thought Chester, *here comes our backup plan*. He felt thoroughly confident that Mark and Gilda would never succeed in finding anything of interest. Consequently, he felt the backup plan was foolproof.

Dr. Meyer grabbed the frame of his glasses and moved them closer to his eyes, a nervous tic. "This information is very sensitive and could cause a negative reaction in the Christian world. That is one of the reasons Mr. Weeks is here. He is a good barometer on the Christian world's possible reaction. Because of a potential negative reaction that could impact Israel, some believe information contained in the Mount Sodom Dead Sea Scrolls needs to be independently verified before it can be released."

"What do you mean by 'independently verified'?" asked Gilda.

"It means that before we can release this information, other information, independent of the Mount Sodom Dead Sea Scrolls, needs to be found to support the travels of Jesus during this eighteen year period."

"And how do you propose to do that?" Mark asked.

"Not just me, Dr. Malloy. I'll be part of a team that includes you and Dr. Baer. Together, we will attempt to find this information," Dr. Meyer said with quiet aplomb.

Secretly, Dr. Meyer was excited about this prospect. He knew that Jacob thought this was a showstopper and expected them to find nothing worthwhile, but Dr. Meyer thought this effort might actually lead to something of archeological value. Based on what he read in the scrolls, he had ideas he wanted to pursue. He thought it would be an ironic twist if they made an archeological discovery because the funding for this effort was coming from Chester, the one who most strenuously opposed the release of the scrolls.

The genius part of the plan, thought Chester, unaware of Dr. Meyer's own aspirations, was that he would be able to keep close tabs on Drs. Malloy and Baer. It followed the adage "keep your friends close and your enemies closer." By keeping an eye on the two and sending them on a wild goose chase leading to nothing, Chester felt assured the scrolls would never be released.

"I propose," continued Dr. Meyer, "that we pursue corroborating information together. The two of you, Dr. Baer and Dr. Malloy, have valuable talents useful in this pursuit. As for me, in addition to my archeology experience, I am familiar with several ancient languages. Together, I believe we have an excellent chance of finding the required information, especially given what I have learned from the scrolls."

Although Dr. Meyer hoped they would find corroborating information, per his agreement with Jacob Cohen, if he and his team found anything of interest, he was obligated to report it immediately to Jacob before the news leaked out. Dr. Meyer did not like this arrangement. However, in order to conduct this scientific study, he felt compelled to comply with Jacob's desires. At least he would be present if anything were found.

"And how do you propose to support and fund this expedition?" Mark said.

"If I may, Dr. Meyer," interrupted Chester, who had been sitting quietly in the back of the room, "I can address that question. Dr. Malloy, that is where I come into the picture."

There was a pause.

Finally, Chester smiled and spoke. "My church, the FCGC, is interested in this project and very much wants to possess, uh, be informed of any of your findings. For that reason, we will happily fund this effort." Chester beamed with satisfaction.

"Why? Why would you of all people want to fund this study?" Gilda asked incredulously. Everything about Chester reeked of manipulation and disingenuousness.

Slyly, Chester smiled. He was prepared for this question. "The FCGC is closely connected with Israel, and we are very interested in Jesus. However, we believe the stories contained in the scrolls are a radical departure from our traditional Bible. The scrolls you found could have been written by some religious crackpot." Chester paused to let his concerns register.

For Mark, Chester's comment triggered thoughts of many fundamentalists in the United States.

Chester continued, pulling Mark back into his monologue. "For that reason, it is vitally important, indeed, our obligation to make absolutely certain this new and somewhat controversial information is correct before we release it. That's why we will provide funding for this scientific study." He ended with a broad, devious smile, his words stated as if sacrosanct.

This strategy is brilliant, thought Chester. *Using this plan, we track and control Malloy and Baer, we keep them busy and away from the press, and in the unlikely event they find something, we will learn about it and take appropriate action. The cost of this endeavor is a small price to pay given all the benefits. And in the end, if need be, there is always the final solution—to eliminate the problem.*

Chester was quite pleased with himself. He continued haughtily, "You should understand my unique position here. I'm not a big supporter of science, so to fund this effort is a significant concession on the part of my church. Supporting a scientific expedition goes against my very nature. I hope you appreciate the exception I am making for you." He thought his offer was such that the two scientists would have to accept and be happy for it.

Mark and Gilda's eyes met. In that instant, both were appalled and united against Chester. To Gilda, Chester was a serpent in the form of a man. Mark became more annoyed; the scrolls were being withheld for dubious reasons. Now science was being attacked by the same person who prevented the scrolls' release. He could not let Chester's comment pass without protest.

"First of all," snapped Mark, "if you supported the release of the Mount Sodom Dead Sea Scrolls, this expedition you're funding would be unnecessary. The scientific community would be able to scrutinize the scrolls and eventually determine their authenticity. Second, Jesus was an intelligent person who was interested in the truth. I'm sure he would have been a supporter of science. Why aren't you?"

Chester replied self-righteously. "Science," he said, drawing out the word, "is imperfect. Certain hypotheses and theories that scientists develop are later proven incorrect. I don't think you can trust the results of science. Take the theory of evolution or the age of the earth, for example. The first chapter of Genesis tells us that God created everything in six days and he rested on the seventh. I don't think you can believe theories concerning evolution and the age of the earth because they are contrary to what Genesis tells us."

Mark had heard and debated against these wearisome arguments before. "Yet when there is a problem with the country's food or water supply or a new disease is discovered, people like you, who do not trust science, immediately turn to science for a solution," he said.

"Your distrust in science is very selective. Science embodies a process where hypotheses are continually tested as new data or information become available. The beauty of science is that it allows for change in ideas as new information dictates those changes. Science embraces new information; it doesn't fear it or a potential change to the status quo, as you seem to be doing."

As Mark spoke, he became angrier. He continued briskly, "And what about evolution? I don't see why the concept of evolution can't coexist with the teachings in the Bible. God gave man a brain with which to observe minute changes, the evolution of species. Those species, including man, change as they adjust to different environments over time. These changes can be viewed, if desired, as ones made by God."

Mark paused to catch his breath as Gilda joined the discussion. "As for the age of the earth, the first chapter of Genesis can be interpreted many ways. It is not a clearly written description of creation. Some believe it is a metaphor for creation and should not be taken literally. Others believe it is a myth."

Gilda, waving her hands in dramatic fashion, hit her stride. "To ancient man, a day was a period of sunlight followed by a period of light from the stars and moon. But, according to Genesis, God did not create the sun, moon, and stars until the fourth day. So, how much time passed during the first three days of creation when 'day' was not defined until the fourth day when the sun that fills the day with light was created? And how long is a day, which we now define as one turn of the earth on its axis, when 'earth' was not specifically defined until the third day? This uncertainty allows room for different interpretations."

Mark admired Gilda's eloquence as she argued the point about the age of the earth. Fired up, he continued to press Chester, "One more thing … back to evolution. There are multiple lines of evidence supporting the theory of evolution. Recent DNA studies, not available in Darwin's time, show that small discrete changes in our genes have occurred and accumulated over time, providing independent evidence of evolution."

Mark thought of something else and quickly asked, "Do you take flu shots?"

"Yes," Chester responded, "every year. What does that have to do with anything?"

"That a new flu virus appears every year is evidence of evolution. It is well known that viruses reproduce, mutate, and evolve quickly. If you receive flu shots, you implicitly buy into evolution. If evolution didn't occur, you wouldn't need to take a flu shot every year."

To add insult to injury, Gilda added, "How do you think herbicide-resistant weeds and pesticide-resistant insects develop?" Quickly answering her own question, she said, "Evolution to the chemical changes we impose on their environment, that's how."

Red-faced, Chester gawked in silence. He didn't anticipate a lecture on science. He hated having his own words used against him. His dislike for Mark grew with every word exiting his mouth.

Mark changed the topic and said, "What I would like to point out is that your church does use science, but it recognizes it selectively. You do not believe the science behind evolution, but you readily accept science to establish the point at which human conception occurs. In Biblical times, people didn't understand the detailed biology of reproduction. They could not have determined when conception occurred with their limited knowledge. Do you think the ancients understood cell division that leads to the development of an embryo?"

Mark briefly paused for effect, then said, "Of course not. Yet you use this knowledge gained through science to fight embryonic stem cell research. The knowledge that allows you to determine the point of conception only came about because of more recent scientific studies. So you are willing to trust and embrace science, but only when it conforms with or supports your beliefs. Your use of science is biased and steeped in hypocrisy and inconsistencies. Science relies on data and knowledge and should not be used selectively only when it suits your needs."

Chester was beside himself. He was becoming more frustrated with each outburst from Gilda and Mark. He was ill-equipped to argue science versus religion. Memorizing the conservative talking points against science, he possessed little substance to win that argument.

On the other hand, Dr. Meyer thoroughly enjoyed Mark and Gilda's performance. He especially took pleasure in watching Chester squirm.

Chester could take no more, demanding, "Dr. Malloy, are you interested in my offer of financial support or not?"

Uncomfortable with Chester, but wanting to accept his offer, Mark asked, "What strings are attached?"

"None," Chester lied without so much of a hint of his duplicity.

Dr. Meyer added, "As I mentioned, my only condition is that we work as a team. I believe we will be more effective that way."

Pausing briefly to assess the proffer, Mark acquiesced. Begrudgingly, he answered, "Yes, I'm interested, but this task is like finding a needle in a hay field with many hay stacks."

Gilda added, "I, too, am interested, but I agree with Mark that this is a nearly impossible task." She wanted to participate in the study but resented Chester's involvement.

Quiet filled the room. Mark's respect for Dr. Meyer significantly influenced his decision. He hoped his trust was not misplaced. Resigned, Mark sighed, turned to Dr. Meyer, and asked, "Alright. Where and when do you suggest we start?"

"Actually, Dr. Malloy, I've already considered that question and performed background checking based on information in the scrolls. Some of the early official church discussions on Jesus took place at the Council of Nicaea," answered Dr. Meyer, adjusting his glasses again. "So we'll start in Iznik, Turkey, the location of the Council of Nicaea."

Mark and Gilda looked at each other, recalling their discussions about the Council of Nicaea they had the first day they met.

Chapter Ten

It is not enough to have a good mind; the main thing is to use it well.

—Descartes

Winter 2002, Jerusalem, Israel

Before traveling to Turkey, Mark and Gilda put their individual affairs in order. Mark was responsible for one course on hydrogeology at the university and had asked a colleague to teach it for him. Now he needed to let his colleague know that his help would be required a bit longer.

Another person on his list to contact was his graduate student, Jesus Lopez. It would be a while longer before Mark could review his thesis. He also needed to follow up with Jesus on the translation project recently underway.

Gilda was in the middle of a number of projects she needed to put on hold. For others, she made arrangements with GSI colleagues to cover for her.

Being a US citizen, Mark needed a visa to enter Turkey. He was surprised to learn that a Turkish visa was not required for Israelis. Gilda teased him about the fact that he needed a visa, while she did not. "Obviously, Israelis are more trustworthy. One needs to keep tabs on those Americans."

The time planning was well spent, both professionally and personally. While Gilda continued working at the GSI, Mark learned about Iznik, Turkey, and the Council of Nicaea. In the evenings, they could hardly keep their hands off each other. Their relationship was so intense that it was hard to focus on their upcoming trip and the new information about Jesus.

Mark knew Matthew mentioned that Jesus was taken to Egypt shortly after his birth to protect him from King Herod, who wanted to eliminate threats to his throne. He lived there until Herod's death. There were even rumors about Jesus' travels to the British Isles, but that he instead traveled east was a revelation to Mark.

As they lay in bed late one afternoon recovering from their latest intimate encounter, a sheet covering most of their bodies, Mark's mind drifted back to Jesus. He thoughtfully commented, "You know, all four gospels—Matthew, Mark, Luke, and John—are silent on the eighteen years between Jesus' twelfth and thirtieth years. Jesus returned at age thirty and was dead by age thirty-three. So we only know about fifteen years of Jesus' life and nothing about the other eighteen years."

Gilda followed the math. "From a time-period perspective, we have information on less than 50 percent of Jesus' life. It seems odd that nothing about those eighteen years is included in the Bible."

"I agree," said Mark. "Jesus became a man during that time. The missing time includes his teenage years up to age thirty. This is a period in many people's lives when they are most productive. Einstein wrote his paper on the theory of relativity when he was twenty-six. Alexander the Great conquered his world by age twenty-five. For Jesus to have done nothing memorable and noteworthy during this period is hard to believe. I wonder why this portion of Jesus' life is omitted from the Bible."

Gilda rose on one elbow and looked at Mark. "It's interesting that there are some who believe Jesus spent those eighteen years in Nazareth. But if that were true, the gospels should include local history during that time. Information from those eighteen years would be in the Bible."

Mark sat up in bed, crossing his legs under the sheet. "It's believable that Jesus left present-day Israel given this absence in his historical record. In fact, his absence is somewhat supported by the Bible. Do you remember when Jesus returned, he was seen as a stranger, not recognized by people like his own cousin, John the Baptist? Had he been in Nazareth the whole time, his cousin and others certainly would have interacted with him and known him. He would not have been perceived as a stranger."

Gilda concurred, saying, "Being away for those eighteen years, he would have changed, becoming a man. It is understandable that his relatives and former acquaintances wouldn't recognize him upon his return to Nazareth. So I guess our working hypothesis is that Jesus was not in Nazareth; he traveled east."

Mark nodded in agreement. Then he bent down and kissed her, temporarily losing interest in the life of Jesus.

Were Jesus' travels to the east even possible? That was the question that nagged at Mark and Gilda. To find an answer, they spent a great deal of time reviewing the immense bank of valuable information on the internet and at the University of Jerusalem library. Various topics arose during their discussions, like languages at the time of Jesus and trade routes Jesus may have taken. Leaving the library one afternoon, Mark thought of a different approach to answering the "Was it possible?" question.

After walking in the sunlight to a crowded park next to the library, they sat on a bench in the shade of a large eucalyptus tree. "What do you suppose might have been barriers limiting Jesus' travels?" Mark asked.

He began addressing his own question, "One barrier to travel may have been language. What languages did Jesus speak?"

"Most scholars believe Jesus spoke Aramaic and perhaps some Hebrew and Greek," answered Gilda. A light breeze blew, causing the leaves to rustle.

Mark smelled the faint odor of menthol cough drops. "Do you smell that?"

"Yes, it is from the eucalyptus tree we are under. Don't you have these trees in Florida?"

"No," replied Mark. He continued, returning to his thoughts about the languages Jesus likely spoke. "As I recall, when you were telling me about the Qumran Dead Sea Scrolls, those scrolls were written in those same three languages. Is that correct?"

"Yes," responded Gilda.

"The New Testament was originally written in Greek. I would have guessed Jesus' primary language was Hebrew. And I would have been wrong. What is Aramaic?" Mark asked.

Drawing on her college history studies, she replied, "Aramaic is a Semitic language about three thousand years old. After starting in the Assyrian Empire along the Tigris River in present-day Northern Iraq, it spread through most of the Middle East from Egypt to the Persian Gulf. Aramaic was, and in some cases still is, spoken in many parts of the Middle East."

"Speaking Aramaic, Jesus would have had no language problems traveling through much of Arabia and Persia, allowing him to travel almost as far as India and China without encountering language difficulties," considered Mark.

"Yea, I think that is correct," agreed Gilda. "Recall, at Jesus' birth, the magi or wise men came from the east. They were thought to have come from Persia, so travel that far was possible based on the Bible." Then she thought of something else. "Another barrier to his travels may have been finances. How did Jesus support himself during those eighteen years?"

Mark had researched Jesus' occupation and responded, "That's a good question. The Bible indicates Jesus was a carpenter. But as a geologist, look around. Ignoring the one we are sitting under, you don't see much in the way of trees for lumber. Do you? What do you see?" He gestured with his arms.

"Rocks," said Gilda.

"Right," agreed Mark. "Some believe that Jesus' profession was incorrectly described as a carpenter, the result of a translation error. The original Greek word in the New Testament was translated to Latin as 'carpenter,' but it actually meant a skilled craftsman in metal, stone, or wood. In the time of Jesus, as today, wood was scarce in the Middle East, whereas stone was plentiful. It is likely that Jesus and his father, Joseph, were both stonemasons. As such, Jesus could have found work in the various locations he traveled because stone was the construction material of choice in many places in ancient times. Being a stonemason, I like to think Jesus was an amateur geologist."

Gilda smiled at Mark's reference to Jesus being an amateur geologist. He always managed to find the geology angle.

"Don't forget," she added, "Jesus also was a rabbi, a religious teacher. During his time, there were many religious teachers preaching a variety of beliefs and they were able to support themselves. So perhaps Jesus supported himself by teaching religion."

"Hmm ... good point," agreed Mark.

Gilda thought of another potential obstacle. "Travel in those times was not unusual. We know that Paul went on missions to present-day Syria, Turkey, Cypress, Greece, and even Italy shortly after Jesus' crucifixion. But how would Jesus have traveled those great distances east?"

"The major eastern route in ancient times," replied Mark, "was the Silk Road. The road earned its name from the Chinese silk trade conducted along the route. Of course, silk wasn't the only commodity transported along the Silk Road. Other commodities included satins, musk, spices, and precious gemstones. They were carried by camels and other pack animals in caravans."

Mark added, "In addition to being used by traders and merchants, the Silk Road was used by pilgrims, monks, missionaries, and soldiers. It was a major axis along which religion, especially Buddhism, was spread and religious ideas exchanged. Historically, the Silk Road is primarily known for trade, but we can't underestimate the importance it had in the exchange of cultural and religious ideas."

"I know of the Silk Road. From what I recall, there were actually several east-west passageways in Asia and Europe," Gilda added.

"Yes, the Silk Road was a network of interconnected trade routes stretching from Asia on the east to Europe on the west. Did you know that part of our knowledge about the Silk Road comes from geology?"

Here we go again, she thought, even though she was finding this conversation interesting. "No, what's the geology connection this time?" Gilda asked, poking Mark in the ribs with her finger.

"Hey, I can't help it. It's just my nature."

She responded, "Okay, just don't go pulling my arm."

"What I am about to tell you is the truth, so I won't be pulling your leg. The expression is pulling your leg," Mark said, laughing.

"Whatever," Gilda responded, brushing her hair behind her ears with her hands.

Mark finally answered, "In the ancient world, the only known source of the popular precious blue gemstone lapis lazuli was in present-day northeastern Afghanistan, where it's still mined today. There is evidence that before the birth of Jesus, lapis lazuli was traded as far away as Egypt, present-day Pakistan, and present-day northwestern India. In Egypt, for example, it is common to find a lapis lazuli scarab buried with the dead to protect them in the afterlife. Knowing the ancient source of lapis lazuli and mapping where the gemstone was distributed, we know these trade routes were extensive."

"So how extensive does your geologic evidence tell you it was?" Gilda asked, humoring Mark.

Mark knew she was goading him, but he continued. "It is commonly believed, based on geology and other information, that there was a northern trade route and a southern one. The northern route started in present-day Xi'an, pronounced 'SHE An,' in China, which by the time of Jesus' birth was the capital of the ancient Chinese empire. The route headed west through present-day Iraq and Iran, and joined the eastern boundary of the Roman empire, which included Israel. The southern route included present-day northern India."

Gilda pondered what Mark had said. They knew from the scrolls that Jesus had traveled east, but that far east! She hadn't considered the possibility that Jesus traveled such distances. "So using the Silk Road, do you think Jesus could have traveled as far as India and China?" Gilda asked with incredulity.

"In theory, that's possible," replied Mark, slowly absorbing Gilda's question. He was trying to sort out the possibilities. "Traveling such long distances in those days would have been slow-going and required a tremendous amount of time. Maybe that's why Jesus was away for eighteen years. That length of time is consistent with a long journey in ancient times, especially if Jesus made stops along the way."

"But why do you think Jesus might have traveled to India or China?"

"I don't know that he did, but with the Silk Road, he could have. That's what I hope we find out."

Mark continued, "One thing that's particularly interesting is that the Silk Road incorporated what was called the Persian Royal Road. I've been reading about it in preparation for our trip and learned it extended from the lower Tigris River in Iran to the ancient port of Smyrna on the Aegean Sea. Guess what Smyrna is near?"

After a moment, Gilda replied, "I give up, what?"

"Iznik, Turkey. It's just to the northeast of ancient Smyrna."

"The same place where the Council of Nicaea took place?" Gilda asked, surprised at the connection between Iznik and the Silk Road.

"Yep, correct. Iznik was an important city on the trade route, being just southeast of Constantinople or present-day Istanbul. Nicaea, now Iznik, was selected for the council because of its central location and easy access off the trade routes for the bishops who attended this momentous gathering."

Mark eagerly anticipated the prospect of perhaps traveling on these same trade routes during his upcoming trip to Nicaea. He wondered what else he might discover.

Gilda interrupted Mark's reverie, "Well, Mark, I think we are as prepared as we can be for our trip to Nicaea. We've studied Nicaea's geography and history. We reviewed the history of the Council of Nicaea and we've explored various aspects of Jesus' life."

Gilda added, "Plus, we know that Dr. Meyer selected Iznik based on something in the Mount Sodom Dead Sea Scrolls. I understand he has been focusing on Arius, who was a prominent figure at the Council of Nicaea. I guess we will learn more about the Arius connection when we see Dr. Meyer in Turkey."

Gilda looked around. The park was now practically empty. She asked, "So, are you ready to go?"

"I'm not only ready to leave this park, I'm ready for our adventure in Iznik to begin."

Chapter Eleven

I doubt, therefore, I think; I think, therefore I am.

—Descartes

Winter 2002, Iznik, Turkey

Only two and a half hours from Jerusalem by plane, Istanbul, a thriving metropolis of over twelve million people, is located on the Istanbul Strait or Bosphorus connecting the Black Sea and the Sea of Marmara. Appropriate for a major city, the Ataturk Airport was a bustle of activity with passengers from all over the world.

Their flight had been turbulent. It was late afternoon, and Mark was happy to be on the ground. While Gilda and Dr. Meyer gathered their luggage, Mark, with only backpack in tow, found the rental car center and picked up their car. He was grateful they drove on the same side of the road here as in the United States and Israel.

Dr. Meyer sat in the passenger side while Gilda volunteered for the backseat given the car's limited size. The car's standard transmission did not present a challenge to Mark, who could drive a stick shift. He actually enjoyed it.

As he drove out of the crowded airport exit, he noticed construction projects surrounding them and contributing to the traffic congestion. Waiting in traffic, Mark recalled, "Istanbul is in an earthquake zone, and epicenters of nearby historic and recent earthquakes are inexorably moving closer and closer. In the near future, seismologists predict Istanbul will be at the center of a major earthquake expected to cause considerable damage."

As Mark knew, the earth consisted of a thin layer on the surface called the crust. Below the crust was a thick liquid mantle of hot molten rock material, with a solid core in the center of the earth. The liquid beneath the crust was in constant motion, like convection cells in a pot of heated water, causing the earth's surface to move very slowly. The crust was not continuous but made up of a series of zones or plates that moved independently, a process called plate tectonics.

Where the plates slid into each other, earthquakes occurred. Wave energy generated by the quakes passing over and through the earth allowed seismologists to "see" the earth's layering.

Mark added while shifting gears, "Istanbul is located where several crustal plates bump into each other, and therefore earthquakes have commonly occurred in this region over the last two thousand years."

"Let's hope the big one does not occur while we are here," Dr. Meyer said, looking at a map to help Mark navigate Istanbul's streets.

Gilda leaned up and asked, "Did you know that Istanbul is the only city in the world located on two continents, Europe and Asia?"

"Yes, I did know that," responded Dr. Meyer. "Istanbul has played a long and significant role in both continents throughout its history."

Exiting the airport on the European side, they bypassed crowded Old Istanbul, crossed the Golden Horn waterway, and eventually drove into Asia via the Bosphorus Bridge, a large suspension bridge connecting Asia and Europe. It reminded Mark of San Francisco's Golden Gate Bridge. With the smell of the salt air and the abundance of sea gulls, Mark's thoughts drifted back to his boyhood and time spent on the Gulf of Mexico.

The drive covered 125 miles around the east side of the Sea of Marmara to Iznik, old Nicaea, capital of the former east Roman Empire. The trip took almost three hours. Although traffic was heavy in Istanbul, it thinned a short distance beyond the city. Beautiful panoramic views of the Sea of Marmara, its choppy surface stirred up by the wind, could be seen along the way. Being near such a large body of water, the climate in this part of Asia Minor was moderate, but temperatures were still in the low forties. Iznik received about thirty inches of rain a year, and winter was the rainy season. As if to prove this point, gray clouds hung heavily overhead, the likely cause of their bumpy plane ride.

As they drove, Dr. Meyer told them what he knew about the Council of Nicaea. "The Council was convened by Roman Emperor Constantine I, the first Christian emperor, in the summer of 325 CE. Bishops came to Nicaea from the entire Christian world, including western and eastern Europe, North Africa, and the Middle East. Represented were the Assyrian church of the East, the Oriental Orthodox, the Eastern Orthodox, the Roman Catholics, the Old Catholics, and a number of western Christian groups."

Mark marveled at the political structure of the Christian church and at how many different groups had splintered off from the oral teachings of Jesus Christ in less than three hundred years. "In such a relatively short period of time, how could so many different churches have developed from the words of Jesus?" Mark questioned, checking his rearview mirror as he began to pass a slow truck in front of him.

Gilda answered, "It's probably because of inadvertent changes to stories as they were repeated orally from group to group, resulting in slightly different beliefs developing. In addition, unique interpretations were made by various individuals who put their own spin on Jesus' teachings."

The diversity of Christian beliefs and Gilda's explanation reminded Mark of a childhood game where children stood in a circle and one child started the game by whispering a short story or phrase to the child standing to his or her left. It was whispered from one child to the next until the story reached the child who originated it. The original and final stories were told to the amusement of all the children because the stories were always so very different. Mark wondered if an adult version of this children's game contributed to the large number of Christian groups growing out of the teachings of Jesus, who originated the story.

Mark asked, "If there are multiple stories, how do you determine which one is the correct version when the person who originated the story is no longer around?"

"That was one of the challenges facing the Council of Nicaea, and in particular, one important issue needed resolution." Dr. Meyer explained. "The Council needed to resolve disagreements over the spiritual relationship between Jesus and God. The disagreement was known as the Arian controversy, named after the followers of Arius, a Christian priest from Alexandria, Egypt."

Dr. Meyer adjusted in his seat so Gilda could hear him. "Arianism, the philosophy of Arius, called into question the divinity of Jesus. How would the Council resolve this issue? The attending bishops, under the strong influence of Constantine, settled the matter by voting."

Mark said sarcastically, "What better way to resolve a spiritual issue than by coerced bishops voting?"

He could only imagine the posturing and politics that occurred behind the scenes. "I wonder what Jesus' reaction might have been to such behavior. Jesus would have been more interested in spreading his message than in how man interpreted his relationship to God."

Gilda and Dr. Meyer did not respond.

Instead, Dr. Meyer continued. "Arius taught that Jesus was not the same substance or matter as God and that before Jesus was born, he did not exist. Some in the church believed that Arius's teachings suggested Jesus was human."

Mark interrupted while keeping his eyes on the road, saying, "That's certainly counter to the concept of the Holy Trinity, which promotes the unity of the Father, Son, and Holy Spirit in one God." As he said this, Mark recalled a passage in John where Jesus states that "my Father is greater than I," which was at odds with the Holy Trinity concept.

Dr. Meyer responded. "That is correct. An outcome of the Council was the Nicene Creed that explicitly affirms the divinity of Jesus, setting the stage for the Holy Trinity. Arius's teachings were deemed heretical."

With the mention of this word, Mark became agitated and injected, "The term heretical was unknown to Jesus and has nothing to do with him. Heresy is a term made up by the church to describe those who don't follow their establishment's doctrines."

"I agree," said Dr. Meyer. "Arius was eventually excommunicated from the church."

Mark interrupted again, saying, "Excommunication is another term that has nothing to do with Jesus' teachings. Jesus would never have kicked anyone out of his church. Not even Judas when Jesus knew Judas would betray him!"

Gilda had had enough, and she said, "Mark, drive and stop interrupting Dr. Meyer."

Mark bit his tongue and remained silent. It was anathema to him how the simple teachings of Jesus could be twisted into a complex set of rules by power-hungry people.

Dr. Meyer added, "Some of Arius's teachings also addressed the entirety of Jesus' life, including the eighteen years absent from the New Testament."

Gilda asked, "Is that why we are here?"

Dr. Meyer responded thoughtfully. "That is a major reason. I believe some of Arius's teachings are consistent with what is in the Mount Sodom Dead Sea Scrolls. Because Arius had knowledge of information contained in the scrolls, Iznik seemed to be the logical place for us to begin our investigation."

Mark understood why other bishops disagreed with the implication that Jesus was human, but why would they object to learning about the missing eighteen years of Jesus' life? What could Jesus have done during those years that would be so disagreeable to the bishops, causing them to omit this information from the New Testament?

Mark thought it ironic that the Arian controversy was resolved, concluding that Jesus was the same substance as God, in Turkey of all places, which was now dominated by Muslims who believe that Jesus was only a prophet, not God. The Muslims and Jews had this belief in common, as Jews did not accept Jesus as the messiah or the anointed one. Mark could not help but wonder what Arius and his followers knew about those missing years that led them to question the divinity of Jesus, reaching a similar conclusion to that of Jews and Muslims. He was aware that Buddhist missionaries had proselytized as far west as Alexandria and may have influenced some of the beliefs in the Gnostic gospels found in Egypt. Could the Buddhists missionaries have influenced Arius? These questions might never be resolved, Mark knew, because Arius's writings on these subjects no longer existed.

Dr. Meyer interrupted Mark's thoughts. "Constantine ordered all of Arius's original writings and supporting documents burned. The emperor's orders were carried out for the most part, but some of Arius's letters were saved and still exist today. Three of them are in Alexandria, Egypt, but aren't very helpful to the debate because they are more administrative in nature than representative of Arius's religious teachings."

Gilda asked, "Didn't you go to Alexandria recently?"

"Yes. I visited there within the last month, studied these letters, and obtained a copy of one of Arius's letters in Greek," Dr. Meyer said. "The letter is an apology to Constantine for Arius's role at the Council of Nicaea. My hope is that this letter helps with our investigation in Iznik."

Arriving just outside the city center, the sky, even darker, was filled with rain-laden clouds. With difficulty, they found their hotel's understated entry, its name over the door in small letters. Mark parked the car on a nearby street. Gathering their belongings, they headed for the entrance. Fortunately, the hotel clerk spoke broken English. The small, white stucco hotel was just a short distance to the ruins of the St. Sophia Cathedral, seat of the Council of Nicaea.

"Dr. Meyer, Mark and I plan to take a walk. Care to join us?" Gilda asked after checking in.

"No, thanks," responded Dr. Meyer. "I will be in my room reviewing some documents. When you are ready for dinner, give me a call."

They dropped their backpacks and suitcases in their rooms and headed out. Newly arrived in Iznik, Mark and Gilda walked to the city center, which was encircled by an ancient wall about 2.8 miles long and about thirty-five feet high. They read this on a plaque next to the wall. It was originally constructed by the Greeks and later rebuilt by the Romans. The wall's remains were one of Iznik's top tourist attractions.

That the wall was in such good shape was amazing, thought Mark, because Iznik was located in an earthquake-prone or tectonic valley. Their hotel was next to the north gate, an entrance through the wall known as the Istanbul Gate. Above the gate were triple arches with masks of a man and a woman. When Mark saw the gate with the masks, he thought of Gilda and himself.

He said, "The wall around Iznik reminds me of the Old Testament story about the walls of Jericho."

Jericho was located a few miles northwest of the Dead Sea near a fresh water spring in cavernous limestone associated with a fault zone or break in the earth's surface along which earth movement can occur. The city was located there because of the source of drinking water the spring provided. The location of Jericho was controlled by the spring; its location was controlled by geology, thought Mark.

"Gilda, do you remember the weekend we explored the area around Jericho during my sabbatical?"

"Yes," she said. "I also remember the description of how those walls came down. The Biblical story described a battle between the Israelites led by Joshua and the Canaanites who occupied Jericho. The Canaanites were named for an area called Canaan, the ancient name for modern Israel and the Palestinian territories. According to the Bible, during the battle, Joshua and his men circled the city and once each day blew ram-horn trumpets. On the seventh day, they made a long blast with the horns and Jericho's walls fell down."

"That's right," agreed Mark. "You remember, geologists and archaeologists who studied Jericho concluded that a strong earthquake occurred around the time of Joshua's attack. We observed evidence of earthquake damage during our visit there. The destruction of the walls of Jericho was likely due to a scientifically explainable occurrence—an earthquake."

It would have been an incredible coincidence, thought Mark, if the earthquake occurred at the same time as when the horns were trumpeted. Certainly, blowing horns made a more interesting story, especially at that time when earthquakes were not understood by ancient man. Mark could understand why a storyteller would use a device such as horns as an explanation or embellishment. Horns or no horns, the story of the walls of Jericho tumbling down was yet another example of the intersection of the Bible and geology. Mark wondered how much longer the walls at Iznik would continue to stand.

Gilda interrupted Mark's thoughts, saying, "I think it is ironic that we are in Iznik, formerly occupied by the Greeks and Romans, exploring proceedings of the Christian church concerning the divinity of Jesus, believed by many to be God on earth. The irony is that in Greek and Roman mythologies, many of their gods came to earth in human form. I wonder if these mythologies influenced early Christians and their interpretation of Jesus' presence."

Continuing to walk down random streets, Mark said, "That's possible. Those mythologies and how the gods were portrayed could have influenced Christian perceptions. I recall seeing statues of the Greek god of lust, beauty, love, and intercourse, Eros, one of my favorite Greek gods by the way. Having wings, Eros statues could have been the model for angels depicted in Christian art."

Eros must have worked his charm because Mark suddenly had a strong desire to return with Gilda to the hotel.

That evening, Mark, Gilda, and Dr. Meyer settled into their small, charming Turkish hotel. It had a local, quaint flavor. The building was only three stories tall, and their rooms were on the top floor. There were no elevators. At the front desk, they asked for dinner recommendations and were directed to a nearby Turkish restaurant.

Outside, a fine mist began to fall. Reaching the restaurant, they had lamb kabobs and couscous with mixed steamed vegetables, along with local wine. Mark was somewhat knowledgeable about European and American wines, but this was his first time drinking Turkish wine. The waiter recommended Yakut, which means ruby, the gemstone. It was a dry and fruity red, and its name had a geology connection.

Mark commented, "Hmm, this wine is surprisingly good."

Dr. Meyer informed Mark lightheartedly, "Wine has been produced in the Anatolia Region of eastern Turkey since 4000 BCE. They probably figured wine making out by now."

Mark smiled ruefully, remaining silent. He was definitely in unknown wine territory.

As they finished their dinner, Dr. Meyer continued discussing the Arius letter, which he copied and brought from Alexandria, Egypt. He pulled it out of his inside jacket pocket. "This letter is Arius's required confession to Constantine following the Council of Nicaea, which Arius attended and argued his position. He lost by an overwhelming majority of votes by the bishops. The confession was required following the Council if he wanted to remain in the church."

Dr. Meyer paused to take a sip of wine, acknowledged its pleasant taste, and continued, "In effect, Constantine forced Arius to give up his beliefs, to admit he was wrong in teaching them and to beg for forgiveness, not from God but from Constantine so he could remain in the church. The tone of his confession letter, however, is not one of contrition, but more a statement of defiance in the guise of a confession."

"What do you mean?" Gilda asked.

"Some passages seem totally out of place. Arius refers to his speech in the St. Sophia Cathedral and compares his eloquent arguments to the beautiful tiles inside the cathedral. As I was reading the letter, I could not help but wonder if these passages were an attempt by Arius to somehow tie his arguments to the cathedral tiles."

"How so? I'm not sure I understand." Mark moved forward in his seat, increasingly gripped by Dr. Meyer's revelations.

Dr. Meyer explained. "I'm just speculating, but from pictures I have seen, some of the tiles in the cathedral contain patterns, but some of the tiles also contain writings. I have a strong suspicion that Arius left behind a message in those tiles. Tomorrow, our search of the ruins at the cathedral should focus on the tiles."

Excited, Gilda said, "You really think the tiles could reveal aspects of Arius's teachings that would be consistent with the scrolls?"

"Based on everything I have read by Arius and what is in the scrolls, I believe it is possible."

"You know," said Gilda, "I actually have a piece of pottery from here. Iznik is famous for its centuries-old pottery and tiles. Iznik pottery has been described by some as the most technologically refined in the long history of Islamic ceramics."

Suspecting the source of the clay used for the pottery, Mark said, "Iznik lies on the eastern tip of a large lake. I'll bet the lake deposits provide a source of good clay for making pottery and tiles."

Smiling, Dr. Meyer was amused at Mark's geology comment. He said, "Arius spoke to the gathering of bishops in the Imperial Room of the cathedral. I suggest we attempt to locate that room tomorrow and focus our examination there."

They ordered coffee and continued their discussions, turning to other locations in Turkey. Gilda pointed out, "Ephesus is a little south of here. Legend has it that St. John brought Virgin Mary to Ephesus after the crucifixion, where she spent her final days. So Jesus' mother may have lived and died near here."

Dr. Meyer added, "Mary was proclaimed the official Mother of God in Ephesus by the Third Ecumenical Council in 431 CE."

"I didn't know that," responded Mark. "There's more Christian history in Turkey than I realized." After taking a sip of his coffee, he added with mile surprise, "Wow, this is great coffee!"

"It should be," said Dr. Meyer. "After all, Turkey introduced coffee to Europe. Just be sure not to drink the muddy grinds at the bottom of the cup."

"Speaking of Christian history," Dr. Meyer added, "this area was once part of the Byzantine or Christian Empire, ruled from Constantinople and reaching its zenith around the ninth century CE. A schism occurred between the eastern or Orthodox and the western or Roman churches in about 1054 when leaders of both churches excommunicated each other."

"This sounds like another example where Jesus' message was corrupted," Mark chimed in.

"Wait," said Dr. Meyer, "it gets better. The gradual alienation of Byzantium from the west led to open conflict, reaching a low point in 1204 with the sacking of Constantinople during the Fourth Crusade."

"You mean some of the Crusades involved one Christian church fighting another Christian church?" Mark asked incredulously.

"Yes," said Dr. Meyer.

Mark shook his head. He was dismayed at how little he knew about Turkey.

Finally, they finished their after-dinner Turkish coffee and walked back to the hotel. It was a cloudy night with no stars visible, leaving the narrow cobbled street dark except for the occasional spill of light pouring out from a shop window onto the wet surface. Perhaps it was because it was so dark or maybe it was because the three were lost in conversation about tomorrow's prospects that they failed to notice the darkly clad figure lurking nearby, intently watching them. The figure was a tall, heavyset man with a scar over his right eye. He was visible at night only because of the smoldering glow at the end of his cigarette.

For appearance's sake, Mark and Gilda requested separate rooms. Dr. Meyer likely knew they were dating, but he was probably not aware how serious their relationship was. After Dr. Meyer bade them good night and retired, Mark made his way to Gilda's room. The two embraced passionately.

Mark looked into her eyes longingly and then said, "I'm excited about tomorrow, but more excited about tonight." Then, holding each other tightly, they fell into Gilda's bed. Unfortunately, it was a single bed. Mark hated single beds.

Outside, the dark figure looked up at Gilda's third-floor hotel room window. It began to rain lightly and the tip of his cigarette hissed as he stared upward.

Chapter Twelve

To know what people really think, pay regard to what they do, rather than what they say.

—Descartes

Winter 2002, Iznik, Turkey

Mark and Gilda awoke early, kissed good-bye, and prepared for the day separately in their respective rooms. They met Dr. Meyer for breakfast in the small hotel restaurant.

During breakfast, which consisted of strong Turkish coffee, delicious Turkish yogurt, fresh fruit, and baked goods, Dr. Meyer explained, "Iznik was first established in 310 BCE. As you've likely seen, it is a city with many well-preserved ancient structures."

"I noticed several mosques during our walk yesterday," recalled Gilda.

"That's correct." Dr. Meyer said. "Mostly Muslim now, the focus of tourism is largely on the city's beautiful mosques. Attention on the mosques is to our benefit because the ruins of St. Sophia Cathedral are largely ignored. Plus, the ruins are in a less popular, somewhat isolated part of the city. This time of year, tourism is very low; it's the off-season, and it is likely that we will be the only ones exploring the cathedral ruins."

He paused, taking a sip of coffee. "Still, we must respect the ruins and any artifacts they may contain. Is that clear?"

Mark and Gilda nodded in agreement.

Shortly after finishing their breakfast, they began walking with their backpacks the short distance to the ruins of St. Sophia Cathedral. Bundled in their winter coats, they carried rain gear as a precaution against the troubled gray sky. Entering the central part of the city through the Istanbul Gate where Mark and Gilda explored the day before, they turned right. Heading west toward the lake, they approached the cathedral ruins near the water. Walking briskly without speaking, Dr. Meyer led the way.

Mark was surprised when they arrived. "Wow. The ruins are much larger than I expected."

"They cover several acres," Dr. Meyer pointed out.

Some walls were still standing and some floors were still intact, but the ceiling and many walls had collapsed, and rock and rubble lay everywhere, with vegetation growing in many locations. Even through the mess, Mark could see some of the colorful tiles that had once adorned the inside of the cathedral. Intricate patterns of blue, purple, and green lay against a whitish background.

Looking at them, Gilda commented, "I can't believe how many tiles still remain after all these years. And the colors are amazing."

Mark said, "The blue comes from cobalt oxide, the purple from manganese, and the green from copper oxide." As he said this, he pointed to the colors on a nearby tile.

"And what about the white background?" Gilda asked.

"The white color is a natural color in the kaolinite clay and sand or silica, brought out by the glazing process. The tiles made in Iznik are composed of about 85 percent quartz, leading to their long-term resilience. Exactly how the tiles are created is a closely held secret of the artisan making the tile."

"How do you know so much about tile making?" she said.

"Just part of my background reading. I was interested in anything related to geology." Mark grinned.

Despite a roped-off path snaking through various parts of the ruins on which tourists were required to stay, the three veered off to more fully explore their surroundings. "We need to begin by mapping the floor of the cathedral beyond the roped path to determine where the Imperial Room was located. The cathedral was destroyed by an earthquake in the sixteenth century, so keep in mind that some of these standing walls may not be too stable. Keep your eyes open and take care as you move about. We don't want any accidents. That's my health-and-safety message for the day," said Dr. Meyer.

Mark thought the earthquake that destroyed the cathedral was another example of the confluence of geology, archeology, and religion. He started to speak, thought better of it and kept that observation to himself.

Starting at the front entrance of the cathedral, they began working, taking care not to disturb any of the ruins. Mark and Gilda retrieved their field books to log information, and Mark slung his small state-of-the-art digital camera around his neck. He examined and photographed each and every tile or group of tiles they saw. As tiles were discovered with writing, Dr. Meyer would interrupt his work and interpret the newly found lettering. This tedious process slowed progress, yielding translations of only fairly standard biblical passages. Like continents drifting on the earth's surface, their investigation, although slow, nonetheless moved forward.

Some of the tiles formed mosaics, many of the Virgin Mother and some of Christ as a baby and adult. In all cases, there were halos circling their heads and Jesus' eyes were dark and penetrating. Mark recalled that halos had been used previously in Greek, Hindu, and Buddhist art to represent religious figures. He couldn't help but wonder if early Christians borrowed the halo from other religions.

All three took turns making measurements with a cloth tape, and Gilda painstakingly prepared a detailed sketch of the cathedral floor. Taking care to avoid piles of rubble and making sure their footing was secure as they cautiously moved around the ruins made the mapping process proceed slowly. Puddles of standing water stood in many locations from the previous night's rain, causing the floor to be slick. The wet floor created further challenges, restricting their movements. At times, Mark thought their careful motions and slow progress were sloth-like. By noon, after several hours work, they had completed mapping only a portion of the ruins.

Breaking to eat, they walked about four blocks to a cafe they passed on their morning trek to the cathedral. Chilly from the morning's undertaking, they ordered soup and hot coffee to warm up. While eating, the partial map of the cathedral floor Gilda had reconstructed was the focus of their attention.

Mark pointed to the map and said, "Here is the main entrance leading to the central body of the cathedral where services would have been held—what I think my old art history professor called the nave. Surrounding the nave are smaller chambers used for crypts or smaller prayer group services. Toward the middle of the nave is the altar that would have faced the cathedral entrance. Behind that altar, there appears to be a large area or room, which we haven't examined yet."

"That large room could be the Imperial Room," said Dr. Meyer, pointing to the large area on the map. "We know it had to be big enough to accommodate close to three hundred bishops and the assisting clergy who attended the council. After lunch, why don't we focus our attention on the area behind the altar? Remember, we are looking for a message Arius may have left, probably in the tiles."

Gilda and Mark agreed. After warming themselves at lunch, they returned to the ruins and began working in what they thought might be the Imperial Room. Starting at the back of the altar, they worked their way outward. Again, the mapping process was slowed by the rubble and wet floor. In some instances, the rubble prevented them from entering certain areas. At other locations, there were standing walls that did not look stable, and for safety concerns, they avoided them. For these areas, Gilda's map had to be estimated.

As the day wore on, the sun began to set, and darkness, enhanced by gathering dark clouds, fell over the ruins. Frustrated that the day was almost over, Mark thought how much he disliked the shorter daylight of winter. A cold wind picked up, signaling an approaching storm. It became gloomier by the minute, and a chill settled in as they approached the northwest corner of the large room.

Gilda reached the corner first. Looking around, she observed, "The area here could have been the location of another altar." She pointed excitedly and said, "The rock structure there is consistent with an altar, likely made of wood, rotted away long ago." She thought she felt a drop of rain and glanced upward. The sky, with dark and billowing clouds, looked eerie. At that moment, a gust of cold wind hit her face, causing a shiver to move up her spine.

Two partial walls forming the corner behind the possible altar still stood, barely. They held firmly against the wind, which increased in intensity.

"Be careful. Those walls could fall over at any moment," Mark shouted, making himself heard above the wind.

Examining the walls more carefully, Gilda yelled, "They're more stable than they look. It should be okay to examine this area."

Cautiously, Mark and Dr. Meyer approached and began observing the floor just as more raindrops fell. Having the walls nearby offered some protection from the wind.

The floor beneath the possible altar location was made of tile. Much of it was broken or missing. But some ceramic squares were still connected. Mark pulled out his flashlight.

"Look here," said Gilda, also now using her flashlight, "there are two different groupings of tiles."

Looking more closely, she continued, "There's a block of them that appears to be slightly different in color and texture from the surrounding ones. Perhaps they were made by a different artisan. Is it possible that the tiles in the middle of the pattern were replaced and are newer than the surrounding ones?"

Studying the tiles more carefully, she added, "Look, there are words written on the middle group and only decorations on the surrounding tiles."

As they gazed at the middle group of tiles, Mark asked his two colleagues, "Do you suppose that after the Council met, Arius and his followers replaced some of the tiles under the very place where he stood at this altar and defended his teachings?"

"That is possible," responded Dr. Meyer excitedly.

Mark understood this would have been Arius's way of saying "screw you" to Constantine. He pondered for a brief moment and then smiled, remembering his readings at the library in Jerusalem and what Dr. Meyer had told them. "I read something to the effect that several of the bishops who followed Arius's teachings worked at St. Sophia Cathedral. They had access and motive to preserve Arius' teachings in this way. Covertly, they could have replaced the tiles and protected them from being discovered and removed."

"I read that as well," responded Gilda. "It makes sense and would explain why the tiles were never discovered by Constantine."

Dr. Meyer said, "Yes. Placing the newer tiles here would have been an obvious act of defiance against Constantine's decision and the bishops who discredited Arius's teachings. It is known that Arianism continued to spread and cause division in the church during the remainder of the fourth century CE. Several of the strongest proponents of Arianism were located here in Nicaea."

Dr. Meyer continued. "Leaders of the church opposed to Arianism might have been able to burn Arius's writings, but it would have been more difficult for them to destroy a message in tiles that they were unaware of and protected by Arius's followers. What irony that the message would be placed on the very spot where Arius stood and defended himself? The tiles would have been preserved, keeping Arius's teachings available for future believers."

As Gilda had noticed, many of the tiles under the altar were missing and others were broken and not very legible. The newer block of tiles was similarly fragmented but clearly had lettering scattered on its surface. "Look, isn't that Greek writing on the middle tiles?" Gilda was so captivated she didn't notice that raindrops were starting to fall more heavily.

"Yes, it is." Dr. Meyer fell to his knees and attempted to translate the fragmented Greek words on the newer tiles still in place. Starting at the top of the block of tiles, he was only able to make out a few disconnected words. His finger tracing the writings, the first word he recognized was "Jesus," which he pointed to and called out. Gilda wrote this down in her field notebook.

Overhead, the black clouds boiled and the wind intensified, almost blowing Gilda's field book from her hands.

Dr. Meyer had difficulty translating some portion of the tiles; it said something like "eastern spirit." Further down, he made out the word "traveled" and finally further down, he read "Babel Tower." There were the words "human substance." At the bottom of the block, he recognized the name "Arius." As Dr. Meyer yelled these words to be heard over the wind, Gilda continued to write them down.

Dr. Meyer continued to yell, "That's all I can make out for now until we reconstruct the dislocated tiles. Unfortunately, it is insufficient to reveal the essence of Arius's message."

While Dr. Meyer translated, Mark tried to take photographs, but found it difficult given Dr. Meyer's position over the tiles and with the interference of the walls and rubble. He did not want to disturb Dr. Meyer while he translated and would have to wait until later, once Dr. Meyer was out of the way, to take more complete photographs.

Although he could not read the Greek words, he noticed a roman numeral on one of the newer tiles. It was the number eighteen. Mark had no idea of its significance, but he pointed it out to his colleagues. Gilda wrote it down.

Looking up from her field book, Gilda pointed out, "There are loose and broken tiles all around. Hopefully we can put them back together like a jigsaw puzzle and develop a more complete picture of what the tiles say."

"Yes, I agree," Dr. Meyer said, rising to his feet, "but I think it's getting too late to do that now—it would be best if we return tomorrow when we have better light and it is warmer."

At that moment, a bolt of lightning rocketed across the sky, lighting up the ruins of St. Sophia Cathedral in a surreal pale black and white. Mark and the others flinched in response to the loud and instant clap of thunder. The wind blew harder, and a heavy rain began to pour down.

"We need to leave," yelled Dr. Meyer. "We do not want to be out here in lightning."

Mark and the others pulled rain gear out of their backpacks and hurriedly put it on. They packed up the rest of their gear and left the cathedral site as the rain fell in torrents.

Exhilarated over their find but disappointed about the delay in studying it, the three scientists walked purposefully through the downpour, leaning forward into the wind and making their way back to the hotel. Large raindrops stung their faces. As they walked, Gilda commented, "I can't believe our good fortune to have discovered the tiles so soon."

Leading the way, Mark turned and teased her, "Oh ye of little faith." Even though he, too, was amazed at the speed of their breakthrough.

It was just after sunset, and in the distance, the Muslim call to prayer began. It was the fourth of five calls for prayer that day and came from the minaret high above a mosque a few blocks away. The musical call of a single male voice echoed in Mark's mind as he trudged through the downpour.

They arrived at the hotel and agreed to meet back in the lobby in fifteen minutes. They went to their rooms to dry off. For the sake of convenience, they returned to the same restaurant where they had eaten the night before. It only required a short walk through the wind and rain, which continued at a steady pace.

Dr. Meyer selected a white wine. Once poured, he offered a toast in celebration. "To our success. May the Mount Sodom Dead Sea Scrolls soon be released." His festive mood was infectious with Mark and Gilda clinking wine glasses and drinking with delight.

After ordering food, Dr. Meyer began discussing the day's discoveries. "Even though the tiles are in bad shape and my limited translation makes it difficult to decipher, combined with the Mount Sodom Dead Sea Scrolls, I believe they make sense. As we discussed in the conference room in Jerusalem, the scrolls indicate Jesus traveled to the east of Israel between the ages of twelve and thirty. The information in these scrolls, the details of which will have to remain confidential along with the cathedral tiles we have just found, supports the premise that the former Tower of Babel was one of Jesus' first stops."

"Are you saying the scrolls we found indicated Jesus traveled to Babel?" Gilda asked.

"Yes," Dr. Meyer responded, carefully watching her reaction.

Gilda slowly leaned back in her seat, lost in thought.

"It makes sense," said Mark. "Given his intellect, Jesus must have been inquisitive. At age twelve, the Bible describes him as having a level of knowledge and wisdom that far exceeded that of others in his age group. With that sort of intellect, why wouldn't he want to explore his world, including outside his home in Judea?"

Gilda eagerly jumped into the conversation. "Certainly the Tower of Babel story, told in Genesis, would have been known to him from the oral teaching of the Old Testament and would have been part of his world. Traveling to Babel, an area where his forefathers once lived, would likely have been a location of interest."

Recalling the Silk Road, Mark added, "Jesus could have traveled the Silk Road, perhaps working on a caravan heading east. He would have likely left Nazareth, traveled through present-day Syria into present-day Iraq and on to Babel. A relatively short trip, it would have been manageable for a bright young man."

"The story of the Tower of Babel is in the book of Genesis," recounted Gilda. "My recollection is that this story occurred in the city of Babylon. The people there spoke a single language and were united in an effort to build a tower that reached the heavens. Unfortunately, their purpose in building the tower was not to honor the magnificence of God but to honor themselves. This displeased God, who did not like being second best. So he made each person speak a different language, which confused them. Giving up the construction project, they ended up scattering all over the earth. That is what Christians who take the Bible literally believe to be the explanation for the world's diverse languages."

Mark shook his head, saying, "To me, this story illustrated the pettiness of man's perception of God, assigning the emotion of jealousy to him." Then he added sarcastically, "I wonder if there were Chinese, Indians, Native Americans, and other such peoples who helped build the Tower of Babel—or did their languages develop in a different way?"

Dr. Meyer gave him a quizzical look. Mark realized that his sarcasm was getting the better of him and quickly bit his tongue. Dr. Meyer's admonitions made him realize that above and beyond being a language-creation myth of questionable authority, the story of Babel did illustrate the importance of communication.

Dr. Meyer broke the awkward silence and said, "So the Mount Sodom Dead Sea Scrolls, along with the broken and incomplete St.

Sophia Cathedral tiles, suggest that Jesus traveled to Babylon in present-day Iraq." Then he added, "I'll be more comfortable with this interpretation once we have the opportunity to study the tiles in more detail tomorrow. Putting more tiles together, we should have a better understanding of what Arius said. There appears to be much more to the message than Jesus' travels. His followers felt this message was important enough to risk excommunication from their church to see that the message survived."

Mark agreed. "Because the risk was so great to Arius's followers, there must be more in the message than a simple trip itinerary. Arius's big difference with the rest of the church concerned the very substance of Jesus—whether he was the same substance as God or a lesser substance. In the extreme, was Jesus spirit or human? It seems logical that any message Arius left would have addressed this issue as well, as it was the primary controversy addressed at the Council of Nicaea."

Looking at Dr. Meyer, Mark added, "You did translate the words 'human substance.' Correct?"

Before Dr. Meyer could respond, Gilda said, "Dr. Meyer, do the Mount Sodom Dead Sea Scrolls contain information on the Arian controversy?"

"The scrolls obviously were written before the time of Arius. But I do not recall any discussion concerning the substance of Jesus, Gilda, but it is an interesting question. I'm not sure why Arius questioned the divinity or spirituality of Jesus."

Mark hoped that Dr. Meyer was being forthright and not holding back because of his agreement with Jacob Cohen. Then he asked, "What about the number eighteen? What's the significance of that number? And what does 'eastern spirit' mean?"

"I do not know the meaning of 'eastern spirit' and I'm not even sure I translated that correctly. Other than the eighteen years of Jesus' life missing from the Bible, I do not know the significance of the number eighteen. Sorry," Dr. Meyer said.

Gilda said, "This is likely unrelated, but many Jews give money in multiples of eighteen as presents to someone celebrating a special event, like a wedding. This is because the number eighteen has a special meaning in the rabbinic system of numerical symbolism. In this system, each letter of the Hebrew alphabet represents a number. The word *chai*, meaning *life*, consists of two Hebrew letters: *het*, equivalent to the number eight, and *yud*, equivalent to the number ten.

Thus, the letters in chai sum to eighteen. Using this system, many believe that the number eighteen means life."

"The word life can be linked to Jesus in many different ways," commented Mark. "I just don't see the connection."

The three sat quietly for a while, lost in thought.

Mark considered the tiles and the possible message from Arius. "We know from the Mount Sodom Dead Sea Scrolls that Jesus traveled to the east and the message on the tiles seems to confirm this. If Jesus did indeed travel east, why did the Bishops at the Council of Nicaea destroy Arius's writings about Jesus' travels during those eighteen years? What did Jesus do during that time, compelling the bishops to destroy the evidence?"

Gilda responded, "We know based on the scrolls and perhaps the tiles that there was information available on Jesus' life during those eighteen years. Roman Emperor Constantine I destroyed this information so it could not be included in the Bible."

Mark spoke softly as if talking to himself, "It wasn't an accident. Those eighteen years of Jesus life were intentionally left out of the Bible. But why?"

Mark and Gilda looked at Dr. Meyer expectantly.

Dr. Meyer looked at Gilda and then at Mark. He was stalling for time, trying to organize his thoughts. "All I know is Arius's teachings were deemed heretical and his writings destroyed. I am not sure what motivated Constantine and the bishops to do this. The Mount Sodom Dead Sea Scrolls contain discussions that may shed light on this matter, but I cannot yet share that information with you."

Having finished their meals and their conversation, all sat deep in thought.

Eventually their silence was disturbed by the waiter. They ordered coffee, and Mark, feeling indulgent, asked the waiter to recommend a dessert.

He recommended "asure," explaining that it was a pudding of cereal grains, sugar, and raisins. Mark was sold on asure when the waiter told them, "According to a legend, asure was originally concocted in the galley of Noah's ark from whatever was left in the pantry toward the end of their voyage when supplies were low." If Noah allegedly ate it, Mark wanted to try it.

After the waiter left, Gilda pointed out, "Some believe that Noah's Ark ended up in Eastern Turkey, which was part of Armenia, on Mount Ararat near the border with Iran. But this has never been proven. As I'm sure you know, Mark, Mount Ararat is a volcanic mountain almost seventeen thousand feet tall and void of sediments that would have been laid down by a major flood in Biblical times."

Before Mark could respond, the waiter returned with the asure and three spoons, saying, "Eat sweetly and speak sweetly," which he explained was an old Turkish saying.

After tasting it, Gilda said, "This is very good."

Dr. Meyer agreed.

The asure tasted better than Mark anticipated it would. "Noah and crew must have eaten well," Mark observed. Then he wondered if Noah was ever tempted to slaughter his cargo for food. Maybe that's why there are no more unicorns around. He imagined one of Noah's relatives saying, "We're out of meat and the children are hungry. We already have regular horses, Noah; no one will miss the ones with the horn in the middle of their heads." Then he shook his head at his terrible sarcasm.

Observing him, Gilda asked, "What are you doing?"

"Nothing," responded Mark, too embarrassed to share his thoughts.

Eventually, they left the restaurant, walked back to the hotel, and retired for the evening. Mark and Gilda followed the same routine as the previous evening, with Mark slipping into Gilda's room.

When Dr. Meyer reached his room, he picked up the phone and made a call.

Chapter Thirteen

No problem can withstand the assault of sustained thinking.

—Voltaire

Winter 2002, Iznik, Turkey

In the morning, the three met for breakfast. By his third cup of coffee, Mark realized how much he enjoyed the strong Turkish drink. He didn't usually add milk, but here, the whole milk, not his usual 2 percent, added flavor. The freshly baked breads and the creamy unsalted butter had more flavor than back home. Judging by the lack of conversation, the others were enjoying breakfast as much as he.

It was hard for Mark to contain his excitement. Sleep had not come easily. His mind raced thinking about what more the tiles might contain. Tossing and turning during the night, at one point Gilda told him to leave so she could sleep. "I can't help it," he had said. "I want to get back to the tiles. I keep waking up thinking about what we might learn."

"I understand," Gilda had responded sleepily as he was heading out the door, clad only in boxers, pajamas in hand. "I'm anxious, too, but the two of us sleeping in this narrow single bed only works if you stay still." He had reluctantly returned to his bedroom; however, sleep there was no easier. To Mark, along with the Mount Sodom Dead Sea Scrolls, the evidence supported Jesus' travels to the east, at least as far as Babylon to visit the site of the Tower of Babel.

The sky was partly cloudy and the cold persisted, but luckily the wind had subsided somewhat. Sunshine peeked through the clouds, warming the streets, which were still damp in some locations. Walking briskly back to the ruins, unlike the previous morning when Mark was so focused, this morning he cheerfully took in his surroundings. All around the city were rolling hills punctuated by tall, spiky cypress trees. Fruit orchards and vineyards were plentiful.

Pointing to the vineyards, Mark said, "Maybe the local wine we drank came from one of these vineyards." What a beautiful countryside, thought Mark.

Dr. Meyer looked up at the vineyard, a topic he knew something about. "Turkey, including Iznik, was one of the earliest wine-producing regions in the world. Turkey is the world's fourth-leading producer of grapes, most of which are used for table grapes and raisin production, given Islamic dietary laws."

"What laws are those?" Mark inquired.

"The one forbidding the consumption of alcohol."

"That's right. But the Muslims consider Jesus a prophet, and Jesus drank wine. In fact, his first miracle was turning water into wine." He paused. "I would have a hard time being a good Muslim," mused Mark.

Walking down the cobblestone street, Mark noticed that stone was the common road-building material. The city center housed numerous ancient well-preserved buildings. The architecture was varied and different from what Mark was used to. Some buildings were made of pale white stone, others of dark, rich-colored red brick. Most buildings were low, only one to two stories high, but there was a sprinkling of taller buildings, six to eight stories tall, including mosques, mixed in with the lower lying ones. The passages between the buildings were extremely narrow and not conducive to automobile traffic, with the tall buildings casting shadows on the walkways. He noticed that all buildings were adorned with beautifully colored ceramic tiles, similar to the ones they had observed at St. Sophia Cathedral.

As Mark's mind returned from sightseeing back to their task, he realized they had arrived at the cathedral entrance. Walking into the ruins, their pace quickened as they followed the trail past the middle altar and back to the site where they worked the previous evening. The cathedral floor was sopping wet, with standing water in many places. Picking their way through the area assumed to be the Imperial Room, they approached the northwest corner.

"What the hell? What's happened?" exclaimed Mark loudly, shocked as he saw the spot where the altar had been. The two walls defining the corner no longer stood. They had collapsed inward, covering the altar. He ran the last few steps to where the tiles had been.

Gilda ran after Mark, stopping next to him, looking wildly about. Stunned by the sight, Gilda exclaimed, "How can this be? I was just near these walls yesterday and carefully examined them. They were unstable, yes, but not unstable enough to fall over last night, even accounting for the high winds."

This was too coincidental, thought Mark, having the walls collapse the evening after the tiles were discovered. Grimly, he said, "Help me remove some of this rubble. We should still be able to retrieve the tiles."

Arduously digging into the rubble, Mark and Dr. Meyer carried away large pieces of stone together while Gilda tossed aside smaller pieces. It took about thirty minutes to remove enough of the heavy, broken wall material to see the floor underneath.

It hit him like a punch in the stomach. "The tiles are gone!" cried Mark, breathing heavily from the physical labor. In their place, he noticed several cigarette butts, flattened by the weight of the rocks.

Dr. Meyer pointed, "Those cigarette butts were not there yesterday when I translated writings on the tile."

Mark glanced quickly at Gilda, then at Dr. Meyer. His mind a complete jumble, he tried to calm himself, to think rationally. Only the three of them knew about the tiles. One of them must be involved in the theft. By the process of elimination, he concluded that Dr. Meyer must share some of the blame.

"This is no accident," he proclaimed, acute frustration driving his words. "The tiles were removed and those walls were pushed over by someone to cover up the theft. The person who did this had to know about our find last evening. Dr. Meyer, who did you tell about our discovery?" he asked accusingly.

"I don't think I like your tone, Mark," responded Dr. Meyer. "If it's any of your business, I reported our progress to Jacob Cohen, as I was instructed to do. You may not believe this, but I'm on your side. I, too, want the Mount Sodom Dead Sea Scrolls released. I, like you, am a scientist and would never do anything that would cause these ancient ruins to be destroyed. I would protect them!"

Mark thought about what Dr. Meyer said. He believed Dr. Meyer would not destroy antiquities. It just didn't make sense. He said, "I'm sorry, Dr. Meyer. I'm just angry and disappointed. We were so close."

"I understand, Mark. This is very upsetting to me, as well."

All remained silent for a few moments, staring down at where the tiles had been each in their own thoughts. Finally, Mark asked, "Do you know if Jacob Cohen told anyone else about our discovery, like Chester Weeks?"

"It is possible. Jacob and Chester seem very close. I must admit I do not understand their relationship," Dr. Meyer answered, wondering if his discussion with Jacob might be connected with the theft of the tiles.

Someone had taken the tiles. As Mark saw it, there were only two possible suspects, given his confidence in Gilda and Dr. Meyer. One was Jacob Cohen. Mark found it hard to believe the Israeli government would be involved in the theft. The risk was too high and the reward was…. He couldn't even think what the reward or motive would be for the Israeli government to be involved.

That left one other person who knew about their quest: Chester Weeks. It was clear to Mark from their earlier conversations that Chester did not want the Mount Sodom Dead Sea Scrolls released. By stealing or destroying supporting evidence, Chester could keep them under wraps indefinitely. Destroying antiquities was not beyond Chester, thought Mark.

For Chester to have been involved, he would need someone here in Iznik. Suddenly, Mark felt uneasy, like someone was watching them. He looked around the ruins and beyond. He saw no one.

They stood quietly for a long time, looking at the rubble where the altar had been. The wind picked up and blew cold in their faces.

Finally, Dr. Meyer said, "I believe our options at this point are limited. We can stay and report the theft and destruction of antiquities to the authorities. In which case, they will likely hold us for questioning. I don't see a positive outcome from this option."

Mark and Gilda nodded in agreement. Gilda said, "If we tell the authorities, we may have to explain why we are here, which would be difficult without mentioning the Mount Sodom Dead Sea Scrolls. Plus, the chances of solving this crime are probably pretty remote."

Looking around the cathedral, Mark shook his head and added, "We don't know who did this and have no evidence other than the missing tiles and destruction of the walls, which now look like many of the other nearby ruins."

Mark felt utterly depressed. Shaking his head, he said, "I can't believe it. These tiles were protected by Arius's followers, they survived earthquakes, lasting hundreds of years, only to be lost or destroyed right after we find them. Our discovery contributed to their demise. We were unknowing accomplices."

The three continued to stand silently, looking down and overwhelmed with disappointment.

The wind picked up, causing the air to swirl in the small excavation they had just created. The flattened cigarette butts began to move slightly, a fluttering motion, in response to the swirling air, as if mockingly waving good-bye.

"If we are in agreement that there is nothing more we can do here," a frustrated Dr. Meyer said, "then I think it is time to return to Israel."

Chapter Fourteen

A witty saying proves nothing.

—Voltaire

Winter 2002, Jerusalem, Israel

The next morning in Jerusalem, the three met with Jacob Cohen and Chester Weeks. Chester had delayed his return trip to the United States for a few days, remaining in Israel to see if anything developed as a result of the team's trip to Turkey. He had told Jacob, "I don't mind staying; the hotel I'm in is very accommodating."

Chester was surprised how quickly the trio had located something of importance. Jacob's reference to their trip as a fool's errand had proven to be wishful thinking. The group met in the same conference room as before.

"Well, what did you find in Turkey?" chortled Chester, a slight hint of a sarcastic smile playing at the corners of his mouth.

Not liking Chester's attitude, Dr. Meyer responded forcefully, "We found twelve floor tiles in the cathedral still in place containing Greek writing. Many other tiles were scattered around, some broken, but we did not have time to examine them or put them back together for a more complete picture. We suspect the tiles were positioned in the St. Sophia Cathedral by Arius or his followers. The text on the tiles suggests that Jesus traveled to Babylon to visit the site of the Tower of Babel. My interpretation of the tiles is consistent with the Mount Sodom Dead Sea Scrolls."

"What physical evidence do you have to support this claim?" asked Chester with a smirk on his face.

Mark had examined the photographs he took while at the cathedral ruins the evening of their discovery, but none showed the tiles clearly. The photos mainly showed Dr. Meyer's backside as he was translating the Greek script. Not his better photography, Mark thought.

"We have no physical evidence," Mark responded dejectedly. "The site was destroyed and the tiles taken before we could examine them further and take pictures."

Surprised, Jacob asked, "What do you mean 'the site was destroyed'?"

Dr. Meyer responded, carefully selecting his words, "The night I called to inform you of the tiles, someone removed them and pushed over nearby walls, which collapsed onto the location where the tiles had been." He paused for a few seconds, and then added, "The two events are strangely coincidental."

Dr. Meyer wanted to make his point but not actually accuse anyone without evidence. The reaction to his statement was immediate.

"Do you think your call to me had something to do with this theft? I can assure you that I had nothing to do with these tiles disappearing," Jacob shot back. He could not help but wonder if his communication of this information to Chester triggered the tiles' demise.

"Now who in the world would have taken the tiles?" queried Chester, smiling like the Cheshire cat from *Alice in Wonderland*.

"That's the exact question I have for you," responded Mark, looking sharply at Chester and feeling repulsed.

"Why Dr. Malloy, whatever do you mean?" Chester asked in a saccharin-drenched voice.

"Someone knew what we discovered and stole or destroyed the tiles before we could complete our study," responded Mark, trying to remain calm but failing. Chester infuriated him.

"Do you think I had something to do with that? Why would I do that? After all, I'm the one funding your study, remember?" Chester's voice was draped in feigned indignation.

Mark's face reddened as he leaned aggressively toward Chester. "You're the one who won't let the Mount Sodom Dead Sea Scrolls be released until we find corroborating evidence," Mark said. "It doesn't seem like you want them released at all."

"Our agreement was that you need to find independent information to support what's contained in the scrolls before they can be released. And you haven't yet done that," Chester said in a snide way, intending to provoke.

"We had independent information until it was taken from us," Gilda said, clearly upset and glaring at Chester.

"Sorry, that wasn't our deal. Our deal was for you to provide independent proof before the scrolls could be released. Your word that you found something doesn't cut it." Pleased with his performance, Chester felt in control.

"Why not release the nine noncontroversial scrolls?" Gilda demanded angrily, looking determined.

"Not just yet. If we release the nine scrolls now, it'll be delicate to explain the other two scrolls if and when released. I think the all-or-none principle applies," Chester said, anticipating this question.

Frustrated and perplexed, Mark considered Chester's response ridiculous. Why did Chester have so much power? Being a pure scientist, Mark had never been interested in money. Consequently, he didn't comprehend the reason for Chester's power based on his financial influence in Israel.

Jacob thought Chester was overplaying his hand, making his involvement in the tiles' disappearance suspect. He wanted to change the focus away from Chester. Diplomatically, he offered, "While Chester's position is a consideration, the decision to find corroborating evidence as a condition for the scrolls release was my decision as the Israeli government representative. Chester's role here is solely to provide financial assistance."

Silence filled the conference room. Mark didn't believe this to be true but considered it fruitless to argue with Jacob.

Finally, Jacob asked Dr. Meyer, "Is that the end of your investigation? Do you have any other ideas concerning where to look?" He hoped the answer would put an end to this elusive effort.

Dr. Meyer looked at Gilda, then at Mark. Turning to Jacob, he said, "If we think Jesus went to Babylon, then we should follow the trail there. The remains of Babylon are about fifty-five miles south of Baghdad, Iraq. The problem is that Saddam Hussein ruined Babylon, the city once known for its hanging gardens. He reconstructed it in his own image, so to speak, without the help of archaeologists or any experts. He had his name inscribed on every brick, trying to make it a monument to himself. The result was an archaeological disaster. It would be a waste of time to go there. The antiquities saved from Babylon are now in Baghdad at the Iraq National Museum. That should be our next destination."

"I agree with Dr. Meyer," Gilda said, eager to continue the search.

Mark remained quiet. His instincts told him that supporting this effort could have a potentially negative effect on the outcome, especially if Chester controlled the decision. The response they received was a surprise.

"That's not possible at this time," said Jacob. "The American government is currently amassing troops on the border of Iraq, and I hear they may invade at any time. Travel to Iraq at this time is simply out of the question."

"But the United Nations weapons inspectors didn't find any evidence of weapons of mass destruction in Iraq during their most recent investigation. The United States isn't going to invade Iraq if there are no WMD there!" Mark argued, his face intense with concern.

"Of course we will!" Chester rejoined self-righteously. "Saddam Hussein is an evil man. He even kills his own people. The American people will stand up for freedom." Chester was familiar with the hawkish, narrow-minded, pro-war talking points and used them at every opportunity.

Mark wasn't even sure what "stand up for freedom" meant in this case. People like Chester talked in general sound bites that appeared logical and rang true, but upon further reflection made little to no sense when applied to the specific situation.

The build up to war was very good for business, thought Chester. He knew there were many evil leaders in the world who killed their own people. But those leaders didn't have huge reserves of oil. That distinction was going to cost Saddam his country. Chester thought that Mark might say Iraq's geology was going to be the downfall of Saddam Hussein.

Gilda leaned in close to Mark and whispered, "So much for your Christian government following the peaceful approach offered by Jesus."

Mark acknowledged Gilda with a brief nod and a frown, unhappy with his president's decision. He didn't respond to Chester. He wondered how his president, who claimed to be a Christian, could start a preemptive war, especially given the lack of evidence of WMD. He could think of no reason to engage in a war halfway around the world. Could the president have information unavailable to the public? The Iraqis had not been the ones who attacked the United States by crashing planes into New York's Twin Towers on September 11, 2001. It just didn't make sense. Starting a war certainly was not Christ-like. It just seemed so wrong ... maybe it wouldn't happen after all.

***

The push to attack Iraq was going on before Chester came to Israel, and he had continued to follow news about the impending invasion. While back in the States, Chester thought of ways to take advantage of the drumbeat to war. A popular slogan, "Support the troops," had been resurrected, and Chester encouraged Pastor Bob to use the slogan as often as possible, especially before the collection plate was passed. The slogan "Support the troops" always helped increase contributions.

Preaching about Biblical battles was another way to support the invasion and generate revenue. The Battle of Jericho was a popular theme for Pastor Bob's sermons. It seemed an appropriate sermon topic to Chester because the Battle of Jericho was the first battle of the Israelites during their conquest of Canaan. Chester loved the part about blowing horns and having the walls come tumbling down—like the St. Sophia Cathedral walls, which didn't need horns to fall, thought Chester, inwardly smiling. He hoped the invasion of Iraq was just the beginning—an expansion of Christianity—and therefore an expansion of more potential financial contributors. This war was definitely good for business.

He also thought the slogan "Support the troops" was great to throw in the face of anyone who opposed the war. You could accuse them of not supporting the troops any time they said anything against the war, even if they actually did support the men and women in uniform but were just against putting troops in harm's way for a questionable reason. What was amazing was that this transposition of words, "troops" for "war", worked—it got lots of people very agitated. Even the naive media fell for the switch. It was an effective, convenient putdown for those against the war. Chester supported the war, and he didn't tolerate anyone who was against it.

***

Jacob interrupted Chester's reverie and said, "Whatever the reason for war, the American troops and a limited number of troops from other countries are gathering southeast of Iraq in Kuwait. The United States wanted to build up forces in Turkey, where you just were, but Turkey would not allow it. My guess is that the invasion will take place before the heat of summer. The American administration believes it will be a short war requiring few troops. One reason to believe the war will be short is the administration's estimated cost of the war, which is quite low. There are some associated with the administration who even suggest that Iraqi oil revenue can easily pay for the war.

"So for now, your expedition is on hold," continued Jacob. "It's likely the invasion will occur sometime this spring and, if the American administration is correct, it won't last long. After that time, we should be able to arrange for you to go to Baghdad."

As optimistic as Jacob was trying to sound, the news deflated Mark and Gilda. Not being able to immediately pursue their quest was one thing, but the thought of invading a country and putting American troops in harm's way without a clear reason was daunting to Mark. He supported the troops and hoped they were being used wisely.

Jacob wrapped up, saying, "We will follow the situation in Iraq, and when it is safe, you can go." Jacob had talked to Chester conceptually about additional travels for the trio and felt that a trip to Baghdad was within the parameters of their original agreement. He heard no objection from Chester.

Chester, on the contrary, wanted to suggest they go to Iraq before the shooting war started in hopes the perpetually irritating Mark might find himself in the cross fire.

With the meeting over, Mark and Gilda headed for her apartment. On the way, Mark, disappointed, said, "I have to return to the States." After reflecting about not seeing Gilda for a lengthy period of time, he added shyly, "I'd love for you to visit me and see the life I lead in Florida. Is there a chance you could take time off and visit me between now and when we go to Baghdad? If we do, in fact, go to Baghdad." His reasons for inviting her were selfish—he wanted to introduce her to his life in the States and hoped she might acquire a fondness for Tallahassee.

"Great minds think alike," responded Gilda cheerfully. "I was thinking about visiting you. I have about a month's vacation saved up. Let me check with my office and try to arrange things. Before the Turkey trip, I shifted some of my work to colleagues, lightening my workload. Now might actually be a good time for me to take some time off."

She added with a smile, "And I'm not pulling your chain."

Mark laughed, "That time you got the idiom correct." Elated, he suddenly felt on top of the world.

Back at Gilda's apartment, they alternated between being intimate and discussing the "what ifs" of finding and then losing the tiles from St. Sophia Cathedral. Their discussion eventually returned to who might have taken the tiles.

"I'm sure Dr. Meyer's conscientious report back to Jacob is connected with the theft. Do you think your government was involved with taking tiles?" asked Mark while lying next to Gilda in bed and stroking her hair.

"I guess it is possible, but doubtful," responded Gilda. "Chester Weeks seems the most likely candidate to me. He is unlike any Christian I know."

"True," Mark responded. "Most Christians I know are compassionate and want to help those less fortunate. They tend to follow the teachings of Jesus. Not Chester."

Gilda lay next to Mark, her arm and leg draped over him, her face nestled against his chest. The clean smell of her hair had an intoxicating effect, while the warmth of her body felt soothing. As she napped, Mark lay on his back, an arm under his head and a doubled-up pillow. He could not stop thinking about Chester. Chester was lying, he knew it, in violation of the Ten Commandments. As was Mark's habit, his mind wandered, connecting various thoughts, starting with bearing false witness, meandering to the Ten Commandments. Some people postulated that the Biblical Jews borrowed the concept of the Ten Commandments from the ancient Egyptians after their Exodus from Egypt. More specifically, the Ten Commandments may have originated from the Egyptian *Book of the Dead*, which included a list of conditions one must follow in order to enter the afterlife.

These Egyptian conditions were remarkably similar to the Hebrew Ten Commandments, only the *Book of the Dead* had more than ten conditions. The Egyptian *Book of the Dead* had been written approximately three centuries before the Ten Commandments were handed down to Moses on Mount Sinai. It was as if Moses, who had been reared as an Egyptian and surely had read the *Book of the Dead*, had picked the best conditions or rules from the older text and adopted them for his own people. Regardless of the origin of the Ten Commandments, Chester certainly was not following them.

Returning from his reverie, Mark leaned down and gently kissed Gilda's forehead, waking her. "We should begin planning our trip," he said softly. Gilda smiled, kissed him, and climbed out of bed. As she walked away, he took pleasure in watching her movements, from her messed hair cascading down the nape of her neck to her hourglass-shaped midsection and finally her well-toned legs. Perhaps the trip planning could wait a bit longer. He called Gilda back to bed. She happily complied.

***

Beginning to make the necessary calls, Gilda notified her office of her desire to take time off. Holding the mobile phone, she stood completely nude, unconsciously stroking her hair and untangling it with one hand. As Mark watched, she hung up and turned toward him. He did not notice the frown on her face. Disappointed, she said, "I can't get away for about a month."

Looking up and catching her eyes, he reassured her. "That's okay. I will leave now and you can join me later. We were apart longer than a month following my sabbatical so I think we can manage, but I will miss you." He added, "The image of you on the phone should sustain me."

Gilda looked down at herself, phone still in hand. "Is this your idea of phone sex? I hope you remember more than this." Placing the phone down, she moved toward him.

"Hmm, I will remember more, your sense of humor for one thing."

They embraced; Gilda pressed her breasts tightly into his chest.

Excited at the thought of sharing his life in Tallahassee with Gilda, Mark was nevertheless apprehensive. His hometown certainly was no Jerusalem—Tallahassee was smaller, had no significant history, and had a much different climate and geology. For that matter, Tallahassee wasn't even an Iznik. He hoped she would see the same beauty in northern Florida as he, but Tallahassee was going to be a tough sell to someone with Gilda's cosmopolitan background.

Chapter Fifteen

Anyone who has the power to make you believe absurdities has the
power to make you commit injustices.

—Voltaire

Spring 2003, Tallahassee/Panama City Beach, Florida

Tallahassee, with its Southern charm, offered ideal weather and
bountiful flowering flora in the spring. White and pink dogwood trees
abounded, often in concert with multicolored azaleas, all bathed in
sunshine. Gilda had been in Tallahassee for almost two weeks. During
that time, she visited Mark's office and other sites in the area. While
on campus, Mark introduced her to his graduate student Jesus Lopez,
who dropped by to discuss his thesis and project with Mark. But
mostly, they spent time just being together.

Gilda stayed with Mark in his home south of the FSU campus.
His one-level, brick house was nestled in a group of hardwood trees
draped in Spanish moss. Among the hardwoods, tall pine trees rose
skyward, their needles scattered about the yard. Covering his property
were large and small azalea bushes in full bloom, providing visual
splashes of pink, red, light purple, and white in all directions.

While at home, much of their time was spent on a large,
screened-in porch attached to the house. Mark treated the porch as an
extension of his home, and when the heat and humidity permitted, he
practically lived out there, with his laptop, notebooks, and papers
strewn about. The overhead fan stirred the air, keeping the porch
comfortable. It was pleasant to be outside but sheltered from the many
insects thriving in this area.

They sat on the porch. It was dusk, and the trees blocked the little
remaining sunlight. The fragrance from the azaleas, together with the
smell of pines, wafted through the air; the Spanish moss waved gently
in a soft breeze. Somewhere above them a mockingbird sang. Mark
and Gilda sat in comfortable patio chairs surrounding a round glass
table. Mark lit candles and opened a bold cabernet sauvignon from

Napa Valley. It was one of his favorites, and he enjoyed sharing it with Gilda, drinking out of large wine glasses that allowed the deep purple liquid to breathe.

As they sat enjoying the evening and the wine, Mark asked Gilda with some trepidation, "So how do you like Tallahassee so far?"

"Well," she responded, taking great care to select her words, "the weather has been pleasant. Better than I expected." She paused, having started this delicate conversation with a neutral topic. She did not want to be critical.

Mark rambled nervously, "In the name of full disclosure, spring is a great time of year here. Given the dry climate you're used to in Israel, you wouldn't like the summers in Florida. You'd wilt. During summer, most people hurry from their air-conditioned cars to their air-conditioned homes or offices. Winters are pleasant enough. In this part of Florida, you actually see a change of seasons. It gets downright cold here. We rarely get snow though. Only once do I remember snow falling and laying on the ground. But I also remember that it melted by noon. The humidity makes the cold more penetrating. Our falls can be pleasant except for the, you know, occasional tropical storm or hurricane."

With a twinkle in his eye, he muddled on, "Then you just stay indoors and have a hurricane party, as long as the storm isn't too bad." Mark realized he wasn't being a very good salesman. He kept pointing out Tallahassee's bad points instead of emphasizing the positive ones.

Gilda listened attentively to Mark's discourse on the weather. *Funny how these Americans are fixated on weather forecasts and weather, per se*, she thought. They had to know the weather forecast before they made any plans. What other country would have a 24/7 TV station dedicated entirely to the weather? In her country, the weather was what it was. Of course, the weather didn't change all that much in Israel.

A green house lizard ran up the wall near Gilda. It was a Florida chameleon or anole. It stopped, and with a few up-and-down jerks of its head, expanded a skin flap under its neck and displaying a flash of red; then it continued up the wall.

She switched subjects and said with enthusiasm, "You know, I really liked your campus."

Hope sprang into Mark's heart; he responded optimistically, saying, "I'm glad. I like it, too, as you can imagine. This university used to be a college for women. They began accepting men after

World War II. When I was in school here, there were more girls than boys. It definitely had its advantages."

Gilda took a sip of wine. As she did so, the mockingbird became still, and other animals began their evening performance, croaking in a melodic rhythm with tenor voices that seemed too great to come from their small bodies. She had heard them previously, but never paid close attention. This time, she cocked her head, listening to the new sounds, looking at Mark quizzically.

"What you hear," Mark explained, "are tree frogs. They sing me to sleep most nights. In fact, when they're quiet, I sometimes have trouble falling asleep."

Gilda glanced toward the sound, unable to see the small frogs. Taking another sip of wine, she added, "I'm really glad we were able to visit some of your local sights outside Tallahassee. I enjoyed Wakulla Springs the most."

Also one of Mark's favorites, Wakulla Springs, a major spring in northern Florida, was about a thirty-minute drive outside of Tallahassee. "What I like about the springs is that during the last ice age, they attracted both animals and man. As you know, much of the earth's water was tied up as ice in glaciers, causing sea levels to be lower than now. Consequently, the water level in the springs was lower, causing spring flow to cease and converting the spring opening to a cave, which provided shelter for ice-age man. Once the ice sheets melted, sea levels rose and the cave flooded, becoming a spring again. Fossils of mastodons have been found in the springs, along with evidence of the presence of ice-age man."

Mark refilled Gilda's glass and continued. "Wakulla Springs is a great archeological site that demonstrates the link between archeology and geology. A stone knife was found near the springs, providing evidence that people lived in this part of Florida about fourteen thousand years ago. The knife was found buried in sand that was analyzed using optically stimulated luminescence or OSL."

"What is that?" Gilda asked.

"It's an age-dating tool that determines when sand grains were last exposed to sunlight. Because scientists were able to date the sand adjacent to the knife to fourteen thousand years ago, we know people were already living here."

Mark added jokingly, "It's not quite the history you have in Jerusalem, but Tallahassee's history is longer than you may have imagined."

Gilda nodded in agreement about the history of Jerusalem. "Jerusalem does have a long history, but I had no idea people inhabited this area for so long," Gilda said, interested in the local archeology.

The breeze momentarily increased, rustling the trees and almost blowing out the candles. Mark thought about what Gilda said and responded, "This time period corresponds approximately to the beginning of Clovis people or Paleo-Indians. What is ironic is that there are some people who don't believe that man lived here fourteen thousand years ago."

"Why? What do they think?" Gilda asked.

"Tallahassee is in what we call the Bible belt, where some take the Bible literally. They believe the earth and man are only about six thousand years old."

Gilda found it difficult to believe that some people thought the earth was so young given the scientific evidence indicating otherwise. "I've heard Creationists believe that, right? Where in the Bible is the earth dated?"

Mark paused, recalling what he read years ago. "It's based on the timing of notable events in the Bible. An archbishop named James Ussher determined the earth was created in October 4004 BCE."

Gilda interrupted, "But fossil evidence indicates much older origins and that the cradle of mankind is Africa."

"Good point. But many people believe the six thousand year age and say that the OSL determination or other scientific dating methods cannot be correct. These are the same people who believe man and dinosaurs lived together when everything we know about the fossil record tells us that can't be. When I talk with people who believe Ussher's earth age, they simply say they don't trust radiological age dating and myopically accept his interpretation."

Gilda shook her head in utter disbelief. "It is so illogical to think that man and dinosaurs lived together. It's not a hard concept to grasp—sediments are laid down by water, with older sediments deposited first, and then eventually covered by younger sediments. We know that dinosaur fossils are found in the older sediments without a fossil record of man, and human fossils are found in much younger sediments without a fossil record of dinosaurs. You don't even *need* age dating providing a specific date range. To believe that humans and dinosaurs coexisted defies simple logic." Gilda's hands, always in motion, nearly knocked over her wine glass as she made her final point.

"I agree," said Mark, smiling at Gilda enjoying her passionate argument. "But you know what? Some people believe that either Satan or even God placed fossils in the ground to confuse us. Of course, there's nothing in the Bible or anywhere else to support this harebrained notion. Who knew God was such a jokester? Hopefully, through education, science can influence and change some unrealistic religious beliefs. After all, there was Galileo's experience."

"What do you mean?" Gilda asked.

Before Mark could answer, there was a rustling of pine needles nearby. Emerging from the disturbance were two grey squirrels, one chasing the other. They left the ground and ran up a pine tree, one after the other, bark flying off in their wake. Mark knew the squirrels' mating chase was a high-speed affair. He explained this to Gilda and then answered her question.

"Galileo invented the telescope and made observations showing the earth revolved around the sun. The Catholic Church, at the time, supported the theory of a geocentric universe based on its interpretation of the Bible."

"How did the Catholic Church come to the conclusion that the sun revolved around the earth?" Gilda asked.

"The Bible doesn't actually say that the earth is the center of the universe, but there are scriptures about the world being firm and never moving. This is an example of how the words in the Bible can be interpreted differently by different people and how these interpretations can change with time," Mark said.

He continued, "For publishing his scientific results, Galileo was called to Rome by the Catholic Church, was found guilty of heresy and sentenced to life imprisonment. He died almost ten years later while still under house arrest. Yet Galileo's views of the earth revolving around the sun spread, and eventually, under pressure from the growing population who believed his teachings, Galileo's theories were accepted by the church. His scientific discovery changed religious beliefs, but the cost he paid was high."

Gilda remained silent, deep in thought, eyes focused on the flame from one of the candles.

Mark ended by saying, "There's hope that science can actually change religious beliefs on evolution and the age of the earth. I'm just glad that geologists today in most parts of the world don't have to fear going to jail or being put to death for their ideas when they don't coincide with religious dogma. Of course, that doesn't apply to some areas of the world, like those controlled by fundamentalist Islamic groups such as the Taliban. Still, I can see why some people who cling to their religious beliefs so strongly feel threatened by scientists who offer a different perspective."

Gilda knew part of the reason Mark was promoting Tallahassee was to explore her possible interest in living there. They already had several conversations on the matter. In a more serious tone, trying to be sensitive to his feelings, she said, "Mark, Tallahassee is a nice place to visit. I realize how dear it is to you. Everyone has an appetite for their hometown, but what may be caviar to you may be unappealing fish eggs to someone else. Tallahassee is not somewhere I could live."

Disappointed, Mark had anticipated this sentiment from Gilda based on previous discussions. He had given the matter considerable thought and was willing to relocate to Jerusalem to be with Gilda. His research and teaching could be performed anywhere, and the geology in Israel was more interesting than that in Florida. From a personal viewpoint, he could always visit his father, or his father could come to Israel.

Thoughtfully, he said, "Gilda, I thought as much. I love you and want to be with you." He hesitated, and then asked, "How difficult do you think it would be for me to get a job in Jerusalem?"

Gilda, surprised at his willingness to give up his life at FSU but at the same time delighted, replied gently, "Mark, I love you, too, but I can't ask you to come to Jerusalem. Not now anyway." She paused, and then she said, "Let's not rush this. We are in the middle of a significant discovery. Let's postpone major decisions about relocation until the issues concerning the Mount Sodom Dead Sea Scrolls play out."

Mark reluctantly agreed to put off career-changing decisions and instead decided to simply enjoy Gilda's company to the maximum for the next two weeks while she was with him. An idea occurred to him. Why not make the two-hour drive over to Panama City Beach and show her the beautiful white sand beaches with the turquoise Gulf of Mexico waters? He wanted her to have good memories of his home and the Gulf beaches in Panama City Beach should help.

***

Driving west, they crossed through northwest Florida's cypress swamps, pine forests, farmland, and small towns. They passed from one time zone into another, over to Panama City Beach. For four nights, they stayed at a beachfront condominium overlooking the Gulf at the end of Thomas Drive. The condo was near St. Andrews State Park, a sandy point with the bay on one side and the Gulf of Mexico on the other.

After checking into the condo, Mark and Gilda put on their bathing suits and went to the beach. Walking into the clear, warm water, waves crashed against them, and they felt the smooth soft sand beneath their feet. After the water became waist-high, they swam out to a sand bar. Between the beach and the sand bar, the water depth changed from ankle-deep to over their heads. On the sand bar, the water was only knee-high. Swimming back toward shore, they bodysurfed on the small, gentle waves, and later they just relaxed on the beach. Mark thought Gilda looked stunning in her black bikini.

While sunbathing, Mark pointed out, "We're lucky. It's early enough in the season that there aren't many people on the beach. This area is renowned for spring breakers, but college kids have not yet descended on the town."

"That's fine with me," Gilda said. "The beaches in Israel are usually crowded. This feels like our own private beach."

That evening, they took a long walk on the beach down to the jetty, which was the entrance to the bay on which Panama City was built. In front of them, fiddler crabs, with their one large claw outstretched, dove into holes in the sand. Sandpipers ran along the beach, following the waves moving to and fro.

The jetty, lined with large gray and brown boulders, was part of St. Andrews State Park. From the beach, they watched the sun set slowly over the Gulf. Walking back to their condo, they could see the bioluminescence as the Gulf waters softly sparkled in the dark.

After their walk, they went to a popular restaurant with an outdoor deck overlooking the bay. Sitting outside, they ate fresh seafood and enjoyed each other's company listening to the waves softly lapping against the breakwall. During dinner, Gilda commented, "I love how the moon shimmers off the water. It's almost mesmerizing."

The days merged into one another, where one day seemed like the next. Mark and Gilda played in the surf and took long walks along the beach each day.

One moonlit evening, after dinner, arm in arm, they slowly sauntered down the beach to a popular local hangout. Approaching, they heard the band playing New Age music. They found a table on the outside deck and ordered drinks. The warm evening breeze, the slow, melancholic melodies, and Gilda at his side made Mark feel comfortable and content.

"Would you like to dance?" he asked suddenly.

Gilda had not been on a dance floor in ages and wasn't sure if she still knew how. Mark pulled her to her feet and smiled, closely studying her face. She easily fell into his arms. He held her close, and she rested her head on his shoulder. It seemed there was no one else on the dance floor, that they were totally alone.

Before they knew it, the band was packing up. The spell broken, they walked back to the condo on the beach. Along the way, Mark commented, "When I was in high school, I would bring dates here under the guise that we could watch submarine races."

Gilda stopped. Looking at Mark with an odd expression, she said, "You can't see submarines, especially at night, if they're under water."

"Exactly," responded Mark with a smile so large it could be heard in his voice.

"Oh," Gilda said, pushing his shoulder in response to her realization as to what "watching submarine races" meant.

Mark grabbed her hand and pulled her into a passionate kiss. They held each other closely, continuing to walk back to the condo. Arriving, they fell into bed still holding each other.

Their tenth-floor condo overlooked the Gulf. Each morning, Mark made coffee and breakfast, and they ate out on the large balcony. Sharing the magnificent view with Gilda, Mark felt very relaxed. In the distance, dolphins bobbed up and down in the water, and further out, the commercial fishing boats lined up as they headed out to deeper fishing grounds. Brown pelicans flew by in formation near eye level.

After one group of pelicans passed, Mark pointed out, "About thirty years ago, you wouldn't have seen brown pelicans here. The pesticide DDT used for mosquito control wiped out all the brown pelicans in the Florida panhandle. They've only returned to this area in the last fifteen years."

Occasionally, F-22 Raptors flew overhead in a formation very similar to that used by the brown pelicans. The similarity between two pelicans in formation and two jets flying in formation was striking, and upon seeing this, Gilda asked, "What are those jets?"

"Those are the latest fighter jet, the F-22 Raptor, based at Tyndall Air Force Base just on the other side of Panama City. The air force trains its elite fighter pilots at Tyndall."

During the day, the land heated the air near its surface, causing air to rise. Cooler air from the Gulf was drawn in to replace the rising air, causing an onshore breeze. At night, the land cooled faster than the water, causing air to flow in the opposite direction, creating an offshore breeze. Consequently, there was always a gentle, refreshing wind on their balcony.

From their room, they could hear the rhythm of the waves softly hitting the beach. The sound was calming, and at night, they left the door to the balcony open and listened to the waves until they fell asleep.

One morning, they discussed the water currents that the waves created and the associated sediment transport. They could see the waves come into the beach at a slight angle. This caused some of the wave's energy to be directed along the beach in what were called long-shore currents. The resulting erosion of the sand was a complex process that resulted in an ever-changing beach. After some major storms, the beach even had to be restored by pumping sand from offshore onto the beach in a renewal program.

Gazing out over the water, Mark asked, "Did you know that Albert Einstein's son Hans Albert Einstein was a hydraulic engineer who studied sediment transport like the kind we see on the beach every day?"

"I did not know that." Pausing, Gilda added, "Hey, did you know that Albert Einstein was Jewish?" Gilda never lost an opportunity to show her Jewish pride. She watched him for his reaction.

"I knew that," responded Mark with a smile. "But above all, he considered himself a pacifist and humanitarian. He once said that Gandhi's views were the most enlightened of all political men of his time. Albert Einstein was a New Testament, uh, the Jesus part, kind of guy. But I find it interesting that his son ended up studying geological processes."

"I'm glad you corrected yourself on the New Testament comment," Gilda said with a sly grin. "Albert Einstein was smart. It is interesting that he was a fan of Gandhi's views. There are ideas that we can learn from all religions."

***

Back in Tallahassee, their remaining time together was spent following the news. Each day, the unrelenting progression brought the United States closer to war with Iraq. They read newspapers, online news reports, blogs, and followed TV and radio coverage. War appeared inevitable as the press coverage seemed to cheerlead for war instead of providing investigative journalism. The press simply repeated administration talking points, especially the mostly conservative local papers in the Florida panhandle. Mark and Gilda were both concerned about how a war between the United States and Iraq would impact their respective countries. And of course, they were concerned about the effect of tensions on their upcoming trip to Baghdad.

After watching the news one evening, Gilda wondered aloud, "I have read everything I can get my hands on concerning the intelligence data that your administration is using as the drumbeat to war. I just don't see sufficient evidence to support an unprovoked invasion of a sovereign nation."

"Neither do I, but I have to give our president the benefit of the doubt. He must know something not available to the public. There has to be more damning intelligence than what we're seeing in the news. He would not take the extreme position of war otherwise." At least, Mark hoped that was the case.

When Gilda first arrived in Tallahassee, her intended month-long stay seemed like it might be an eternity. Would she be bored? It was the longest period of time she'd ever been away from work. Yet it went by incredibly fast. It felt to her as if she had just arrived, and now it was time for her to return home.

"I can't believe you're leaving already," said Mark as they ate breakfast on the day of her departure. "If our trip to Baghdad is postponed much longer, I'll come to Jerusalem to visit you. The university's spring break is not too far off, and I could come then."

Both Mark and Gilda felt gloomy. They barely spoke while she packed her suitcases. It was only a fifteen-minute drive to Tallahassee's small airport. The first leg of her trip would take her north to Atlanta, as it would for just about every flight out of Tallahassee.

Mark explained, "There's an expression down here that when you die, in order to get to heaven, you must first pass through Atlanta." Gilda laughed despite herself.

At the airport, Gilda looked up at Mark with tears glistening in her eyes and said, "Mark, I'll miss you greatly. I love you. My father is probably rolling over in his grave. He would have had a hard time accepting me with a Gentile. But I think he would have grown to like you. One way or another, we will be together soon." She kissed him hard and held him for a long time before finally letting go.

"I love you, too," Mark said softly, and then he added, "Perhaps the administration is correct and this will be a short war."

With that, she boarded her flight for Israel via Atlanta and London. Mark left the terminal and went outside. He stood there until her flight took off. He continued standing there, watching her small jet rise higher into the deep blue, cloudless sky until it was completely out of sight. Feeling incredibly lonely, he dreaded going back home to his empty house, his empty porch. Instead, he drove to the FSU campus and stayed up all night working in his office.

He finally went home thirty hours after Gilda left. At home, he felt lost, looking around, expecting Gilda to be there. Exhausted, he still had trouble falling asleep. He struggled to get through each day following Gilda's departure. Even daily conversations or e-mails with her did little to ease his longing.

Two weeks after Gilda returned to Israel, the United States invaded Iraq's sovereign soil on March 20, 2003.

Chapter Sixteen

To believe in God or in a guiding force because someone tells you to is the height of stupidity. We are given senses to receive our information within. With our own eyes we see, and with our own skin we feel. With our intelligence, it is intended that we understand. But each person must puzzle it out for himself or herself.

—Sophy Burnham

Spring 2003, Jerusalem, Israel/Baghdad, Iraq

A week and a half after the war in Iraq began, Mark left for Israel. He brought Jesus Lopez's thesis to read on the plane.

Jesus gave Mark a ride to the airport. Mark told him, "I'm taking a leave of absence from the university and don't know when I'll return, but I'll e-mail you comments on your thesis. I'm going to Israel to be ready to go to Baghdad as soon as we're given the green light." He added, "Please continue on the project. I'll stay in touch to track your progress. And remember, it's only between the two of us. Please don't discuss your work with anyone else."

"I understand, Professor. Thanks for trusting me with this important task. I won't let you down." Jesus had made significant progress and was excited about his findings thus far.

As he left for the security line, Mark turned and said, "Thank you for everything, Jesus."

Jesus waved good-bye, "Good luck, Professor. Keep your head down."

Mark felt at home when he landed near Jerusalem. As he walked through the now-familiar airport, waiting in the long line at passport control, and finally passing through customs, his heart raced in anticipation of seeing Gilda. There she was—standing in a black shirt and pants with her black hair tied back in a ponytail. He had never believed the adage "Absence makes the heart grow fonder" until now.

They kissed and held each other for a long time before finally leaving the airport.

Returning to her apartment, Mark noticed for the first time a beautiful piece of pottery. "Is this your Iznik pottery?"

"Yes." Gilda held it up. It was a small vase decorated in white hyacinths and yellow carnations accented with smaller blue tulips and red roses.

The pottery brought back memories of the beginning of their adventure and searching for independent evidence to support the Mount Sodom Dead Sea Scrolls. It also triggered questions about what lay ahead for them. Mark had apprehensions about going to Iraq, but he knew it was necessary.

"Do they have any idea when we might go to Baghdad?" he asked.

"The Americans are making rapid progress, and our military thinks it will be over soon, but no one knows exactly when. As soon as it is deemed safe enough, we will go. In the meantime, we need to be ready."

While they waited to leave, they spent time together, exploring each other's bodies and minds. Her imagination carried him to new places. She had a unique perspective on many topics, which made him see everything from a different viewpoint. Yet on many topics, they were like-minded. Given their different backgrounds, it was amazing how similar their religious philosophy was. While together, they discussed a vast variety of topics, from politics to religion to personal matters, but the war was foremost in their minds.

On one occasion, religion was their focus, and Gilda asked, "Mark, what do you believe?"

"What do you mean?" Mark asked.

"I know your intellectual outlook on religion, but what do you actually believe?"

"That's a tough question. It's easier for me to tell you what I don't believe. I don't believe in organized religion. I know religious groups do much good, but all too often a religious group collectively thinks its beliefs are more correct than the beliefs of other groups. Often differences in various groups' beliefs are trivial. It's almost like group narcissism. This feeling of superiority has led to many wars. In fact, it seems to me that more people have been killed in the name of organized religion than any other factor throughout the history."

Gilda nodded but added, "You know, there are other factors, such as land. Often, groups fighting over land are of different religions, so it is hard to distinguish the exact cause of war. My own country is a prime example. People with religious differences fight because they believe they have a right to the same land. Perhaps people could coexist if organized religion was not such a barrier."

"You make a valid point," agreed Mark.

Gilda pressed, "Now that I know you are not a fan of organized religion, what do you believe?"

Mark became more pensive. "I've spent a lot of time trying to figure out God and what I believe," he answered slowly. "So far, I have nothing to show for my efforts. I couldn't figure it out, so I quit trying. Perhaps there is a God, but I can't tell you the specifics of what I believe because I don't know. There are times I envy people who are so certain in their beliefs, but I'm not one of those people."

He let out a long sigh. "I'm not an atheist because that would require believing in something—that there is no God. I guess I'm an agnostic. I can't sort it out and give up." As he said this, Mark thought, *If I give up, why do I enjoy discussing religion so much?* It was an enigma.

"What about you? What do you believe?"

Gilda thought about the question and replied, "I'm a little like you. I'm not a very religious person, but I do abide by the more important holidays and traditions of Judaism. I certainly do it more out of my cultural heritage than any strong religious beliefs. My Jewish traditions are very important to me. Because Jews have been treated so horrifically throughout history, I want to make sure my traditions continue, more as an act of solidarity than any religious beliefs."

She continued, "I believe the fear of death is a strong motivation for religion. There are times when I think that mankind is arrogant and cannot accept death as final. An afterlife was conceived to satisfy the idea that we are too important to just end at death; we must continue after death, perhaps in spirit, whether in paradise, in heaven, or back on earth reincarnated. The promise of an afterlife appeals to many people; it eases their fears of death and gives them hope. It is amazing how many religions include the premise of an afterlife. Given the extensive history of burial practices, the afterlife concept may have started with the Neanderthals."

Mark said, "What's interesting is that the religion a person follows is random, depending largely on where he or she was born. Had I been born in Israel, for example, I would likely be Jewish. Had you been born in America, you would likely be Christian. People generally take the religion of their parents and those closest to them, and they are usually taught not to question it."

Gilda asked, "What religion did you learn from your parents and your location?"

"I was reared as a Methodist, but had friends from many religious backgrounds." Mark recalled some statistics he had read and said, "What's amazing is that worldwide there are only about eleven million Methodists, whereas there are forty-three million Baptists and seventy-five million Presbyterians. But guess what? There are over a billion Roman Catholics. These numbers give perspective on some of the more popular Christian denominations, at least those in America."

Gilda asked, "Isn't your president a Methodist?"

"That's what he claims," said Mark, feeling very uncomfortable about a Methodist invading Iraq. Mark slowly shook his head with a look of disgust. He said, "He further claims that God told him to start the war. I don't believe Jesus would command anyone to start a war. We are taught that we are all God's children, so why would God command you to kill his children?"

Mark's agitation and voice were building. "We are given freewill and we make mistakes. But for that, would God order us killed? Look at the thief next to Jesus on the cross—he made mistakes but was still forgiven. Invoking God's name to initiate a war is a way to manipulate the masses. Manipulating people to go to war is not a Christian act." This last sentence was said forcefully.

"Whoa, I didn't mean to upset you with my question," Gilda said.

"Trust me, you're not the one upsetting me."

Mark eventually calmed down and continued with their religious discussion. "What is interesting is that many Christian groups have slightly varying beliefs. I know there are differences between Eastern Orthodoxy and Roman Catholicism, but perhaps the most significant differences in beliefs in the Christian world are those between Catholics and Protestants."

Mark continued, saying, "You may recall the Protestant Reformation was initiated by Martin Luther in 1517 when he nailed his ninety-five theses to the door of the Castle Church in Wittenberg,

Germany. The dispute was with Roman Catholic Church clergy over abuses, including those associated with confession and absolution. This was during the Inquisition. That action by Luther gave birth to the plethora of Christian denominations."

He paused, trying to remember his point. "You don't have to look any further than Ireland to see the outcome of Protestant/Catholic differences, albeit as you point out, land also is an issue. It's ironic that the Bible on which the Protestants rely was selectively compiled by their rivals, the Catholics, at councils like the one at Nicaea."

"And yet," said Gilda, "we see the same thing with the Qur'an. From one religious document, different Muslim groups have developed, like the Shia and Sunni, who fight each other."

"Plus," Gilda added, "look at the way Christians have persecuted Jews throughout history. Some Christians blame the Jewish community for the death of Jesus when Jesus was trying to help the Jews against the yoke of Roman occupation. Jesus was killed by the Romans and a few corrupt Jewish leaders. Out of that Roman culture grew the Roman Catholic Church, yet the Roman contribution to Jesus' death seems forgotten."

Mark responded, "Actually, there are a number of fundamentalist Christian groups that think the Roman Catholic Church is evil and was complicit in misinterpreting the Bible and keeping it out of the hands of 'true' Christians. It's probably hard to find a religion that doesn't have its detractors. That seems to be the nature of religion."

Mark thought for a moment and added, "Not only were the Romans involved in Jesus' death, they persecuted early Christians, who were forced to worship surreptitiously in the catacombs, underground burial places in Rome. Then a thousand years later, the Roman Catholic Church possessed the spoils of the Roman Empire as evidenced by items in the Vatican Museum and began persecuting those with beliefs other than their own during the Inquisition. The more things change, the more they stay the same."

Shaking her head, Gilda asked, "Do you still attend the Methodist Church?"

"No, but sometimes I listen to music from *Godspell* on Sunday mornings," Mark responded with a big smile.

"What's *Godspell*?"

"It's a musical about Jesus' life that has some really good music. Haven't you ever heard of the song 'Day by Day'?" He proceeded to sing a few lines.

Gilda rolled her eyes. That was answer enough.

While in Israel, Mark and Gilda followed the progress of the war with great interest as Americans, British, and other coalition allies traversed Iraq. Finally, the US Army's Third Infantry Division made a mad dash across the desert, reaching the outskirts of Baghdad. First captured was the Baghdad International Airport, ten miles west of downtown Baghdad. Then, on April 9th, Baghdad abruptly fell, only twenty-one days after the invasion began. The coalition troops, mainly Americans, had done their job. Only time would tell how well the war planners had performed theirs. Everyone in the administration thought the war was over, that the mission had been "accomplished."

***

Chester Weeks did not come to Israel in the spring of 2003. Instead, Jacob Cohen arranged a conference call with him that included Mark, Gilda, and Dr. Meyer. Once again, Chester agreed to fund another trip for them, this time to Iraq.

With any luck at all, Chester thought while hanging up the phone, maybe Mark would catch a stray bullet and that would end this whole episode. If that didn't work, there was always his backup plan, which had worked so well in Iznik.

***

Jacob Cohen, the epitome of organization, had begun working with other parts of the Israeli government, which, in turn, made appropriate calls to the US government. The governmental discussions had the desired result. The Israelis, Dr. Meyer and Gilda, and the American, Mark, would be allowed to enter Baghdad. They were provided a special flight from Jerusalem to Baghdad. Their ultimate objective was the Iraq National Museum to explore artifacts from the time Jesus might have visited Babel.

Their descent into Iraq began without warning. It was the first time Mark had experienced a corkscrew landing, used to prevent being hit by a missile. Even though he considered himself a seasoned flyer, nothing had prepared him for the jet's slow downward spiral toward the ground. Images from the History channel of World War II bombers spinning downward after being shot down flashed in his mind. He grabbed the armrests with white-knuckled fingers while his stomach lurched. The motion never seemed to end, and nausea consumed him.

The bump caused by the wheels hitting the ground made his heart skip a beat and bile rose to his throat. Once he realized they were on the ground, he began to relax. He swallowed to remove the bad taste from his mouth, and his stomach began to return to normal. Never had Mark been more delighted to be on terra firma, albeit Iraq. He tried to act nonchalant, hoping no one observed him during the landing. Perhaps his companions, too, were engrossed in their own fears as the jet descended.

After landing at the Baghdad International Airport on April 10th, they found one of the few available taxis. The taxi driver spoke little English, but Dr. Meyer had a card with the name of their hotel written in Arabic. The driver greeted them warmly and encouraged them into his taxi. Despite the white flag tied to the antenna, Mark noticed bullet holes in the sides of the taxi. Pointing them out to Gilda and Dr. Meyer, he asked, "How recent do you think those are?"

Gilda was nervous about the situation, too, and tried to calm her nerves with humor, saying, "Probably his last fare. I'm happy to sit in the middle between the two of you."

Mark looked out the window as they traveled along the Baghdad Airport Road. It was a long ten-mile stretch from the airport to downtown. That thought did not please Mark. It was unclear how dangerous the drive would be, but they made the trip without incident.

Still, they saw troop movement and the grotesque aftermath of war. It was one thing to see the damaged vehicles from the air; it was all together different seeing them on the highway. From the air, burned-out automobiles looked like shattered toys. On the ground, it was obvious human beings had been injured or died here. Quite a few bombed-out buildings were razed to the ground and still smoldering. Rubble lay everywhere, slowing their trip as the taxi maneuvered around objects in the road. Damaged vehicles were abandoned in place. The sights were all too familiar to Gilda and Dr. Meyer, but foreign to Mark. It made him a bit frightened. Had this been a good idea? What had he gotten himself into?

Their destination was the Sheraton Hotel on the east bank of the Tigris River, where they would stay for the next few days. The hotel, unaffiliated with the famous Sheraton brand, had once been first class, but the war and years of sanctions on Iraq had taken their toll.

Despite years of hardship, the hotel was a decent place to stay—likely much better than where the troops were, thought Mark. This time, Mark and Gilda dropped the pretense and asked for one room, which was on the tenth floor overlooking the city. That they asked for one room came as no surprise to Dr. Meyer, who was entertained by their love-smitten antics. The front desk clerk warned that services at the hotel were limited and that electricity was intermittent, but the hotel backup generator worked most of the time, that there was running water for the most part, and that there was a limited menu in the hotel restaurant.

"All the comforts of home," said Mark in jest.

Through their respective governments, Dr. Meyer had made arrangements to meet with a senior staff member at the Iraq National Museum named Sadik Rasheed. Their meeting was scheduled for the next day. The museum was about a mile east of the hotel. US Army CPT Joe Wilson and an interpreter would accompany them and drive them the mile in a heavily fortified army vehicle. Mark hoped they would travel in a Humvee—he had seen one on TV. Thank goodness for acronyms, thought Mark—the car was actually called a high mobility multipurpose wheeled vehicle, which was a bit of a mouthful.

Dinner at the hotel was their only alternative. It was not prudent to leave the heavily secured hotel. Because of the restaurant's limited menu, they ended up ordering simple pizzas and imported beer.

Drinking warm beer while waiting for the pizzas, Mark said, "Saddam Hussein's Baath Party wanted a secular state like Turkey. That's why we can drink alcohol here. Now that Saddam Hussein is out of power, I wonder if religious factions will fill the power void in Iraq like they did in Iran."

"It's hard to say," responded Dr. Meyer pensively.

The pizzas finally arrived and looked meager by Mark's standards. They appeared to be some sort of cheese-like substance on top of pita bread. Mark took a bite and said, "This is pretty bad, but better than no food at all."

Being in Baghdad, Gilda recalled Biblical stories that may have been based on Babylonian legends. She said, "In addition to the story of the Tower of Babel, there are other stories in the Bible that are thought to have their origins in Babylon."

She took a bite of pizza, made a face, and continued, "For example, there was a poem about a man, the righteous sufferer, in

Babylon, who lost his wealth and position but did not lose his faith in the Babylonian god Marduk. For his loyalty to Marduk, the man, referred to as the Babylonian Job, had his wealth and happiness restored. This poem is thought by some to be the inspiration for the story of Job in the Bible."

"In the Bible, Job's loyalty to God was tested when God threw difficult and negative situations Job's way. Because Job stood strong and did not lose his faith, God rewarded him," said Mark. "I wonder what kind of God toys with his creations in such a manner. I've always believed that the author of the Job story was assigning human-like traits to God and those traits were not man's better ones."

Mark could not help but feel a connection between the devastating story of Job and the overwhelming devastation caused by man that he saw on the drive from the Baghdad airport. Man was certainly capable of causing tremendous devastation to his fellow man. *Now we will have to restore and rebuild Iraq, similar to God rewarding Job after he destroyed him*, Mark thought.

Mark's thoughts were interrupted by Gilda, who continued, "There's also the story of Noah and the flood. That story could be based on the Babylonian epic tale about Gilgamesh. Many early civilizations were established near rivers for a convenient source of water for irrigation, cleaning, and drinking, plus for the mode of transportation offered by the river. The problem with rivers, especially before dams were built, was they often flooded."

Gilda continued her logical progression, saying, "Consequently, many early civilizations have flood or deluge stories simply because they were located in floodplains of major rivers. Babylon, being built between the Tigris and Euphrates Rivers, was no exception to flooding and the resulting flood stories. One story described Gilgamesh, who was told of Marduk's plan to destroy life through a great flood. He was told to build a vessel for his family, friends, and cattle so they could survive. Some believe that the Gilgamesh story was the basis of Noah's deluge story in the Bible. Certainly, Jews were in the Babylon area and likely heard the story of Gilgamesh."

Poking at his last slice of pizza, Mark recalled the dessert they had in Iznik that allegedly was first made in the galley of Noah's vessel. A vision of a unicorn came to mind. He smiled as he recalled his sarcastic thought about Noah's crew eating the last pair of unicorns, giving rise to their absence today.

He couldn't help but say, "The storytellers of Noah's adventure apparently embellished the Gilgamesh story. Instead of bringing just cattle, Noah loaded up all animals, two by two, a male and a female." Mark's scientific mind slipped into gear. "Ignoring the diverse flora, how did Noah gather up all the different insects in the world? After all, insects are animals, too, so they had to be there. And how did Noah gather up all the numerous animal species in rainforests? Living in a desert region, this must have been problematic. What about the unique species, like marsupials, that evolved in Australia because of the continent's isolation? Did Noah travel to Australia and pick those up? Then there were the species that lived in cold climates in the mountains."

Mark realized by the stares that he was going overboard, and calmed down. "The embellishment of the Gilgamesh story may have made the Noah story more interesting, but it also made it less believable to modern man. Of course, back in Biblical times, the Noah story was more believable because people only knew about their local animals, which were much more manageable to load into an ark or boat. Plus, they would not have cared about insects."

Gilda said, "Because of the flooding of the Tigris and Euphrates Rivers, the area around here is underlain by thick alluvial or river-deposited sediments, much of which consist of very fine-grained silt. That silt near land surface is a major contributor to the sandstorms in and around Baghdad. Sooner or later, the American military will have to deal with those silty wind storms."

That comment turned their discussions to the war, and soon they were silent, each keeping their thoughts private. It was clear that the evening meal and discussions were over. Dr. Meyer asked for and paid the bill. They bade their goodnights and went to their respective rooms. Mark and Gilda's room was worn and needed a facelift, but at least it had a double bed. Mark was happy. He stripped and jumped into bed. Gilda followed suit. Soon the thought of careless, destructive gods and the war-ravaged city outside their window was lost in intimacy.

After a quick breakfast the next morning, the three gathered near the hotel entrance, ready for their US Army escort to arrive. While they waited, Dr. Meyer discussed some of what he knew about Babylon. "The Assyrian Empire was followed by the Babylonian Empire. Babylon, which was rebuilt by Nebuchadnezzar in about 690

BCE, was its capital. It was at that time that Babylon was known for its famous hanging gardens."

Dr. Meyer paused as some of the hotel guests, who appeared to be reporters, walked past them and out the front door. "The area surrounding Babylon is known as Mesopotamia or the Mesopotamian plain and is between the Tigris and Euphrates Rivers here in present-day Iraq. A large number of impressive and historically significant antiquities have been found nearby. Many of these are preserved in the Iraq National Museum, and we are quite fortunate to be able to visit the museum today. Saddam Hussein treated the museum as his private collection, allowing only his friends to visit."

Walking briskly through the hotel entrance was a handsome black man in a captain's uniform. He looked around, saw them, walked toward them, and asked, "Are you Dr. Meyer?"

"Yes," responded Dr. Meyer as he reached for the captain's hand.

Introductions were made, and as Mark shook CPT Wilson's hand, he asked, "Where are you from, Captain?"

"I grew up in St. Davids, Pennsylvania, just down the road from Villanova University, where I went to college."

"That's a good school," commented Mark. "I attended a conference at Villanova once—beautiful campus and chapel. Isn't that area called the Main Line?"

"Yes, sir, after the commuter train line."

CPT Wilson was anxious to get moving and ended the small talk. He brought them up to speed on the situation at the museum. "First of all, you should know that we took great care to protect the museum during our invasion. Our forces avoided bombing the museum, so it has not been damaged by air strikes. The day before Baghdad fell, Iraqi forces, in violation of the Geneva Conventions, engaged our forces from within the museum. We did not return fire for fear of damaging the museum and only just recently secured it. So your timing couldn't be better."

Dr. Meyer acknowledged CPT Wilson's summary. "Thanks for that update, and thank you very much for your help."

CPT Wilson asked, "Are you ready to go?"

All three responded, "Yes."

Mark got his wish. They traveled in a Humvee with an escort to the Iraq National Museum. Pulling into a large courtyard in front of the museum, before them was an entrance with two gigantic double doors, each at least twelve feet tall and four feet wide. Sadik Rasheed, who was dressed in Western-style shirt and slacks, met them at the entrance. Before entering the museum, Gilda pulled the scarf she had around her neck up around her head as a symbol of respect. Having grown up in this part of the world, she knew the importance of proper etiquette and generally accepted it as a way of life.

Sadik spoke fairly good English. He explained that the museum had been established in 1926 with the help of British traveler and author Gertrude Bell. As a consequence, the exhibits were labeled in both English and Arabic. Documents not on display were stored by date. Sadik knew they were interested in the time period around 50 to 300 CE, when writings concerning Jesus' travels may have been recorded, and so he led them toward the appropriate area deep inside the museum.

As they walked through the museum, Mark saw many large artifacts. Huge, intricately carved stone panels depicted battle and hunting scenes. Large stone statues of winged bulls and winged lions with heads of men sporting wavy hair and beards appeared to guard entranceways into museum rooms. Ancient coins, jewelry, and other gold, silver and bronze pieces were on display. It was an amazing sight. Mark was in awe and wished he had more time to slowly meander about the fantastic museum.

Gilda paused in front of a stone relief displaying a lion killing a bull, a gigantic struggle. Sadik noticed and explained, "This killing represents spring replacing winter, symbolic of renewal."

It was spring, and Mark thought of other symbolism where the American forces were defeating Saddam's forces. He was proud of the American troops and thinking of them as lions seemed appropriate.

Eventually, Sadik took them down a steep, narrow marble circular staircase leading to an underground vault. He explained, "Antiquities are so numerous in Iraq that many have not been studied and are simply stored in these vaults." Inside the vault were rows of dusty locked storage cases containing documents and small artifacts organized according to time periods. Mark dug into his backpack and pulled out his digital camera and his field book for taking notes.

Finding the documents for the appropriate time period, Dr. Meyer said, "I will take the cases here, why don't you two work on those over there?" He pointed to the right side of the room. They began the deliberate, wearisome process of carefully examining the contents in the cases.

They were slowed by the fact that neither Gilda nor Mark could read Aramaic. When they found a scroll or tablet with writings, they had to wait for Dr. Meyer to finish what he was doing before he could review and interpret it. Dr. Meyer read Aramaic, but not at a very rapid pace, and he needed to refer to his dictionary repeatedly, further slowing down the review process.

Still, they made progress, working through lunch under the watchful gaze of Sadik. By early afternoon, about three quarters of the way through the storage cases, Gilda noticed a curious-looking scroll. It was much more ornate than the others she had seen that day. Thinking it might be important, she eagerly handed it to Dr. Meyer and said, "This scroll looks different from the other ones I've come across. I'm not sure what that means, but you should take a look at it."

She returned to searching through the cases. Dr. Meyer began the slow process of reading and interpreting the Aramaic scroll. As he painstakingly translated the words on the scroll, he became more animated, saying, "Gilda, this may be what we have been looking for." Mark and Gilda stopped searching the storage boxes and rushed to his side, trying to read his notes.

"What is it?" Gilda asked impatiently.

"I'm going as fast as I can. Translating this is very tedious. This scroll discusses a visitor 'from the west.' One who taught and exchanged ideas, especially on religion. One who was interested in the area's people and history, especially of Babel. This visitor was in the area only a short period of time and then he continued his travels to the east. He was highly regarded, impressing the local population with his kindness and mysterious deeds. They refer to him as *Issa*." Dr. Meyer paused, looked up at Mark and Gilda, and said, "I have seen that name before and believe this may have been Jesus."

Issa, thought Mark, as he was taking notes, *could this really be Jesus? And if it was Jesus, why did the scroll use the name Issa?* Dr. Meyer seemed to be familiar with the name, but Mark had never heard it before.

Just as he was getting ready to ask Dr. Meyer about the name, Mark felt, as much as heard, a loud rumble pass through the museum. He glanced fearfully at Gilda and then at Dr. Meyer.

"Did you feel that?" he inquired nervously.

Gilda nodded, but Dr. Meyer kept right on with the task at hand.

Mark was concerned, but at the same time he reasoned they were in a museum constructed of thick, reinforced concrete, and they had

CPT Wilson and his men to protect them. Still he was on alert, carefully listening and glancing toward the door.

A minute or so later, CPT Wilson ran into the vault and announced in a loud voice, "There was a nearby explosion. We need to quickly head back to the hotel. Now!"

Dr. Meyer stopped his translating and returned the scroll to Sadik, who had moved next to the three.

Dr. Meyer asked Sadik, "May we please take this scroll with us?"

"No," responded Sadik, "it belongs to Iraq and must stay here."

"May we come back, perhaps tomorrow, to view it again?" Dr. Meyer pressed.

"Yes, of course," answered Sadik, slightly lowering his head.

CPT Wilson came closer to Dr. Meyer and said with authority, "We must leave immediately. Your safety is my responsibility. Gather your belongings and follow me."

As they left the museum, Mark had an ominous feeling of déjà vu. He recalled the last time they were this close to learning more about Jesus' travels—the tiles in Turkey had been taken.

Chapter Seventeen

The religion that is afraid of science dishonors God and commits suicide.

—Ralph Waldo Emerson

Spring 2003, Baghdad, Iraq

Quickly whisked to their vehicles, the trip back to the Sheraton Hotel began without incident. Although the staccato sound of automatic weapons could be heard nearby, Mark, Gilda, and Dr. Meyer remained quiet, bouncing about as their Humvee raced through the streets. Sweat running down his face, Mark peered out the window that offered little protection, rapidly scanning the horizon but not sure what to expect in the Baghdad neighborhoods.

As they approached, most people, clad in loose-fitting clothing capable of hiding a weapon, ducked into homes and shops, many of which had windows knocked out. Sunlight glistened off the remaining intact glass, making it hard to see who might be behind those openings. Ghostly images appeared, but Mark was unsure whether they were the result of his imagination or were real. Litter was everywhere, some mounds large enough to conceal a gunman or a bomb.

At one intersection, burning tires in the street slowed their progress. With diminished visibility, they cautiously approached, not knowing what was beyond the billowing black smoke. Guns locked and loaded, everyone was at alert. CPT Wilson told them to lower their heads. Carefully maneuvering around the blazing blockade, no one was there. All relaxed momentarily. Looking out the windows again, it amazed Mark how nerve-racking simply driving down the street was. Finally reaching the hotel, the three quickly exited the Humvee, bade everyone thank you and good luck and rushed inside.

During their drive, the group failed to notice a taxi following some distance behind. Its single occupant—a tall, heavyset man with a scar over his right eye—sat in the backseat chain smoking. When the group got out of the Humvee and entered the Sheraton, the taxi turned, heading back in the opposite direction.

In the hotel, the three began to unwind, searching for privacy in the surprisingly comfortable lobby, which was paneled in dark cherry wood. They found large leather chairs in an empty corner. Keeping their voices low, the three began their discussions.

Mark asked, "So who is this Issa? Have either of you ever heard of him before?" He suspected Dr. Meyer had.

"I haven't," replied Gilda quickly, now looking toward Dr. Meyer.

After a moment to gather his thoughts, Dr. Meyer responded, "Yes, actually, I have, but I had forgotten about it."

"What have you heard?" Mark asked eagerly, feeling his heart beat faster.

"Issa, or Saint Issa, is discussed in a book written in the late 1800s by a Russian medical doctor, Dr. Nicolas Notovitch. I have a copy of his book back in Israel. I read it some years ago, but never took it seriously. That is, not until now."

"And?" probed Gilda, as excited as Mark with this new finding.

"Well, in the 1880s, Dr. Notovitch was traveling through present-day Afghanistan, India, and Tibet when he fell and broke his leg. While recovering, he was introduced to ancient scrolls located in northern India that discussed a person named Issa. He concludes that Issa and Jesus were the same person. I will have to reread the book to be sure of the details."

"Wow! I wonder if Jesus did, in fact, go to India. And if so, why?" Mark pondered aloud.

"I do recall something being said about that. Dr. Notovitch asserts that Issa or Jesus went to India to study Buddhism and Hinduism. Apparently, he became so proficient in both religions that he not only studied under holy men, but also became a holy man himself and taught religion. I have to tell you that some of this fits with what is described in the Mount Sodom Dead Sea Scrolls, but the name Issa is never used. I never put the two together until now."

Mark and Gilda straightened in their chairs and watched Dr. Meyer, anxiously awaiting more information, but none came. Mark kept forgetting that Dr. Meyer had knowledge about what they were searching for and that he was guiding their investigation based on what he had learned from the scrolls.

"Studying and teaching religion sounds like something Jesus might do, being a rabbi," commented Gilda softly, leaning forward in her seat so she could be heard. "The possibility that Jesus traveled to northern India to study religions other than his own is fascinating."

"At the time of Jesus' travels, it is possible there were Hindu and Buddhist missionaries visiting Babylon. I guess it's plausible that Jesus met one or more of them as he traveled the Silk Road. Maybe he became interested in their beliefs and decided to learn more by traveling to northern India, the cradle of Buddhism," Mark suggested.

Gilda added, "If memory serves me correctly, at that time in Jesus' life, both Hinduism and Buddhism were established religions. Hinduism is one of the world's oldest religions currently practiced and has diverse traditions. It is the third largest religion in the world after Christianity, which only began at the time of Christ, and Islam, which began much later in about the mid-seventh century CE."

Mark asked, "When did Hinduism start?"

"Its roots date back as far as 2000 BCE."

"How does that date compare with the start of the Hebrew religion?" Mark followed up.

"Many people would say that the Hebrew religion started with Abraham, also about 2000 BCE. Others might say it started around the time of the exodus from Egypt. At that time, the scattered tribes from Abraham became a single nation, adopting Yahweh as their god and forming the first monotheistic religion," Gilda responded, happy she could recall past teachings.

Hearing no further questions, she continued. "Buddhism began in about 400–500 BCE in ancient India. It was established in large part to help the suffering find peace through renunciation of worldly matters, meditation, and physical exercises."

"Isn't yoga associated with Buddhism?" Mark asked.

"Yes," responded Gilda. "Meditation and physical exercises are sometimes combined in what we today call yoga. Experts in yoga are amazing and appear to be able to exert control over voluntary muscles of the body as well muscles we think of as involuntary, like the heart."

"So the scroll we just saw in the Iraq National Museum appears to indicate that Jesus made it as far as Babylon and then continued his trek east. Dr. Notovitch's book indicates Jesus traveled further east, at least as far as northern India. The Babylonian scroll, for lack of a better name, may have more to tell us. I could not read the entire document before we were forced to leave. I hope when we return tomorrow I can perform a full and complete translation," said Dr. Meyer.

Mark recalled the Council of Nicaea and the destruction of Arius's writings. Reevaluating the Council's decision in light of the new information gleaned from the Babylonian scroll raised questions. "Dr. Meyer, did Constantine destroy Arius's writings and keep Jesus' travels during those eighteen years out of the Bible because the writings showed that Jesus was influenced by Eastern religions?"

Dr. Meyer hesitated, then decided to be forthright, "I think that is likely, but it cannot be established without release of the Mount Sodom Dead Sea Scrolls. Recall, the Council produced the Nicene Creed, establishing the divinity of Jesus. Another group of bishops wanted to distance Christianity from other religions, like Judaism. For example, the celebration of Easter was separated from Jewish Passover."

Mark followed the logic. "If Arius's writings and documents questioning the divinity of Jesus were based on the travels of Jesus and possible influence of Eastern religions on him, then those writings would be counter to the Nicene Creed and the desire to make Christianity a stand-alone religion. Those documents would need to be destroyed."

"Exactly," said Dr. Meyer. "When one is growing and spreading a juvenile religion, it is counterproductive to show a reliance on an older, well-established religion."

Listening to this discussion, Gilda thought about their current situation. "The Council suppressed information on Jesus' travels during the missing eighteen years of his life to make sure it would not become part of the Bible. Now Chester Weeks is attempting to do the same thing the Roman Catholic Church did in 325 CE. All because of a fear that knowledge of Eastern religions' influence on Jesus might undermine Christianity?"

"That appears to be the case," replied Dr. Meyer. "That's why we must secure the Babylonian scroll and use it to ensure the Mount Sodom Dead Sea Scrolls are released."

Mark simply shook his head, struck by church politics and hypocrisy. He knew the answer but asked rhetorically, "How could religious leaders who claim to promote honesty and truth go to such lengths to lie and hide the truth?"

No one responded. They sat quietly for a time. Mark, lost in thought, casually scanned the lobby. It was spacious and elegantly decorated. The floors were covered in large black and white marble squares. The furniture was sizeable and comfortable, reminding him of what might be found in an old English drawing or smoking room. Scattered around the lobby, next to some of the chairs, were huge potted plants; the greenery made the lobby pleasant visually. It gave him the feeling of being in an oasis in the middle of a desert.

Finally, after a long silence, Dr. Meyer suggested, "Why don't we take time to get refreshed and meet later for dinner?" After agreeing on a time to meet in the hotel restaurant, they climbed the stairs to their rooms.

There wasn't much time before they were to reconvene for dinner. In their room, Gilda laid down to rest, while Mark went out on the balcony. He was interested to observe but careful not to make himself a target. Baghdad was still in upheaval. He could see signs of chaos in all directions. There were few cars on the streets and bands of men, some armed with what he thought were AK47s, freely roamed below. Black smoke rose at several locations. Occasionally, he could hear gunshots in the distance. Mesmerized by the street violence, this felt like an out-of-body experience, so surreal.

CPT Wilson had informed Mark that law and order had yet to be fully restored in the city. There was absolutely no sign of any police and only limited signs of military troops. The situation was disconcerting. He had been told that the American military was stretched to the limit. He was grateful for the assistance of CPT Wilson and his men, but felt badly that his presence might be diverting CPT Wilson from more important assignments.

On the other hand, he believed he was performing a task worth pursuing. His presence in Iraq was justified. Understanding what Jesus had done during the eighteen years of his life missing from the Bible was significant. He further believed that making this new information available to the public was paramount. It might change the Bible or people's perception of the Bible, but it would not change the teachings and basic tenets of Jesus. The public could make their own determination whether to accept the new information or not, think it through, and assess how it might affect their views.

He heard the door slide open behind him and turned to see Gilda emerge.

She joined him in his corner on the balcony overlooking Baghdad, put her arm around his waist, and commented sadly, "The area surrounding the Tigris and Euphrates Rivers is so beautiful. Can you imagine Babylon with its hanging gardens near here? Where did we go wrong? Why did humankind have to spoil this beautiful region?"

"I don't know," Mark replied sadly.

Feeling uncomfortable out in the open on the balcony, he told Gilda they should go back inside. As they turned to head back indoors, he heard a whizzing sound followed by the crack of brick and concrete being smashed. A small explosion of dust and rock fragments caught his attention just off to the right. He reacted instantly, pushing Gilda through the door, ducking in, quickly sliding the door closed, and pulling the blackout drape behind it. They crawled away from the window.

Mark held Gilda closely on the floor in a corner of the room. "That was close! It was stupid to stand out on the balcony," he said, holding Gilda tightly, her warmth calming him down.

Gilda gently stroked his hair. "Fortunately, we're okay. Who would have thought Baghdad was still so hostile."

He held her closer. He thought he felt her shaking, but realized it was himself.

Later, they found Dr. Meyer standing outside the restaurant ready for dinner. Sandwiches and drinks from the very limited menu were the selection for the evening's meal. Dinner, which should have been a happy occasion marked by finding the Babylonian scroll, turned instead into a rather somber one.

The gloom resulted from being in a war-torn city and being confined to their hotel due to the potential violence lurking outside. Gilda shared with Dr. Meyer the story of nearly being shot. Visibly upset and concerned, Dr. Meyer chided her, "You should never have gone out on the balcony. This country is in a state of war. This is serious business, and you must behave accordingly." Gilda felt like a schoolgirl being admonished by her teacher. Dr. Meyer was correct.

Further contributing to the subdued evening was the interruption of their evaluation of the Babylonian scroll. Given the circumstances, they did not know what awaited them in the morning. The occurrences in Iznik were foremost on their minds. Other than polite small talk, there was little conversation over dinner. As the plates were cleared, Mark asked, "Dr. Meyer, did you call Jerusalem and report our findings?"

"I tried, but was not able to get through. The front desk told me the phone service is intermittent, but I was not successful." He paused, adding, "My efforts to contact Jacob were halfhearted. To be honest, my enthusiasm for reporting to him has waned."

That was music to Mark's ears, but still he responded halfheartedly, "Well, perhaps after tomorrow we'll have more to report."

After dinner, they bade each other goodnight and retired for the evening. Mark and Gilda went to bed early, but had a restless night's sleep, in part due to the street noise below their bedroom window. The sound of gunshots throughout the night was very unnerving to Mark. After each shot, he expected to hear the shatter of glass. During his waking moments, his thoughts alternated from flights of fancy about the Babylonian scroll to profound concerns about their very safety.

In the morning, they awoke to find Baghdad even more chaotic. Carefully looking out from behind the curtain, they saw many more people in the streets, many of them removing items from broken shop windows. Individuals carried goods, either on their backs or on their heads, while groups of men carried larger items. To Mark, it appeared that the entire city was being looted in the absence of police or troops to prevent crime. There seemed to be more smoke in the air. They could smell it, even inside their room. The entire lawless scene made Mark very nervous, and he shared his observations and apprehension with Gilda.

At breakfast, he told Dr. Meyer about his unease.

"For now, we must rely on the American army for protection," was Dr. Meyer's response, "but I share your concerns."

As they were finishing breakfast, CPT Wilson came into the hotel and saw them in the restaurant. He walked over to their table, his field uniform rumpled. He was unshaven, his face drawn and eyes gaunt. Judging from the dust and grime, he had been out on the streets most, if not all, of the night. "I have some bad news for you," he said apologetically. "Unfortunately, with our limited troop levels, we haven't been able to gain control of the city. People are running wildly through the city, knocking out windows of shops and grabbing what they can. Even the Iraq National Museum was hit last night."

"How badly?" Dr. Meyer asked.

"Bad enough," responded CPT Wilson. "From what I've heard, many antiquities have been stolen. The area around the museum is now secure; that was a priority." He glanced at the three of them. Each looked worried. "Since you're ready, let's go and you can see for yourself."

They left with CPT Wilson immediately and drove as quickly as possible to the museum. Along the way, they saw damage caused by looters but luckily encountered no obstacles. When they finally arrived, the large museum doors were wide open, but no one was around.

As they cautiously entered the museum, they were greeted with a menacing and deafening silence. The electricity was off and darkness surrounded them except for the beams of their flashlights. CPT Wilson's men had checked out the museum earlier, but the three were still uncomfortable. Searching around for Sadik Rasheed, they called out his name, but all they heard were the echoes of their voices bouncing off the stone walls. Slowly retracing their path to where they had found the scroll yesterday, they noticed many items missing.

Broken glass and pottery crunched under their feet as they went deeper into the museum. Gilda looked at Mark, horrified, and said, "This is terrible!" She thought of the Babylonian scroll, adding, "I have a bad feeling about this."

"I've had a bad feeling since arriving in Baghdad," Mark replied, looking around while slowly moving forward.

There was a noise behind them. Mark's heart discharged a slug of adrenalin, causing him to tense. They turned to see one of CPT Wilson's men letting him know his men were in position outside.

Finally, they reached the underground vault. It, too, was open, with no evidence of forced entry. The same was true of the storage cases. Many were wide open with no damage to them. They immediately went to the Babylonian scroll storage case. Looking into it, Gilda cried out in anguish, "Oh, no! It's missing."

The case was wide open and empty. Mark's heart sank. Not again, he thought. They quickly scanned the floor, hoping to see it there. Nothing was found.

After slowly walking around the room and carefully examining the doors and storage cases, CPT Wilson approached the Babylonian scroll storage bin, peered inside, and stated assuredly, "This looks like an inside job given there are no signs of anyone forcing their way in here and there's no damage to the storage cases. The thieves knew this area of the museum very well and had keys to get into the locked areas and files."

Mark wholeheartedly agreed with CPT Wilson's assessment, especially given that this area was not even part of the museum open for viewing and was not easily accessible. Mark wondered if their host the previous day, Sadik Rasheed, was somehow involved—he was missing, wasn't he?

Mark recalled that Dr. Meyer had not been able to make his call last night, so Jacob Cohen did not know about their finding the Babylonian scroll. Therefore, Jacob could not have provided information to Chester. Was this theft really just a coincidence, or was it related to the missing tiles?

Mark felt ill. Each time they got close to providing proof needed to confirm Jesus' travels, it was taken from them. He erupted, "First missing tiles and now a missing scroll! The two thefts have to be related."

The others looked at Mark in silent agreement.

Finally, Dr. Meyer said, "I don't think there is more we can do here."

CPT Wilson said, "I concur. We should leave. I'll escort you back to the hotel. Then I must attend to other matters. I suggest you leave Baghdad as soon as possible. Conditions here are likely to get worse before they get better."

It would eventually be determined that the looting of the Iraq National Museum was, in fact, an inside job conducted by several of the museum staff. What the investigations never revealed, however, was that there was one outsider who participated in the theft. That one outsider now had the Babylonian scroll in his possession.

***

On April 12, 2003, the Associated Press reported that the famed Iraq National Museum, home of extraordinary Babylonian texts, sat empty except for the shattered pottery and glass littering the floor. This news sent shock waves around the world. Not only were important antiquities missing, but the looting of the famous museum became a symbol of a mistake made by the war planners.

Disappointment weighed heavily on Mark, Gilda, and Dr. Meyer, but all were happy to leave Iraq. Later that day, they returned to Jerusalem on an Israeli charter flight, arranged by Jacob on short notice.

Chapter Eighteen

If there is any religion that could cope with modern scientific needs it would be Buddhism.

—Albert Einstein

Spring 2003, Jerusalem, Israel

Back in Jerusalem for only a day, they again met with Chester Weeks and Jacob Cohen. Chester had returned to Israel in anticipation of this meeting. Gilda made a mental note of this and wondered how Chester knew to return to Jerusalem at exactly this time.

Describing events in Baghdad, Dr. Meyer informed Jacob and Chester about finding the Babylonian scroll. "The scroll was written in Aramaic and told of a traveler from the west who visited Babel and its surroundings, who was interested in religion, in peoples' beliefs, and who eventually continued traveling east. The person in the scroll was named Issa." He paused, before saying in a solemn tone, "I believe Issa and Jesus are the same person."

Utter silence filled the room. Dr. Meyer continued quickly, emphasizing, "That Jesus traveled east is consistent with the Mount Sodom Dead Sea Scrolls." After looking down for a moment, he inhaled deeply, raised his head, and said regretfully, "The bad news is the Iraq National Museum was looted the very evening after our preliminary examination of the Babylonian scroll, which was taken and is now missing."

"Missing? What do you mean missing?" Chester asked, acting surprised. He had learned about the looting the evening it happened. Upon hanging up the phone with his man in Baghdad, he had caught the first available flight to Jerusalem.

"It was taken from the vault where we examined it the day before. Whoever took it knew where it was and had keys to unlock the vault and case that held it. We suspect museum staff was involved," Dr. Meyer said.

"Why do you think Issa and Jesus are the same person?" asked Jacob, disbelief in his voice.

Reaching into his briefcase, Dr. Meyer pulled out a book and placed it on the conference room table. "See this? It is entitled *The Lost Years of Jesus: The Life of Saint Issa* written by a Russian medical doctor named Nicolas Notovitch in 1894. Dr. Notovitch based his book on scrolls found in northern India. I read this book some time ago and just yesterday scanned it prior to this meeting. In his book, Dr. Notovitch provides evidence that the person referred to as Issa was actually Jesus."

Mark picked up the book and paged through it.

"What was Jesus doing in northern India?" Jacob asked, still rather doubtful.

"Consistent with being a rabbi, he was there studying and teaching religion. But together with teaching Judaism, it appears that Jesus—or should I say Issa—took an interest in the religions of Buddhism and Hinduism."

Chester responded crossly, "That's pure speculation. There's no evidence that any of that is true. Jesus' teachings came from God!"

Seeing the incongruity in what Chester had just said, Mark simply shook his head. Chester also was speculating without evidence. Mark saw no point in arguing.

"Why would Jesus change his name?" Jacob pursued skeptically.

"I do not think he did change his name," responded Dr. Meyer. "It may have been the way the locals pronounced his name and subsequently spelled it phonetically. In Aramaic, his name was Yeshua while in Arabic, his name was Isa, sounding closer to Issa. Or his followers may have changed it. It was not uncommon for that to happen. The founder of Buddhism was originally named Siddhartha Gantama, but his followers renamed him and called him the Supreme Buddha, the Awakened One."

"Are the scrolls that Dr. Notovitch found still in India?" Chester asked in a tone of arrogance and disbelief.

"No, they are missing," responded Dr. Meyer evenly.

"What happened to them?" Gilda asked.

Dr. Meyer pulled out some notes and adjusted his glasses. "In 1887, Dr. Notovitch visited the city of Leh, capital of Ladakh in northern India. It was and is a center for Tibeto-Buddhist culture and, as it did in Jesus' time, attracts scores of Buddhist pilgrims annually. Leh is on the Indian border near Tibet in the mountains and was a bustling market along the Silk Road used by caravans of trans-Himalayan traders. It is home to the Buddhist Hemis Monastery. The Hemis scrolls, as I shall call them, were discovered by Dr. Notovitch in the monastery."

Dr. Meyer paused to clear this throat, and then continued while the group listened attentively, "Dr. Notovitch had the scrolls translated and made a record of the results, the basis of his book. As you can imagine, skeptics of Dr. Notovitch's book abounded. I was one of them. Several of these early skeptics traveled to Leh and elsewhere to confirm the existence of the Hemis scrolls. In every case, the skeptics returned convinced that Dr. Notovitch's account was correct and that the scrolls did, in fact, exist. The most recent confirmation of the scrolls was in 1925 by an archeologist who was part of a German mountain climbing expedition. At that time, the Hemis scrolls had been moved from the Hemis Monastery to the Sera Monastery in Lhasa, Tibet."

After scanning his notes, Dr. Meyer resumed, "The Hemis scrolls were last reported as missing by monks who escaped from Tibet through the mountains into northern India. The scrolls disappeared during the Chinese Revolution around 1950, presumably taken by the invading Chinese."

"If the scrolls are missing, this is a nonissue," suggested Chester gleefully. "Dr. Notovitch's account should not be believed without proof of the scrolls as back up."

"Not so fast," countered Mark, placing Dr. Notovitch's book back on the table. "Just because Dr. Notovitch copied from scrolls that no longer exist today isn't sufficient to disregard what he copied. The Ten Commandments were copied from stone tablets. Those stone tablets no longer exist, yet we—and I assume you—accept the Ten Commandments."

Mark could not help but give Chester a hard stare before continuing. "A more recent example of a missing original text is the Book of Mormon, which Joseph Smith copied from golden plates in the early 1800s. The Book of Mormon is believed by more than ten million Mormons worldwide, even though the original golden plates no longer exist. If one believes the Ten Commandments or the Book of Mormon, using similar logic, one could also believe the Hemis scrolls."

Chester sat quietly, at a loss for words, a dour expression reflecting his mood. He hated when Mark used logic he could not dispute. It happened so rarely at home—Pastor Bob never argued like this. He didn't believe in the Book of Mormon, but he never criticized Mormons, at least publically, because they were needed allies for his church's social agenda. He certainly couldn't argue against the Ten Commandments, even though he took them more as loose guidelines rather than actual hard-and-fast rules.

Instead of arguing, Chester asked a question he knew would annoy Mark, "Well, it seems convenient that your little scroll has gone missing. How in the world did you manage to lose the Babylonian scroll? You're zero for two so far in this little adventure of yours, aren't you? And now you probably want to go after another set of scrolls that we're not even sure exist?"

Chester's antics enraged Mark, but he refused to give Chester the satisfaction of showing it. He bit his lip, momentarily remaining silent.

Restraining himself, he looked directly at Chester and replied calmly, "I'm sure that the theft of the St. Sophia Cathedral tiles and the looting of the Babylonian scroll are linked. Someone obviously doesn't want us to obtain the independent corroborating evidence that would allow release of the Mount Sodom Dead Sea Scrolls."

Mark stopped for a moment, looking around the room, then he inhaled deeply before putting himself out on a limb, saying, "Chester, you're the only one I'm aware of who fits that description and has the inside information to make the thefts possible."

Before Chester could reply, Gilda quickly added, "By the way, Chester, how did you know to return to Israel at this time? How did you know we would be returning from Baghdad now?"

Red-faced, Chester snapped, "My business in Israel isn't your concern." Still agitated, he added, "With the so-called Hemis scrolls missing, there seems to me no reason to pursue them. At this point you've hit a wall and your little adventure is over." The heated words oozed out of his mouth like lava from a slow volcanic eruption.

"No," Dr. Meyer blurted. Tension filled the room as Dr. Meyer gathered his thoughts. Finally, he said, "I believe we need to go to Tibet to see what we can find. We need to visit the Sera Monastery in Lhasa, the last place the Hemis scrolls were seen, to learn what we can about them."

Given Dr. Meyer's position, Jacob felt a break from the current conversation was needed, giving everyone a chance to calm down and regroup. He slowly looked from person to person and suggested, "Why don't we take a break now and reconvene after lunch?"

Mark and Gilda looked toward Dr. Meyer, who slightly nodded. Everyone agreed. While Chester and Jacob remained, the others left the conference room.

Once the three were gone, Jacob closed the door and sat across from Chester. "Dr. Meyer appears eager to go to Tibet to follow up on these Hemis scrolls. I believe it will be difficult to stop him, with or without your financial support. Let me remind you that with your support, you will maintain some control over them; otherwise, you will lose it."

Chester thought about what Jacob said. This trip would once again occupy Mark and keep him out of the way. In the meantime, their trip could even lead to more undesired information about Jesus that Chester could remove from potential public exposure. So far, his investment had paid off handsomely and eliminated two items he believed did not conform to his viewpoint, his order of things. Another trip for the trio might be worthwhile after all.

"Jacob, you offer sage counsel. Let me think more about it over lunch. May I order a sandwich and stay in the conference room?"

"Certainly, I need to go to my office, but before I leave, I will find someone to help you." Jacob left.

***

Chester sat alone in the conference room, eating his sandwich and letting his mind wander. He leaned back in his chair and considered the cost of the trip. Money really wasn't an issue. The Iraq War had gone well, increasing contributions to his church. Who cares if some museum was looted? Now the Coalition Provisional Authority (CPA) had been formed to run and rebuild Iraq. They would take care of the situation. The CPA's ranks were being filled by people who agreed with Chester's agenda, many of whom came from politically conservative organization. Even though the president had campaigned against "nation building," rebuilding Iraq represented an opportunity to grow Chester's business.

Responsibilities for the CPA lay within the Pentagon instead of the State Department, which historically handled such situations, an arrangement Chester wholeheartedly agreed with. Prerequisites for working for the CPA were to answer the following in the affirmative: "Yes, I voted for the president; yes, I support the way the president is fighting the War on Terror; and finally, yes, I am prolife and against the Supreme Court Roe v. Wade decision." In other words, to work for the CPA, you needed to be a "good Christian." What more did one need to know in order to rebuild a simple and backward country like Iraq, thought Chester? It was all about proper order.

Chester smiled, knowing the Roe v. Wade case was code for having a prolife stance, meaning being against abortion. Chester loved the term prolife, but thought it was a misnomer. The irony of the term always made him laugh. How could anyone be prolife and support the death penalty or war? Plus, many who called themselves prolife didn't care about the babies once they were born. Little to no effort was made to help with the child's healthcare or education. After all, that would require additional taxes. "Probirth" was the term Chester thought better described his position, but "probirth" was not a good catchphrase. It certainly wouldn't generate the money that the term prolife generated in his fundraising activities. The careful selection of words was so important, especially where raising money was concerned, which was Chester's primary focus. "Activist judge" was another of Chester's favorite expressions, applying it to any judge who did not actively pursue his beliefs.

He was calming down and enjoying his sandwich. He continued thinking about selecting the right words to manipulate people and another catchphrase came to mind. He was fond of the term "intelligent design" (ID). He knew what Mark's reaction would be if he mentioned ID. ID was a term he and others helped coin to make religious-based creationism sound more scientific.

Chester supported teaching ID as science in public schools, even though he knew it wasn't really science. He was financially supporting the election of school board members throughout the country who were trying to insert ID into the "gaps" associated with the theory of evolution. If there were insufficient data or a gap in the fossil record, so that every step of the evolutionary process could not be supported, ID was there to fill those gaps. Supporting ID was a good investment because his efforts helped raise even more money, some of which he donated to, or as he preferred to say, reinvested in the ID cause. There was a good financial return on this investment. Yes, Chester continued to think, money for the trip to Tibet is not an issue.

Chester's thoughts returned to Iraq. Given their prolife position, and for that matter, ID, Chester knew that the right people were running the CPA in Iraq and things would go well. This would be another opportunity to spread the Gospel, his Gospel, to the Muslims in Iraq. Then he remembered the line in the movie *Jerry McGuire*: "Show me the money." Everything was going his way. His offshore bank accounts were larger than ever. Chester thought it ironic that he had a Swiss bank account in, of all places, the Cayman Islands.

He had only been to the Cayman Islands once to set up his accounts. The contrast of the efficient Swiss compared to the laidback nature of the locals was striking. Since opening that account, his biggest problem was making sure his wire transfers were less than $10,000 so as not to attract the attention of the government. Ever since 9/11, he had to be especially careful about how he moved money around. He hated Bin Laden for the destruction he helped cause, but the difficulties in transferring money gave him another reason to despise Bin Laden.

Chester finished his sandwich and thought about home and his most recent efforts to raise money there. Chester knew the Pentagon and the CPA needed money, and so did he, so he convinced Pastor Bob to preach on the topic of giving money to both the government and to the church. It's like "killing two birds with one stone," he thought. Of course, this needed to be effected subtly. He suggested building sermons around the statement by Jesus, "Give to Caesar what is Caesar's and to God what is God's." Caesar, in this case, meant government taxes.

Normally, Pastor Bob's flock did not like hearing about giving money to the government or paying taxes. But when tied to patriotism and defense, it worked like a charm. Chester had even suggested that his church send inexpensive care packages to the troops, and he used this hook to increase donations, only a small portion actually being used for the packages. Contributions poured in. Yes, money was no object to financing their next trip, and if it kept Mark and Gilda out of the way, so much the better. Tibet was a rugged place; maybe Mark would fall off a mountain and break more than a leg.

***

A knock sounded at the door; Chester returned from his reverie as the others once again gathered in the conference room. Everyone settled in and Jacob asked Chester, "Now that you've have had some time to think about the trip to Tibet, what have you decided?"

Chester informed them in a pious manner, "I've reconsidered, and I agree to support the trip. I believe it may be worthwhile. When do you plan to leave, and what are your travel plans, Dr. Meyer?"

"Chester, I didn't expect such a sudden agreement. What changed your mind?" asked a surprised Dr. Meyer.

"Jacob Cohen is a very persuasive man. He helped me see the good in your proposed trip." Chester seemed impatient. With his mind made up, he was ready to leave. He didn't want to spend more time in a room with Mark than necessary.

It took Dr. Meyer a moment to gather his thoughts. Referring to his notes, he said, "In addition to rereading Dr. Notovitch's book, I read about Tibet in preparation for a possible trip there. As you likely know, Tibet is part of the People's Republic of China, so we will need to obtain visas, which will take a few weeks. We can fly into China through Beijing. From there, we can fly to Golmud in Qinghai Province and then take a train to Lhasa, Tibet. By taking the train on the last leg of the trip, we can try to avoid altitude sickness. We want to be able to function at Lhasa's twelve thousand feet."

"Well, then, I guess you'll be on your way to Tibet," Chester said. "Let me know the cost and I'll wire the money for your trip when I get back home. I plan to return to the United States as soon as I can get a flight back." With that, Chester left the conference room without a handshake or a good-bye. Jacob followed close at his heels.

In the hall, out of earshot of the others, Chester turned said, "Jacob, like before, please keep me posted on when they leave and on the progress of their travels. I am particularly interested in any findings they stumble upon."

Jacob agreed and walked Chester out of the building.

Back in the conference room, Mark looked at Gilda. "Obviously, the meeting is over."

Gilda said, "I wonder what changed Chester's mind?"

"Whatever the reason," said Mark, "I don't think it's because he's benevolent. There has to be an ulterior motive."

"I agree," Gilda chimed in. "What's the saying? I think I smell a cat."

"Close," responded Mark, "but it's a rat. 'I think I smell a rat.'"

"Right ... rat, whatever. I still don't trust that man," asserted Gilda.

"That makes two of us." Mark turned to Dr. Meyer. "Concerning the trip, do you need anything from me for the visa application?"

"No, I do not think so. I believe everything we need is in the file you filled out when you worked for the Geological Survey of Israel and when we obtained your visa for Turkey. We may need a passport picture, but I will get back to you on that."

His sabbatical at the GSI seemed so long ago. Mark was about to leave, but he thought he would bring up the subject of Chester.

"Chester leaves me cold. It's not a coincidence that two pieces of evidence disappeared shortly after we discovered them. Plus, I agree with Gilda, I find it extremely odd that Chester anticipated our return from Baghdad and came to Jerusalem in order to meet with us. We need to be careful about what we tell Mr. Weeks." Mark paused. Trying to be as polite and respectful as he could, he continued, "That means, Dr. Meyer, you need to be careful what you tell Jacob Cohen."

"I agree, Mark. I have a duty to my country, but my country is not involved in the thefts; my sense is that only a few individuals are involved. I, too, suspect that Chester funds our trips in order to keep tabs on us and eliminate any of our findings. You have my word that I will provide Jacob only information absolutely necessary to continue our exploration."

"Thank you," said Mark, once again hoping his trust in Dr. Meyer was justified.

Gilda wasn't in the mood to return to her office. "Why don't we go to a cafe for a drink?" She wanted to discuss the meeting with Mark.

Mark agreed and they left.

They took advantage of the spring weather and sat outside at a street cafe and took in the warm sun over a glass of wine. Gilda drank a white while Mark enjoyed a local red. After several minutes of silence, Mark turned to Gilda and said, "I've never been to China before, let alone Tibet. Have you?"

"No, but it is a place I've considered visiting to learn more about its history."

"Speaking of China's history, why isn't that history captured in the Bible? Have you ever wondered why the Bible is so Middle East–centric?" Mark asked. "Everything seems to happen right around here, from the beginning of time until the end."

"You know, actually, I have," answered Gilda. "I know that the Old Testament is a relatively good history of the Jews, whose homeland of course was in the Middle East. Look at the New Testament; it's about Jesus' life, which also was centered in the

Middle East, at least the part of his life that we know about from the Bible. But at the time of Jesus' life, there was a whole other world out there that the Bible ignores."

"Right," agreed Mark. "There was ancient India. There was ancient China. There were the Americas. Australia. There were large populations and other religions existing at the same time as the history covered in the Bible. If God is the God of all people, why are these other people and their histories ignored in the Bible?"

"Maybe they weren't ignored by Jesus," suggested Gilda. "Maybe areas outside the Middle East are discussed in the Mount Sodom Dead Sea Scrolls, but somehow they just didn't make it into the final edition of the Bible."

"Yes," agreed Mark, "probably with help from the Council of Nicaea and similar councils."

"With luck, we'll learn more when we're in Tibet."

Gilda barely finished her sentence when a tremendous boom occurred. The noise startled Mark; he jumped and ducked almost simultaneously. His heart leaped, sending a shiver through his body. Even though the sound came from a few blocks away, he could see ripples in his wine glass.

"What was that?" He exclaimed.

"A bomb," replied Gilda coolly. "Probably a few hundred meters away." She seemed calm on the surface, but Mark sensed her anger.

"Should we go see if we can help?" Instinctively, he felt the need to do something to counteract the violence that had just disrupted the afternoon. But birds were already beginning to chirp again.

"No. It occurred too far away. By the time we get there, others will have already called for help. We will just be in the way," she explained with a bitter tone he rarely heard in her voice.

Not counting Iraq, it was the first time Mark had been anywhere this close to a bomb, and it was very unnerving. If it could happen a short distance away, it could happen where they were sitting. He began to appreciate the difficulties of living in Israel. He knew he may have to accept living under these conditions if he joined Gilda here, but for now, he was anxious to leave Jerusalem and go to Tibet. The visas to enter China couldn't come soon enough.

Chapter Nineteen

Science is organized knowledge.

—Herbert Spencer

Summer 2003, Golmud, China

After two weeks, their China visas were ready. Uncertain about the time required to obtain the visas, Mark had stayed in Israel. During this time, Gilda learned a little Chinese while Mark studied Tibetan history and geography. A day after receiving the visas, the three made the six-hour flight to Beijing. Landing, Mark watched out the window; gray-brown air pollution hung thickly over the capital city.

From Beijing, a short domestic flight west to Golmud placed them on the ground in the late afternoon, Chinese phrasebooks in hand. Starting the land excursion in Golmud, elevation of about ninety-two hundred feet, allowed them to gradually adjust to higher elevations as they traveled to Lhasa. Leaving the airport by taxi, they headed for the downtown train station.

Out the taxi window, throngs of black-haired people hustled along the streets. China obviously wasn't a mixing bowl like America, where hair color varied widely, Mark thought.

While riding, Mark shared what he learned about the city with his colleagues. Pulling out notes, he said, "This is what I found out about Golmud. It's the third largest city on the Tibetan Plateau. South of here lies the Himalayan Mountain Range. The plateau, also known as the Roof of the World, has an average elevation of about sixteen thousand feet, the highest region in the world."

Dr. Meyer added, "When I read about Golmud, I focused on health and safety issues. At these elevations, the oxygen level and atmospheric pressure are about half that at sea level. So don't exert yourselves on the first day and be cognizant of altitude sickness, which has symptoms of headaches, dizziness, fatigue and stomach upset. Also, solar and ultraviolet radiation is twice as strong here compared to sea level so use plenty of sun block. We could have flown directly to Lhasa, but going by train gives us an opportunity to see this beautiful area's landscape while we adjust to the elevation."

"And geology," Mark inserted.

"Of course," said Dr. Meyer jovially.

Their taxi ride was longer than anticipated, prompting Gilda to say, "What type of industry here supports such a large population?"

"There are salt lakes nearby," responded Mark. "In fact, the city has the largest inland salt lake in the world. The salt lakes contribute to a chemical industry that produces potassium, magnesium, and salt. I don't suppose you want to hear how the salt deposits formed, do you?"

"No," Gilda and Dr. Meyer quickly replied in unison, looking at each other and smiling.

Mark reacted with a sheepish grin and kept his geological knowledge to himself.

As the taxi pulled up to the train station, the large crowds prompted Mark to say, "All these people remind me of an article I read about the thriving tourism here. It's grown largely due to the Qinghai-Tibet Railway, the railway system we'll take to Lhasa, which is at the end of the line." He finished his comment as he retrieved his backpack from the taxi.

The Golmud train station was modern and clean. To guarantee their comfort, first-class tickets were purchased for the next train leaving early the following day. "Why not go first class?" Mark said. "After all, Chester is paying for it."

Gilda playfully pushed Mark. "You're terrible."

All three traveled lightly, carrying only backpacks. They found information at the station about nearby hotels and selected one. After checking into a small hotel and dropping off their backpacks, they went for a walk to explore the area around the train station.

It was a bustling neighborhood; there were small shops and stalls everywhere, selling a variety of wares from food to electronics. Even with the lively crowds, there was no trash on the ground. As they walked along the crowded streets, elbow-to-elbow, Mark realized they were the only non-Chinese. That fact was not missed by some who passed by and stared.

Gilda went into one of the stalls to purchase bottled water and tried the Chinese she had learned in preparation for the trip. She greeted the shop owner, saying, "Ni hao," pronouncing it "Nee Ha-OW."

The shop owner responded "Ni hao" and then said something in Chinese to his young son, who looked to be about ten years old.

The boy turned to Gilda and said, "Hello."

Surprised, Gilda responded, "Hello. Do you speak English?"

"Yes, a little," answered the boy. "We learn English in school."

Wow, thought Mark, impressed with the youngster's early command of the English language. *I wonder why children in America aren't learning other languages at such a young age? It would surely make us more competitive in a global market, which judging by the education system here in China, is one of many advantages we sorely need.*

Gilda asked for bottled water and paid in yuan, performing the transaction with the boy in English.

As they were about to leave, Mark turned to the boy and said, "I notice you speak English with an American accent. Why?"

"We have the choice to learn English with an American or British accent. Most Chinese prefer the American accent because it sounds more pleasant to us." He smiled up at them.

Gilda said thank you in Chinese, "Xie xie," which was pronounced as "she-she" and left.

The boy said, "You are welcome." Then he turned and began speaking excitedly in Chinese to his father.

As they left the shop, Mark thought it interesting that an American accent sounded better to most Chinese. To him, a British accent sounded refined, and he enjoyed listening to it.

Heading back to the hotel, along the way they found a restaurant that looked acceptable. "Acceptable" in this case meant finding something suitable on the menu they recognized and could eat. Around the room was a variety of unidentifiable dishes. Mark nodded over to a nearby table and said, "Does that look like chicken feet to you?

Gilda glanced over and saw the characteristic three toes, lightly breaded and fried. "Yes, it does," she grimaced.

Luckily, the undecipherable menu displayed pictures of food choices. Deciding to share three dishes, Gilda made the selection. She was the pickiest eater of the three, and whatever she selected would be fine with Mark and Dr. Meyer. She selected chicken, beef, and vegetable dishes. When the food arrived, the waitress placed it on a Lazy Susan in the middle of the table, making it easy to spin to the desired dish. Gilda's choices were pleasing to the palette and went well with their Chinese beer, Tsingtao.

As they were finishing dinner and enjoying a second beer, Mark brought up Chester Weeks, saying, "I understand why Chester wants to hold back the release of the Mount Sodom Dead Sea Scrolls. New information that potentially changes the traditional Bible would pass through the Christian community like a tectonic wave of about 8.5 on the Richter magnitude scale."

Gilda pushed her plate away, sat back in her padded chair, and said, "On that, I think we are all in agreement, especially if the new information shows that Jesus' teachings were influenced by Eastern religions."

Mark paused and stared at his beer on the table, picking at the label on the bottle. He added, "No one wrote down the words of Jesus at the time he actually spoke them. For years after he died, Jesus' words were passed down orally. Once written down years later, the individual writings were subsequently repeatedly copied by hand for distribution and the original writings eventually lost. We don't know exactly what Jesus said."

Dr. Meyer set his beer on the table, adding, "Some of these individual writings were eventually combined to form the Bible, which also was copied by hand. No original copy of the Bible exists; some of the oldest known Bibles were written in Greek and were eventually translated with some passages misconstrued and modified. Throughout this process, humans made decisions concerning what to include and how to make the translations. There were numerous opportunities for mistakes, omissions, or misunderstandings. We saw from the Council of Nicaea that some material was selected and other material intentionally omitted."

"I agree," Gilda joined in. "But many people believe that God supervised the Bible's compilation, that he guided those who made the decisions and copied it so there would be no mistakes."

"That's inconsistent with what's stated in the Bible," argued Mark, now leaning forward in his seat, thoroughly engaged. "The Bible says that one makes one's own decisions using free will. According to the Bible, mankind has the responsibility to exercise free will and is commanded by God to do so. Those who promote free will often refer to a passage in Deuteronomy where we are instructed to choose between life and death, blessing and cursing. Why would God give us freewill, except in compiling the Bible?"

"I don't know," responded Gilda.

The waiter came by and Dr. Meyer, who did not speak Chinese, motioned for the check.

As the waiter walked away, Mark continued, saying, "Support for free will in compiling the Bible is provided by mistakes and inconsistencies contained within it. Additional information about early versions of the Bible will help us understand what Jesus actually did and said. That is why releasing the scrolls is so important."

"Mark, I agree with you," Dr. Meyer said, leaning closer into the table. "I promise when our trip to China is over, I'll do everything I can to see that all the scrolls are released so everyone can know the truth for themselves."

By the time they left the restaurant, darkness was upon them. It felt like they could reach up and simply touch the bursting constellations above.

"Can you believe how bright the moon and stars look from here?" Gilda asked. "There are so many more stars visible than back home."

Unlike many other parts of China, air pollution in Golmud was almost nonexistent in the thin air, and the lights from the city did not compete with the bright night sky.

As they looked up, a falling star shot across the horizon. "Did you see that?" Gilda asked.

"Yes," replied Mark. "You get to make a wish."

Gilda reflected a moment. "My wish is that we find what we need and are able to keep it, guaranteeing the Mount Sodom Dead Sea Scrolls are released to the world."

With the loss of sunlight, the evening cooled despite its being the height of summer. They threw on light jackets. Mark and Gilda walked the rest of the way back to the hotel with their arms around each other. It helped keep them warm and also gave Mark a good feeling inside. Dr. Meyer enjoyed seeing young love and smiled when they showed affection toward each other.

In the small hotel lobby, before parting, Dr. Meyer suggested, "Why don't we meet at 6:30 in the morning and make our way to the train station? Our train departs at 7:30 sharp."

Leaving Dr. Meyer in the lobby, Mark and Gilda retired to their room. It was small and had twin beds. "Do you want to push the beds together?" Mark asked with a smile.

"How about if we start the evening in your bed and then I move to mine so we can get some sleep?" Gilda responded. "It has been a long day, and we have an early departure."

"That works for me. But if you get cold during the night, feel free to rejoin me," he said.

The evening started off with a bang. Unfortunately, the small bed was like a lumpy trampoline. In the middle of an intimate moment, both almost bounced off the bed. Their avoidance of the floor was short-lived as Gilda began laughing. Her giggling was contagious; soon, both were laughing uncontrollably, inching closer to the edge with each outburst. Mark was first to hit the floor, which was hard and cold. Lucky for Gilda, she landed on top of him. Climbing back under the blankets, still chuckling, they held each other tightly, mainly for warmth—the mood had passed.

Chapter Twenty

Science is the great antidote to the poison of enthusiasm and
superstition.

—Adam Smith

Summer 2003, Lhasa, Tibet

Still half asleep and groggy, they met Dr. Meyer early in the hotel
lobby. Sleep had been difficult for Gilda because of the time change—
it was five hours later in China. Mark looked at his watch and realized
it was only 1:30 AM in Jerusalem. Sleeping part of the night in a single
bed together hadn't helped. Still, the thought of that bouncy bed
brought a smile to Gilda's face.

Dr. Meyer, on the other hand, greeted them with an enthusiastic
"Good morning!" Mark and Gilda grunted something in response.
Trudging slowly behind Dr. Meyer, they made their way to the train
station. Despite the early hour, the area near the station was a beehive
of activity.

Walking along the platform next to the twenty-car train that
would take them to Lhasa, they found their first-class accommodations
near the front and boarded. They were pleasantly surprised at the
modern train car. Greeted by a conductor, they were shown to their
plush seats, which were spacious and comfortable. The car was only
about half full, and Mark and Gilda sat next to each other while
Dr. Meyer sat alone directly in front of them.

"You can have the window seat," Gilda told Mark, her eyes half
closed. "I know you want to see the terrain. I plan to sleep awhile.
Maybe we can switch later."

Their conductor, in surprisingly good English, explained that the
Qinghai-Tibet Railway was built only recently. He provided them with
oxygen masks, which were standard issue for passengers needing help
adjusting to the high altitude. He said, "Oxygen levels in each train car
are monitored, and passengers will be notified if and when to use the
oxygen masks."

Their train car, as did all the cars, had an easy-to-see digital display of the altitude, outside air temperature, train speed, and distance to the next station. Mark was very impressed with the technology.

Looking at the advanced, modern infrastructure in China, Mark said, "Many people think China is still backward in its road and rail network, but this makes some of our infrastructure in the United States pale by comparison."

Dr. Meyer said, "Prior to the railway, the only connection between Golmud and Lhasa was the Tibet Highway, a narrow, pockmarked, and windy road with many treacherously steep grades, curves, and switchbacks. Construction of the railway was controversial because some saw it as exploitation of Lhasa and Tibet by introducing increased tourism."

The literature on the train indicated that the ride on the Qinghai-Tibet Railway from Golmud to Lhasa took twelve hours. As Gilda read it, she gave Mark the highlights. "The train's early departure is designed to maximize our daylight hours so we can see as much of the Tibetan Plateau terrain as possible. We will be heading southwest, traveling at fifty-five miles per hour, and passing through areas of geological interest, landscape variety, and biological diversity. You should enjoy that, dear."

She paused, smiling sleepily at Mark, then continued, saying, "We will cross four significant mountain ranges, as well as five major rivers, including the Yellow, Yangtze, and Mekong Rivers."

Mark replied mockingly, "Thank you, dear." Then more seriously, he said, "I'm really going to enjoy this trip." Being the highest-elevation passenger train in the world was its claim to fame, but even without that distinction, the journey was unique and beautiful enough to be worth the trip halfway around the world.

"Well, I think it's bedtime for me," Gilda said, leaning her chair back and adjusting her headrest.

Half-teasing, Mark asked "Should I wake you if I see something interesting?"

Gilda tossed her head, laughing as she curled up in the seat. "It better be really interesting. I would say don't wake me for the next couple of hours. I haven't finished my beauty sleep yet." It didn't take her long to nod off.

While Gilda slept, the train pulled away from the station on time. Leaving Golmud behind, Mark could see the landscape, which was treeless and sparsely vegetated. Once out of city, there were few villages along the train's route. Majestic snow-capped mountains were visible in the distance, some with large glaciers glistening in the early sun. These glaciers, Mark knew, had built up over long periods, one snowflake at a time.

After traveling for only an hour, a breakfast service came by, offering tea or coffee, fruit juices, and baked goods with butter and jams. Gilda woke up, and they shared a light breakfast. Mark said, "Was the smell of food too irresistible?"

Ignoring his usual teasing, she replied contentedly, "It may be awhile before I eat again, so I thought I better wake up." After eating only a few bites, however, she drifted back to sleep.

Because of the grade, Mark knew the train was rising and was pleased with the oxygen supplied to their car. He continued looking out the window and saw wide valleys with streams meandering in their centers and large alluvial fans flanking the valley walls. Alluvial fans had been formed by erosion off the sides of the valleys, the accumulated sediments spreading out over the valley floors like open Chinese fans tilted at a low angle.

Extensive fields of sand dunes occupied some valleys where strong and constant winds had picked up the sand previously deposited by water and blown it into piles or dunes. Following the direction of the wind, these dunes slowly migrated across the vast valley floors, one sand grain at a time.

Gilda began to stir, and Mark gently kissed her forehead. When she was fully awake, he excitedly related the scenes he had witnessed, insisting they change seats so she could have a better view. Before sitting down after the seat swap, Mark checked on Dr. Meyer. The aisle seat next to him was vacant, so Mark asked, "May I join you?"

"Of course."

They chatted for awhile. Mark realized Dr. Meyer was enjoying the train experience as much as he. After a brief period, Mark moved back next to Gilda, who was looking out the window.

Around noon, an attendant in a black and white uniform served them lunch in their seats. While they ate their chicken, Mark and Gilda continued watching the landscape pass. The train continued southwest, and Mark noticed the countryside became greener and more populated. There were villages and flocks of sheep and yak, an animal he had only seen in pictures.

At times, the train passed close to the narrow Tibet Highway, where small trucks heavily loaded with a variety of goods could be seen. The trucks looked well worn, having taken many years of punishment from the highway. There were Buddhist monks in colorful robes walking, making their pilgrimages to the holy shrines in Lhasa. Mark had heard about the intolerance of the Chinese government to those who practiced any religion. Yet it seemed that intolerance only went so far. He saw that many Chinese practiced Buddhism with little interference from their government. He also knew from the literature he read before the trip that active Buddhist temples were located throughout China.

Mark recalled that while walking in Golmud, they had passed a Buddhist temple and stopped to watch the crowds in the courtyard. A number of people entering the temple purchased handfuls of incense sticks and lit them. Thick smoke drifted up from the burning incense and filled Mark's nostrils with a smell he found more pleasant than he expected. Upon leaving the temple, a man approached them and said hello in English. The man further said, "May I speak with you? I need to practice my English."

They spoke with him for some time, and Mark commented, "I thought your government discouraged the practice of religion. How is it that you are able to support a Buddhist temple and light incense as a religious practice?"

The man smiled with a sparkle in his eye and said, "Oh, I do not practice Buddhism. I am simply superstitious." With that, he bade Mark good-bye and walked away.

Mark concluded from this exchange that the man did practice Buddhism, but to be on the safe side, he referred to his practice as being "superstitious." The Chinese government probably thought all religion was superstitious so calling his religious practices superstitious safely played into his government's biases. *Clever*, thought Mark.

But the Chinese government's religious tolerance only went so far. The Dalai Lama, the latest in a long line of spiritual leaders of Tibet who carried the name, was in exile as a result of Chinese rule over the territory.

As they traveled through one mountain pass, the emergency warning light came on with an announcement that passengers could use the oxygen masks. A generator producing oxygen for the train cars apparently had stopped working. All three decided to comply. Mark noticed that the purer oxygen from the mask produced a nice, somewhat euphoric feeling.

"Not bad," he mused.

All returned to normal after about thirty minutes.

Mark checked with Dr. Meyer again. "How's your oxygen level?"

"I'm fine," replied Dr. Meyer.

The thought of oxygen caused Mark to think about the earth's atmosphere, and he said, "Speaking of oxygen, do you know much about the evolution of our atmosphere and why we have oxygen today?"

"No, but I bet geology is involved in this story." Dr. Meyer winked at Mark. "But you know what? I am interested, so please do tell me about the evolution of our atmosphere. But remember, I am an archeologist, not a geologist, so don't make it too technical."

Mark sat down next to Dr. Meyer. "Well, you're right about the geology part," Mark said, grinning, pleased to be accommodated. "The story begins inside our earth. Based on the analysis of energy waves generated by earthquakes and passing through the earth, we know we live on a thin crust, below which is the mantle, composed of molten rock in constant motion. Below the mantle is a core in the center of the earth. The core is a solid center with liquid surrounding it. The motion of the solid center relative to the surrounding liquid creates the earth's magnetic field, which helps maintain the atmosphere by preventing gases, like oxygen, from escaping into space. So the first step in the development of our atmosphere was establishment of the magnetic field to capture any gases that formed on earth.

"Are you with me so far?" Mark asked.

"So far, so good."

"Okay." Mark adjusted in his seat, turning more toward Dr. Meyer. "The earth's early atmosphere did not contain oxygen. We know this based on older rocks composed of minerals, which only form in a nonoxidizing environment."

He glanced back and noticed Gilda was bent forward in her seat, listening to his story. This encouraged him to continue. "About three billion years ago, bluegreen algae evolved and began to create oxygen by photosynthesis as they do today. We know this because of evidence of oxygen formation in the rocks. First, there is a fossil record of the algae found only in rocks that age and younger. Second, prior to that time, oceans were acidic and contained large amounts of dissolved iron. The iron readily reacted with the newly produced dissolved oxygen. This produced banded iron formations, a major worldwide source of iron."

The train began a long turn, and they leaned toward the window in response to the centrifugal force caused by the train's motion.

Mark continued uninterrupted, "These formations likely started out as mud deposits that continued to accumulate until all the iron in the oceans was consumed by chemical reactions, causing the iron to form a solid and fall out of the water. Only then, after all the dissolved iron was used, did oxygen start to leave the oceans as a gas and enter earth's atmosphere. This eventually led to the atmosphere we have today. The oxygen in our atmosphere allowed evolution of species that depend on oxygen, leading eventually to man. The story of evolution extends beyond biology."

Pausing to take a deep breath, he continued, "After that time, the rock evidence indicates there was oxygen in our atmosphere. This is typified by deposits known as red beds, with a rust color indicating weathering or oxidation of iron in the presence of oxygen. These red beds are only found in younger rocks, after oxygen was introduced to the atmosphere."

Dr. Meyer thought about what Mark had just told him and said, "Have there been times in the past when there was more oxygen in earth's atmosphere than we have today?"

"Good question," responded Mark, happy for Dr. Meyer's interest. "The answer is yes. One such time occurred about three hundred million years ago and was called the Carboniferous Period. During this time, carbon was removed from the earth's atmosphere by tremendous plant growth and subsequent burial, the processes that formed our present-day coal beds. This resulted in oxygen levels increasing due to all the plant life. While oxygen is excreted by plants, it's used by animals to produce energy. The additional oxygen gave insects the energy to grow to enormous size because of their unique breathing system of tracheal tubes running throughout their bodies. These are the so-called giant bugs, like dragonflies with two-and-a-half-foot wingspans we find in the fossil record from this period."

Surprised, Dr. Meyer said, "I'm glad we do not have giant bugs today. Thank you, Mark, for sharing that story with me. Geology and archeology have much in common—they both use science to sort out what happened in the past, only the past I deal with is much more recent. You might say we are forensic scientists. I can see why you are so fascinated by geology." He smiled and said, "Now every time I take a breath, I will think of the bluegreen algae ... and giant bugs."

Mark smiled, rose in his seat, stretched, and turned back toward Dr. Meyer. "I guess I'll return to my seat now. See you in Lhasa, Dr. Meyer." Mark returned to sit next to Gilda.

Gilda teasingly asked, "You weren't telling Dr. Meyer geology stories about giant bugs, were you?"

Mark's smile enlarged as he looked at Gilda. He leaned into her and kissed her lips, saying, "I thought you liked my geology stories."

Gilda, feeling warmth spread through her, smiled back and responded, "Your geology stories may drive some people up a tree, but I generally find them interesting."

"It's 'Drive some people up a wall,'" Mark said, smiling and shaking his head.

As she touched his arm, she said, "My point is your geology stories don't annoy me."

As they once again came close to the Tibet Highway, Gilda spotted a group of people on horses and camels herding sheep and bringing truck and car traffic to a standstill.

Pointing out the scene to Mark, she observed, "What a strange juxtaposition of various modes of transportation, especially given that we are observing all of this from a modern train."

Seeing the people on horses and camels, Mark said, "Jesus may well have traveled the Silk Road by the same mode of transport nearly two thousand years ago. And to think some people still travel by horse and camel in this area today. It's remarkable how some things don't change."

As they approached Lhasa, mountains could be seen in the distance. Tibet was home to some of the world's tallest mountains, including Mount Everest, the highest mountain on earth. Pointing, Gilda told Mark, "These mountains may have played a significant role in evolution."

"How so?"

Gilda describe the progression, "The Himalayas, including Mount Everest, were formed by plate tectonics when the Indian plate crashed into the Southwest Asia plate. The constant pressure between the two plates gave rise to the Himalayas, which advanced upward over millions of years and still continue today. The birth of these mountains is thought to have contributed to the monsoon climate in India and may have changed the climate in Africa. Some scientists believe the Himalayas are a major contributor to the development of Earth's cooler temperatures starting forty million years ago. In addition to becoming cooler, Africa became dryer, converting some forests into grasslands. This forced tree-dwelling primates to survive on the ground. The process of natural selection finds the optimal adjustments to new environmental conditions. To see above the grass, primates began walking on two legs over four million years ago, eventually evolving to man."

Dr. Meyer, who had been listening, turned back and said, "In other words, if it weren't for geological processes forming the Himalayas, we might not be here."

"That's correct," responded Mark jokingly. "I bet you never knew how important geology was."

Chuckling, Dr. Meyer turned forward.

At seven, the train finally pulled into the Lhasa station, which was surrounded by older buildings in stark contrast to the modern facility. The sun, nearly down, yielded to the moon and stars, once again brightening the evening sky. It was a relief to arrive. Though the train ride featured wonderful creature comforts and gorgeous views, after twelve hours it had become long and tedious. Rising from their seats, they stretched, gathered their backpacks, and left the train station.

Knowing they would arrive late, they had made reservations at a hotel near the train station. Dr. Meyer retrieved a map showing the hotel's location. "Follow me. I think I know how to get to the hotel."

The path to the hotel was uphill, zigzagging through ancient structures. At each turn in the path, spectacular views revealed intricately laced buildings silhouetted by surrounding mountains. As the temperature dropped, the cold sharpened. Trails of smoke meandered through the air as evening fires were lit. As Gilda zipped up, she declared, "I'm glad we brought our jackets." While packing for this trip in Jerusalem, it was hard to believe they would need them.

Still unaccustomed to the thin atmosphere, they stopped multiple times to catch their breaths, taking in the views before finally reaching the hotel. As he panted at one stop, Dr. Meyer asked jokingly, "Where are the bluegreen algae when you need them?"

Mark laughed, "That's a good one, Dr. Meyer." All were ready to be in the warmth of the hotel and rest after their strenuous walk in the cool night air.

The hotel was small but altogether adequate. Inside, a fire crackled in a stone fireplace, giving off warmth and a slight pleasant smell of burning wood. Best of all, a small restaurant was connected to it. Tired and hungry, they checked in and went to their rooms before dinner. Mark and Gilda's room was small, and the walls and floor were made of wood. Mark was disappointed. Once again, they had twin beds. Gilda made things worse by laughing at his disappointment.

"It's okay, dear. We can push the beds together," Gilda said sympathetically. Pushing the beds together was fairly easy given the layout of the room. They did so and remade the beds so they could dive in when they returned from dinner.

They met Dr. Meyer in the restaurant. Nothing on the menu looked familiar. They decided to just pick something and hope for the best. Mark was not sure what it was he ordered, but after his first bite, it tasted so bad that he thought it must be yak. He imagined that with a name like yak, it must taste bad. He tried to wash it down with a beer. He told the others of his suspicions.

Dr. Meyer said, "Yak actually tastes like beef. I'm not sure what you ordered, but it is probably not yak." After seeing the look of disgust on Mark's face, he added, I'm glad we are not sharing our dinners tonight." After which Dr. Meyer and Gilda laughed while Mark stared at his plate.

As he carefully picked through his food, Mark asked, "So what's our plan for tomorrow?"

"We're headed to the Sera Monastery," Dr. Meyer replied. "I have a map of Lhasa showing its location. Let's meet up tomorrow morning for breakfast and then head to the monastery," answered Dr. Meyer.

"I don't know what time the monastery opens, but I vote for sleeping in tomorrow," said Gilda. Despite her nap on the train, she still felt tired.

They all agreed and decided to meet for breakfast later than usual. They retired for the evening, and Mark and Gilda headed for their chilly and drafty bedroom. They got ready for bed and jumped in, huddling and cuddling under the covers. Their sheets were cold, but soon their combined body heat had the sheets warm. They held each other closely and drifted off to sleep.

***

At a nearby hotel, a tall, heavyset man with a scar over his right eye also was trying to fall asleep as he gasped for air in between coughing fits. Sleep was hindered by a tremendous headache booming in his temples with each heartbeat. The throbbing continued despite the handful of aspirin he had washed down with tap water that tasted like iron. Having flown into Lhasa earlier that day, he was awaiting further instructions from Chester Weeks.

Chapter Twenty-one

Doubt is not a pleasant condition but certainty is an absurd one.

—Voltaire

Summer 2003, Lhasa, Tibet

Located on the north bank of the Lhasa River and sandwiched by colossal mountains, the city of Lhasa was settled thirteen hundred years ago, long after Jesus' lifetime. The name meant "Holy Land" or "Buddha Land." The city boasted many Buddhist shrines and structures, including the grand palace where the Dalai Lama lived until his exile in 1959.

Before the Chinese invasion, the Tibetan government was nominally ruled by the Dalai Lamas, a line of Tibetan spiritual leaders. Forced to flee through the mountains into northern India, the Dalai Lama established the government of Tibet in Exile in northern India, not far from where the Hemis scrolls were originally found.

Dr. Meyer explained that the Sera Monastery was located on the east side of Lhasa and was quite a trek from the hotel where the three had spent the night. "Are you up for a long walk this morning at this altitude?"

"If you can make it, Dr. Meyer, I think we can," responded Gilda cheerfully. Being in the high foothills close to the Himalayas, the surrounding landscape was rugged. Gilda welcomed the walk in the bright sunshine after sitting on the train the day before. The view of the mountains was breathtaking. With the thin air, however, Gilda had little breath to spare.

Leaving the hotel, Mark felt a little light-headed. A strong, dry wind blew steadily. He heard, then saw multicolored flags of all sizes flapping—there were rows of short flags on single strings and lines of narrow, vertical flags on long poles, all dancing in the wind. The constant sounds produced by the wind and flags had an oddly calming effect.

A short distance from the hotel, they passed three metal wheels on spindles. "I know what these are," Gilda announced gleefully. "They're Tibetan prayer wheels."

Looking more closely, writings in Sanskrit appeared on each wheel. "That's a mantra," she explained, "that should be repeated as you spin the wheel."

Continuing to walk, Gilda spun each wheel in a clockwise direction. "That's for good karma. Hopefully, we will gain wisdom during our search for the Hemis scrolls today." The wheels clattered their song behind her.

Shaking his head, Mark said, "It's just a little ironic—a Jewish woman using a Buddhist prayer wheel to gain wisdom about the founder of Christianity. Perhaps you should cross yourself for good measure."

"You never know," she responded, smiling and continuing to walk along the narrow path behind Dr. Meyer.

Past the prayer wheels, their path became steeper. When they stopped to catch their breath, they took in the majestic mountains in the distance. While resting, Mark wanted to share some of what he had read about Tibet in preparation of their trip and asked the others if they knew the history of the area. They knew a little but were interested in what Mark had to say.

"Keep it short," Gilda teased after his comment at the prayer wheels.

Mark began, "Okay, I'll try. Tibet has an interesting history, but what may be most important to us starts at the beginning of the twentieth century. At that time, the British still occupied neighboring India, the crown jewel of their empire. The British believed Russia was trying to expand its sphere of influence, so in 1904 they invaded Tibet. At that time, the Dalai Lama was exiled to Mongolia. So even before the Chinese came along, the Dalai Lama had been exiled by our friends the British."

Mark recalled that near the end of the British Empire, the Brits had changed the geography of numerous locations around the globe. These changes in borders had led to many of the conflicts in the world today, including those in Israel and Palestine, India and Pakistan, and Iraq, where they had been just a few weeks ago.

"Anyway," continued Mark, "the British invasion of Tibet led to two important outcomes. First, a trade agreement was established between Britain, and therefore India and Tibet. This agreement established a trade connection between Leh and Lhasa, in addition to the existing Buddhist connection. Given the prominence that Lhasa had gained in the world of Buddhism, this trade agreement would have made it easy to move the Hemis scrolls discovered by Dr. Notovitch in Leh to the Sera Monastery here in Lhasa."

"And the second outcome?" Gilda inquired.

"The Chinese became concerned that the British were expanding their sphere of influence so the Chinese expanded westward into parts of Tibet. This expansion was interrupted by internal affairs in China, namely the Chinese Revolution of 1911. But it set the stage for the subsequent invasion of Tibet in 1950 by the People's Republic of China. That led to the eventual disappearance of the Hemis scrolls. So goes the law of unintended consequences. Had the British not invaded Tibet, would the Chinese have stayed out as well? Who knows?"

After Mark's story and their brief respite, the three continued their trek to the monastery. After fifty arduous minutes, with multiple stops, they reached the Sera Monastery, a series of single-story buildings on a relatively flat piece of property. In front of them, they saw a courtyard covered with a layer of gravel. A wide variety of trees and bushes were scattered throughout. By midmorning, it had warmed, and groups of monks sat outside in circles with their legs crossed. A monk stood in the center of each circle. It was evident from the movement of their hands and bodies that the standing monks were teaching the others around them. All wore the typical garb of a Tibetan monk: a red and yellow robe.

Seeing the robes reminded Mark of another inconsistency in the Bible as to what color robe was placed on Jesus by the Roman soldiers. Matthew indicated it was scarlet, whereas Mark and John said it was purple. It was remarkable that monks dressed today as they did at the time of Jesus.

Not wanting to interrupt the teaching, Mark, Gilda, and Dr. Meyer watched and waited. After a short period, one of the standing monks noticed them and approached. Explaining why they were there, they quickly learned the monk did not speak English. He turned and spoke to one of the sitting monks, who, after listening intently, rose and left the area.

The monk returned in a few minutes with a colleague, who said in good English, "Hello. How may I help you?"

Introducing themselves as scientists, they gave a brief description of their quest and asked to speak with someone who might know about the scrolls discovered by Nicolas Notovitch in Leh, India, at the Hemis Monastery at the end of the 1800s and subsequently transferred to this monastery in the early twentieth century.

Silence ensued—the monk was clearly unhappy.

Finally, the monk asked cautiously, "Why do you seek this information?"

Dr. Meyer responded politely, saying, "We hope to learn where the scrolls are and what they contained." He further explained his background and that of his colleagues.

The monk stood silent in thought, appearing unsure how to proceed, so Dr. Meyer added, "We believe these scrolls discuss a part of the life of Jesus Christ, who you may know as Issa. We have reason to believe that Jesus traveled the Silk Road to Babylon where he may have met Buddhist and Hindu missionaries. We further believe he may have continued traveling east along the Silk Road and eventually stopped at Leh to study and teach religion. The scrolls we seek may support our findings and provide additional evidence about Jesus' travels."

The monk remained perfectly still. He seemed to be absorbing this information. Dr. Meyer wasn't sure if his explanation had been understood. The monk showed no reaction. Suddenly, the monk asked them to follow him. Quietly, they walked up a few steps to a low-lying building with a covered porch surrounding it. Removing their shoes, they went inside to find a large, poorly lit room constructed of wood. The room was mostly empty with a few decorative pillows strewn about on the floor, which was adorned with beautiful, rich-colored rugs. Similar textiles hung on the walls. The monk took them to a corner of the room and curtly said, "Wait here." He abruptly turned and left.

The three stood looking around the room and at each other for almost ten minutes, awaiting the monk's return.

When he reentered the room, in his wake was a small, hunched-over elderly monk wearing glasses with thick lenses and black frames. Like most of the other monks, the old monk's head was completely hairless and egg-like.

"This is Sakya Pandita," said the English-speaking monk. Presenting the man at his side, he continued. "He was here when the scrolls were. He is the only one left who is familiar with the scrolls and has agreed to talk with you, to share his knowledge before he also passes. You may ask him questions, but he speaks no English. I will need to interpret."

Mark, Gilda, and Dr. Meyer bowed slightly toward Sakya, who bowed his head in acknowledgement and smiled, revealing several missing teeth, and looked impishly through his glasses. Sakya appeared friendlier than the other monk.

"Please be seated," the English-speaking monk said, gesturing toward the floor.

They sat on a brightly colored rug and introduced themselves to Sakya. Dr. Meyer took the lead in explaining the reason for their visit. Before they got too far into their discussion, Dr. Meyer asked if it would be acceptable for Mark and Gilda to take notes during the conversation.

"Yes," he replied through the interpreter, adding, "You must try our tea."

While Mark and Gilda retrieved notepads from their backpacks, the younger monk left. During this time, Sakya observed them in silence. The monk returned, offering them small bowls filled with a hot, milky-colored liquid. Mark hesitantly took a sip, experiencing a slightly salty taste. He inadvertently made a face. Looking up, he saw Sakya watching him. Smiling, Sakya asked through the interpreter, "Do you not like our yak butter tea?"

Mark took another sip, forcing a smile, and said, "It's good, but not what I expected. Thank you." His mind flashed back to his terrible meal he had thought was yak.

With the pleasantries over, Dr. Meyer asked if he could begin the interview. "Yes, I am ready," said Sakya through the interpreter. Mark gladly sat his tea down and grabbed a notepad. Gilda did the same.

Dr. Meyer spoke slowly, taking frequent breaks so his words could be translated. He waited to see Sakya's reaction. Sakya said nothing, even when he noted Dr. Meyer's interest in the Hemis scrolls. Sakya seemed to focus on a symbol in front of him that was part of the rug on which he sat, but Dr. Meyer was sure he was listening intently. After the brief history of their travels and findings, Dr. Meyer posed his first question: "Do you know where the scrolls are?"

"No," responded the interpreter after Sakya's very brief answer.

"Do you know what happened to the scrolls?"

"Yes."

Excited, Dr. Meyer continued.

"What happened to them?" he asked eagerly, wondering if they might be within his grasp.

"Like many of our sacred relics, they were taken by Chinese soldiers during the 1950 invasion."

Even though he suspected this was the case, Dr. Meyer felt like a balloon with its air being released—disappointment yet again.

So, thought Mark, Chinese communists have the scrolls and are keeping them from the public. Chester's attempt to keep the Mount Sodom Dead Sea Scrolls hidden was something he had in common with the Chinese communists.

"Did you see the scrolls?"

"Yes."

"Did you read the scrolls?"

"Yes."

"Can you tell us what was contained in the scrolls?"

Sakya thought about this question and seemed to be searching for the right words. Finally, he looked up and stared, one by one, at each of their faces with a sparkle in his eye. After a few moments, he began to speak. He was speaking so quickly the interpreter had trouble keeping up.

"I studied the scrolls before they were taken. They gave an account of Issa's travels and his time spent at Leh studying and teaching. It was clear to me from the scrolls that Issa and Jesus were the same person. Issa had an intense interest in all religions, wanting to understand different people's beliefs and the basis for those beliefs. In addition to learning, he enjoyed teaching, often combining common aspects of different religions into a coherent notion. Just as people do today, his followers and students would sit around him and learn from his teachings. He was an accomplished teacher."

Mark had the image of the monks in the courtyard and of the way the one lead monk taught the small group surrounding him. He wondered if the Buddhist method of teaching inspired Jesus to gather a small group of disciples or students around him and teach them outside in nature. His teaching method certainly departed from the way rabbis taught inside a temple.

Sakya continued, "According to the scrolls, some believed Issa could perform miraculous feats. He was described as a master at yoga, having an uncommon ability to control his body with his mind. He could slow his heartbeat and breathing so that to those around him, he appeared dead. After awhile, he would allow his heart and breathing to return to normal, and those who observed this said it was as if Issa had returned from the dead."

Sakya paused. Mark and Gilda looked at each other in amazement while Dr. Meyer leaned back in contemplation.

Like a landslide, it hit Mark, his brain synapses immediately firing to recall the memory of Jesus on the cross and his resurrection three days later. Had Jesus really died or had he controlled his heartbeat and breathing, slowing both, making the Romans think he was dead?

Mark had studied the crucifixion. There were very few non-Christian sources on the subject. He knew there were many uncertainties with the crucifixion, including the chronology of events, the date, the place, even the identity of those who witnessed it. The four gospels give different and varying accounts that contained discrepancies. Gospel Mark, for example, indicated that Jesus was crucified the day after Passover, whereas John indicated he died the day before.

According to the account by John, Roman soldiers pierced Jesus' side with a spear to confirm death. The spear is sometimes referred to as the "Holy Spear" or "Spear of Destiny." John said that immediately blood and water came out of Jesus' side. That the spear-pierce actually occurred had been questioned, and none of the other gospels discussed it. Certainly, a body, alive or dead, did not yield water. This aspect of the story called into question its authenticity.

Like an epiphany, Mark thought about the spear-piercing story in a new light. He knew from his readings about the crucifixion that Jesus died in less time than other crucified people. So the question again was, "Was he really dead? Or had he gone into a yoga trance, resulting in a seemingly quicker death?" Mark thought Jesus had mental and spiritual strength, and he could not image Jesus dying before others; if anything, Mark thought, Jesus would have outlasted most. So maybe he wasn't really dead. If Jesus was dead and John's account was true, then why did his blood immediately rush out? An autopsy of a dead person produces negligible blood. *In order to bleed, you need a heartbeat.* Some blood would leak from a dead body, but John's account that blood immediately rushed out, if true, suggested that Jesus had a heartbeat and was still alive.

The monk's words about Jesus being a master at yoga made Mark question Jesus' death on the cross. It may still have been a heroic act of spirituality and transcendence, but a very different one than that described in the Bible. He also thought back to the Council of Nicaea and the Arian controversy. What did Arius know about Jesus' life that caused him to believe the substance of Jesus was different from the substance of God? Did he, in fact, believe that Jesus was human, as the

Jews and Muslims believe? Did Arius have information about the crucifixion that led him to question the resurrection? It made Mark wonder all the more what the Mount Sodom Dead Sea Scrolls might say on this topic.

After a moment, Sakya resumed, "Issa, according to the scrolls, along with practicing yoga, could meditate, what you might call pray, for hours. It was not unusual for him to stay up all night in meditation. While here, he practiced Dzogchen meditation. This is a natural type of meditation practiced in Tibetan Buddhism. Issa was experienced in meditating before arriving and became proficient in Dzogchen meditation much faster than most. He was one of our best students and teachers. It was said that everyone was sad when he left."

That Jesus meditated triggered other possibilities. The night before Jesus was betrayed by Judas, he was up all night praying, perhaps meditating. Praying was more an external practice where you appealed to God. Meditation was an internal practice, a prolonged period of perfect concentration and contemplation. When perfected, Buddhists believe it could lead to a holy trance. As capable as Jesus was, it was believable that he would have perfected his concentration. Mark was gaining even more respect for Jesus and his uncommon abilities and talents.

Sakya continued, "According to the scrolls, Issa was a very good stonemason and took charge of expanding the Hemis Monastery in Leh. Some of his construction efforts at the monastery still exist there today."

Wow, Mark thought, so Jesus really was a stonemason, and a good one at that. Once again, the thought of Jesus being an amateur geologist made Mark smile with pride. And to think, he could go to Leh and see some of Jesus' work today. That was a trip Mark would make someday.

Dr. Meyer finally asked another question, "How long was Issa in Leh?"

"Issa loved Leh and the exchange of religious ideas Leh offered, but he only stayed for seven years."

"Did the scrolls indicate where he went after he left Leh?"

"Toward the end of his stay, Issa became interested in Taoism. He journeyed to where he could learn more about it. One day, Issa left with a caravan heading east. Their destination was Xi'an. More specifically, the Big Wild Goose Pagoda. Travelers to Leh told Issa about the Big Wild Goose Pagoda, which was maintained by Buddhists but had a strong Tao influence. Issa wanted to go there and continue his education. Today, the Big Wild Goose Pagoda still exists in Xi'an."

Dr. Meyer had visited Xi'an and knew it was about fifteen hundred miles northeast of Lhasa and the easternmost terminus of the Silk Road. It was established as the capital of China under China's first emperor around 200 BCE. Before that, it had been a cultural, religious, and industrial center, starting in the eleventh century BCE. It was a well-established city accessible via the Silk Road by the time Jesus would have visited there.

Dr. Meyer had no further questions. He asked Mark and Gilda if they had any. The group sat quietly, trying to absorb the information. With so much swirling in their heads, it was difficult to organize thoughts in order to think of additional questions.

Mark rose to the occasion and after several moments asked, "As I understand, you are the only one here who read the scrolls. Is that correct?"

"Yes, I am the only one left who read the scrolls before they were taken away. I cannot tell you who in the Chinese government has read them," Sakya responded sadly.

Mark continued, "Is there any other information about Issa you can tell us?"

"I read the scrolls a long time ago, and my memory is not what it used to be. I've told you what I can remember."

Mark was disappointed but realized that Sakya had last read the scrolls fifty years ago. He said, "I have one last question. Why didn't you come forward with this information?"

Sakya, with arms outstretched, said, "Look at me. Who would believe me? Without the scrolls, I have no proof of Issa's travels."

Nodding his head in agreement, Mark understood. He hungered for more information but could think of no further questions.

Dr. Meyer looked at Gilda, then Mark. Neither reacted, so he assumed the question-and-answer period was over. He thanked Sakya and the translator for their help and bade them good-bye, bowing prior to exiting.

As they were putting on their shoes outside, Gilda commented, "Sakya indicated Issa was experienced in meditation prior to arriving in India. Kabbalah meditation has been practiced by Jewish spiritual leaders for over two thousand years. Perhaps Jesus was exposed to Kabbalah before leaving Judea. The Jewish and Buddhist meditation techniques are similar."

Leaving the monastery, Mark added, "That Jesus only spent seven years in Leh means he would have spent substantial time in Xi'an, assuming he was there for the remainder of the missing eighteen years. It's fascinating that he became interested in Taoism. Tao means 'path,' and that 'path' is made up of three parts: compassion, moderation, and humility. These certainly were qualities Jesus exhibited later in life."

Dr. Meyer stopped and turned to Gilda and Mark, then said, "I think we should leave today and fly to Xi'an to see if we can pick up Jesus' trail there. I've been to Xi'an and know where the Big Wild Goose Pagoda is located."

Excited, Mark and Gilda responded in unison, "I agree."

Then Gilda added, "It feels good to complete our study here without being interrupted by storms or explosions. Hopefully, we will have the same success in Xi'an." She looked at Mark and smiled, "Maybe those prayer wheels worked."

Mark laughed and shook his head. "We can use all the help we can get."

As they walked back to their hotel, Mark brought up the subject of Jesus being a master at yoga. "Expert yogis can demonstrate controls over internal organs, blood flow, and breathing. The ability of some yogis to even stop their breathing and heart beat completely for a period of time has been demonstrated under laboratory-controlled conditions." He paused, considering the magnitude of what he was about to ask. "Is it possible Jesus did not die on the cross but controlled his heartbeat and breathing, making the Romans think he was dead?"

They stopped walking and stood, shocked by Mark's idea. Gilda and Dr. Meyer, lost in thought, did not respond. Overhead, a solitary hawk soared, catching the thermal updrafts and slowly climbing. Breaking the silence, the hawk cried out its hoarse scream.

Looking up, Mark said in a low tone, "The Gospel of John describes an event at the end of the crucifixion where a Roman soldier pierces Jesus' side with a spear to prove that he was dead and blood immediately comes out."

Gilda understood right away. "For a body to bleed profusely, the heart needs to be beating to pump the blood out."

"That's right," agreed Mark. "So if Jesus bled immediately, he may have not been dead. He may have meditated, using yoga, through the crucifixion. He died in only three hours before most crucified, which is hard to believe."

"What about his ordeal before crucifixion?" Gilda asked.

"Although he was flogged, Simon of Cyrene carried the cross for him. His suffering was no worse than others crucified. Luke even portrays Jesus as being impassive during the ordeal, not displaying any emotion of defeat."

Pausing, Mark continued, "At the end of the day of the crucifixion, Joseph of Arimathea asked Pontius Pilate, the Roman governor of Judea, for Jesus' body. Pilate granted the request, and Jesus' body was wrapped in linen cloth and laid in a tomb, a small cave."

Gilda added, "That was consistent with Mosaic Law, the ancient law of the Hebrews whereby the body had to be buried before sundown the day death occurred. Jesus' body would have been removed fairly quickly, before sunset."

"Mary Magdalene and other women saw where Jesus was buried. What if they used the linen to bind Jesus' wounds and feed and nursed him back to health? Given his wounds, it easily could have taken him three days to recover to the point where he could walk," said Mark.

Gilda added, "It is commonly believed that the guards at Jesus' tomb were Jewish. Although they were ordered to seal the tomb, the seal may have been purposely imperfect. The women could have entered the tomb repeatedly, and Jewish guards could have let them pass with food and water. Many Jews were sympathetic to Jesus, who was thought to be a resistor to Roman rule."

Mark wondered if the scenario Gilda just suggested could have contributed to Jews rejecting Jesus as the messiah, then said, "All four gospels report that several women were the ones to find Jesus' tomb empty. Women were the first to announce Jesus' resurrection. Had they been nursing him, it makes sense they would be the first to learn of his exit from the tomb. But why would they have called it a resurrection?"

Gilda thought a moment and answered, "A recently found stone tablet predating Jesus' birth contains the concept of bodily resurrection after three days. The tablet was found in Israel, and the story is believed to be a metaphor for the redemption of all Jews. This story, if widely known, could have given the Jewish women the idea for the resurrection."

"That's possible." Mark continued his thoughts, saying, "The disciple Thomas doubted the resurrection, gaining the name Doubting Thomas. He was only convinced after touching Jesus' wounds, but this event occurred after the resurrection and doesn't prove that Jesus actually died. Jesus returned home to Galilee, perhaps to say his good-byes. According to the gospels, Jesus appeared on different occasions during a forty-day period after the resurrection. Why did he wait forty days before leaving? What was he waiting for, perhaps a caravan heading east or a ship heading west? The question I have for you, Dr. Meyer, is any of this discussed in the Mount Sodom Dead Sea Scrolls?"

Dr. Meyer looked from Mark to Gilda. Catching their eyes, he said emphatically, "There is nothing in the Mount Sodom Dead Sea Scrolls that would lead me to believe Jesus did not actually die on the cross. That Jesus was a master at yoga is interesting new information that can lead one to all sorts of speculation. But as far as I know, there is no documentary evidence in the scrolls that contradicts the New Testament version of the crucifixion and resurrection."

Dr. Meyer hesitated adding, "It is interesting, however, that the Gnostic gospels from Nag Hammadi, Egypt, suggest an Eastern religious influence on Jesus and that he did not die on the cross as traditionally described.

"There is one other thing that may call the resurrection into question," Dr. Meyer said. "I didn't think anything of it during our translation of the scrolls, but the account of the Gospel Mark omitted the final verses describing the resurrection. This omission is consistent with other early copies of the gospels, such as those found at St. Catherine's Monastery near Mount Sinai, Egypt."

"What does that mean?" Gilda asked. "Were the verses describing the resurrection subsequently added by another?"

"It is unclear," responded Dr. Meyer. "But that is what some have concluded."

Gilda remarked softly, her voice trailing off, "This is starting to feel like a conspiracy theory." With that said, the conversation ended.

Mark felt the issue was unresolved. There was the Arian controversy, the Gnostic gospels, and now the insight about Jesus being a yogi. Did Arius's writings suggest Jesus didn't die on the cross? Were his documents destroyed by the bishops at Nicaea to conceal the truth about the crucifixion? Now there was the information that Mark's Gospel was subsequently altered to include the resurrection. Did Saint Mark fail to discuss the resurrection because he knew it didn't actually occur? Maybe they would learn more in Xi'an.

As if reading his mind, Gilda said, "I agree with Dr. Meyer. Let's go to the Big Wild Goose Pagoda and continue our investigation there."

They returned to their hotel, hastily checked out, and walked to the train station. From there, they took a taxi to the Lhasa airport and bought tickets on the next flight to Xi'an. The flight took about three hours and would arrive in Xi'an by evening. Mark thought, *With our snap decision, no one in Israel or the United States knows our itinerary or destination. Chester cannot foil our plans this time.*

Chapter Twenty-two

Judge a man by his questions rather than by his answers.

—Voltaire

Summer 2003, Xi'an, China

During the flight to Xi'an, Dr. Meyer described his previous visit to the former Chinese capital. "I attended a conference in Xi'an. As part of that trip, I toured many of the historic landmarks and am somewhat familiar with the city."

"Did you go to the Big Wild Goose Pagoda?" Gilda asked.

"No, but I believe it is downtown and easy to reach," Dr. Meyer replied.

Approaching the airport, Mark peered through the window to see the large, eight-million-person city below in a valley surrounded by low, green mountains. Xi'an was in a bowl with thick gray-brown air pollution hanging over it. Coming from Lhasa's clear sky, the air pollution seemed even more dramatic.

The Xi'an international airport was, as Mark had begun to expect, new and modern. He went to the hotel phone bank and booked rooms at the Hyatt Regency Xi'an. Next they grabbed a taxi.

The valley surrounding Xi'an was mainly farmland. Dr. Meyer said as they drove by fields, "This area produces a significant amount of food for China."

The countryside near the airport had few people, but the change was striking as they approached the city. Xi'an, a very active, lively city, had all the traffic problems that come with modern society. As the sun lowered on the horizon, the taxi entered a twenty-foot-thick gate through a high ancient brick wall.

"Another walled city," Gilda observed. "A reminder of mankind's nature to fight, persisting throughout history."

Located within the ancient wall, which surrounded the historic city center, the Hyatt was a few minutes away. The hotel, bounded by dense urbanization, had a large, attractive, and inviting open area outside the front entrance.

A Western-style hotel, it had a spacious, warmly decorated lobby and a modern restaurant. Mark was amazed at all the people behind the reception counter—there must have been five or six staff greeting newcomers. Labor must be cheap, and providing jobs appeared to be a priority, thought Mark, who was ready for the comforts of a well-known hotel chain after his experience in Tibet.

Checking in, they decided to meet for dinner later. Mark and Gilda went to their room. Although a bit worn, it was very clean, and best of all, it had a queen-size bed. Mark was happy. He dropped his backpack and jumped onto the bed, motioning Gilda to join him.

She did, jumping on and straddling him. Looking down, her long, black hair formed an intimate curtain around their faces. Smiling, she asked, "Is this bed more to your liking?"

In answer, he pulled her head down and kissed her.

They were almost late for dinner. The restaurant where they met Dr. Meyer was a large open area with buffet stations in the middle. The three sat in a booth and considered their many options for food, ranging from Chinese to Western. Rather than partake of the buffet, they ordered from the menu.

Mark declared meekly, "I know this is going to sound tacky, but I'm in the mood for a cheeseburger and fries. Sometimes I get a craving for a burger, especially after whatever it was I ate in Lhasa." He made a face.

"You're right," responded Gilda. "Wanting a burger and fries in Xi'an is tacky."

But then she decided on a chef salad, which Mark pointed out also wasn't Chinese. Dr. Meyer was the only one to eat local food.

The waitress took their orders, and Mark asked for a French burgundy white wine that would go well with Gilda's salad and he thought would be a reasonable complement to his and Dr. Meyer's meals.

When the requested wine arrived, Mark tasted it. Upon his approval, the waitress poured it for the others. Dr. Meyer held up his glass, "To success at the eastern end of the Silk Road." They clinked glasses. Dr. Meyer went on, "Last time I was here, I learned that Xi'an is the birthplace of the ancient civilization in the Yellow River Basin and has been inhabited for over three thousand years. Xi'an was the first capital of the ancient Chinese empire under the Qin Dynasty in about 200 BCE when the first emperor consolidated neighboring states under his rule."

"It's amazing that Xi'an has existed for so long and was connected to the west via the Silk Road during much of that period," Gilda observed as she watched some of the other guests. "I see from some of the beautiful and colorful silk dresses around the room that silk is still very popular here."

Dr. Meyer and Mark followed Gilda's gaze and observed the silk dresses to which she referred and the petite, well-proportioned figures they adorned. Dr. Meyer continued knowingly, "That impressive wall we passed through was initially constructed beginning around 600 CE using earthen materials. It was rebuilt in the 1500s with the brick we saw today. It is about forty feet tall, with a wide path at the top extending over eight miles."

This made Mark think about the wall that surrounded Iznik, Turkey, where they had begun their search. It seemed like such a long time ago. Since then, they had traveled to Baghdad, Iraq, and Lhasa, Tibet, and now here they were in Xi'an, China.

"Isn't Xi'an the location of the famous terracotta warriors?" Gilda inquired.

"Yes, it is," answered Dr. Meyer. "The life-size, terracotta soldiers were buried almost twenty-two hundred years ago to protect the first emperor of China. They have been partially excavated in a number of large pits. In one pit alone, there are estimated to be about six thousand warriors, including archers, foot soldiers, and cavalrymen, each one distinctly different from the next. It is truly an impressive archeological site, and the excavation continues."

Mark, familiar with the history of finding the soldiers, added, "The terracotta warriors were discovered in 1974 when a local farmer, drilling a water well, encountered large pottery fragments. You might say that if it weren't for groundwater, the terracotta warriors may not have been discovered."

Both Gilda and Dr. Meyer groaned loudly.

Fortunately for Mark, at that moment, their food arrived.

Mark jokingly said, "Okay, for that I won't tell you about the clay that was used for the terracotta warriors."

Dr. Meyer and Gilda smiled, then Gilda said, "That's a relief."

Undaunted, Mark savored his cheeseburger. Being able to catch one's breath was easier here than in Lhasa and added to their enjoyment.

They ordered coffee and continued their discussions. Mark asked Dr. Meyer nonchalantly, "Have you reported to Jacob?"

"Not yet. I want to see what we find out tomorrow before I inform him where we are and what we are doing. Right now," he said, pausing to stir his coffee, "I would prefer that Chester not be aware of our activities."

Relieved, Mark said, "I've been thinking about Jesus' interest in the Eastern religions of Taoism, Buddhism, and Hinduism. When I was a child, I remember being confused over the way God was portrayed in the Old Testament versus how he was portrayed in the New Testament. I asked my pastor why God had changed from being a vindictive and mean-spirited God in the Old Testament to a kinder, gentler God in the New Testament. His response was that God had not changed; man's perception of God had changed."

Mark took a sip of coffee before saying, "Now, based on what we've discovered, it seems to me that maybe Jesus' perception of God changed. What I mean is that in his travels, Jesus was influenced by Eastern religions promoting self-awareness and a loving kindness. This influence altered his religious views. If he is the same as God, then God's relationship with mankind changed. Jesus, hence God, displayed a loving kindness."

Pausing, he continued, "The message from God in the Old Testament is 'Accept my love or I will damn you to hell.' The message of Jesus is one of compassion, forgiveness, and love. Jesus' message in the New Testament is 'Turn the other cheek' in response to aggression. This message is consistent with the teachings of Eastern religions."

"Mark," said Dr. Meyer as he finished his coffee, "that is the point made in Dr. Notovitch's book on Issa. He wrote that Jesus was influenced by Eastern religions. What he teaches in the New Testament represents a cross pollination between his traditional education and teachings in Judaism and what he learned from Eastern religions."

"Jesus may have found the complete opposite of his knowledge of Judaism in his study of Taoism here in Xi'an," suggested Mark. "Taoism has no dogma, no ritual, and no mythology. It stresses the unity of humanity and the universe—being one with nature. There is no need for a physical structure, such as a temple, church, or mosque, in which one has to gather to worship God. It is interesting that Jesus' sermons were delivered outside the confines of a physical structure. This may have been a Tao influence. By the time of Jesus' life,

Taoism was a pervasive part of the Chinese psyche, so Xi'an would have been an appropriate place for Jesus to come and study. In China, there was a convergence of the Taoist and Buddhist religions and the development of the concept of Zen."

"You know," said Gilda, "I've never been sure what 'Zen' means ... do you know?"

Mark organized his thoughts and responded, "One goal of Zen is to lead a life in harmony with nature, which may have inspired Jesus to be more in touch with his environment. There are some Christians who now interpret the New Testament to mean that one should be more environmentally conscious. This focus on nature by Jesus could have been a Tao influence."

A large group walked by their booth, heading to a table further back in the restaurant. Their laughter and talking interrupted Mark's discourse. When they passed, he continued, "Zen is the pure condition of life, free of constraints, beliefs, and doctrines. One must release preconceptions, negativity, biases, and doubt to be prepared to accept enlightenment. In other words, it requires the ultimate in open-mindedness."

He pressed on, "For that reason, a powerful imagery in Taoism is water. Remember that Jesus used water for baptism, and baptism is analogous to a rebirth. At birth and presumably rebirth, one has unconditional receptivity and is prepared to accept enlightenment. The coincidences of these Christian traditions with Taoism are striking. There seems to be a connection with what's in the New Testament and what Jesus may have learned from Eastern religions."

Gilda immediately objected, saying, "Wait a second. There also is an ancient Jewish ritual involving submersion in a water pool, called a mikvah, and Jesus would have been aware of this ritual. He didn't need Taoism to learn about submersion in water. The mikvah usually was a natural body of water where a person immersed herself or himself to become pure prior to a significant event. Most frequently, it was used by married women who were readying themselves for sex, which, I think you will agree, has something to do with birth as opposed to rebirth." Gilda ended her comment with a big smile.

Once again, Gilda had grounded Mark using her knowledge of Judaism. He yielded, "You're correct, Gilda. It seems likely that Jesus borrowed from Eastern religions, but he certainly had many beliefs and traditions from Judaism." He added, half jokingly, "Your comment is very Zen-like."

"I'm glad you have an open mind," she said. "You know, I'm still not sure what Zen is. Your explanation was very nebulous. Why do you know so much about Taoism anyway?"

"I became interested in it a few years ago and read several books on Taoism and its relationship to Buddhism. Taoism is concerned with the dynamic balance between yin and yang, two opposites, often interpreted as good and evil, traits we all possess. Jesus understood this balance, teaching that God is good, and the Devil is obviously bad. Have you ever wondered why the almighty God did not simply destroy the Devil? It would disrupt the balance. Without evil, what is the meaning of good?"

Mark polished off his coffee. Gilda had already finished. The waitress came over with the check.

When she left, Mark returned to the topic of Buddhism. The wine seemed to have loosened his tongue more than normal. "Buddhism also appears to have had an effect on Jesus," he said. "Buddha was an advocate of the poor, and his teachings, or dharma, supported love and compassion to others. In Jesus' Sermon on the Mount according to Matthew, or his Sermon on the Plain as Luke conflictingly refers to it, Jesus lists his blessings, with the first one being 'Blessed are the poor in spirit.'

"Like Buddha, Jesus was an advocate for the poor and preached love and compassion. Buddha was the son of a king, but gave up all his riches. Jesus said it is hard for a rich man to enter the kingdom of heaven ... it is easier for a camel to go through the eye of a needle. Jesus preached radical change to the poor who were oppressed physically and spiritually by the Romans. Jesus' new message, breaking from traditional teachings, is consistent with the message in Buddha's dharma. Plus, both men helped the sick and disenfranchised, giving them hope for a better life. The similarities between the teachings and actions of the two men seem clear."

As he finished, another idea occurred to Mark. "Let's assume Jesus incorporated ideas from Buddhism, Hinduism, and Taoism. That would have been akin to the early Hebrews borrowing tales from earlier religions, like the story of Babylonian Job and the Ten Commandments from the Egyptian *Book of the Dead*. The Eastern religions predated Christianity and are considered by Christians to be pagan religions, but if the stories and ideas have value to Jesus' message, why not utilize them?"

Dr. Meyer responded, "Mark, what you say makes sense. It is consistent with Dr. Notovitch's book and the Mount Sodom Dead Sea Scrolls. Perhaps we will learn more at the Big Wild Goose Pagoda tomorrow. I think we should meet for breakfast, then go to the pagoda."

Agreeing, they separated for their rooms. Mark went through the motions of getting ready for bed, but his mind was preoccupied with Jesus' life and on the next day's prospects. They were approaching what Mark thought was the end of Jesus' travels. Maybe they, too, were reaching the end of their search.

Chapter Twenty-three

We don't actually have the original writings of the New Testament. What we have are copies of these writings, made years later—in most cases, many years later. Moreover, none of these copies is completely accurate, since the scribes who produced them inadvertently and/or intentionally changed them in places.

—Bart D. Ehrman, *Misquoting Jesus*

Summer 2003, Xi'an, China

The Big Wild Goose Pagoda, located in the Da Cien Temple complex just outside the city wall, was about two and a half miles away. Dr. Meyer sat in the front of the taxi while Mark and Gilda squeezed into the back, with barely enough room for Mark's backpack. As they crept along at glacial speed in the morning rush-hour traffic, the three sat quietly lost in their thoughts, observing the street.

Dr. Meyer broke the silence, pointing to the right and saying, "There in the distance is the pagoda." It stood tall within the temple complex, surrounded by an urban environment—densely packed streets with a cacophony of noise and constant commotion.

Approaching the pagoda, they glimpsed other temple features. Within the complex, a small park, an island of greenery, offered a welcomed escape from the hustle and bustle of the city. In the middle of the park stood a simple water fountain surrounded by a white stone footpath with the stations of the compass. Seeing the greenery, Gilda observed, "That park has good feng shui, providing a pleasant and energizing escape from the city."

Directly in front of them, the pagoda loomed large, a seven-story brick structure. It was constructed out of seven squares, stacked one on top of the other. Each higher box had wide eaves but was slightly smaller than the one below, like a big, square, multilayer wedding cake, thought Mark. Arched entranceways adorned all four sides of each story, and on top was a roof that tapered to form a high point. It was a simple but grand masterpiece of Buddhist construction.

As the taxi crept closer to the pagoda, Mark opined, "Walking may have been faster."

Finally arriving close enough, they exited the taxi at the curb of a busy street and walked the rest of the way. Monks with shaved heads stood nearby wearing maroon robes that wrapped around their bodies in an intricate manner. On the street, several tourists snapped pictures of the popular attraction. A sign in several languages requested that pictures of the monks not be taken. They passed the sign and entered the grounds of the pagoda.

Monks scurried to and fro performing a variety of tasks. Just as in Lhasa, the three searched the faces of the monks to see if any looked their way. Dr. Meyer took the lead and approached one of the young monks and asked for someone who spoke English. With some difficulty, he made his request understood, and the monk disappeared inside the pagoda.

They waited a short time, continuing to observe the monks and their surroundings. The young monk returned with an older one in tow. "Do you speak English?" Dr. Meyer asked of the older monk.

"Yes," he replied politely. "How may I help you?"

"We would like to talk to someone familiar with the early history of this pagoda."

"You are in luck," responded the elder monk. "I am that person."

They all introduced themselves. The elder monk's name was Naku Chu. He said, "You may call me Naku." He was short and wiry, reminding Mark of Gandhi without glasses.

"Thank you, Naku," said Dr. Meyer. "You may call me Amos."

Mark and Gilda looked at each other with raised eyebrows. As long as they had been with him, they always addressed him as "Doctor Meyer."

Dr. Meyer continued, "We would like to explain why we are here and ask you some questions. This could take an hour or two. When would be a good time for us to meet with you?"

"Actually, Amos, I am free now if that is convenient for you."

"That is very kind of you. Meeting now is fine."

"Follow me, please. Would you care for tea?"

"Yes, please," the three replied in unison, Mark hoping it would not be yak butter tea. Removing their shoes, they followed Naku inside the pagoda.

The inside was modern and well lit. The wooden planking on the floor creaked as they walked across it, and the pagoda smelled musty.

The walls were painted with red symbols and covered with framed photographs of monks and the pagoda itself. Naku led them to a low table, where they were invited to sit on colorful rugs. Naku said something in Chinese to a nearby monk, who left, presumably, to get the tea. Naku sat with them in a cross-legged, straight-backed lotus position at the table, and soon the tea arrived. To Mark's relief, it was green tea. As before, Mark and Gilda prepared to take notes and let Dr. Meyer lead the discussion.

"Please, why don't you start?" suggested Naku to Amos.

"Our story begins in Israel about a year ago, when Mark and Gilda found ancient scrolls describing the life of Jesus Christ—in particular, the eighteen years of Jesus' life not discussed in the Bible. These scrolls indicate that Jesus traveled east along the Silk Road, apparently wanting to visit locations discussed in the Old Testament. He journeyed to the city of Babel, near present-day Baghdad. We found additional evidence, another scroll, of Jesus' trip to Babel in Baghdad's Iraq National Museum, but that scroll was stolen in the midst of our investigation. This scroll and an 1894 book by a Dr. Notovitch indicate that from Babel, Jesus traveled to Leh in northern India. We hypothesized, based on information in these documents, that Jesus met Buddhist and Hindu missionaries traveling the Silk Road and became interested in those religions. Furthermore, we believe that while in Leh, he studied Buddhism and Hinduism at the Hemis Monastery for approximately seven years. While there or perhaps before, Jesus was given the name Issa."

Dr. Meyer paused, letting Naku process this information, and then he said, "Dr. Notovitch's book was based on scrolls found in Leh that he had translated. Those scrolls, which we refer to as the Hemis scrolls, are missing and presumed taken by the Chinese government. They were last seen in Lhasa, Tibet, where we were yesterday. We spoke with a Buddhist monk there at the Sera Monastery. The monk had read the Hemis scrolls before they were taken and learned from them that Jesus—or Issa—became interested in Taoism and left Leh, again traveling on the Silk Road and arriving in Xi'an. The monk told us that Jesus came here to this pagoda to study Taoism. As you know, this would have occurred about two thousand years ago. That is why we are interested in the early history of your pagoda."

Dr. Meyer paused, taking a sip of tea, and said, "We hope you can tell us what you might know of this story and perhaps add to it."

Naku sat, quietly absorbing Dr. Meyer's history of Jesus' travels. His long silence made Mark, Gilda, and Dr. Meyer anxious. Finally, he replied, "I have heard legends about such a person coming to study and teach here. What is interesting about these stories is that the religious man in the legends left Xi'an, but returned years later to continue his studies and teachings. He stayed in Xi'an until the end of his life, which was well into his eighties, an old age for that time. The person in these legends is believed by some to be Issa, whom you know as Jesus."

Mark was stunned. His mind raced. Could Jesus have left Jerusalem after the crucifixion and returned here? Based on his discussions with Dr. Meyer, he knew the Mount Sodom Dead Sea Scrolls did not support an alternative to the crucifixion. Still he wondered if it were possible that Jesus meditated through the crucifixion, survived, and returned to Xi'an to continue his religious work. Before Mark could ask any questions, Naku continued.

"I have read your Bible and know about Jesus. Perhaps it would help if I told you the history of our pagoda. It has served as a center for religious teaching and study for more than two thousand years. It was first built in about 100 BCE, so it would have existed during the time of Jesus. In the beginning, it was a smaller structure with only five stories. The focus then was Taoism, but with time, Buddhism became more popular. In early 600 CE, the pagoda was destroyed by an earthquake.

"In 652 CE, the pagoda was rebuilt by an important Buddhist leader, Xuanzang. Xuanzang's story is similar to the one you just told of Jesus. He also traveled the Silk Road, only starting in Xi'an and traveling west. He, too, went to northern India to study and teach. He was in Leh at some point, but this was some five hundred years after Jesus. Like Jesus, Xuanzang was away exactly eighteen years, traveling to many countries.

"Returning to Xi'an, he was a major force in expanding Buddhism in China, where he taught our religion. He brought back Buddha relics and numerous documents on Buddhism, which are housed here in the Big Wild Goose Pagoda. Xuanzang eventually wrote a book about his journeys entitled *Pilgrimage to the West*. The similarities in his story and travels are a mirror image of Jesus' travels. The symmetry is striking."

Naku paused, lost in contemplation. He poured more tea, then continued his story, "Because of Xuanzang, this pagoda houses many manuscripts related to Buddhism. Prior to Xuanzang, it contained manuscripts related to both Taoism and Buddhism, but many of those were destroyed during the earthquake and subsequent fire that damaged the original pagoda. There are a few rooms below ground where some older materials survived the earthquake. For superstitious reasons, those rooms were left as they were after the earthquake, and the new pagoda was built on top. It was thought to be symbolic of a rebirth. That area of the pagoda is somewhat dangerous and restricted because of loose rocks forming the walls. Very few of us go into that area. I am one of the few monks here who has access and goes periodically to those underground rooms."

Naku paused again, organizing his thoughts before proceeding.

"On one of my trips to that basement area, I discovered a scroll that may be from the timeframe when Issa was in Xi'an. The scroll is contained in a terracotta jar with a lid. I removed the lid and slipped the scroll partially out of the jar, enough to see that it was in very poor condition. I observed the text was written in Chinese. I saw writing on the edge and I recall the name Issa written in Chinese characters. For fear of damaging the scroll, I did not try to read more than what was on the edge."

Gilda gasped slightly. Dr. Meyer tried to control his excitement and asked, "May we visit that area and see the scroll you're talking about?"

Naku hesitated. "As I mentioned, it is a somewhat dangerous area, but your investigation is important so I can make an exception and take you down there myself. I just want to make sure you are aware of the potential danger. Are you sure you want to take the risk?"

Without hesitation, all three replied an overwhelming, "Yes!"

"All right," he continued. "We will need flashlights. The subterranean area has no power. Give me a few minutes to prepare, and I will lead you to the scroll. You should retrieve your shoes."

As they were putting on their shoes, Naku returned with flashlights and asked them to follow him. They moved to a central hallway lined with yellow statues and turned left, heading toward the back of the pagoda. They reached a door on the right at the end of the hall. Naku inserted an old-fashioned, large, metal key into the lock and opened the door. Following Naku into a small room, they came upon another locked door on the opposite side. Jingling his keys, Naku found the right one and unlocked the door. As it creaked opened, Naku shined his flashlight on a spiral staircase leading down into darkness.

The metal steps were narrow and slightly damp with humidity. The staircase had a small railing that looked unstable.

With flashlights illuminating the way, they proceeded down the steep and narrow stairwell, spiraling precipitously downward. Bolted loosely to the wall, the stairwell wobbled with each step into the subterranean darkness. Bringing up the rear, Mark stepped cautiously behind Dr. Meyer. About midway down, Dr. Meyer slipped on a wet step. Mark tried to catch him but missed. Dr. Meyer collided with Gilda, who was below him, and they both started to fall. Gilda caught herself, dropping her flashlight in the process. Leaning into Gilda's back, Dr. Meyer was able to regain control.

Embarrassed, he said, "I am so sorry, Gilda. My foot just slipped, and I was not holding on as well as I should have been. Thank goodness you caught me. I stress health and safety, and I'm the one who slipped. Did I hurt you?"

"I'm okay, Dr. Meyer, glad I could help," Gilda responded, trying to reassure him. Thankfully, she had just paused, not wanting to bump into Naku, and was holding tightly onto the railing when Dr. Meyer fell into her. Dropping her flashlight and grabbing the handrail with her other hand had stopped the fall just in time. She felt a flash of pride, which quickly faded under the realization of the role luck had played.

After the near mishap, everyone took special care stepping down the steep staircase, making sure to hold on tightly to the railing. As they descended, a musky odor penetrated Mark's nostrils.

At the bottom of the stairs, Gilda retrieved her undamaged flashlight. Natural rock and tight clay lined the basement, which was about fifteen feet below the first floor. Large wooden beams positioned overhead supported the ground-level floorboards. The basement floor contained debris, including several boulders, and a heavy layer of dust. The jagged boulders strewn about had fallen out of the walls, along with dust from the fine clay matrix that had been between boulders. On the wall, Mark could see gaps between the rocks and clay, suggesting that the rocks were not firmly held in place. Naku was correct, thought Mark, this was not a safe place. Except for the light from the flashlights, it was pitch black. Their eyes slowly adjusted.

Following Naku across the large room, they picked their way around boulders and into a smaller room, one of several, that was crudely dug into the rock and clay. The walls were uneven, the ceiling low. In the smaller room were many terracotta jars side-by-side on the floor. Naku carefully searched, selected one jar, and picked it up. He turned to them, saying, "This is the scroll I told you about."

He squatted, then gingerly placed the jar on the floor between them and cautiously removed its lid.

Naku instructed them, "Please do not shine your flashlight directly on the scroll for I fear the light could damage it."

Naku carefully removed the scroll partially from the jar. Through the low, indirect light from the flashlights reflecting off the walls and floor, Mark could just make out the writing on the scroll. Pointing to Chinese characters, Naku said, "This is the name Issa."

Dr. Meyer asked, "Can you unroll it and translate more of the scroll for us?"

Naku refused to unroll it because of its fragile and damaged condition. "Any further work on this scroll needs to be performed under laboratory conditions to minimize damage."

"Why haven't you already performed the laboratory analysis?" Dr. Meyer asked politely.

Naku looked at each one of them carefully before answering. "That type of analysis requires the involvement of my government. You indicated earlier that you suspect the Chinese government took the Hemis scrolls. I fear that the involvement of my government with this scroll could lead to its disappearance as well. I have chosen instead to keep the scroll concealed here for its protection."

"May I examine the terracotta jar itself?" Mark asked.

"Yes, of course."

Mark lifted the jar and examined the outside. It was about a foot tall and made out of sandy clay. Holding the jar, some sand grains could be removed by rubbing.

"Can you remove the scroll entirely so I can examine the inside of the jar?" he asked. "You wouldn't need to unroll it."

Naku reluctantly agreed and carefully removed the scroll.

Mark then slowly slipped his hand into the wide-lipped jar and felt around. He cautiously moved his hand deeper into the jar, unsure of what he might find. On the bottom, he felt something. It was loose, fine sand, likely weathered from the inside of the jar or introduced at the time the jar was made. He had an idea.

He grabbed his backpack, removing a small metal soil sample container with a screw cap. "Naku, may I take a sample of the sand that's on the bottom of the jar?"

"Sand? I didn't even notice there was any. Yes, you are most welcome to take a sample."

Mark asked Gilda for her assistance. She held up her flashlight so he could see. He uncapped the soil sample container. With the assistance of the indirect light from the flashlight, Mark slowly dipped the container into the jar and carefully scooped up some fine sand. He immediately sealed it with the screw cap.

Naku carefully returned the scroll to the terracotta jar, capped it, and returned it to the location where it was when they entered the room.

Dr. Meyer asked, "Would you permit us to take the scroll out of the country and analyze it properly?"

"I do not think so. It is a treasure of our pagoda," Naku said, shaking his head. Looking at the three scientists' faces, he added, "But I will take your request under consideration. I have shown you the scroll because I believe it is important and could end up being lost forever. The quest you have undertaken has moved me, and I am sympathetic to your cause. But I am reluctant to give up protection of the scroll."

Dr. Meyer tried to reassure Naku, saying, "I understand your concerns and promise you we will take every precaution to ensure the scroll's safety. Let me make some phone calls and see what I can arrange for the scroll's transport. May we return and meet with you tomorrow?"

"Yes, that would be fine."

Naku headed back toward the larger basement room and to the stairs. The others followed him in silence, each wondering what promise the scroll offered.

They retraced their footsteps out of the basement, taking special care with the steep steps of the spiral staircase.

Back on the main floor of the pagoda, Mark recalled the tiles at the ruins of the St Sophia Cathedral with the number eighteen on them. Given that both Jesus and Xuanzang traveled for eighteen years, he asked Naku, "In Buddhism, is there anything special about the number eighteen?"

"Yes," responded Naku, stopping in the hallway to explain. "There are eighteen dharmas that a Buddha must possess. Dharmas are universal truths that underlie all physical and mental domains.

"In addition," said Naku, pointing to two rows of figures lining the pagoda hallway, "these yellow figures are found in most Buddhist temples. They are called Lohans, the historical followers of Buddhism who have achieved full spiritual fulfillment. These followers have reached nirvana or complete bliss, delight, and peace. If you count these figures, you will note there are eighteen of them. In China, including Tibet, Buddhist temples contain eighteen Lohans, whereas Buddhist temples in other countries have only sixteen."

"Why is that?" Mark asked.

Naku paused before answering. Finally, he said softly, "There are legends that the two additional Lohans in China are Xuanzang and Issa. According to legend, these two Lohans were added in China because of their significant contributions to Buddhism here. I did not tell you this previously because, again, these are only oral legends, and I did not want to overwhelm you with stories having no proof."

A shiver ran through Mark's body. He asked, "Is there any way to confirm that Xuanzang and Jesus, or rather Issa, are the two additional Chinese Lohans?"

"Not that I am aware of," responded Naku. "Our written history on this matter is lacking and likely destroyed in the earthquake that ruined our original pagoda." Pausing, he added, "There is something else I want to show you. Please follow me."

Naku took them toward the back of the pagoda where the last two Lohans sat. He said, "The two rows of Lohans are lined up on the east and west walls of the pagoda." Pointing to the last of the Lohans on the east wall, he said, "I believe this is Xuanzang."

Turning to the west wall, he said, "I believe this is Issa. He is on the west wall, representing the direction from which he came." Issa and Xuanzang faced each other.

Mark looked carefully at the yellow Lohans and focused on the one thought to be Jesus. He quickly noticed the differences and pointed them out to the others. "This figure is the only one with Semitic features. Plus, it has a long, full-faced curly beard, which is missing from the other Lohans."

Gilda readily agreed, "This figure also appears taller than the other Lohans."

Naku followed up, "The Chinese figures have limited facial hair or facial hair that is cropped short. The long beard is unusual."

With a pleasant smile, the Jesus figure had its arms in its lap with palms up in an inviting manner. Mark leaned in and looked more closely. The others watched Mark and noticed what he saw. In the center of each palm was what appeared to be a scar. Mark thought it was his imagination, so he reached out and touched it. The wooden hands were smooth except for a small, rough spot in the center of each. It wasn't his imagination. Mark suddenly had goose bumps. He felt a paradoxical mix of disbelief and a desire to believe.

Excited and pulling his hand away, Mark asked, "Do you see what appears to be a scar in the center of each hand? Could this be proof that Jesus was here after the crucifixion? It suggests he survived and returned to Xi'an, consistent with Naku's legend."

"Mark," said Dr. Meyer, "it could just be a coincidence. We likely will never know. But it is odd that of all the Lohans, this is the only one with scars ..." Dr. Meyer caught himself and corrected his statement, saying, "I mean flaws on his hands."

Staring at the Jesus figure's hands, Gilda added softly, "Mark doesn't believe in coincidences, and in this case, neither do I." She approached and gently held Mark's arm. After awhile, he had seen enough and turned. Still holding his arm, Gilda and Mark led the group as they moved down the hallway toward the front of the pagoda and away from the Lohans.

The three thanked Naku, bade him good-bye, and started to leave the pagoda.

Having turned and taken a few steps, Naku turned back and called out, "I just remembered. The number eighteen has meaning in Chinese tradition as well. It can mean one who is going to prosper. It is desirable to live on the eighteenth floor. Buildings with floors numbered eighteen are often very expensive in China."

Mark turned and thanked Naku again. Walking away, he thought that to prosper generally meant to gain financial wealth, but it also could mean to gain spiritual wealth. He found it interesting that in both the Jewish and Chinese traditions, cultures Jesus had influenced, the number eighteen imparted positive connotations.

On the way out of the pagoda, they passed a collection jar used for donations. All three pulled out money and placed it in the jar. It was the least they could do for all the help Naku had given them.

For their return to the hotel, they decided to walk and consider their next steps.

Chapter Twenty-four

If you would be a seeker after truth, it is necessary that at least once in your life you doubt, as far as possible, all things.

—Descartes

Summer 2003, Xi'an, China

"I can't get the Jesus figure out of my mind. Just think, his teachings may have influenced many more than just the small group in Judea," Mark excitedly said as they walked down the street outside the pagoda, a torrent of traffic rushing past. Turning to Dr. Meyer, he said, "Are you sure there's nothing in the Mount Sodom Dead Sea Scrolls concerning an alternative to Jesus dying on the cross?"

Speaking loudly to overcome the traffic noise, Dr. Meyer responded, "There is nothing in the scrolls you found contradicting the story of the crucifixion. To be honest, I, too, was moved by the Jesus figure, but we need to focus on this new scroll and how to obtain and protect it."

Dr. Meyer paused, making sure Mark was paying attention. "In order to convince Naku to turn the scroll over to us, we need a way to safely transport it to a laboratory, one likely located in Jerusalem."

Due to the street noise and wanting to think without distraction, Dr. Meyer suggested, "On our way back to the hotel, let's use the time to think independently about various approaches to getting the scroll out of China. Once back at the Hyatt, we can brainstorm our ideas together. Is that acceptable?"

Gilda agreed. Mark hesitated and then said, "I will try, but I tend to think better out loud."

Gilda almost laughed. "I can attest to that," she said. "In fact, I bet Mark will talk about this before we reach the hotel. Any takers?"

Dr. Meyer smiled but decided not to accept what he thought was a losing bet.

Shaking his head, Mark responded, "I know myself too well to take that bet."

Walking away from the pagoda, they were mindful of the huge volume of cars on the streets. Twenty years ago, most Chinese rode bicycles, but in today's economy, one goal for each Chinese family was to own a car. That goal seemed to have been fulfilled in Xi'an. The switch from bikes to cars added significantly to the pollution.

Despite the thick air, the sun shone warmly on their backs. A light breeze blew, offsetting the warm temperatures. Xi'an has a temperate climate and was generally warm and humid, but today, the humidity was low.

After walking only a short distance, Mark's mind sped through the possibilities, given the new information about Jesus and Xuanzang. They stopped on a corner, waiting for the light to change. Mark couldn't contain himself—he asked, "What do you think about reincarnation?"

Before anyone could respond, he answered his own question. "I don't believe in it, but did you know reincarnation was taught in the Roman Catholic Church until about 550 CE, when it was eliminated by a narrow margin of 3–2 at the Council of Constantinople? I wondered if Buddhist monks visiting the West had an influence on early Christian thinking concerning reincarnation."

Gilda smiled and said, "I would have won my bet if there had been takers." She looked at Dr. Meyer, who nodded and smiled. The light changed, and they crossed the street.

Responding to Mark's original question, Gilda said, "Some Jews also believe in reincarnation. Actually, there are several Jewish sources dealing with the subject. In Hebrew, it is called *gilgul ha'ne'shamot*, which means the recycling of souls. So Jesus may have known about the concept of reincarnation prior to traveling east."

Mark stopped, becoming somewhat excited, and said, "I didn't know that. So, for these Jews, some early Christians, and certainly for Buddhists, Jesus could have been reincarnated."

Both Gilda and Dr. Meyer stopped and turned back toward Mark. This time Dr. Meyer spoke, "Mark, you have left the realm of science. As scientists, we will never be able to prove or disprove reincarnation. Although an interesting topic, it is one that we will never resolve. Besides, most people today do not think the Bible supports the concept of reincarnation."

"I agree, Dr. Meyer, but you have to admit the lives of Jesus and Xuanzang are so similar that a spiritual connection seems possible. The symmetry of their lives is undeniable," Mark argued feebly.

"Mark, I understand your point," said Gilda sympathetically, "but Dr. Meyer is right. Besides, I think we have more pressing matters to resolve—like how to get the Xi'an scroll to a laboratory for proper analysis."

Dr. Meyer reiterated, "We need to concentrate on our primary goal of protecting and interpreting this Chinese scroll."

Resuming his walk, Mark tried to concentrate his thinking on the scroll. They were about half way back to the hotel. Reaching the city wall, they turned right, walking parallel with the wall. Outside the fortification was a water-filled moat with an adjacent tree-lined park. Strolling along a sidewalk through the park, the wall and moat were to their left. It felt good to be in the shade provided by the trees. Mark watched several children in the park, enjoying their playfulness. After a short distance, they came to the south gate in the wall, known as Yongning or eternal peace. Instead of entering the beautifully decorated gate, Dr. Meyer suggested they walk up the many steps to the top of the wall.

At the top, Mark was surprised at the huge expanse of the structure. People rode bikes several abreast on a wide path running the entire length of the wall. Even with the bikers, there was plenty of room for people to walk leisurely. Mark noticed three nearby gate towers that had been converted into shops, including one that rented bikes.

The view from the top of the wall was grandiose, marred only by the pollution that wreathed the wall and obscured the views. Near the south gate, they could see the tall and ancient bell tower in the center of the city.

Recalling his previous visit here, Dr. Meyer explained to them, pointing, "The bell tower was used as an early warning system in the event of an attack by rival rulers in ancient times."

He continued, pointing to the left, "Nearby you can see the drum tower, the time piece in ancient times. The beating of a large drum inside the tower was used to mark the passage of time, similar to a medieval cathedral's clock."

After their brief sightseeing stop, the three walked down the stairs and passed through the gate in the direction of the bell tower. The bell tower was surrounded by a large traffic circle bustling with vehicles of all sizes, honking and maneuvering their way around the circle. The three followed the sidewalk abutting the traffic circle.

Passing by a large shopping center, money-changers accosted them. Wanting dollars in exchange for Chinese yuan, the rate they offered was guaranteed to be better than the official exchange rate. The scene reminded Mark of the story of Jesus' encounter with money-changers at the temple.

Eventually they turned right onto the street where the Hyatt was located. From there, they walked about seven blocks through crowded streets with a variety of shops. By the time they reached the hotel, all were eager to eat and decided on a late lunch in the hotel restaurant.

Mark and Dr. Meyer had sandwiches, while Gilda ordered a salad.

Mark could wait no longer. He was anxious for the others to come to the conclusion he reached. If only he could be more persuasive. He asked, "According to legend, Issa, or Jesus, returned to Xi'an after a period of years. Don't you think Jesus could have returned here after the crucifixion … assuming he survived? It would be consistent with the scars on the hands of the Jesus figure."

Gilda said, "Mark, many things are possible, but it is best not to read too much into legends passed down through so many years. We should concentrate on the scroll."

"I know," replied Mark, unable to drop the subject, "but legends often have some glint of truth behind them. Remember, the Bible was passed down orally for many years before the stories were written. These oral stories are considered legends by some. The act of writing those stories should not increase their believability, nor should the act of not writing them diminish their credibility."

He saw Dr. Meyer shaking his head and realized he was off on a tangent. As difficult as it was, he knew he had to refocus his thinking. He sighed, saying, "You're right. Our goal is to release the Mount Sodom Dead Sea Scrolls. And to do that, we need the Xi'an scroll."

Their meals arrived, and after taking a few bites, Dr. Meyer asked, "Why did you take that sediment sample?"

Mark eagerly responded, "Naku wasn't sure when the scroll was written. If the scroll was placed in the jar around the time it was written, and if the jar was made around that time as well, we should be able to date the scroll using that sediment. It is likely that the sediment weathered from the inside of the jar. We should be able to determine a minimum date for the jar and, therefore, the scroll."

"How do you plan to date the sediment?" Dr. Meyer asked.

"There's a dating technique that's been proven reliable for a variety of sediments. It's been benchmarked against locations where dates are known by other means and has proved accurate. The method was used at Wakulla Springs near Tallahassee where I live—Gilda, you remember, right? The method is called optically stimulated luminescence or OSL for short. In effect, the OSL clock in sediment, composed of quartz and feldspar, is reset by its last exposure to sunlight prior to deposition."

Taking a bite of his sandwich, he continued, saying, "In our case, exposure to sunlight ended when the terracotta jar was sealed. After burial, the geological luminescence accumulates at a defined rate that can be used to determine the length of time the sediments have been buried—hence, the date of burial. The analysis to determine the age can be performed in an appropriate laboratory within a couple of days."

"So this will help determine if the scroll was sealed in the jar near to or shortly after the time of Jesus' travels to Xi'an," Dr. Meyer summarized.

"Exactly," said Mark.

Dr. Meyer finished his sandwich and changed subjects. "I've been thinking about ways to get the scroll out of China. Israel has a consulate here in Xi'an. I need to call and check in with Jacob Cohen. He will likely not be happy with our trip to Xi'an, but I'll deal with that. I want to explore with Jacob the possibility of sending the scroll to Israel in a diplomatic pouch. That should be a safe way to get the scroll out of China without its being confiscated. Once in Israel, we can perform the necessary laboratory work to read and interpret the scroll."

Gilda responded in a low voice, saying, "The Chinese likely will consider removing the scroll from China a criminal offense. This is very serious, and we need to be fully aware of the potential consequences of the actions we are proposing. Are we certain we want to do this?"

"I hadn't thought about it in that way," said Mark. With little hesitation, he added, "But I believe it is important to make the contents of the scroll public, and it will allow release of the Mount Sodom Dead Sea Scrolls. I'm in."

Dr. Meyer took some time before responding. Finally, he said, "I, too, believe the reward is worth the risk. No government should keep important archaeological findings from the public, and that includes Israel."

Finally, Gilda said, "I'm in, too. But I don't like the idea of bringing Jacob Cohen into the plan." Turning to Dr. Meyer, she asked, "Is there no better way?"

"Not that I have been able to determine. If you have other suggestions, now is the time to share them."

Having none, Gilda and Mark reluctantly agreed with Dr. Meyer's plan. At this point, they needed Jacob's help.

After a short period of silence, Dr. Meyer said, "Why don't you two stay here, and I will go to my room and call Jacob? I should not be long and will let you know what I find out."

While they waited, Gilda and Mark sat in the booth and drank hot black tea. Gilda said, "That's a good idea, using OSL to date the sediments in the jar. We need all the evidence we can get to support our conclusions about the travels of Jesus."

Before Mark could respond, Dr. Meyer returned very agitated.

"What's wrong?" asked Gilda.

"Jacob wants us to return to Israel immediately," Dr. Meyer said rapidly. "When I asked why, he did not give me a clear reason. I do not like what is happening, and I no longer trust Jacob. I told him I would return. He demanded that we all return, so I dropped the subject. I will fly back, but I want you to stay and return to the pagoda tomorrow to see if you can talk Naku into giving you the scroll."

"Then what do we do?" asked Gilda.

"For now, we should take one step at a time. I can catch a flight later today, arriving in Jerusalem early tomorrow morning. I will see Jacob and get to the bottom of this. This charade has gone on long enough. You need to obtain and protect the Xi'an scroll before something happens to it. We've already lost too many pieces of evidence."

Gilda inquired, "Did you tell Jacob about the scroll?"

"Yes, because I wanted his help in using the diplomatic pouch."

"Do you think he will help?" she asked.

"We didn't get that far, but I will pursue it in Jerusalem. I will give you the details if and when they are worked out."

Mark grabbed his backpack. "I know you have a lot to do tomorrow when you reach Jerusalem, but take this sediment sample and have it analyzed as soon as you can." Mark handed Dr. Meyer the sample container.

"Okay. I'll take care of it and get back to you with the results as soon as I receive them. For now, I need to pack and head to the airport."

Mark stood and shook hands with him. After being together for these past few days, Gilda felt that a hug was more appropriate than a handshake. She embraced him lightly and wished him a bon voyage. With that, Dr. Meyer said good-bye and left them in the restaurant. Disconcerted, they watched him leave.

"I'm tempted to return to the pagoda right now," said Mark. "But we told Naku we would return tomorrow. I guess we'll just have to wait and be patient."

"Plus," said Gilda, "we need to come up with a plan to reassure Naku about how we'll protect and transport the scroll out of China."

Chapter Twenty-five

Traveling is almost like talking with those of other centuries.

—Descartes

Summer 2003, Oklahoma City, Oklahoma

Jacob Cohen angrily hung up the phone. Dr. Meyer was becoming increasingly troublesome, too independent. Jacob felt a gnawing sensation in the pit of his stomach. His concern grew.

Looking at his watch, he decided that despite the time difference, an immediate call to Chester was necessary. He had kept Chester informed of the trio's activities from the start and felt compelled to relay the newest information. Having the lucrative Israeli tourism business negatively impacted by those three mischief-makers was something Jacob did not want to happen.

***

A "megamansion" is difficult to define, but when you see it, you know it. Chester's massive house was built on two adjacent lots in an exclusive gated community. Built on three acres, the house was constructed of a light red, oversized brick, surrounded by a seven-foot matching brick wall. It wasn't for defense like the walls surrounding ancient cities; Chester just liked his privacy. The two-story house had seven bedrooms, seven bathrooms, and a five-car garage containing a variety of cars, including a hot sports car and his classic Bentley. Chester enjoyed the toys his job afforded him. The house also included a first-class media room in the basement where he enjoyed watching old movies, especially those starring Ronald Reagan. It had to be one of the largest houses in Oklahoma City, and Chester called it home.

Chester's pride and joy was the outside living area behind his house. Included were a swimming pool, an outside kitchen and lounge, and a beautifully landscaped waterfall and small stream surrounded by massive rocks. The artificial stream ended in a fishpond containing koi.

Even though it was the middle of the night, Chester was wide-awake and couldn't sleep. His wife, or the "little lady" as he liked to call her, had retired hours ago. He sat alone outside, enjoying the quiet solitude of darkness. He was savoring the taste of a Dos Equis beer right out of the bottle with a slice of lime pushed into it. Bottle opener in hand, he recalled that it was sometimes referred to as a "church key." He chuckled and wondered how it got that name.

He took another pull from the bottle and looked around, admiring his stream and waterfall. The large rocks lining the stream had been imported from out of state. Chester thought these may be the only rocks in Oklahoma City, which was built on a flat plain. The delight provided by the unique view of the rocks was interrupted when a thought jumped into his head.

He couldn't help but wonder what that smartass Mark Malloy would think of his backyard rocks. He didn't understand how anyone could be interested in rocks the way Mark was. It seemed to him that science, particularly geology, was anti-Christianity. Even though he found it hard to believe the stories in the Bible, they were certainly more plausible than interpretations based on a bunch of rocks.

The phone rang, interrupting his thoughts.

Chester took the call in his outside living area so he could continue listening to the gurgling water as it flowed over the rocks. The small liquid crystal display on his phone flashed the caller's name, and he knew it was Jacob Cohen. He picked up the phone apprehensively, given the hour, and said, "Hello, Jacob. What's going on?"

"Hello, Chester. Is this too late to call?" Jacob sounded anxious.

"No, I'm still up. What's on your mind?"

Jacob took a moment to organize his thoughts. He was still bubbling with fury over Dr. Meyer's usurping his authority. As calmly as possible, he went on, "As we expected, our threesome was unable to locate the Hemis scrolls in Lhasa, but they were informed by a monk who studied the Hemis scrolls that Jesus left northern India and traveled further along the Silk Road to Xi'an, China, where he continued his religious studies focusing on Taoism. Dr. Meyer decided to go to Xi'an without my permission or letting me know of their plans until they were already there."

"Where?"

"Xi'an," Jacob replied, pronouncing it slowly and distinctly.

Chester paused. He repeated the name, having no idea where it was. Then asked, "Did they find anything there?"

"Yes," Jacob answered. After taking a deep breath to soothe his taut nerves, he continued, "They found another scroll that may document Jesus' travels to Xi'an. The scroll is located at the Big Wild Goose Pagoda, a Buddhist temple there. I ordered them back, and I think Dr. Meyer is returning to Israel, but I fear that Mark and Gilda may have stayed. I suspect they will try to obtain the Xi'an scroll because Dr. Meyer was exploring ways to remove the scroll from China. With Dr. Meyer returning, I now have no way to keep tabs on the two geologists."

"I can't believe they found another scroll! They must be the luckiest scientists in the world." If he didn't know better, Chester thought they might be receiving divine help. "Do you know where Mark and Gilda are staying?" Chester was now regretting his approval of this latest trip. When he relented, he never dreamed they would find anything else.

"Yes, at the Hyatt Regency in downtown Xi'an."

"Is there anything else I should know?" Chester asked.

"That's everything I have for now."

"Okay, thanks, Jacob," said Chester, concern in his voice. "Your call is very helpful. Please let me know as soon as you learn anything further when Dr. Meyer returns."

"I will," agreed Jacob.

Bidding their good-byes, Chester hung up. Jesus was quite the traveler, Chester mused; his proper order of things would have been undisturbed if only Jesus had stayed in Judea.

He thought about his options. Although concerned, he felt he still had control over the situation. He knew his next step. It was time to contact his cousin, Mickey, again.

Mickey and Chester grew up together in Oklahoma. Whereas Chester gravitated to the church to scam money, Mickey became involved with organized crime. He began by providing muscle for protection schemes, loan shark payments, and various forms of extortion. He was good at what he did. With more and more successful jobs came more responsibility. He became one of the best "fixers" in the business. If you had a problem, Mickey was the one to call; he could fix it.

Chester used Mickey's services from time to time. Once an investigative reporter who was exploring the First Church of God's

Chosen got a little too close for comfort to the money angle. Chester called in Mickey, and the investigation was dropped after the reporter's home burned down under mysterious circumstances.

When Mark and Gilda began their quest, Chester called on Mickey once again. Mickey had traveled to Iznik, Turkey, and shadowed Mark and Gilda at the St. Sophia Cathedral. He hired some local thugs, and together they removed the tiles and destroyed the altar area.

Using his political connections, Chester found a way to get Mickey into Baghdad when the trio traveled there. Mickey traveled as a security consultant to one of the private contractors operating in Iraq and then followed the scientists to the Iraq National Museum. He offered the museum staffer Sadik a nice sum of dollars for the Babylonian scroll. The timing was perfect. Sadik and his colleagues were planning to steal jewelry and gold artifacts from the museum anyway. Taking money for what he considered a worthless scroll was a pretty good proposition for Sadik.

Now Mickey was in Lhasa, Tibet. He had followed the threesome there, but he lost their trail and was awaiting Chester's instructions.

Mickey picked up on the third ring, finding it difficult to even say hello.

"Mickey, I know where they are," Chester said. "They left Lhasa and flew to a place called Xi'an." Chester spelled it out for Mickey. He continued, "It's in China. They are staying at the Hyatt Regency there. It seems they've found another scroll at a place called the Big Wild Goose Pagoda. Can you believe it?"

"No. What dumb luck," Mickey said in a raspy voice.

"I agree," Chester said in a menacing voice, adding, "Mickey, you know what to do."

"I'll leave for this Xi'an place right away. Hey, you owe me extra for coming to this Lhasa place. It sucks, and I've felt like hell ever since I got here. I have one hell of a headache I can't get rid of. This place is so high up, I can hardly breathe." Mickey sat in his hotel room trying to inhale gulps of air.

"Maybe you should give up smoking, Mickey." Chester waited for a reaction. When none came, he continued, "Let me know what you find out in Xi'an."

"I will. Don't worry." With that, Mickey hung up and lit a cigarette, instantly succumbing to a coughing attack.

Mickey was in his early fifties, his black curly hair turning grey. He was a big man, just less than six feet, three inches. Except for the damage caused by smoking, he was in good shape physically, although with age, he had bulked up. He weighed 225 pounds and had a paunch where his flat stomach used to be. Having been an enforcer, he knew how to fight, and his scars proved it. One scar over his right eye looked particularly bad—or impressive, depending on your point of view.

Not well educated, Mickey wasn't stupid. Many people in his past had assumed one with the other, underestimating him; that had been their undoing. He had street smarts, and as he recently traveled the world working for his cousin, he found that street smarts were pretty much the same everywhere, and money was the universal language. He had been using this knowledge to his advantage while following the three scientists at the behest of his cousin. *They might be smart*, he thought, patting himself on the back, *but I've been able to outfox them every step of the way.*

Mickey checked out of his hotel and took a taxi to the Lhasa airport. He didn't wait long for a flight to Xi'an. Arriving a little after dark, he called the Hyatt and was able to get a room. He caught a taxi to the hotel. Checking in, he went to his room. Already he was feeling better because of the lower elevation. He called Chester, letting him know his new location.

He decided to have dinner in the hotel restaurant with the hope of running into Mark and Gilda. On his way to the restaurant, he passed by the concierge area with its many tourist pamphlets. He saw one on the Big Wild Goose Pagoda and grabbed it to read at dinner. The pamphlet gave him directions to the pagoda and related its history. He read that the pagoda was a major center for the study of Taoism around the time of Christ and later, around 500 CE, became a major center for the study of Buddhism. Mickey had trouble comprehending these dates. To him, the 1960s were ancient history.

He wondered how the pagoda got its stupid name, and his question was answered in the pamphlet. Zen masters, who studied and taught Taoism, were traveling nearby and ended up at the location of the future pagoda. They hadn't eaten in days and were hungry. As they meditated, a flock of geese flew overhead. The lead goose broke its wing in midflight and fell to the ground near the Zen masters. Their hunger was alleviated. That event led to the construction of the pagoda near where the goose fell, giving the pagoda its name.

Mickey laughed out loud. *What a dumb story*, he thought. Then again, if meditation could bring down a goose in midflight, maybe he should try it. He really didn't know what meditation was, but that wasn't going to stop him.

On a whim, he began to focus on an image of Mark and Gilda, thinking this to be meditation. Five minutes into his meditation, in walked Mark and Gilda, who sat nearby. Mickey was not much of a Christian, but he thought that there might be something to this Taoism.

Consumed in conversation, Mark and Gilda took no notice of their surroundings. The woman's hands moved rapidly. They seemed very excited, and Mickey stared hard at his menu as he strained to overhear their conversation.

Chapter Twenty-six

Maybe when Mark says that Jesus was crucified the day *after* the Passover meal was eaten (Mark 14:12; 15:25) and John says he died the day *before* it was eaten (John 19:14)—maybe that is a genuine difference.

—Bart D. Ehrman, *Misquoting Jesus*

Summer 2003, Xi'an, China

By morning, no brilliant plan to remove the Xi'an scroll from China had come to mind. Mark stood shaving at the bathroom sink, Gilda taking a bath behind him. Water glistened on her body in the mirror, not helping his concentration on either the scroll or his shaving. She was clearly lost in thought. She broke the silence, asking Mark, "What if we check the scroll as luggage or ship it to ourselves?"

"Either might work, both are risky. It could be damaged or, worse, discovered and confiscated."

"It may be a risk we have to take," she insisted.

Mark finished shaving, managing to cut himself only once while watching Gilda, and then joined her in the oversized tub. For the moment, they lost interest in the scroll.

After getting dressed, their discussion continued. "What about smuggling it across the border by land?" asked Gilda.

"I'm not sure how we could do that. I think border crossings in China involve considerable scrutiny."

"Then we are back to Dr. Meyer's idea of using a diplomatic pouch. I hope he is successful in dealing with Jacob," said Gilda.

"Maybe so," agreed Mark. "But I'm not sure how helpful Jacob will be."

Considering their immediate situation, Gilda asked, "Do you mind walking back to the pagoda this morning?"

"Sure, I'm all for walking."

Following breakfast, they left the hotel and followed the route taken the previous day. Unbeknownst to them, a tall, heavyset man with a scar over his right eye followed them at distance. Mickey knew he didn't have to follow too closely; he already knew where they were heading. He took his time, enjoying another morning cigarette. He looked up at the sky and thought that his cigarette smoke could not be any worse for him than breathing the brownish air.

Mark and Gilda welcomed the walk, taking note of sights and sounds they missed the day before with Dr. Meyer. The peasant beggars on the streets made a particular impression on Mark. He asked, "Don't you think it odd to see beggars in a communist country? I thought everyone was supposed to benefit equally under communism."

"China is a communist country in some ways and capitalistic in others," she explained. "What I find interesting is that the facial features of the peasant beggars are not typically Chinese. They look more like the faces we saw in Tibet."

"That makes sense," Mark mused. "Tibet is losing much of its culture. As part of the Chinese invasion and annexation, the government has encouraged Chinese from other parts of the country to relocate there. In turn, Tibetans have been forced to leave their homeland to find work elsewhere. Some have ended up on the streets."

They made it back to the Big Wild Goose Pagoda in less time than the previous day. Removing their shoes and entering the pagoda through the arched door on the first level, they found several monks and asked for Naku. After waiting about ten minutes, Naku met and greeted them. "Where is Dr. Meyer?"

"He was called back to Israel," Mark responded. "We have not yet finalized exactly how we will transport the scroll out of China, but if possible, we would like to take it with us today for safekeeping. Other artifacts have mysteriously disappeared after we located them, and we want to prevent that from happening here."

Naku was slow to respond. "You ask a great favor, one that I am reluctant to grant." Behind his stiff shell of reticence, Naku recognized the potential benefit of releasing the scroll.

He gestured for them to sit before continuing. "I have given considerable thought to the scroll and its importance. It may very well prove a connection between Christianity and Buddhism, as well as other Eastern religions. I view that connection as a positive association highlighting commonalities of our religions and the strength and importance of their teachings. My hope is that the release of the scroll might contribute to a world of mutual understanding and harmony."

Pausing, he continued, "Plus, the scroll is aging and may disintegrate to the point where it can no longer be translated. Consequently, I have decided that it is better for the scroll to be made public in order to highlight these religious connections rather than keep it hidden, even though there are many risks involved in moving it, and even if it means that our community here will lose it. But I must know—how will you avoid the scrutiny of the Chinese government?"

"We are as concerned as you about the safety of the scroll," Gilda said. "We know the Chinese government took the Hemis scrolls, and if the Xi'an scroll is discovered, they will confiscate it as well. Plus, we will likely be arrested. But, like you, we believe the risk is worth the potential reward. We have put considerable thought into this and believe our best solution is to use a diplomatic pouch to remove it with the help of our consulate here in Xi'an. Absent that, our next choice is to smuggle it out of the country, but the details for that have not yet been worked out."

Silence followed. Naku seemed hesitant. After a pause, he nodded his head affirmatively. "I will trust your judgment."

Mark's eyes locked onto Naku's as he promised, "I will do all I can to prove your trust is well placed." Still sensing some uncertainty on Naku's part, Mark asked reluctantly, "Are you sure?"

"Mark," Naku answered politely, "the Chinese have a saying, 'The rice is cooked,' meaning the decision is made."

After a moment, Mark suggested, "If you have a light blanket, perhaps we can wrap the terracotta jar and slip it into my backpack."

Naku agreed with this plan and left to retrieve a blanket. He returned with a beautiful handwoven wall covering and asked, "Will this do?"

"Yes, that's perfect. It should provide good protection while not being too large."

Naku produced flashlights and handed one each to Gilda and Mark. He asked, "Shall we?"

After retrieving their shoes, Mark and Gilda once again followed Naku to the central hallway and toward the back of the pagoda. No other monks were around. At the end of the hall with the yellow Lohans, they entered the small room containing the stairwell. Carefully, they descended the steep spiral stairs and went through the main basement room into the smaller, cave-like room containing the terracotta jars. As they crossed the room, Mark stopped for a second, hearing the large wooden beams above them creak, but then he moved forward, thinking nothing of it.

***

Mickey hoped the squeaky floor did not give him away. He slowly, quietly made his way down the spiral stairwell. He did not have a flashlight, but could see his way using the light given off by those ahead of him. As he neared the bottom, he carefully pulled out his .38 pistol. He silently watched Mark, Gilda, and the old monk.

***

Naku picked up the jar they had examined the day before and opened it. He lifted the lid and felt inside to confirm the scroll's presence. Replacing the lid, he carefully wrapped the jar in the wall covering. Mark dug through his backpack to see what he could eliminate to make room. He pulled out water bottles and empty sample containers. Naku slipped the terracotta jar into the backpack, and Mark tightened the straps to secure it.

Naku said, "Please take the utmost care of the scroll."

"I will," promised Mark.

Suddenly, from behind, a gruff voice said loudly, "I'll take that now."

They turned to see a tall, heavyset man with a scar over his right eye pointing a gun at them. Mickey's snub-nosed .38 wasn't a big weapon, but to Mark, staring right down its barrel, it seemed like a cannon.

"Who ... who are you?" Gilda stammered.

Mark slowly straightened up from his squatting position, backpack still in hand, transfixed with indecision.

"That's not important. Just give me the backpack. Now!" yelled the man, turning the gun directly at Mark.

Mickey slowly edged closer. He figured the old monk and the woman were no threat. He focused on Mark, who stood motionless, dumbstruck as he held the backpack. Mickey stepped toward Mark to grab it.

Suddenly, Gilda sprang forward, twisting her body and delivering a roundhouse kick with her right foot and knocking the gun out of

Mickey's hand. Before he could recover, Gilda threw a straight kick, again with her right foot, catching him squarely on the nose.

To Mark, it sounded like a fist hitting and breaking through the rind of a watermelon. He grimaced and watched as the assailant's head flew back and blood from his nose sprayed over the rock and clay. As the man fell backward into the larger room, his head hit on a rock on the ground. Their attacker was out cold.

"Wow!" exclaimed Mark, utterly stunned. "I didn't know you could do that!"

Gilda responded, "The first day we worked together, remember I told you I trained with the Israeli Army and knew the art of self-defense."

"Right, but I had no idea just how skilled you were." Then he whispered to himself, "Boy, I'm glad I never made you angry."

Gilda heard, but her slight smile faded quickly as she glanced at the unconscious man lying prostrate on the floor. "Could this be the same person who took the tiles when we were in Iznik and the Babylonian scroll when we were in Baghdad?" she asked Mark.

"If not, it's awfully coincidental that he shows up here just when we find the Xi'an scroll."

Mark, finally able to move, handed his backpack to Naku, who was standing in shock, and forcing him out of his trance. He moved toward the man on the floor, whose nose and head were bleeding profusely, bent down and checked his pulse. "He's alive, just knocked out."

Mark's mind raced; he had a plethora of questions. What to do with the gun-toting man? Did he know the whereabouts of the St. Sophia Cathedral tiles and the Babylonian scroll? Should they involve the local authorities? If so, would the existence of the Xi'an scroll be revealed?

Leaving Gilda with their attacker, Mark moved back to the smaller room to consult with Naku, who was still guarding the backpack.

Suddenly, Mark felt the earth sway under his feet as the room moved to and fro. He heard the ancient floorboards above squeaking. Not sure what was happening, he felt oddly disoriented and helpless. He looked at Naku and saw that he was grasping the side of the wall to keep his balance, fear in his eyes. In that instant, Mark realized: it was an earthquake.

Chapter Twenty-seven

All men are born with a nose and ten fingers, but no
one was born with a knowledge of God.

—Voltaire

Summer 2003, Xi'an, China

At first, the ground trembled slightly. The shaking intensified until the floor moved violently. Mark was thrown down, dropping his flashlight. Dust kicked up everywhere, dulling what little light emanated from the fallen torch. In addition to making it difficult to see, the fine particles of clay made breathing laborious. He heard Naku coughing. Mark felt helpless, hearing rocks falling and timber crashing down nearby. He was frightened—not just for himself, but for Gilda also. He couldn't see her; he had no idea what was happening to her. He called out her name, but there was no response.

After what seemed an eternity but was probably less than a minute, the shaking subsided. Calm returned; an eerie silence filled the basement. During the uncomfortable stillness, Mark lay on the floor, trying to regain his bearings. He felt his body with his hands, tried to move his legs, and determined he was unhurt. He searched for his backpack, found it beside him, and could tell it was undamaged. He grabbed his flashlight and looked around. The settling dust was thick, especially near the floor, causing him to cough. He needed to stand above it to see and breathe.

Scrambling to his feet, a motion off to his right caught his eye. It was Naku. Mark, now fully upright, made his way to Naku and helped him to his feet.

"Are you hurt?" Mark asked.

After a moment, Naku responded, "No, I think I am all right."

Mark and Naku had been in the smaller cave-like room, whereas Gilda and the stranger had been in the main basement under the wooden floor when the earthquake struck. Mark pointed his flashlight in that direction. It was difficult to see very far.

Advancing, the first thing he noticed was the man. He was partially buried under rubble—the rock wall near his head had collapsed, and only the lower half his body was visible. He was not moving.

Mark's priority was to find Gilda. He moved the light, searching to the right of the fallen man. One of the large wooden beams that had supported the floor above had fallen and lay at an angle, one end still attached to the rafters above. His eyes followed the beam to its other end where it rested on the basement floor. There he saw her, lying perfectly still on her back.

Mark rushed to Gilda, his heart in his throat, and knelt by her side. There was an enormous gash on the top of her head; blood was everywhere. He recalled that even minor head wounds produced considerable blood. *Don't focus on the blood*, he told himself, *the wound may not be that bad*. He placed two fingers on her wrist, trying to feel a pulse. Nothing! Never very good at feeling someone's pulse, he kept trying. After an agonizing period of time, he finally heard her breathing and felt a weak pulse. He could see her chest shallowly moving up and down.

Greatly relieved, he forced his fears into an imaginary compartment and locked them there. Examining her, he observed no other obvious wounds or broken bones. He ran to retrieve his backpack. Picking it up, he also grabbed the water bottles he had discarded only moments earlier. He quickly returned to Gilda. Reaching into his backpack, he pulled out a small first aid kit.

Naku followed him and asked, "What can I do to help?"

"Use the water to clean her wound," instructed Mark. Naku did as requested. Mark applied antiseptic, gauze, and tape, trying to stop the bleeding. As he finished applying the dressing, the ground again began to shake.

"Naku, help me move her to the smaller room." While trying to maintain their balance, the two gently pulled her by the shoulders to the smaller room. Pieces of the wooden floor fell from above, and additional side walls collapsed in the larger room. But the smaller room remained in tack.

"An aftershock," explained Mark. "It shouldn't be as severe as the first earthquake." As the shaking subsided, feeling vulnerable, Mark said, "We need to get out of here before there are more."

Dust stirred up again. When it became still, Mark turned to Naku and asked, "Can you stay with Gilda? I need to check out the guy over there. I'll only be a moment."

Naku nodded agreement, and Mark moved slowly and warily through the debris in the larger room until he reached the man lying to the right of the staircase. He smelled of stale cigarette smoke mixed with sweat. Blood had pooled around him, darkening the red clay. Mark felt for the man's lower arm and checked his pulse. He waited and waited … but felt nothing. The man was dead. Mark yelled his unpleasant finding to Naku.

Feeling carefully under the dead man's body, Mark finally located his billfold in a back pocket. A considerable amount of effort was required because the man was pinned to the ground by the rocks and rubble. In addition, the man's dead weight was considerable. Eventually, Mark removed the man's billfold and examined it using his flashlight. He pulled out an American-looking driver's license.

Michael Weeks was the name on the license; he was from Oklahoma City! Looking further through his billfold, Mark spotted other cards. A video rental card gave the name Mickey Weeks.

Mark returned to Gilda and Naku, and put Mickey Weeks's billfold in his backpack. "We need to leave. Can you help me with Gilda?"

"I'll try. If you take the lead with her shoulders, I'll follow behind with her feet," Naku suggested.

"That's a good idea." But before they set off, Mark told Naku, "Wait here, and I'll try the stairs to see if they can support our weight. I'll also check the condition of the pagoda."

Using his flashlight, Mark moved toward the stairs. He pulled on the staircase, finding it loose but passable. He walked up a couple of stairs and jumped on them; they held. He continued up the remaining stairs and entered the upper part of the pagoda. Furniture and wall hangings were strewn all over the floor, but the building was intact. Mark walked into the hallway and could see an unobstructed way to the outside. He quickly made his way back down the staircase and over to Gilda and Naku.

"We can make it all the way to the outside. The staircase is a little shaky but should hold us. Are you ready to go?"

"Yes," Naku said hesitantly.

After putting on his backpack, Mark lifted Gilda by the shoulders. Naku grabbed her feet. They slowly moved toward the stairs. Mark, walking backward, tripped twice on large rocks, but continued his tight grip on Gilda.

Reaching the stairs, he slowly stepped up. Going up the narrow stairs was tricky, especially now that the staircase was loosened by the earthquake. With their combined weight, Mark feared another aftershock might cause the stairs to fail. He wanted to ascend the stairs quickly, but in order to synchronize their movement, they had to pause after each step. The staircase shook more violently with each step as they inched upward.

Finally, Mark reached the first floor and pulled Gilda out of the staircase. As Naku stepped onto the first floor, his back foot pushed forward off the last step. Suddenly, the staircase gave way, falling behind Naku, who lost his balance, stumbling forward and dropping Gilda's legs.

Still holding Gilda's arms, Mark called out, "Are you okay?" The thought of Gilda asking him if he was okay when he fell into the sinkhole flashed through his mind.

"Yes, I'm okay," Naku said shakily, lying next to Gilda. The noise of the staircase banging against the rocks as it fell could be heard behind Naku, his foot still hanging over the void. As the noise abated, Naku looked up at Mark. Their eyes locked for a moment as they both realized how close they had come to falling with the staircase.

Naku slowly rose to his feet. They resumed carrying Gilda into the main hallway. Mark noticed several of the Lohans had toppled over, and he gingerly stepped through the rubble as they moved toward the front of the pagoda. He quickly glanced back at the figure Naku thought was Jesus. It was still upright and looked the same as it did the day before. It appeared to Mark that the Jesus figure was watching him. They hurried down the hall, able to move faster on the first floor of the pagoda. Approaching the front of the pagoda, another aftershock hit.

This one knocked them out the front door, all three falling on the ground. As they fell forward, the back portion of the pagoda, where they had just been, partially collapsed, causing a blast of air and debris to fly out of the front door and settle on top of them. Mark thought of the Lohans in the back of the pagoda, including the one of Jesus, now buried under the remains of the ancient structure.

Naku softly spoke, saying, "That was close." Looking around, he asked, "Can I leave you here with Gilda? I need to check on the other monks."

"Of course," Mark responded, still shaken.

Naku stood, dusted himself off, and left, walking around and talking with various groups of monks. Some of the monks were helping others with injuries.

Mark dragged Gilda further away from the pagoda in case more of it collapsed. He sat, holding her head in his lap and stroking her hair. The bleeding had stopped, but she was still unconscious. Her breathing was labored and she occasionally moaned.

Mark knew head injuries could easily be fatal, especially if there was any bleeding around the brain. He looked around, considering how to get her to a hospital in a damaged city where so many others were likely injured.

As if reading his mind, Naku came by and told him, "Several of the monks have been injured, and ambulances have been called. Because of the damage and injuries throughout the city, it may take a while. We have three monks who are medically trained. I've asked one to come by after he has treated the more seriously injured."

"Thank you, Naku."

Naku touched Mark's arm as a reassuring gesture, turned and left. Mark looked around the city. Collapsed or damaged buildings were everywhere. Some buildings were on fire. He could smell smoke. He had experienced minor earthquakes previously, but this was his first major earthquake, and the devastation was shocking.

He felt Gilda move and looked down just in time to see her open her eyes. As she tried to focus on the smoke in the sky and Mark's dirt-stained face, a look of confusion filled her eyes. "What happened?" she asked, wincing as she tried to sit up. She fell back into his lap.

"Earthquake," Mark said. "You were hit on the head in the basement of the pagoda."

Gilda tried to process the information. "Is Naku okay? The scroll?"

"Yes, he's fine, and I've got the scroll right here. Remember that man with the gun? He's dead. His name was Mickey Weeks, and he was from Oklahoma City. Gilda, does that name sound familiar to you?"

She still looked confused. Mark said, "Don't worry about it. Just rest."

Gilda closed her eyes and drifted off. She was either asleep or unconscious again.

Naku again came by, this time with another monk.

"He knows medicine," said Naku.

The other monk examined Gilda, checking the wound on her head. He lifted her eyelids and checked her eyes as they reacted to the daylight. After the examination, the monk said something to Naku in Chinese.

Naku turned to Mark, "Your dressing on the wound is good and should last until we get Gilda to a hospital. She has probably suffered a concussion. With stitches for the wound and rest for the concussion, she should be fine."

"Is it okay for her to sleep, or should I keep her awake?" asked Mark.

After the translation, the answer was, "Rest and sleep are good for her."

Relieved, Mark still wanted to get her to a hospital as soon as possible. He was coming down from his adrenalin high, and exhaustion consumed him. Bending over, he kissed her forehead. She opened her eyes momentarily and smiled up at him, renewing his strength.

Chapter Twenty-eight

Faith consists in believing when it is beyond
the power of reason to believe.

—Voltaire

Summer 2003, Xi'an, China

Xietong Hospital, an ultramodern facility, suffered only minor damage. It was extremely overcrowded with countless earthquake victims. One was Gilda. Pacing back and forth, Mark had waited nervously with her for almost ten hours at the pagoda before help finally arrived. She slept most of the time. When they arrived at the hospital, it was dusk; a red glow fell over the city, a product of the many fires still burning.

Gilda's head injury required twenty-two stitches. Some of her beautiful, long black hair had to be shaved and a bandage affixed to a large portion of her head. She continued to sleep, partly due to the medication.

While at the hospital, Mark learned that several major faults near Xi'an formed a fault-bounded depositional basin in which the city was located. Tectonically active, no major earthquakes have occurred in Xi'an for hundreds of years … until now.

Lying on her back in the semiprivate room, she appeared as comfortable as could be expected. A "semiprivate" room usually meant one roommate; Gilda shared the room with three other women, all of whom were worse off. The woman immediately next to her had two broken legs and was in considerable pain. The other two patients in Gilda's room also had broken bones and lacerations.

Mark had been at the hospital with Gilda for about twenty-four hours. Given the condition of the city, he had unable to contact anyone outside the country. When he wasn't helping Gilda, he assisted her roommates by giving them water and helping them eat, especially the one with a broken right arm.

Gilda exhibited the classic symptoms of a concussion. Her head hurt and she had some memory loss, especially concerning the minutes leading up to and during the earthquake. The intravenous drip had been removed, but she was not eating much because it made her nauseous. As she slept, Mark realized he needed to do the same, but couldn't settle down. He could only watch Gilda and worry. Fortunately, she was getting stronger with each passing hour. When she awoke, she was staying awake for longer periods of time. Her conversations became longer and more detailed each time they spoke.

Now Gilda was wide awake. She looked around the room, smiled, happy to see

Mark at her side. She reached for his hand and asked for about the third time, "How long have I been here?"

He had answered this question previously, but apparently it had not registered with her. "You've been in the hospital a bit over twenty-four hours. It's been about thirty-four hours since the earthquake. How are you feeling?"

"Better." She slowly pulled herself into a sitting position.

"How's your head?" he asked, bending over to brush a kiss lightly on her cheek.

"Okay. It doesn't hurt all that much anymore." She cautiously tried rolling her neck and moving her head from side to side and was pleased with the results. "Do you think I could leave?" Looking around, she added, "They probably could use my bed."

"Gilda, you've been through quite an ordeal. I know you're anxious to leave the hospital, but I'm not sure you're strong enough."

"I really am feeling much better."

Mark looked dubious, so she started to get out of bed, saying, "I'm fine and want to leave."

He stopped her. Maybe she was well enough. Mark didn't like being in a hospital either and understood her desire to leave as soon as possible. "Let me find someone who can examine you and see if you are fit enough to go."

He gave Gilda a quick kiss and left the room. It took him a while to locate a doctor who spoke English and had time to listen. The doctor, who seemed as tired as Mark, followed him back to Gilda's room and examined her chart. Then she examined Gilda.

She nodded at Mark and told him in broken English, "She leave now but need rest. Stitches out in week."

Mark acknowledged this, and the doctor left. Gathering Gilda's belongings, he made sure to grab his backpack. He helped her change out of the hospital gown into her own dirty clothes. Surprisingly, she was feeling quite stable and not dizzy anymore. Shortly after Mark helped her change, an orderly came into the room with a wheelchair. He pointed to Gilda and then at the chair. Even under these emergency conditions, hospital policies were enforced.

Gilda rose slowly and gingerly settled into the chair, and the young man wheeled her to the hospital entrance near where they had arrived only twenty-four hours earlier. During one of Gilda's sleep periods, Mark had learned by talking with hospital staff that the Hyatt Hotel was still open and had only suffered minor damage. Taxis were running, and they were lucky to catch one at the hospital entrance. It had just arrived, dropping off a patient.

Driving to the Hyatt was a challenge due to the collapsed buildings blocking or partially blocking many of the streets. Most fires were out. Damage throughout the city appeared random, although extensive. Some buildings were heavily damaged, while others appeared unscathed. Mark knew the damage was not random but a function of building construction, and of where and how the earthquake's energy was focused. Power outages were scattered throughout the city. Many traffic lights were out. Fortunately, the Hyatt was in a section of town with electricity.

When they arrived at the Hyatt, Mark helped Gilda out of the taxi and up to their room. Nightfall was upon them, and Mark could barely hold his eyes open. "I'm going to clean up and go to bed. Are you well enough for a shower?"

"That sounds great. I'll join you, but I may be too weak to wash myself," she said sheepishly.

Mark went to turn on the water—and nothing happened. "Guess what? There's no water. I guess we'll just have to sleep as we are." Mark had been looking forward to a nice, warm, prolonged shower to finally wash away the pagoda dust and grime. There was bottled water in the room and they used it to brush their teeth.

Removing their clothes, Mark helped Gilda. Then lay down. Mark's head hit the pillow, and he was asleep immediately. Gilda snuggled close to him and soon drifted off as well.

Ten hours later, Mark awoke feeling fully refreshed. He found Gilda lying in bed watching him with her warm dark eyes. "How do you feel?" he asked.

"I still have a slight headache, but I'm fine." She touched his cheek. "You know, I think you saved my life."

"Look who's talking. You saved mine by taking out the guy with the gun."

"Gosh, I had almost forgotten about him." Gilda raised herself on one elbow. "What happened to him?"

Mark cleared his throat and said softly, "He was crushed to death, Gilda, by collapsing rocks caused by the earthquake." He watched her reaction and said, "I think I know who he was."

Gilda shook her head slowly, trying to process everything that had happened in the basement room of the pagoda. "How?"

"From his driver's license. His name was Mickey Weeks, and he was from Oklahoma City. Does that sound familiar?"

"Boy! What do you think? Is he … that is, *was* he any relation to Chester Weeks from Oklahoma City?"

"He's got to be. I think we now know who took the artifacts we found in Iznik and Baghdad. My suspicions are confirmed."

"You think Chester sent a relative to take the Xi'an scroll as well?" Gilda asked.

"Yes," responded Mark, "but I bet with all the chaos Chester doesn't know what happened. I don't think anyone at the pagoda would know who he was because I took his wallet. I know they were going to report his death to the authorities and get him buried, but he's just a John Doe until I can get his papers to my government."

"What about his passport?" Gilda asked.

"I didn't find one on him," responded Mark. "My point is, for all Chester knows, Mickey Weeks may have been successful and in possession of our latest find. We might be able to use this to our advantage in exposing him for the devious, lying cretin he is when we return to Israel."

Thinking ahead, Gilda said, "I need to contact Dr. Meyer."

"Okay," responded Mark as he rose from bed and disappeared in the bathroom. He reappeared at the door and with a hint of impatience in his voice. "Guess what? There's still no water."

They cleaned up as well as they could and got dressed. Gilda tried the phone. Surprisingly, it was working. She called Dr. Meyer and reached him on the first try. After a fifteen-minute conversation, she hung up.

"Well, what did you find out?" asked Mark.

"Dr. Meyer has contacted the Israeli consulate, informing them of our presence here. The Israeli government is flying earthquake aid to Xi'an, and we need to be at the airport by noon today so we can catch one of the aid flights on its return trip to Jerusalem. Dr. Meyer will call them to confirm that we are to be on that flight."

"Did you tell him about Mickey?"

"No, I thought it best not to share that information just yet," Gilda said contemplatively.

"What about Chinese security? Can we get the scroll out?"

"Apparently, we can. Because of the confusion resulting from the earthquake and much-needed aid, security for our flight is practically nonexistent. Security forces are tied up doing other things, and aid flights are a low priority. We should have no problem getting the scroll out," she said triumphantly. "You still have it in your backpack, don't you?"

"Yes, I sure do." Then he added, "It seems that, as horrible as it is for most people, for us the earthquake might be a blessing in disguise."

Gilda nodded slowly. After a moment, she said, "I'm starved. Let's go down and have some breakfast." Mark agreed, happy Gilda's appetite had returned.

The restaurant had a limited buffet, but the food tasted good. There was plenty of bottled water. Mark realized how little he had eaten while Gilda had been in the hospital and attacked his cereal with relish. Soon his thoughts turned back to their investigation.

"You know, Chester Weeks is the one who set the condition for independent support of the Mount Sodom Dead Sea Scrolls. I'll bet he tracked our every movement and had Mickey Weeks steal anything we found, keeping it out of the hands of scientists—all the while keeping us quiet about the Mount Sodom Dead Sea Scrolls. I don't think he had any intention of releasing the scrolls."

"I think you're right," Gilda said. "But that means either he or his henchmen—this Mickey guy or someone else—must have the St. Sophia Cathedral tiles and the Babylonian scroll. How are we going to find them?"

"I don't know," replied Mark. "Maybe we should let Dr. Meyer know as soon as we return to Jerusalem. He might be able to help."

Gilda asked, "What about Jacob? How involved do you think he is?"

Mark stopped eating. Reflecting, he said, "I suspect he was just a conduit for information, but I'm not sure. We need to be wary of him."

After breakfast they returned to their room to pack.

"Are you sure you're feeling up to traveling?" Mark asked as he led her to a chair, sat her down, and began throwing their clothes into their backpacks.

"I have no choice. But yes, I feel okay to travel. I'm just thinking about our mission now and I want to get back to Jerusalem as soon as possible."

As he closed up their backpacks, she continued, "Because of the damage caused by the earthquake, travel time to the airport is uncertain. We should leave as soon as possible. Once at the airport, we need to find a Mira Dubinsky from the Israeli consulate—Dr. Meyer told me she'd meet us there. She'll be able to tell us where to find our flight."

After checking out, it took twenty minutes to hail a taxi. The trip to the airport took an hour and a half—well over the thirty minutes it had taken them previously. Destruction was everywhere. Even the ancient city wall had suffered major damage, but the gate was still intact. As they left the urban area and drove through the countryside, the earthquake damage seemed worse. Perhaps the country homes were not as well built as the urban dwellings.

Gilda watched sadly as she saw people standing in front of their crumbled homes or children picking through the rubble. She said, "One of the doctors told me that many of the victims, including many of the dead and missing, were children who had been in collapsed school buildings." She sighed, knowing it would take years to rebuild; these people's lives would never be the same.

Mark looked into Gilda's sad eyes. Unsure how to console her, he put his hand on her leg and gently squeezed.

When they arrived for their noon flight, the airport was full of life and chaotic with the movement of people and vehicles. Perhaps because the buildings were modern and well built, there was little damage here. Unlike what they expected, security guards were everywhere. Gilda was surprised and said, "There's more security here than when we flew from Lhasa. We are supposed to meet Mira Dubinsky, but I have no idea where and don't know how to contact her."

Mark looked around. "Does El Al fly into here?"

"I'm not sure," responded Gilda.

"There," pointed Mark. "El Al has a check-in counter over there."

Trying not to draw attention to themselves, they calmly walked over. No one was in line, but there was someone behind the counter— a woman dressed in street clothes.

"We are looking for Mira Dubinsky," Gilda said to the trim woman, who appeared to be in her late fifties, her graying dark hair in a tight bun.

"That's me. Are you Dr. Baer?"

"Why, yes," she said, flabbergasted but relieved. "Please call me Gilda," she said, turning to Mark, "and this is Mark Malloy." Again facing Mira, she continued, "I thought security was supposed to be light."

"It was light until about two hours ago. Then everything changed to what you see now. You are going to have to pass through security and passport control."

Mark and Gilda looked at each other; both had a mask of confusion and fear, but neither spoke.

Finally, Mark turned to Mira and said, "That's a problem because of what I have in my backpack."

"I am aware of your cargo. You can check the backpacks with me. Because of my diplomatic status and my work with the aid flights, I should not have a problem getting these on the plane."

Gilda and Mark were dumbfounded.

Mira handed them some papers. "Take these. You can pass through security with them and with your passports and visas, then head toward the A concourse. I will meet you there and take you to the plane. Give me your backpacks and go. We don't have much time."

With great unease, Mark slowly handed her his backpack. It was difficult for him to part with it. His eyes lingered on it.

Breaking his moment of indecision, Mira said, "You'd better go now."

They did as instructed, heading for passport control and security. There were few people in line. Passengers were moving through quickly, but they were undergoing considerable scrutiny. As they waited to pass, Mark asked, "How do we know that was really Mira Dubinsky? She never showed us any identification."

"You're right. But it must have been her. She knew my name." Then she added, "I guess we will see on the other side."

That didn't make Mark feel better.

The combination of showing the papers that Mira gave them at security and having no carry-on luggage allowed them to pass unimpeded. Arriving at the A concourse, Mira was nowhere to be found. They stood at the entrance to the concourse looking around. Mark began to wonder if he would ever see his backpack again. Then they saw her, but without their backpacks!

"Follow me," Mira instructed.

"Where are our backpacks?" Gilda asked.

"They're on the plane," she said as she passed through a side door. They followed her down the outside stairs onto the tarmac to a huge Israeli military transport plane whose relief supplies had just been offloaded. Mira introduced them to the pilot and copilot, and then took them inside the fuselage, which had a wide-open space for pallets. Along the sides of the fuselage were metal seats with nylon straps. She escorted them to the front of the plane, where they sat down. In the seats next to them were their backpacks. Bidding them "Bon voyage," Mira turned and left.

Greatly relieved to have his backpack back, Mark quickly checked inside. The scroll was still there. He let out a sigh of relief. Next, he strapped his backpack into a nearby seat and helped Gilda get settled. Finally, he strapped himself in. The seats were extremely uncomfortable, but it didn't matter. They were leaving. Leaning back in his rigid metal, unpadded seat, Mark momentarily closed his eyes and exhaled. How fortuitous, he thought, their problem of getting the scroll out of China had been solved by an earthquake.

They had only been on board about fifteen minutes when the plane's large rear door closed loudly, and they began to taxi for takeoff. Mark heard the engines throttle up to full power and felt the plane gain speed as it bounced down the runway. He looked out the small window next to him and saw the view change angles as the plane began to lift off the ground. Soon they were climbing through the pollution and clouds, higher and higher into the bright blue sky. He finally relaxed for the first time in days. They had succeeded in leaving China with the scroll.

Looking down through the window, Mark felt pensive. He could see all the terrible devastation caused by the earthquake. He loved his profession, geology, and all its wonders—for him it was an avocation. Geological forces, however, could be formidable—the natural occurrences that produced physical hazards, and earthquakes like the one that just occurred, were at the top of the hazard list. He thought that even though people might understand what caused earthquakes better than ancient man, the ruin produced by them today was just as bad as in the past.

Gilda looked out her window, also with mixed emotions. She felt guilty to be leaving the devastation and sorry for the affected people and their tragedies. At the same time, she was happy to be heading home to Jerusalem, although she was unsure what awaited them.

Chapter Twenty-nine

I have only ever made one prayer to God, a very short one: O Lord, make my enemies ridiculous. And God granted it.

—Voltaire

Summer 2003, Jerusalem, Israel

By late afternoon in Jerusalem, they landed, exhausted after the long flight and from the earthquake experience. Concerned, Mark reached for Gilda. He warmly caressed her hand. "I saw you trying to sleep. Were you able to?"

"No. All that bouncing around made my head really hurt. Plus, the seats are so uncomfortable."

He helped her up; both stretched. Gathering their backpacks, they exited the plane's rear door and walked slowly across the tarmac toward the terminal. Immediately, they were met inside by Dr. Meyer, Chester, and Jacob.

"Oh, great," Mark whispered under his breath.

Anticipating Mark and Gilda's return once he spoke with Mickey in Xi'an, Chester had caught the first flight to Jerusalem. Not hearing from his cousin in the last couple of days, though, made Chester very anxious about Mickey's well-being given the well-publicized Xi'an earthquake. He convinced Jacob to insist that the five of them meet in a private conference room at the airport immediately upon Mark and Gilda's arrival.

Everyone shook hands perfunctorily and exchanged pleasantries. "Gilda, how is your head?" Dr. Meyer knew about her injury from their phone conversation. Plus, her bandage made it obvious. Chester and Jacob seemed to care less.

"It still hurts a bit, but I'm much better. Thank you for asking."

Chester, tense and agitated, motioned to Jacob with his hands and nodded toward the direction of the conference room. He frowned and said nothing, but the message was clear: Let's get on with it. Jacob took the cue, saying, "I have a conference room here at the airport where we can talk in private. We want to debrief you now, so please follow me."

Before Mark or Gilda could protest, they were ushered off.

After everyone was seated around the large, rectangular, wooden conference-room table, Jacob got right to the point and said, "Tell us what happened in Xi'an."

Gilda said, "We have not had a shower in three days. Is this so important we can't clean up first?"

Mark chimed in, saying, "We just survived an earthquake during which Gilda was injured. She needs rest. Can't this wait?"

Chester piped up sternly, "It is that important. I'm financing your trips, and I want to know what happened in Xi'an. Why did you even go there in the first place?" Bullying, which was second nature to Chester, usually produced the desired effect.

Not intimidated, Mark glared at him while maintaining a cool demeanor. He spoke slowly and as calmly as possible, "What happened? There was an earthquake. Now may we leave?"

"We know that," Chester replied disdainfully, raising his voice with deliberate venom. "No, you can't leave. We want to know what happened to the scroll you found."

Mark gritted his teeth, knowing Jacob had told Chester about the scroll. He recalled their walk back from the pagoda and seeing the money changers, and a passage from the Bible came to mind. He decided to use it. "While recovering from the Xi'an earthquake, I read the Bible," he lied. "Do you know what passage I read, Chester?"

"I don't know, nor do I care," Chester responded an octave higher, agitated.

Mark ignored him. "I read about Jesus at the temple. Do you remember that story, Chester?" This time he drew out the second syllable of Chester's name.

Chester fumed but said nothing and glared at Mark, his heavy breathing heard around the table.

Mark hoped to provoke Chester into making a mistake, revealing his complicity in the theft of the antiquities. "That event took place when Jesus returned to Jerusalem for Passover and he went to the temple. In the temple, Jesus found money changers and merchants selling various items. This angered Jesus, and he rebuked them, saying, 'This is a house of prayer, but you are making it a den of robbers.' He overturned their tables and kicked them out of the temple.

Chester, do you know who that story reminds me of?" Mark looked directly at Chester. Everyone else at the table did the same.

Before Chester could answer, Mark continued, "It reminds me of you. You are the robber in the house of prayer. You are the one who sells and takes money in Jesus' house. You and your corrupt ways don't belong in God's temple. If Jesus were here today, he would kick you out."

Red-faced, Chester was so mad he forgot about the Xi'an scroll. His focus was Mark. Raising his voice further and slamming his fist on the table, he yelled, erupting like a volcano and spittle ejecting from his mouth, "How dare you judge me? You arrogant son of a bitch! You think you're so smart. Your worthless research is over. I'll ruin you! The Mount Sodom Dead Sea Scrolls will never see the light of day!"

Chester's voice sounded like the hissing of a snake. The image of a serpent flashed in Gilda's mind, causing her to recall the Devil's appearance in the Garden of Eden. She could not help but draw a link between the Devil and Chester.

Mark showed no reaction, believing he was finally seeing Chester's true colors. In a flash, he recalled another Bible story that seemed appropriate. Samson was attacked by Philistines along a road. Samson found the jawbone of an ass and defended himself. In so doing, he smote the Philistines with the jawbone of an ass. One might say the Philistines were slain by the jaws of an ass. Mark calmly told Chester, "Now, I know how the Philistines felt when they were slain by the jaws of an ass."

Everyone in the room, including Chester, clearly understood that in using the Biblical passage about Samson, Mark had cleverly called Chester an ass.

Chester, seething and beyond the brink, could take no more. He wanted to know what happened in Xi'an, but not at this price. He believed that with enough financial clout, he could convince Jacob never to release the Mount Sodom Dead Sea Scrolls. Word dueling with Mark was a waste of time. He suddenly stood, his movement knocking over his chair in the process. He began to storm out of the conference room.

As he reached the door, Mark asked, "Don't you want to hear about Mickey?"

Chester's body tensed. He stopped abruptly, frozen in place. Dread paralyzed him. The room fell silent except for the whirring sound of a spinning wheel on Chester's overturned chair. His mind raced. He should leave, but he couldn't. How could they know about Mickey? What else did they know? After a moment, Chester slowly turned toward Mark, crimson-faced and breathing heavily. He asked tentatively, "What did you say?"

"Mickey Weeks from Oklahoma City. A relative of yours?" Mark asked.

The wheel stopped spinning; the room was now perfectly silent. Chester's mood changed dramatically, as if a shadow moved across his face. He was no longer an angry, aggressive man; he became very subdued. In a low tone, he said unconvincingly, "I don't know what you're talking about."

"Sure you do," said Mark. "Mickey Weeks is the one who followed us to Iznik and took the St. Sophia Cathedral tiles. He followed us to Baghdad and took the Babylonian scroll. Does that jog your memory?" Mark was guessing, but he felt confident. He let it sink in and added, "I have his driver's license right here if that helps." He raised it in front of him. Finally lowering his arm, Mark thought he would finally learn the truth.

Everyone in the room looked intently at Chester, who could only say glumly, "I still don't know what you're talking about." Yet Chester did not leave, obviously wanting more information.

"He's related to you, right? Mickey Weeks, Chester Weeks?" Mark said, baiting the trap he hoped he was setting.

Chester stood in silence; his shoulders drooped; he looked like a defeated man.

Mark suddenly felt badly for the news he was about to deliver, despite all that Mickey and Chester had tried to do to him, to Gilda, and to their discoveries. His voice softened slightly, and he said sympathetically, "Mickey's dead, Chester."

Mark thought Chester might collapse as his legs buckled slightly. Slowly moving like a viscous fluid, Chester shuffled a few steps forward, bent down, and righted his chair with shaking hands. He fell heavily into it, slumping down. He swallowed hard, deeply sighing. "I don't know who this Mickey is," Chester insisted in a very low and broken voice.

Mark spoke gently, "Chester, we have Mickey's address. I'm sure it will be easy to connect him to you through your family relationship. I'm very sorry about your loss. But do you really want to continue this charade?"

Jacob had been willing to go along with Chester's plan as long as everything was above board—or at least appeared so. Now he shifted in his seat uncomfortably, anxiety rising. He had his suspicions about Chester's involvement in the disappearance of the St. Sophia Cathedral tiles and the Babylonian scroll, but he was willing to let those slide as long as no one was the wiser.

But now someone was dead. It appeared as if Chester was somehow implicated in this business. It seemed to Jacob that things were not going according to plan, and he no longer wanted to be a part of the arrangements he had made with Chester. Jacob felt the need to separate himself from the situation. Now he joined Mark's questioning, trying to show his lack of involvement in any wrongdoing by asking, "Chester, is any of this true? Did you have anything to do with the disappearance of the tiles and the scroll?"

Chester looked at Jacob, disgust creeping into his stare. He knew what Jacob was doing. *What an opportunist*, he thought. Chester felt totally alone. Jacob was turning against him; Mickey was dead. He felt like a drowning man barely hanging on to a life raft. His life raft was his lie, and he was going to cling to it for dear life. Chester certainly didn't want to admit any guilt or complicity, but he needed to know how much Mark really knew about his plot. And he wanted to know what had happened to his cousin.

Gathering his reserve strength, he said, "Jacob, I assure you I had nothing to do with those thefts. And I don't know who this Mickey is, or was." Chester felt a small amount of confidence returning. He could get through this as long as he continued to deny everything.

Frustrated with Chester's answers, Gilda asked, "Where are the St. Sophia Cathedral tiles and the Babylonian scroll? What have you done with them?"

"I've done nothing with them and have no idea where they are," Chester said.

Attempting to be nonchalant, Chester rose somewhat in his chair, leaned forward in Mark's direction, and said, "Okay, I'll bite, even though I don't know this Mickey character." He cleared his throat. "Who is he and what happened to him?"

Mark studied Chester, trying to determine what to say next. In the end, he told the truth, "He tried to steal the Xi'an scroll at gunpoint, but Gilda disarmed him." Mark paused, checking Chester's reaction, which was unchanged. He resumed, saying, "Then the earthquake struck, and he was crushed to death by falling rocks."

Chester slumped in his chair and said nothing, waiting for more information. He couldn't believe that rocks and an earthquake had killed his cousin.

Now Mark took a bit of liberty with the facts, hoping Chester might yet confess. "Before he died, Mickey told me everything. How he worked for you and what he had taken. He knew he was dying and made a deathbed confession. We know all about your involvement."

Chester fell backward slightly in his chair, feeling like he had been punched in the face. He was confused; he didn't think his cousin would betray him. But if he were dying … could he really have confessed? His indecisiveness abruptly evaporated. Whether Mickey confessed didn't matter, Chester thought, and he said, "I don't know this Mickey, and I don't believe he accused me of anything because I haven't done anything. It's my word against yours, and I've heard enough."

Mark thought Chester recovered surprisingly quickly and was caught off guard. He tried to compose his next words.

Before Mark could speak, Chester stood. He had all the information he needed, and his instincts told him continuing this discussion might put him at risk. He needed to regain control of the situation, including what to do about Mickey and, more importantly, what to do about the findings of Mark and Gilda. Chester glanced at Jacob, giving him an imperceptible nod. No one else in the room noticed. He gave Mark a look of pure hatred, turned, and left the room without saying another word. The door automatically closed behind him.

Mark and Gilda turned toward Jacob, hoping he would stop Chester even though they only had circumstantial evidence in the form of Mickey Weeks's billfold.

Jacob sat there and did nothing except try to avoid the three pair of eyes focused on him. He was relieved to see Chester go. Chester had clearly become a liability. The last thing he wanted was an investigation involving Chester's activities drawing attention to himself. He wanted to avoid an embarrassment to Israel as well. If no one else was going to object to Chester's leaving, he certainly wasn't going to stop him. Finally, he said casually, "I can't believe Chester did these things. He's right; it is your word against his, and we have no legal basis to hold him."

Mark's disappointment with Chester's escape from punishment was tempered by his excitement of having the independent evidence that triggered their search. Evidence that ensured the Mount Sodom

Dead Sea Scrolls would be made public. The triumph of obtaining and keeping the Xi'an scroll was edifying.

After a long silence, Dr. Meyer asked, "Do you have the Xi'an scroll with you now?"

"Yes," Mark replied excitedly. "It's here in my backpack." He realized that Chester left before learning the status of the Xi'an scroll, causing him to smile.

Jacob sat silently, listening intently to the conversation.

Dr. Meyer responded enthusiastically, "I have the results of the OSL age dating of the sediment sample you collected from the terracotta jar. The sediment age is almost two thousand years old. It places the likely date of the scroll around the time of Jesus' life. We still need to translate the scroll, but it looks like Jesus was in Xi'an, which also is consistent with what is written in the Mount Sodom Dead Sea Scrolls."

Dr. Meyer inhaled deeply and looked first at Mark, then at Gilda. The edges of his mouth began to turn upward, ending in a large smile. "After all our travels and disappointments, I believe we finally have our independent corroboration."

Mark couldn't control himself. He jubilantly jumped out of his chair, lifted Gilda out of hers, and held her in his arms, twirling her around.

Gilda, giddy with excitement and trying to catch her breath, said, "If you don't stop, you're going to cause my head to start hurting again." She couldn't stop smiling.

Dr. Meyer glanced at Jacob. Seeing that he looked surprised at Mark and Gilda's behavior, Dr. Meyer winked and smiled at him. Jacob's mood changed little.

When the brief celebration was over, the three turned to Jacob, waiting for him to speak. At last, he said without emotion, "You have met the conditions. I will not stand in your way. You have my full cooperation to publish the results of your findings, including those from the Mount Sodom Dead Sea Scrolls. I will arrange for you to work with the translators who have been decoding the scrolls to get all the information and access you need." Pausing, Jacob added perfunctorily, "Congratulations and thank you for your good work." They stood and shook hands.

Afterward, Jacob said, "I must attend to some urgent matters and return to my office. Good-bye and thank you again." He turned and left the room.

As he was leaving, Mark whispered to Gilda, "Well, he doesn't seem happy."

"Too bad," Gilda responded. "I will not let his attitude dampen my spirits!"

Once Jacob was gone, Dr. Meyer shook Mark's hand vigorously and hugged Gilda, saying "Congratulations" with a full smile on his lips. "We now have the evidence we need showing that during the eighteen years of his life missing from the Bible, Jesus traveled to northern India and to Xi'an, China where he studied Eastern religions before returning to Judea." He thought about this and then said, "You may have just changed the world."

Gilda beamed. "Thank you, Dr. Meyer," she said. "We couldn't have done it without your help." It was a very serious moment, making her feel uncomfortable. To break the weightiness of the situation, she said, "I don't know about changing the world, I just want to change into some clean clothes for now. Can you give us a ride to my apartment?"

"Absolutely," agreed Dr. Meyer with a smile.

Deep in their own thoughts, they spoke little during the twenty-minute ride to Gilda's apartment. At one point, Gilda asked, "What about the St. Sophia Cathedral tiles and the Babylonia scroll? How can we locate and recover them?"

Mark answered, "I'm not sure, but there must be a connection with Chester that can be explored."

Finally, as they were getting out of Dr. Meyer's car, Mark asked, "Is it okay if I keep the Xi'an scroll overnight and bring it in the morning?"

"Yes, enjoy your evening, and I will see you tomorrow." With that, Dr. Meyer said good-bye and drove off.

Mark and Gilda went into her apartment. As soon as the door closed, they walked toward the bathroom, removing and dropping clothes along the way. By the time they reached the shower, they were naked. Finally washing off the pagoda dust and grime felt invigorating. As they stood holding each other and letting the hot water pour over them, Gilda asked, "Did Mickey really have a deathbed confession?"

Mark smiled. "No, but Chester will never be sure. There is no telling what he thinks Mickey may have told me. Chester is going to have a lot of work trying to cover his trail, and who knows, maybe he'll make a mistake along the way and get what he deserves."

They left the shower, barely dried themselves, and headed straight for bed.

As Mark pulled Gilda close, he looked into her eyes and asked, "Are you well enough?"

She said, "If you thought the earth shook for you in Xi'an, wait until you see what it's going to do for you in Jerusalem."

Chapter Thirty

Religion is a cow. It gives milk, but it also kicks.

—Buddha

Winter 2003, Jerusalem, Israel

The gunfire kept repeating. Was he back in Baghdad? Where was it coming from? The shots grew louder and louder, closer and closer. Suddenly, Mark bolted awake from a deep sleep and checked the brightly lit clock on the radio by the bedside, obscured by an empty champagne bottle. It read 4:30 AM. Slowly, he realized where he was: in Jerusalem, not Baghdad. He reached behind him to find Gilda lying peacefully against his back, spooned against him and holding him tightly with her arm. Fully awake now, he heard the sound again: loud, rapid knocking at the door.

"What is it?" asked Gilda groggily, trying to wake up and feeling Mark stir. They had been up late celebrating.

"I think someone's at the door," Mark responded, still trying to clear his head.

"Who could it be this early?" Gilda asked as she rose, looking at the clock and grabbing her robe.

"No idea." Mark lifted himself up. Sitting on the bed, he pulled on jeans.

They went to the door together. Keeping the door chained, Gilda cracked it open to see several men. The one in front spoke. "Are you Gilda Baer?"

For a moment, she couldn't speak. Finally, she managed to respond with a simple, "Yes."

Before she could say or ask anything, he said, "I'm Captain Neumann of the Israel National Police." Displaying his credentials, he continued, "We have a search warrant giving us the authority to search your apartment. Please open your door and allow us to enter."

Confused, Gilda stood motionless, trying to sort out what was happening.

"Ms. Baer, if you do not open your door immediately, we will kick it in."

Still confused, his statement broke her paralysis. She unlatched the chain; Captain Neumann and two policemen quickly entered the room with great panache.

Fully awake, Mark asked, "What's this all about?"

The captain gave him a long stare. Instead of an answer, he asked, "Are you Mark Malloy?"

"Yes."

As Mark spoke, the men accompanying Captain Neumann began searching Gilda's apartment.

"Mr. Malloy, may I see some identification? You too, Ms. Baer."

While Gilda went to retrieve her identification card from her purse, Mark pulled his passport from the front pocket of his jeans. He carried it with him always. They handed their identifications to Captain Neumann, who gave Gilda a search warrant.

As the police officer examined their papers, Gilda read the warrant. She looked up and asked, "You're looking for contraband? What do you mean?"

Captain Neumann put their identification papers in his pocket. "Let's cut to the chase, Ms. Baer. We have it on good authority that you're in possession of stolen property—property with the potential to cause an international incident. Now do you know what we're talking about?"

This can't be happening, thought Gilda. *Are they referring to the Xi'an scroll?*

Before she could speak, one of the policemen walked up to Captain Neumann carrying Mark's backpack. "I think we found it, sir. Look at this."

Neumann looked inside the backpack, reached in, and pulled out the jar containing the Xi'an scroll. He looked at Gilda, then at Mark. "You're under arrest for possession of stolen property. Other charges may follow. We have to handcuff you, but I will allow you to get dressed before we do so. One of my men will stay with you while you change. Please do so now."

Without speaking and accompanied by a policeman, Mark and Gilda went into the bedroom and completed dressing. When they returned to the living room, handcuffs were placed on them and they were escorted to a police car. Sitting in the backseat, a metal grate separated them from the front. The backdoors had no handles on the inside. They were caged. Driving to an unknown location, they simply looked into each other's eyes, filled with questions.

Arriving at a secure-looking building, Mark and Gilda were escorted inside and placed in separate rooms. The officer with Mark unlocked his handcuffs. He was grateful for this simple pleasure of allowing blood to flow back into his hands. His delight of being free of the handcuffs was short-lived. As he rubbed his wrists, the officer told him to sit and his hands were cuffed again, this time in front of him and connected to an iron ring in the table where he sat. The policeman left the room, closing the door, leaving Mark manacled to the table.

He had no watch, and there was no clock in the room. No one came to question him. The room was becoming warmer by the minute, and sweat began to run off him, dripping on the table. It was the first time he had sweat like this since being in Israel. Obviously, the police were trying to make him feel uncomfortable by turning up the thermostat; he had read about this technique.

After what must have been an hour but seemed much longer, a man came into the interrogation room. It was Jacob Cohen.

Mark glared at him.

Jacob sat down across from Mark. Giving him a hard stare, he said stiffly, "Well, Dr. Malloy, are you aware of the serious trouble you have brought upon yourself and others? The Chinese government is aware you stole the Xi'an scroll, a valuable national antiquity. They are about to turn your theft into a nasty international incident, which will cause considerable embarrassment to Israel and America, all because of your actions."

Mark wondered how the Chinese government found out. He suspected Jacob and Chester cooked up this "nasty international incident."

Boldly and incredulously, Mark asked, "Why does a government not acknowledging religion care about a religious scroll?"

Jacob ignored him, saying, "I can't let my country be embarrassed by the likes of you. I've assured the Chinese government that the scroll will be returned in the condition in which it was found. Upon the return of the scroll, they will drop the matter. You, Dr. Malloy, will never see that scroll again."

Trying to remain calm, Mark tensed in anger. His thoughts about the scroll rapidly transitioned to thoughts of Gilda. "I am the one who took the scroll. Gilda had nothing to do with it. In fact, she protested and tried to talk me out of it."

Jacob smiled. "That's funny. She told me it was her idea and that you had nothing to do with it."

"She's lying to protect me. I'm the one responsible."

"Taking responsibility is very noble of you, but you both have participated in a serious crime. You and Ms. Baer could be in jail in Israel for a long time. And our jails are not nearly as nice as yours in America. Your university will not be happy with a professor who is a convicted thief jailed in Israel, especially if it is leaked that your actions may have undermined Israeli security."

"How have I undermined Israeli security?" Mark asked incredulously.

"Perhaps you have, perhaps you haven't. Once the leak is out, it doesn't really matter. Everyone will side with us and believe you are guilty."

Jacob continued, "Then there is the matter of Gilda. Do you know what this will do to her career? Her job at the GSI is over. If she stays in Israel, she will be lucky to find work as a laborer at a kibbutz. That is, after she gets out of jail. You know, it's too bad because jail really ages a woman. Gilda's beauty will disappear rapidly. Plus, with a criminal record, she will not be allowed to enter the United States to visit you, once you are expelled from Israel."

When Jacob stopped talking, the room was still. Mark knew Jacob's threats were real, but he also thought that Jacob was sharing this information to frighten him. He hoped Jacob wanted to make a deal.

Mark decided to press the point. "What do you want, Jacob? What are your terms?"

"With the damage you have caused, do you really think you can get off with a deal?"

"Yes, I do, Jacob. So why don't you cut the crap?"

Jacob looked at Mark for a period of time, sizing him up. Finally he said, "Any reporting of your theft could be a huge embarrassment for Israel. So here is the deal. To save my country from any embarrassment, the Mount Sodom Dead Sea Scrolls will be locked away. You will not have access to them, and for your own sake, you will refrain from discussing them, because as far as Israel is concerned, they do not exist. As you have no proof of their existence, you will be portrayed as a crazed geologist if you attempt to make any information concerning the scrolls public."

Smiling wickedly, Jacob added, "Showing you to be a crazed geologist will not be a far stretch for our propaganda group."

If his hands were not cuffed to the table, Mark was sure he would smash Jacob's face.

"Finally, you will leave Israel immediately and will never be allowed back into the country."

"What about Gilda?"

"She must leave the GSI. That is not negotiable. Other than that, nothing else will appear on her record."

"And if we don't agree?"

"There will be a closed-door trial, and I guarantee you will serve time. Under this scenario, the scrolls will still not be released."

Mark lowered his head. He wondered whether there was anything he could do. Nothing came to mind. Jacob and Chester held all the cards. Using the national security angle, his embassy could offer little to no help. He felt terrible for Gilda—losing the job she loved. Further, he had let Naku down; the Xi'an scroll would be confiscated by the Chinese government after all. After a moment, he looked despairingly at Jacob, "I guess I have no choice. I have to accept your terms."

"You are correct, you have no choice." Jacob rose to leave and said, "There's someone else who wants to see you." He turned and exited the room.

A few minutes later, the door opened. In walked Chester. He sat in front of Mark, a smirk on his face. "You didn't really think we would let you waltz out of here to tell the world about the scrolls, did you? I told you those scrolls would never see the light of day."

Mark fixed his eyes on Chester, remained silent and wondered how he could have ever been so naive.

Chester tossed a billfold on the table in front of Mark. He recognized it as belonging to Mickey.

Finally acknowledging Mickey's relationship to him, Chester asked, "How did my cousin really die?"

Without hesitation, Mark responded, "He died exactly as I told you. The earthquake caused his death."

At this point there was no reason for Mark to lie, but Chester continued to question him. "For God's sake Mark, tell me the truth."

"I am telling you the truth. We were in a hand-dug basement when the earthquake occurred. Part of a wall collapsed on Mickey, killing him. That's the truth! There was a Buddhist monk who witnessed it. He can verify what I'm telling you."

Satisfied this time with the answer, Chester pulled the billfold off the table and put it in his pocket. "He was a good man, very innovative in finding solutions to problems. You know, Mickey paid off Turkish customs officers in order to ship those tiles to me. I was able to send him to Iraq as a security consultant. Then he used the fog of war and my political connections with the security firm to carry the Babylonian scroll out of Iraq and deliver it to me. He will be missed."

It occurred to Mark that he was paying dearly for his transgression while Chester, who performed worse acts, would suffer no consequences. It finally dawned on Mark: money does have its privileges. He was glad to at least now know where the St. Sophia Cathedral tiles and the Babylonian scroll were.

Chester said in disgust, "I hate geology. It killed my cousin."

"Although the earthquake ultimately caused his death, had he not been there doing you bidding, running your evil errands, he wouldn't have died. You can't blame geology for putting Mickey in harm's way. That was your doing, Chester," Mark said emphatically.

Angrily, Chester slammed his fist on the table. "The Mount Sodom Dead Sea Scrolls will never be released. It's as if they never existed. You can talk about them until you're blue in the face, but no one will believe you."

"What about Dr. Meyer?" Mark asked.

"Dr. Meyer has seen the error of his ways. He has no control over the scrolls and thus has no proof either. Such outrageous claims without proof would cost him his job. He's in no position to support the claims of a crazy geologist."

"And Gilda?"

Chester's face beamed with hauteur, saying maliciously, "Did you know she will be leaving the GSI?"

Now Mark was livid. He wanted to lash out. If only his hands weren't shackled to the table. All he could do was sit and take Chester's ranting.

Chester watched Mark, hoping to see a negative reaction. He wanted him to suffer. "She will have no proof of the scrolls and will be portrayed as a disgruntled former employee if she talks about them. Not a very believable character. After that bump on her head, she hasn't been the same. Get the picture?"

Once again, Mark dropped his head, looking down at the table, totally dejected.

Chester piled on, "And if you try to discuss the scrolls publically, you'll be destroyed. Our expression in Oklahoma is that you'll be made to seem like you're 'Two sandwiches short of a picnic.' No one will believe you.

"Well," Chester said, "You have a plane to catch. It's good to know that I'll never see you back in Israel. Can't say it's been a pleasure knowing you. The moral of this story is religion wins over science. You lose, Dr. Malloy."

Mark corrected him, "You mean money wins over science."

Chester snickered, saying, "To me, they're one and the same." His smile grew, his artificially enameled white teeth visible. He rose and turned, and Mark's tormentor left the room.

Shortly after Chester left, Jacob returned. "We've packed your things, which we found at Ms. Baer's apartment and have here at the station. Your flight leaves in four hours. There's space available. You can call and make your own reservation. This time, you pay. Chester's generosity is no longer extended to you."

"I don't have a phone," replied Mark.

"You can use one of the phones here."

"May I see Gilda before I leave? This will be my only chance to say good-bye."

Jacob was torn. In the end, he concluded that their punishment was enough and decided to let them see each other. "Once you've made your flight arrangements, she can accompany you to the airport."

Jacob called in a policeman. He addressed Mark, "I'm going to have you uncuffed now. You know what you have to do, correct?"

"Yes. I will make the necessary calls and leave for the airport."

Jacob instructed the officer to uncuff Mark. "Follow me," Jacob told Mark.

They left the interrogation room and headed to a large room with cubicles. Jacob led him to an empty one with a phone. "Make your call," instructed Jacob and left.

As Mark entered the cube, he noticed his backpack and suitcase in the corner. He looked into the backpack and found his personal belongings, including his passport and billfold, which had the phone number of his travel agent. He called and made the necessary arrangements.

Then he called a second number. It belonged to Jesus Lopez.

"Hey, Jesus." There was a pause as he listened to Jesus.

"Sorry to call at this hour, but I need to know what you found."

After a moment, Mark interrupted Jesus, "Whoa. Slow down, Jesus. I can hear how excited you are, but I'm having trouble following you. Just give the high points. I don't have time now for all the details."

Mark listened intently, becoming more animated with each passing minute. Finally, he said, "This is fantastic information. I will be back in Tallahassee soon, and we can talk more then. Thank you, Jesus!"

Mark smiled with satisfaction as he hung up the phone. "Thank you, Jesus" was a sing-song expression that many Christian evangelicals used when giving thanks for their blessings. At this point, he had something for which to be thankful.

Mark gathered his belongings and found Jacob nearby. "I've made my arrangements and am ready to go. Where's Gilda?"

"She is in the car with Captain Neumann. I will take you there now."

Mark followed Jacob to a waiting police car. Jacob turned and walked away without another word.

"Put your suitcase and backpack in the front seat and get in the back with your friend," Captain Neumann instructed curtly.

Mark did as ordered and sat next to Gilda. They hugged each other as the car pulled away. When they finally pulled apart, Mark looked into her eyes and saw they were red and glistened with moisture. He didn't know what to say; he just held her.

After a few moments, they separated. Mark couldn't talk frankly in the car, but he had so much to tell her. He tried to convey a message to her by telling a story that Neumann would not understand.

"Let me tell you something about myself. It'll make sense later. I attended a meeting once in San Francisco and was walking around one evening when I was talked into taking an evaluation test by Scientologists. I thought it would take a few minutes, but I was in there for over two hours answering more than one hundred questions. My answers were used to develop a psychological profile."

He looked toward the front of the car and saw Captain Neumann watching him in the rearview mirror.

Mark continued, "At the end, a guy provided a debrief, telling me I have a basic distrust of people. Then he asked me to fill out a form that would provide them with my address and contact information. My response to him was 'You've got to be kidding me. You know I don't trust people, and you think I'm going to give you my address.' So I left and never heard anything more from the Scientologists."

Gilda looked at him as if he were crazy. "My life is ruined and you're telling me stories about Scientologists? I didn't think anyone could pull me out of my depression, but you succeeded. Now I'm angry."

Mark heard Captain Neumann chuckle. "I can't explain here, but it will make sense to you later," Mark said.

They remained quiet until reaching the airport. Mark could tell Gilda was still angry; it showed in her eyes, which he tried to avoid.

Captain Neumann parked, let them out of the car, and escorted them inside the terminal. He stayed with them while Mark checked his luggage and obtained his boarding pass. Passing through security was the next step, and Gilda couldn't follow.

Mark turned to Captain Neumann and said, "Can we please have some privacy? We don't know when or if we'll see each other again."

Captain Neumann hesitated and said, "I will wait over by the door. Ms. Baer, when you're finished, please go over there." He pointed to the door where he would wait. He left them alone.

After he walked away, Gilda looked at Mark and asked irritably, "What was that story all about?"

"When we found the Mount Sodom Dead Sea Scrolls, there were twelve scrolls." Mark recalled.

Gilda shook her head, "No, there were only eleven. What are you talking about?"

"When you left to call your boss, remember I stayed behind and took photos. I took more than photographs. I placed one of the clay jars containing a scroll into my backpack after you left. Like the Scientology profile indicated, I didn't trust giving all the scrolls to your government."

Gilda stared at him in disbelief, her mouth open.

Mark continued quickly before he had to leave, "I shipped it to myself and retrieved it when I returned to the States."

Gilda couldn't believe her ears. She asked incredulously, "So you have one of the Mount Sodom Dead Sea Scrolls?"

"Yes, that's what I'm trying to tell you. Not only do I have one of the scrolls, as luck would have it, it's a key scroll."

"What do you mean? I don't understand," Gilda said.

"Like the others, the scroll I took was copper and written in Greek. Do you remember my graduate student Jesus Lopez?"

Gilda tried to recall. "Yes, I met him when I visited Tallahassee."

"Correct. Well, in addition to Spanish and English, he knows Greek and has been translating the scroll for me."

"And?" asked Gilda, grabbing his arm.

"The scroll describes Jesus' travels to Xi'an."

"Travels?"

"Yes, Jesus not only studied and taught in Xi'an in his late twenties, he returned there after the crucifixion, just like in the legend told us by Naku."

Stunned to silence, Gilda could only watch Mark. Finally, she asked, "Why didn't you tell me this before?"

"Jesus Lopez completed his translation while we were in China. I just now found out what was on the scroll."

A look of comprehension filled Gilda's face. She looked around, fearful someone might be listening to them. Softly, she said, "That explains why Dr. Meyer didn't know Jesus survived the crucifixion based on his translation of the Mount Sodom Dead Sea Scrolls. You stole the scroll that discussed those events."

Shaking her head in disbelief, she added, "This may also explain why Arius questioned the divinity of Jesus. He must have known about Jesus' survival. The church couldn't allow that information to be released, so his records were destroyed. Now Chester is preventing the release of the scrolls, but luckily you have the critical one."

She paused. Looking directly into Mark's eyes, she asked, "What are you going to do?"

A sly smile formed across Mark's face as he said, "Jacob and Chester challenged me to talk about the Mount Sodom Dead Sea Scrolls, saying they would make me seem like a crazed geologist. Well, they'll soon get their chance. I plan to announce our discovery, but not discuss the scroll I have. I'll wait for a rebuttal, and then I'll produce the scroll as proof. Plus I have the jar in which the scroll was contained and photographs of all twelve jars as they lay in the cave. "

"You'll be accused of theft, and Israel will demand the scroll back."

Mark again smiled. "To do that, your government will have to admit the scrolls exist. How can they accuse me of stealing something they will have just claimed is a figment of my imagination? Plus, once I produce the scroll as proof, I believe Dr. Meyer will support us."

A slight smile formed on Gilda lips. Maybe there was hope after all.

Before she could say anything else, Captain Neumann appeared next to them startling Gilda. Giving Mark a stern look, he said, "You've had enough time. Move on. You need to leave now to catch your flight."

Mark gazed longingly into Gilda's eyes, and then he hugged and kissed her. Pulling apart slowly, still holding her shoulders, he leaned closer and said, "This isn't over. Watch the news and don't give up. We'll be together soon, I promise."

He turned and walked away to catch his plane, flight number eighteen. Taking the number as a positive sign, a broad smile grew on his lips.

Gilda watched Mark leave, her confidence waning. She wondered if he could overcome the power of Jacob and Chester.

Part way to the security line, as if sensing her thoughts, Mark turned and yelled back, "Remember, don't give up. Keep the faith!"

THE END